It reads like a

Yohanna

I'm not looking for romance. I'd rather just focus on my career; it's what I'm good at. Love? Not so much.

Lukkas

It's been years since I've dated—legitimately. Yes, the paparazzi have shot me with beautiful women, but they're just photo ops. (*shaking his head vehemently*) I'm not looking for love. Not me! Not again!

Yohanna's mum

I tell her all the time, "Get married! It'll solve all your problems!" (breathing exasperatedly) But does she listen? When is she going to learn that Mother knows best?

The Matchmaking Mamas

We haven't met a bachelor or bachelorette we can't match. (smiling sweetly into the camera) Today: single… Tomorrow: in love!

This is what the critics are saying: "Finding your soul mate has never been so much fun!"

HER RED-CARPET ROMANCE

BY
MARIE FERRARELLA

Published in Great Britain 2015
by Mills & Boon, an imprint of Harlequin (UK) Limited,
Eton House, 18-24 Paradise Road, Richmond, Surrey, TW9 1SR

ISBN: 978-0-263-25142-5

23-0615

Harlequin (UK) Limited's policy is to use papers that are natural, renewable and recyclable products and made from wood grown in sustainable forests. The logging and manufacturing processes conform to the legal environmental regulations of the country of origin.

Printed and bound in Spain
by CPI, Barcelona

To
Mary-Theresa Hussey
in loving gratitude
for all the good years

Prologue

Cecilia Parnell reached into her pocket to take out the key her client had given her, then stopped midway and pulled her hand out again.

The initial movement had been automatic. She had the keys to all of her clients' homes. Ninety percent of her clients were at work when she and her cleaning crew arrived; the other 10 percent usually preferred to be out when their homes were rendered spotless from top to bottom.

A firm believer in boundaries and privacy, Cecilia made it a policy never to use the key when she knew her client would be home. And today Yohanna Andrzejewski was home. She knew that because the young woman had specifically requested to see her.

Cecilia assumed the request had something to do with some sort of dissatisfaction with the quality of the work her crew did. If so, this would be a first, since no one had *ever* registered any complaints, not in all the years that she had been in this business.

Pressing the doorbell, Cecilia took a step back from the condo door so that Yohanna could see her when she looked through the peephole.

But it was obvious that her client didn't bother checking to see who was there. The door opened immediately, giving Cecilia the impression that the young woman was standing right behind the front door, waiting for her to arrive.

"Thank you for coming, Mrs. Parnell," Yohanna said, closing the door behind her. She sounded breathless, as if she'd been running.

Or perhaps crying.

"Of course, dear—" Cecilia replied kindly.

She was about to say something else when she turned and really looked at the young woman for the first time. Yohanna, usually so bright and upbeat that she practically sparkled, not only looked solemn but almost drained of all color, as well. Cecilia stopped walking. The mother in her instantly kicked in.

"What's wrong, dear?" she asked, concerned.

Yohanna took a deep breath and then let it out. It sounded almost like a mournful sigh. "I—I'm afraid that I have to let you go," she murmured, appearing stricken and exceedingly uncomfortable.

For the life of her Cecilia couldn't think of a single reason why she and her crew were being dismissed. She screened every one of her people very carefully before she hired them. Her daughter was a private investigator, so background checks were very easy to run. All of her employees had been with her for at least two years if not longer, and each one of them did excellent work.

Something else was going on.

"May I ask why?"

Yohanna's eyes widened as she realized the natural implication of what she had just said. She was quick to correct the misunderstanding.

"Oh, no, it's not anything that you or your crew have done. If anything, they're even better than when you first started cleaning here. I'm really thrilled with the job you've been doing."

Confusion creased Cecilia's brow. "Then, I don't understand. If you're happy with our work, why are you letting us go?" The moment Cecilia asked the question, she saw the tears shining in the younger woman's intense blue eyes. "Oh, darling, what's wrong?" she repeated.

This time, not standing on any formality, Cecilia took the young woman into her arms and hugged her, offering her mute comfort as well as a shoulder to cry on.

Ordinarily, Yohanna kept her problems to herself. She didn't like burdening other people, especially when there was nothing they could do to help or change the situation. But this time, she felt so overwhelmed, so helpless, not to mention betrayed, the words just came spilling out.

"I was laid off yesterday," Yohanna told the sympathetic woman. "I can't afford to pay you."

It was obvious that uttering the words was excruciating for Yohanna.

Cecilia gently guided the young woman to the light gray sofa and sat with her.

"Don't worry about paying me. You've been a wonderful client for four years. We'll work something out.

That's not important now. Tell me exactly what happened," Cecilia coaxed.

Yohanna took another deep breath, as if that could somehow shield her from the wave of pain that came with the words. Being laid off was a whole new experience for her and she felt awful.

"Mr. McGuire sold the company to Walters & Sons," she told Cecilia, referring to the man who had owned the company where she had worked. "The deal went through two days ago, before any of us knew about it. Their head of Human Resources called me into her office yesterday morning and said that they wouldn't be needing my services since they already had someone who could do my job."

Cecilia could just imagine how hard that must have been for the young woman to hear. One moment the future looked bright and secure, the next there was nothing around her but chaos and upheavals.

"That's simply awful," Cecilia sympathized. "Let me make you some tea and you can tell me everything." She rose from the sofa. "Did you know any of this was coming?" Cecilia asked as she walked into the kitchen.

Yohanna followed, looking, in Cecilia's estimation, like a lost puppy trying to find its way home.

"No, I didn't. None of us did," she said, referring to some of the other people she worked with. "I went to work for the company the year before I graduated college. Nine years. I was there nine years," she proclaimed. "McGuire's was like home to me. More," she emphasized, and then added in a quiet voice, "No one there berated me for not having a love life."

Cecilia took a wild guess as to the source of the berating Yohanna was referring to. It wasn't really much of a stretch. "Not like your mother does?"

Yohanna nodded and pressed her lips together, trying to get hold of herself. "I'm sorry I'm such a mess," she apologized, "but I just got off the phone with her."

Admittedly, when she'd told her mother about being suddenly laid off, she'd been hoping for a positive suggestion. Or, at the very least, sympathy. She'd received neither. "My mother's solution for everything is to get married."

"She just wants to see you happy," Cecilia told her as she filled the kettle with water from the tap.

"She just wants grandchildren," Yohanna contradicted. "I don't think she'd care if I married Godzilla as long as she got grandchildren out of it."

An amused smile played on Cecilia's lips. "The subsequent grandchildren from that union would be much too hairy for her liking," she quipped. Placing the kettle on the stove, she switched on the burner beneath it.

"But the immediate problem right now is to get you back into the work force." Cecilia had never been one to beat around the bush. That was for people like Maizie Sommers and Theresa Manetti, her two best friends since the third grade. They were far more delicate and eloquent in their approach to things. She had always been more of a blunt straight shooter. "What is it you do again, dear?"

"A little bit of everything and anything. Make sure that everything is running smoothly, keep track of appointments, meetings, suppliers. Make calls… In short, I guess you could call me an organizer. I take—took," she corrected herself, "care of all the details and made sure that everything at the office was running smoothly."

Cecilia nodded, the wheels in her head turning quickly. "I know people who know people who know people," she said, making something vague sound positive. "Let me make a few calls. We'll see if we can't get you back in the game."

In more ways than one, Cecilia thought. *Wait until I tell the girls we might have another project on our hands.* The mention of the young woman's mother's mindset had not gone unnoticed.

"You really think so?" Yohanna asked, brightening a little. "I'd be eternally grateful for anything you can do to help."

Cecilia smiled at the young woman. "Leave it to me," she promised confidently. Among all the people she and her friends currently knew—and that was a lot, given the nature of their businesses—there had to be someone who could use a sharp young go-getter like Yohanna.

Just then, the kettle emitted a high-pitched whistle. The tea was brewed.

"Ah, I believe it's playing our song," Cecilia said cheerfully, crossing back to the stove. In her head she was already calling Maizie and Theresa. They were going to want to hear all about Yohanna and her present predicament. "Everything's going to be just fine, dear," she promised, filling the teacup to the brim. "You just wait and see."

"I hope so," Yohanna murmured. But at the present moment she was having trouble mustering enthusiasm.

Chapter One

"You know, for a man who currently has the number one movie at the box office for the past three weeks, you really don't look very happy," Theresa Manetti commented to her client as she paused for a moment to stand by Lukkas Spader.

In the catering business for more than twelve years now, Theresa quickly surveyed the large room where she was presently catering the popular producer's impromptu party, a last-minute send-off that he was throwing for his departing assistant, Janice Brooks.

Tall, with broad shoulders and a broader smile—a smile that was conspicuously absent at the moment, Theresa noted—the thirty-six-year-old wunderkind, as those in higher places tended to dub him, shrugged.

"I can't rest on my laurels, Theresa. In this cutthroat business, you're only as good as your next project."

Theresa narrowed her eyes as she studied the young man. That wasn't at the heart of his problem. She could tell by the lost look in his eyes.

"There's something else, isn't there?" the woman asked. "Don't bother denying it, Lukkas. I raised two silver-tongued lawyers, I can see beyond the facade. You're young, good-looking—I'm old so I'm allowed to say that—and the world is currently at your feet. Yet you look as if you've just lost your best friend. What's bothering you?"

Lukkas shrugged. Admitting that the woman had guessed correctly wasn't going to cost him anything. Besides, he liked this woman whose catering service he'd used half a dozen times or so. There was something about Theresa Manetti that reminded him of his late mother.

"You're not old," he told her and then grew more serious when he said, "She's leaving."

"She," Theresa repeated, looking around the room to see if she could spot the woman Lukkas was talking about.

He nodded. "Jan."

Theresa looked at him in surprise. "You mean the young woman you threw the going-away party for?"

She couldn't see them as a pair, but if he didn't want this Jan leaving, why was he throwing this party for her? Why wasn't he trying to convince the young woman to stay?

Lukkas frowned as he nodded. "She's following her heart and marrying some guy in England she met while we were in production on *My Wild Irish Rose*." As if a lightbulb had suddenly gone off in his head, he realized what his caterer was probably thinking. That this was a matter of the heart. Nothing could have been further from the truth.

"Don't get me wrong," he said, quickly setting Theresa straight. "I'm happy that Jan's happy, but I don't know what I'm going to do without her."

"Why?" Theresa asked, curious. "What is it that she does?"

"She keeps me honest and organized," he told her with a dry laugh. Because the woman was still looking at him, waiting for a viable answer, Lukkas elaborated, "I'm the one with the ideas and the energy, the inspiration. Jan's the one who makes sense of it all, who simplifies my chaos and makes sure that everything gets done on time."

Aware of the level of work involved in what Lukkas did, that certainly sounded like a taxing job, Theresa thought.

"And you don't have anyone to take her place?" she ventured. At the same time Theresa realized this wasn't a matter involving the heart. Lukkas seemed genuinely happy that his assistant had found someone to love so this wasn't something that could be fixed with a good match.

A pity, she silently lamented. She and her friends hadn't had a good challenge in almost a month. All three of them ran their own respective businesses, but nothing truly made them come to life like pairing up a couple and moving their lives along; lives that would have otherwise just gone their own separate routes, never bumping into one another, never discovering the pot of gold that was waiting for them at the end of the rainbow.

Thinking of that made her recall the poker game she and her friends had played last Monday. The card game was really just an excuse to get together, unwind and occasionally talk about a possible new opportunity for them to play Cupid. Last Monday, Cecilia had spent most of her time talking about a young woman named Yohanna Something-or-other—the last name was a tongue twister at best. Apparently the young woman had just lost her job and was also too sweet and adorable—Cecilia's exact words—to be without a soul mate.

"Jan is going to be hard, if not impossible, to replace," Lukkas was saying.

Theresa smiled at the much-sought-after producer. He was single. He was exceedingly handsome. He was perfect. "Don't be too sure," she said.

He turned toward her. "You *know* someone?"

Theresa's smile was warm and genuine—and very encouraging. "Dear boy, I *always* know someone." Theresa's eyes were fairly sparkling at this point.

Watching her, Lukkas thought that this woman must have a trick or two up her sleeve. Right now, he needed to find someone to replace Jan. A competent someone. "Tell me more. I'm listening."

A little less than twenty-four hours later Yohanna Andrzejewski found herself standing on Lukkas Spader's doorstep. *The* Lukkas Spader, big-time producer of some very special movies.

Part of her thought she was dreaming. The other part was exceedingly nervous. That was the part that had allowed her knees to feel like Jell-O.

Taking a deep breath and telling herself to calm down, she leaned over and rang the doorbell. And then smiled. The doorbell played several bars from the first movie the producer had ever made: *Dreamland*.

She closed her eyes, recalling the rest of the score.

And that was the way Lukkas first saw her, standing on his doorstep, her eyes shut and swaying to some inner tune.

"Can I help you?"

The voice was deep and sexy. Startled, her eyes flew open.

The man was even better looking than his pictures, she realized as she frantically went in search of her tongue. It, along with her brain, had gone missing in action. It took a second for her to bring about the reunion.

"I'm—" She had to clear her throat before continuing. "Yohanna Andrzejewski. I'm here about the job opening," she added after a beat.

He'd been expecting her. Glancing at his watch, he saw that she was early. A hopeful sign, he thought. "I've been expecting you," he told her. "Follow me."

She fell into step behind him. "You answered your own door," she noted, slightly surprised.

"Had to," he told her. "It hasn't learned to open itself."

She laughed. "I was surprised that you have a house in Newport Beach," she confessed. "You're not all that far from where I live." Initially anticipating a long commute for the interview, she'd been relieved when she was told that he would see her in his Orange County home.

"Things are a little chaotic here," he admitted. "I haven't finished getting all the furniture yet. I think of this as my home away from home. Don't get me wrong, I love Hollywood." Entering a first-floor bedroom he'd converted into an office, Lukkas crossed to his desk, took a seat and gestured for her to take a seat on the opposite side. "But sometimes you just have to get away from the noise just so you're able to hear yourself think."

"Yes, sir," Yohanna responded.

The smile on her lips was almost shy. He was amused but also somewhat skeptical about whether this petite, attractive young woman was equal to the job he needed doing.

"I noticed on your résumé that your last job was with a law firm." He raised an eyebrow as he took a closer look at the dark blonde sitting before him. "Are you a lawyer?" He was aware that most law school graduates had to begin at the bottom of the heap if they were even lucky enough to land a position with *any* firm.

"No, sir."

"Don't do that," he told her.

She hadn't a clue what he might be referring to. "Do what, sir?"

"Call me sir," he specified. "You make me feel like my father—not exactly a feeling I cherish," he added more or less to himself.

Even so, she'd heard him. "Sorry, si—Mr. Spader." She'd managed to catch herself.

"Even worse," he told her. "My name is Lukkas. Think you can manage that?" Yohanna nodded vigorously. "Good," he pronounced.

Letting her résumé fall to his desk, he moved his chair in closer and leaned over, creating a feeling of intimacy. "So tell me, Yohanna with-the-unpronounceable-last-name, just what makes you think that you can work for me?"

As a rule Yohanna had a tendency toward modesty, but she had the distinct impression that the man interviewing her didn't value modesty. He valued confidence. She'd always had people skills, skills that allowed her to read others rather accurately. Lukkas Spader didn't strike her as a man who had the patience to work with meek people.

However she had a feeling that he respected—and expected—honesty. "Mrs. Parnell—"

He held up his hand, stopping her right there. "Who's Mrs. Parnell?"

"She's friends with Theresa Manetti, the woman who—"

He stopped her again. "I know who Theresa Manetti is," he told her. "Go on."

Yohanna picked up the thread exactly where she had dropped it. "She said you needed someone to organize your schedules, your notes and keep up to the minute on all the details of your projects."

He studied her for a long moment. She couldn't glean anything from his solemn, thoughtful expression. "And that would be you?" he finally asked.

Yohanna detected neither amusement nor skepticism in his voice. He was harder to gauge than most. Not to mention that the man was definitely making her nervous. Not because he was so good-looking but because she really wanted to get this job. She wasn't good at doing nothing.

Yohanna pulled herself together. She was determined not to let the producer see how nervous he made her. His world was undoubtedly filled with people who fawned over him. She wanted him to view her as an asset, not just another fawning groupie or "yes" person.

"That would be me," she replied, silently congratulating herself for not letting her voice quiver as she said the words.

The next moment she was relieved to see a smile playing on the producer's lips. The fact that the smile also managed to make him almost impossibly handsome was something she tried *not* to notice.

It was like trying not to notice the sun.

"You're pretty sure of yourself, aren't you?" he asked, amusement curving the corners of his mouth.

Yohanna raised her chin ever so slightly, an automatic reaction when she felt she was being challenged. "I know my strengths," she replied.

"Apparently so does Mrs. Manetti," he told her. "When we spoke, she spoke very highly of your qualifications, and I respect her judgment."

He continued looking at her, as if trying to discern if she was as good as the older woman had led him to believe. The silence dragged on for a good several minutes.

Yohanna had met the woman he was referring to only briefly. They had exchanged a few words and the interview had been arranged. There had been no time for Mrs. Manetti to form an opinion about her abilities one way or another.

She could feel herself fidgeting inside, and her pulse rate began to accelerate. All she could think of was that she really needed this job. She'd only been out of work for a couple of days, but the thought of prolonged inactivity had her already climbing the proverbial walls. Not to mention that she had enough money in the bank to see her through approximately one month—one and a half if she gave up eating.

As a last resort she could always move in with her mother, but as far as she was concerned, living under a freeway overpass was preferable to that. Her mother had been decent enough when Yohanna was growing up, but in the past eight years, only two topics of conversation interested her: marriage and children, neither of which was anywhere in Yohanna's immediate future.

She was fairly confident that living with her mother even for a day would swiftly become catastrophic.

Lukkas continued doling out information. "If you became my assistant, you'd be keeping irregular hours at best. I'm talking *really* irregular," he intoned, his eyes on hers. "And you'd be on call 24/7. Are you up for that?" he asked, looking at her intently.

"Absolutely," she assured him with as much confidence as she could muster.

But Lukkas still had his doubts. "You're not going to come to me in tears a week or two from now, saying that your husband is unhappy with the hours you're keeping and could I give you a more normal schedule, are you?"

"I don't have a husband, so that's not going to happen."

But Lukkas wasn't satisfied yet. "A fiancé? A boyfriend?"

"No and no," Yohanna responded, quietly shooting down each choice.

Lukkas still appeared skeptical. "Really? Not even a boyfriend?" His eyes never left hers, as if he considered himself to be an infallible human lie detector—and being as attractive as she was, the young woman couldn't possibly be telling the truth.

"Not even a boyfriend," she echoed, her face innocence personified.

"You're kidding, right?" he said in disbelief. How could someone who looked like this woman not have men lining up at her door, waiting for a chance just to spend some time with her? He knew this was none of his business or even ethical for him to ask, but curiosity urged him on.

"No," she replied. "I just never experienced that 'walking on air' feeling, si—Lukkas," she quickly corrected herself.

"Walking on air," he repeated. "Is that some sort of code?"

"More like a feeling," she explained then added quickly, "I've never met a man I felt I had chemistry with. In other words, I didn't experience any sparks flying between us. Without that, what's the point?" she asked with a vague shrug.

"What, indeed?" he murmured, thinking back, for a second, to his own solitary life. It hadn't always been that way.

Talking about herself always made her feel uncomfortable. Yohanna was quick to return to the salient point of all this. "The bottom line is that there isn't anyone to complain about my hours even if they do turn out to be extensive."

"No 'if' about it," he assured her. "They *will* be extensive. I'm afraid that it's the nature of the beast. I put in long hours and that means so will you." Again he peered closely at her face, as if he could read the answer—and if she was lying, he'd catch her in that, too. "You're all right with that?" he asked again.

"Completely."

"You haven't asked about a salary," he pointed out. The fact that she hadn't asked made him suspicious. Everyone always talked about money in his world. Why hadn't she?

"I'm sure you'll be fair," Yohanna replied.

Again he studied her for a long moment. He didn't find his answer. So he asked. "And what makes you so sure that I'll be 'fair'?"

"Your movies."

Lukkas's brow furrowed. He couldn't make heads or tails out of her answer. "You're going to have to explain that," he told her.

"Every movie you ever made was labeled a 'feel good' movie." As a child, the movies she found on the television set were her best friends. Both her parents led busy lives, so she would while away the hours by watching everything and anything that was playing on the TV. "If you had a dark side, or were underhanded, you couldn't make the kinds of movies that you do," she told him very simply.

"Maybe I just do it for the money." He threw that out, curious to see what she would make of his answer.

Yohanna shook her head. "You might have done that once or twice, possibly even three times, but not over and over again. Your sense of integrity wouldn't have allowed you to sell out. Especially since everyone holds you in such high regard."

Lukkas laughed shortly. "You did your research." He was impressed.

"It's all part of being an organizer," she told him. "That way, there are no surprises."

There were layers to this woman, he thought. "Is that what you consider yourself to be? An organizer?"

"In a word, yes," Yohanna replied.

He nodded, as if turning her answers over in his mind. "When can you start?"

There went her pulse again, Yohanna thought as it launched into double time. Was she actually *getting* the job?

"When would you want me to start working?" she

asked, tossing the ball back into his court. It was his call to make.

He laughed shortly. "Yesterday." That way, he wouldn't have lost a productive day.

"That I can't do," she told him as calmly as if they were talking about the weather. "But I can start now if you'd like," she offered.

Was she that desperate? he wondered. Or was there another reason for her eagerness to come to work for him? Since his meteoric rise to fame, he'd had friends disappoint him, trying to milk their relationship for perks and benefits. As for strangers, they often had their own agendas, and he had become very leery of people until they proved themselves in his estimation. That put him almost perpetually on his guard. It was a tiring situation.

"You can start tomorrow," Lukkas told her.

She wanted to hug him, but kept herself in check. She didn't want the man getting the wrong impression about her.

"Then, I have the job?" she asked, afraid of allowing herself to be elated yet having little choice in the matter.

"You can't start if you don't," he pointed out. "I'll take you on a three-month probationary basis," he informed her. "Which means that I can let you go for any reason if I'm not satisfied."

"Understood."

He peered at her face. "Is that acceptable to you?"

"Very much so, s-si—" She was about to address him as "sir" but stopped herself, uttering, instead, a hissing sound. "Lukkas," she injected at the last moment.

"I'm currently producing a Western. We're going to be going on location—Arizona. Tombstone area," he specified. "Do you have any problem with that?"

She wanted to ask him why he thought she would, but this wasn't the time for those kinds of questions. They could wait until after she had entrenched herself into his life. The fact that she would do just that was a given as far as she was concerned now that he had hired her.

"None whatsoever," she told him.

"All right. Then go home and get a good night's sleep. I need you back here tomorrow morning at seven."

"Seven it is. I'll be bright eyed and bushy tailed," she responded, thinking of a phrase her grandfather used to use.

"I'll settle for your eyes being open," he told her. "See you tomorrow, Hanna."

Yohanna opened her mouth to correct him and then decided she rather liked the fact that her new boss was calling her by a nickname, even if she didn't care all that much for it. She took it as a sign they were on their way to forming a good working relationship.

After all, if someone didn't care for someone else, they weren't going to give them a nickname, right? At least, not one that could be viewed as cute. If anything, they'd use one that could be construed as insulting.

"See you tomorrow," she echoed. "I'll see myself out," she told him.

Lukkas didn't hear her, his mind already moving on to another topic.

Yohanna had to hold herself in check to keep from dancing all the way to the front door.

Chapter Two

The landline Yohanna had gotten installed mainly to placate her mother—"What if there's a storm that takes out the cell towers? How can anyone reach you then? How can *I* reach you then?"—was ringing when she let herself into her condo several hours later that day.

Yohanna's automatic reaction was to hurry over to the phone to answer it, but she stopped just short of lifting the receiver. The caller-ID program was malfunctioning, the screen only registering the words *incoming call*.

Frowning, she stood next to the coffee table in the living room and debated ignoring the call. Granted, everyone she knew did have this number as well as her cell number, but for the most part, if they called her, it was almost always on her cell phone, *not* her landline. *That* was for sales people, robo calls and her mother.

Which meant, by process of elimination, that the caller was probably her mother.

Yohanna was really tempted to let her answering machine pick up. Talking to her mother was usually exhausting.

But if she ignored this call, there would be others, most likely coming in at regular intervals until she finally picked up and answered. Her mother had absolutely unbelievable tenacity. She would continue calling, possibly well into the evening, at which time her mother would make the fifteen-mile trip and physically come over. Her hand would be splayed across her chest, as she would dramatically say something about her heart not being up to taking this sort of stress and worry.

Yohanna resigned herself to the fact that she might as well answer her phone and get the inevitable over with.

Taking a deep, bracing breath, she yanked the receiver from its cradle and placed it against her ear—praying for a wrong number.

"Hello?"

"It's about time you answered. Where were you? Never mind," Elizabeth Andrzejewski said dismissively. "I'm calling you to tell you that I've got your room all ready."

Yohanna closed her eyes, gathering together the strength she sensed she was going to need to get through this phone call.

Until just a minute ago she'd been walking on air, still extremely excited about being hired. She would have been relieved landing *any* job so quickly, on practically the heels of her recent layoff, but landing a job with Lukkas Spader, well, that was just the whip cream *and* the cherry on her sundae.

However, dealing with her mother always seemed to somehow diminish her triumphs and magnify everything that currently wasn't going well in her life. Her mother had a way of talking to her that made her feel as if she was a child again. A child incapable of doing anything right without her mother's help.

Yohanna knew that, deep down, her mother really meant well; she just wished the woman could mean well less often.

"Why would you do that, Mother?" she finally asked. She hadn't used her room since she'd left for college and moved out on her own.

"So you'll have somewhere to sleep, of course," her mother said impatiently.

"I *have* somewhere to sleep. I sleep in my bedroom, which is in my condo, Mother, remember?" Yohanna asked tactfully.

She heard her mother sigh deeply before the woman launched into her explanation.

"Well, now that you've lost your job, you're not going to be able to hang on to that overpriced apartment of yours. You should sell it now before the bank forecloses on it."

Yohanna was stunned. Where was all this coming from? She'd had this so-called "discussion" with her mother several years ago when she'd first bought her condo. Her mother couldn't understand why "a daughter of mine" would "waste" her money buying a "glorified apartment" when she had a perfectly good room right in her house. She'd thought that argument had finally been laid to rest.

Obviously she had thought wrong.

"The bank isn't going to foreclose on me, Mother," Yohanna informed her. "My mortgage payments are all up-to-date."

"Well, they won't be now that you've been fired," her mother predicted with a jarring certainty.

"Laid off, Mother," Yohanna corrected, trying not to grit her teeth. But there was no one who could make her crazier faster than her mother. "I wasn't fired, I was laid off."

"Whatever." The woman cavalierly dismissed the correction.

"There *is* a difference, Mother," Yohanna insisted. "One has to do with job performance. The other is a sad fact of modern life. In my case, it was the latter."

"Potato, po*tato*," her mother said in a singsong voice. "The bottom line at the end of the day is that you don't have a job."

The words suddenly hit her for the first time. "How did you find out?" Yohanna asked.

She hadn't told anyone about her layoff except for Mrs. Parnell, bless her. Granted, the people that she'd worked with knew, but a lot of them had been laid off, as well. She didn't see any of them sending her mother a news bulletin. They didn't even *know* her mother.

So how had her mother found out?

"I'm your mother," Elizabeth Andrzejewski replied proudly, as if that alone should have been enough of an explanation. "I know everything."

"You're not omnipotent, Mother," Yohanna told her mother wearily. "Spill it," she ordered. "Just how did you find out about the layoff?"

The silence on the other end of the line began to stretch out.

"Mother…" Yohanna began insistently.

Elizabeth huffed. "If you must know, I went to the office to surprise you and take you out for lunch today.

Imagine *my* surprise when I walked in and found out that you didn't work there anymore. Why didn't you tell me?" she asked, sounding as if she had been deeply wounded by this omission of information.

"I didn't want you to worry—or get upset," Yohanna answered.

That part was true, although there were many more reasons than that why she had kept the news to herself. Specifically, she didn't want to have to fend off her mother's offers for "help," all of which revolved around getting her to move back home. She'd moved out once, but she had a feeling that next time would be a great deal more difficult.

"You didn't want me to worry." Elizabeth practically sneered at the words. "I'm your mother. It's my job to worry about you. Now, I won't take no for an answer. I'll come over tomorrow morning to help you pack up your things and—"

Her mother was more relentless than a class-five hurricane, Yohanna thought. But she was not about to throw up her hands and surrender.

"I'm not selling the condo, Mother," she began patiently.

"All right, rent it out, then," her mother advised, frustrated. "That'll help you cover the cost of the exorbitant mortgage until you're about to get back on your feet again—"

"Mother, I *am* on my feet."

She heard her mother sigh again. This time, instead of sounding dramatic, there was pity in her mother's voice.

Irritating pity.

"There's no need to put up a brave front, Yohanna. Lots of people lose their jobs these days. Of course, if you had married Alicia Connolly's son, that nice young doctor, you wouldn't be in this predicament, wondering where your next dollar is coming from."

Her mother was referring to a setup she'd had her hand in. As Yohanna recalled the entire excruciating event, it had truly been the blind date from hell as well as ultimately being the reason she had vowed to *never* allow her mother to set her up with a date again.

"For your information, Mother," she said, enunciating each word so that her mother would absorb them, "I am *not* wondering where my next dollar is coming from."

"Well, then, you should be," Elizabeth told her with more than a touch of indignation in her voice. "The bank isn't going to let you slide because of your good looks, which, as you know, you're not going to have forever," she added, unable, apparently, to keep from twisting the knife a little bit. "Which reminds me. My friend Sheila has this nephew—"

Although she was always somewhat reluctant to keep her mother in the loop—mainly because her mother always found something negative to say about the situation—Yohanna knew that the older woman was not about to stop trying to manipulate her life—big-time— unless she told her mother that she was once again gain-fully employed.

"Mother, stop, please," she pleaded. "I don't need to move back into my room or to rent out my condo."

"Oh, then, just what is your brilliant solution to your present problem?" Elizabeth asked.

I'm talking to my present problem, Yohanna thought.

However, she kept that to herself, knowing that if she ever said those words or similar ones out loud, her mother would be beyond hurt. She couldn't do that to the woman no matter how much her mother drove her up a wall.

"I've got a job, Mother," she told her.

"Honey, I told you that you don't need to pretend with me." It was obvious by her tone of voice that her mother simply didn't believe her.

"I'm not pretending, Mother," Yohanna answered, struggling to remain calm and clinging to what was left of her dwindling patience.

"All right." She could all but see her mother crossing her arms in front of her, fully prepared to sit in judgment. "And just what is this 'job' you've gotten so suddenly?" Before she could tell her, Yohanna heard her mother suddenly suck in her breath. "You're not doing anything immoral or illegal, are you?"

It was more of an accusation than a question. Among other things, her mother, an avid—bordering on rabid—soap opera fan, had a way of allowing her imagination to run away with her along the same creative lines that many of the soap operas she viewed went.

"No, Mother. Nothing illegal or immoral." She really hadn't wanted to tell her mother until her three-month probationary period was up, but, as with so many other things that involved her mother, she found that she had no choice in the matter. "I'm going to be Lukkas Spader's assistant."

"And just what does this man want being assisted?" Elizabeth asked suspiciously.

"Lukkas Spader, Mother," Yohanna repeated, stunned that her mother didn't recognize the name. "The *producer*," she added. But there was apparently still no recognition on her mother's part. "You know, the man who produced *Forever Yours, Molly's Man, Dangerous*." She rattled off the first movies that she could think of.

"Wait, you're working for *that* Lukkas Spader?" her mother asked, sounding somewhat incredulous.

Finally! Yohanna thought. "That's what I'm trying to tell you."

Suspicion leeched back into Elizabeth's voice. "Since when?"

"Since this morning, Mother, when Mr. Spader hired me."

Elizabeth obviously wasn't finished being skeptical about this new turn of events. "And what is it that you say you're going to be doing for him?"

Yohanna silently counted to ten in her mind before answering. "I'm going to be organizing things, Mother. Movie things," she elaborated, knowing how her mother tended to think the worst about every situation. Given the choice of picking the high road or the low one, her mother always went the low route.

As proved by her mother's next question. "Are you telling me the truth?"

Yohanna rolled her eyes. This was *not* a conversation that a thirty-year-old should be having with her mother. Anyone listening in would have thought her mother was talking to someone who was twelve. Maybe younger.

"Of course I'm telling you the truth, Mother."

To her surprise, instead of continuing to harp on the subject, she heard her mother give a huge sigh of relief. "Oh, thank God. Now, remember not to mess anything up, understand?"

"I'm not going to mess anything up, Mother." And then it hit her. She knew what her mother was thinking. Yohanna nearly groaned. Her mother *never* gave it a rest. *Never.* "He's my boss, Mother," she said in a sharp warning voice.

"So?" Elizabeth asked defensively. "Bosses don't get married?"

Enough was enough. She was *not* having this conversation. "I've got to go, Mother. I've got some things to take care of before I go in tomorrow." It was a lie, but it was better than slamming the receiver down in the cradle, which she was very tempted to do.

Rather than attempt to pump her for more information, her mother surprised her by saying, "Go get some new clothes. Sexy ones. These Hollywood types like sexy women."

There was no point in arguing about this with her mother any longer. She had never known her mother to admit she was wrong or that she had overstepped her boundaries. Not even once.

There was no reason for her to hope that her mother would suddenly come to her senses at fifty-seven and turn over a new leaf.

For better or worse, this was her mother.

"Yes, Mother," Yohanna replied in a near-to-singsong voice. "Bye." And with that, she hung up, promising herself to get a new phone—one with a working caller ID—the first opportunity she got.

Yohanna didn't remember when she finally closed her eyes and fell asleep.

All she knew was that it felt as if she'd only been asleep for ten minutes before she opened her eyes again and saw that, according to the clock on her nightstand, it was quarter to six.

Spader wanted her at his Newport Beach home by seven.

Stifling a groan, she stumbled out of bed, then somehow made her way down the stairs and into the recently remodeled kitchen.

If she was going to get anything accomplished, she needed coffee. Deep, hearty, black coffee. Downing one cup fortified her enough to go back upstairs, take a shower and get dressed. All of which she did at very close to top speed. She needed to get out and on the road as quickly as possible.

She didn't anticipate any large traffic snarls from her home to Spader's but there was always a chance of a collision and/or a pileup—and she didn't like leaving *anything* to chance.

She also didn't like calculating everything down to the last possible moment. On time wasn't her style—being early was.

Fueled by an enormous amount of nervous energy, Yohanna was on the road less than half an hour after she'd woken up.

Twenty minutes after that, she was parked across the street from Spader's impressive three-story house. As usual, she was early and, ordinarily, she would walk up to the front door and ring the bell. She just assumed that to most people, being early was a plus. But Lukkas Spader might be one of those people who actually didn't like anyone arriving early, possibly before he was ready to see them.

She needed to find that little detail out before tomorrow morning. In the meantime, she looked at her wristwatch and continued to wait, parked directly across from his slightly winding driveway.

Which was where the patrol officer who tapped on her driver's-side window found her.

Startled by the knock—her mind was elsewhere—Yohanna looked up at the officer. To say she was surprised to see him was putting it mildly.

The officer motioned for her to roll down her window. Which, after one false start, she did.

"Is there something wrong, Officer?" she asked him, even though, for the life of her, she couldn't imagine what that could be, or why he'd want to speak to her in the first place.

"You tell me," he replied, waiting. When she continued watching him without saying a word in response to his flippant remark, the officer appeared to be losing patience as he asked, "Mind telling me what you're doing sitting out here all alone like this?"

"I'm waiting until seven o'clock," she explained. To her, it was all very logical.

"What happens then?" he asked.

She found the officer's tone just slightly belligerent, but told herself it was her imagination. "I knock on Mr. Spader's door."

The officer didn't seem to believe her. "And then what?" he demanded.

"He lets me in." Why was he asking all this? she wondered. She certainly didn't look unsavory.

"That the plan?" the officer said sarcastically.

Yohanna began to feel a little uneasy. "I don't think I understand."

The officer blew out a breath, sounding as if he was struggling to keep from raising his voice. "Look, honey, why don't you just drive off, buy yourself some popcorn and watch one of the guy's movies like everyone else does?"

The officer clearly didn't understand. "But Mr. Spader is waiting to see me."

"Sure he is," the officer said in a humoring voice. "You look like a decent kid. Stalking never ends well. Not for the stalker, not for the person they're stalking. So why don't you just—"

"Wait, what?" Yohanna cried, stunned at the very suggestion the officer was making. "I'm not stalking Mr. Spader," she insisted. "I work for him."

"Suuure you do." He stretched out the word, mocking her before he suddenly became stone-cold serious. "I don't want to take you in, but you're really not leaving me much of a choice here, lady. Now, for the last time, start your car and go home—"

"Ask him," Yohanna cried quickly. "He'll tell you that I work for him. Just go up to his door and knock." She was almost pleading now.

If she didn't show up the first day, she might as well kiss the job goodbye. And even if she wound up having the policeman escort her to Spader's door, the producer still might hand her her walking papers. No one wanted to knowingly work around trouble.

"You'd like that, wouldn't you? So you could tell all your little crazy loser friends that you got to see Lukkas Spader up close and personal-like. Sorry, I'm not in the business of making your pathetic little fantasies come true. Now, this is your last chance to go free—" he began again.

"Please, I'm telling you the truth, Officer. I work for Lukkas Spader. He told me to meet him here at seven this morning and I was just waiting until seven before knocking on his door. I am *not* stalking him," she insisted.

Still apparently unconvinced, the police officer frowned.

"You're not leaving me any choice. I warned you." One hand was now covering the hilt of his service weapon, ready to draw it out at less than a heartbeat's notice. "Get out of the car. Now."

One look into the man's eyes and Yohanna knew the officer wouldn't stand for being crossed. He wasn't the type to suffer any sort of acts of disobedience quietly or tranquilly.

Keeping her hands out where he could see them, Yohanna did as the police officer ordered. She got out of the car slowly.

"Is there a problem, Officer?"

The question came from someone standing directly behind the officer. Yohanna leaned over slightly to look, praying she was right.

She was.

It was Lukkas.

Yohanna's heart went into overdrive.

"No, sir, Mr. Spader. I just caught another stalker. This one's not as intense as the other one was, but she looks like trouble all the same."

Lukkas smiled as he stepped to the officer's side and looked at her. "She does, doesn't she?"

Chapter Three

"Do you want to press charges?" the police officer asked, looking expectantly at the man standing next to him.

Stunned, Yohanna's eyes widened considerably as she stared at the man she had *thought* was her new employer. Had her signals gotten somehow crossed and she'd misunderstood him yesterday?

No, that wasn't possible. He hadn't given her anything in writing, but she remembered every word he'd said and could recite them back to him verbatim. Her very precise photographic memory was part of what made her so good at organizing things. It also helped her take care of what needed to be done—and then remembering where everything was hours, even days, later.

She was about to nudge the producer's memory a little so this officer could move along when she heard Spader tell the man, "No, not at this time, Officer."

The police officer was still eyeing her as if she was some sort of a criminal deviant. She needed her new boss to say something a little more in her defense than a barely negligible remark.

"Mr. Spader, tell him I work for you," she requested with more than a little urgency.

The corners of Lukkas's mouth curved just a hint as he turned toward the officer and said, "She does, actually. This is Hanna's first day. She's here a little early," he commented. "But that's a good thing."

The officer removed his hand from his weapon. "Oh." There was just a sliver of disappointment in the man's voice. He glanced from the producer to the woman who had almost been arrested. "Sorry about that, but it's better to be careful than let things ride and then be sorry."

The apology was halfhearted, but Yohanna considered it better than nothing. She inclined her head, silently indicating that she accepted the officer's rather paltry excuse.

A huge range of emotions swirled through her like the wind gearing up before a storm. This was a whole different world that she was signing on for.

She focused on the one piece of information she had picked up out of all this. "You had a stalker?" she asked Lukkas incredulously. She'd occasionally read about things like that happening, both to famous celebrities as well as to average, everyday people, but it had never touched her life or happened to anyone she actually knew.

Until now.

"What happened?" she asked him.

Lukkas didn't answer her and gave no indication that

he had even heard her. Instead, what he said was, "Ready to get started?"

She took that to mean that the subject of his past stalker was off-limits. While her curiosity was still rather exceedingly ramped up, she could understand why the producer wouldn't want to pursue the subject. This was obviously something out of Spader's private life and she was just an employee—a *new* employee at that—hired on a probationary basis. That didn't exactly make her someone he was about to bare his soul to within the first few minutes of her first day on the job.

So she buried the question as well as her growing and somewhat unbridled curiosity and cheerfully replied, "Absolutely," to his question.

But even with her ready and eager to get started, it turned out that the producer wasn't quite ready to go back into his house just yet.

Instead, he took out what looked like a weather-beaten wallet from his back pocket. When he opened it, she realized that he wasn't holding a wallet. What Lukkas had in his hand was a checkbook.

The next moment he had turned toward the officer who was still standing there. "I heard that the department is collecting ticket money for their semi-annual basketball-for-charity game," Lukkas said as he began to write a more than substantial check to the Bedford Police Department, earmarking it for the basketball game.

Seeing the sum, the officer beamed, instantly forgetting all about the arrest he had been deprived of. "Yes, sir."

"Here." Lukkas tore out the check and handed it to the officer. "This might help a little."

Looking again at the sum the producer had written in,

the police officer's eyes seemed about to fall out of the man's head. Yohanna thought that perhaps the number hadn't quite registered when the man had first glanced at the check.

"Yes, sir, it sure would," the officer said with no small enthusiasm.

"Keep up the good work," Lukkas said, turning his back on the man and striding back to his house.

Yohanna tried to fall into place beside the producer. She found herself all but racing to keep up with him. In the background, she heard the patrol car driving away.

Glancing over his shoulder, Lukkas asked, "Am I walking too fast for you?"

"No," Yohanna answered stubbornly, doing her best to move even faster.

He stopped abruptly at his front door. Fueled by momentum, Yohanna almost crashed into him. Had he not caught hold of her shoulders just then, her body might have wound up vying for the exact same space that his was in.

Hiding his amusement, Lukkas held her in place for a moment. "Never be ashamed to admit the truth," he told her, referring to the answer she'd given him.

Rather than meekly accept the castigation, she lifted her chin ever so slightly and asked, "Does that work both ways?"

He didn't answer her immediately. He took his time, as if he was weighing something.

"Yes," he said after a beat.

She decided to see if he actually practiced what he preached. "Then, did you have a stalker?"

Releasing her shoulders, instead of being annoyed, Lukkas laughed. "Touché," he acknowledged, inclining his head.

Then he pulled open the front door. He'd left it unlocked earlier when he'd come out to see what was going on.

Yohanna just assumed the man was going to leave the question she'd repeated hanging in the air, unanswered. To her surprise, as she started to enter the house, she heard him say, "Yes, I had a stalker. It was a few years ago."

Closing the door behind them, Lukkas began to lead her through the house to the room he'd converted into his office. The same place where he had conducted her interview yesterday.

This time, since she was just a shade less nervous than she had been the day before, she took in more of her surroundings. Rather than modern or austere, the furnishings struck her as comfortable with warm, friendly lines. She wondered if her new boss had done the decorating himself, or if he had hired someone to do it for him.

Maybe he'd left it up to the woman she was replacing, she mused.

"Did they catch the person? The stalker," she clarified. Since Lukkas had opened up a little, she did her best to follow up on the subject. The more she knew about her employer, the more efficiently she could serve him.

"Why do you want to know?" As a rule, Lukkas didn't like being questioned. He turned the tables on his new assistant. Every word she uttered painted that much more of a complete picture of her.

"Just curious if there was still someone out there who felt they had the right to a piece of your life," she told him.

He thought that was rather a unique way of describing his stalker. Maybe there was more to this woman he'd hired than he'd thought, which was all to the good in his opinion.

"There's *always* someone out there, Hanna," he told her. "But if you're asking specifically if that misguided young woman is liable to pop up outside my window at a time of her choosing, the answer's no. To the best of my knowledge, she's still being treated as an inpatient at a psychiatric facility." This time he stopped right outside his office door. "Anything else?"

She got the distinct impression that the topic of conversation was to end right here, at his door. She wasn't quite sure if that meant she had stepped over some invisible boundary, or if the tone of voice he was using was just the way he sounded when he spoke to someone who was working for him.

If he decided to keep her on, she supposed she'd find out.

"Yes," she replied.

"Go ahead." There was no indication that he was running out of patience as far as she could see—which was good.

"Shouldn't I have filled out some sort of paperwork for your human resources department?" Yohanna asked.

Although overjoyed to actually be working, especially for someone like Lukkas Spader, there was still a small part of her that was highly skeptical about the validity of the entire arrangement. That left her wondering if perhaps, at the end of the day, she was not only off the record but completely off *any* books, as well.

Lukkas made no answer.

Instead, he pushed open the door to his office and silently gestured toward his desk.

There, lying on the blotter, away from the rest of the disorganized array that covered more than seven-eighths of his desk, were several pristine white pages stacked one on top of the other.

Crossing over to his desk, Yohanna saw that they appeared to be meant for her. Her first name was written on the top sheet.

"I would have put down your full name," he told her. "But there's no way in hell I would have spelled it right."

She smiled at that. Her last name had been misspelled more times than she could count.

"It took me two days to learn how to spell it when I was a kid. I thought about having it legally changed a couple of times," she confided, even though she had never gone through with it.

"Don't," he told her. "It has character. This is a place that tends to spew out carbon copies," he said, referring to his industry. "Being unique is a good thing." He paused for a moment. "When you finish with those, I'll give you a number and you can fax them to Human Resources," he told her. "Then we'll get down to the real work."

Yohanna had already sat down and begun filling out the employment forms.

Lukkas looked up from the preproduction notes he'd been working on. The center of his back was aching, the way it did when he remained immobile for a long period of time. It was due to an old college football injury, reminding him that he wasn't a kid anymore. He didn't like being reminded.

He glanced at his watch.

It was past seven-thirty in the evening. More than

twelve hours since he'd gotten started. Not that that was unusual. He was used to driving himself relentlessly whenever he was working on a project, especially at the very beginning of it.

He was also used to his people wearing out and leaving before his own day ended.

He had to admit he was surprised that this new woman not only hadn't said anything about the amount of time that had passed since she'd arrived at his house, but she appeared to be keeping up with the grueling pace he had set for himself.

Empty cardboard containers were piled up in the wastepaper basket beside his desk, evidence of the food they'd consumed. He'd sent out for lunch, but that had been close to six hours ago.

He felt his own stomach tightening in complaint, and he was accustomed to this sort of pace. He expected to hear Hanna's stomach rumbling at any second. He had no doubts that the woman probably thought he was some sort of an inhumane slave driver.

Pausing, he studied her unabashedly. She seemed to be oblivious to it, but that was probably an act. She didn't strike him as the type to be oblivious to *anything* in her immediate surroundings.

"You tired?" he asked her.

"No," she answered as she went over the notes he had completed earlier and handed to her. He'd wanted her to familiarize herself with what was involved on his end of preproduction. He planned to take her every step of the way just once. After that, she had to sink or swim on her own.

Raising her head for a split second to look in his direction, she assured him, "I'm fine."

"What did I say about the truth?" he asked her.

"Ah, a pop quiz. You didn't tell me about that." Her quick grin faded as she gave him the answer he required. "To never be afraid to admit it."

He nodded and then said, "Let's do this again. You tired?"

For a second Yohanna debated repeating her denial, but obviously that wasn't what Spader wanted to hear from her.

"Maybe a little," she allowed, even though it was against her nature to complain.

When he kept on looking at her, as if his eyes were drilling right into her mind, searching for the truth, Yohanna mentally threw up her hands and said, "Exhausted, actually."

The smallest of smiles briefly made an appearance on his lips. "There, that wasn't really so hard, was it?" he asked.

"It wasn't actually easy, either," she told him. "Especially since I wasn't sure what it was you wanted to hear," she admitted.

"The truth, Hanna, always the truth," he stressed. He put his pen down. Right now, this was more important than the notes he was making. "You're not going to do me any good if I have to read between the lines anytime I ask you a simple question. I need total honesty from you," Lukkas told her.

She spoke before she could censor herself. "No one wants total honesty. They just want *their* version of total honesty."

The words surprised him and managed to catch him completely off guard. He scrutinized her for a long moment, as if trying to decide something. "How old are you, Hanna?" he finally asked.

"Thirty."

He noticed there wasn't any hesitation before she volunteered the number. Most women over the age of twenty were coy when it came to the age question. She really was unique, he thought.

"Thirty, and already so cynical," he commented.

But Yohanna had a different opinion about her view. "Not cynical," she contradicted. "Being completely honest a hundred percent of the time is really cold and unfeeling."

He leaned back in his chair, rocking slightly as he regarded her. "How do you figure that?"

"For instance, if a girlfriend asks you if what she has on makes her look fat, she really doesn't want to know that she looks fat. What she really wants is to hear how flattering the outfit she's wearing looks on her."

"But if it really does make her look fat?" Lukkas asked, curious as to what her thought process was. "Aren't you doing that friend a disservice by *not* telling her the truth?"

Yohanna shook her head. "If it really does look bad on her, she'll figure it out on her own. She wants to hear flattering words from you."

"You can't be serious," he protested.

"Completely," she insisted. "What your friend will come away with is that you cared more about her feelings than making some kind of point by being a champion of the truth."

"In other words, you're saying it's all right to lie," he surmised.

"If you can't bring yourself to tell her a little white lie,

21 Aug 2019 2:17 PM

Her red carpet romance / Marie
Ferrarella A millionaire for Cinderella,

Date Due: 14 Sep 2019

To renew your items:
Go online to librariesireland.com
Phone us at (01) 842 1890
Opening Hours Mon-Thu 10am to 8pm
Fri Sat 10am to 5pm

say something nice about the color. Maybe it brings out her eyes, or makes her skin tones come alive."

"In other words, say anything but the word *fat*," he concluded.

She nodded. The smile began in her eyes and worked its way to her lips in less than a second. He found himself being rather taken with that. "*Fat* only belongs in front of the word *paycheck* or *rain cloud*."

"That's two words," Lukkas pointed out, not bothering to hide his amusement.

Yohanna suddenly became aware that she had been going on and on. Her demeanor shifted abruptly. "Sorry, I talk too much."

"You do," he conceded. "But lucky for me, so far it's been entertaining." Lukkas grinned, then after a beat, asked, "How's that?"

She wasn't sure what he was asking her about. "Excuse me?"

"I just threw in the truth, but then said something to soften the blow. I was just asking how you thought I did, if I got the gist of your little theory."

For a moment, as her eyes met his, Yohanna didn't say anything.

Was he being sarcastic?

Somehow, she didn't think so, but that was just a gut reaction. After all, she didn't really know the man, didn't know anything about him other than the information she'd gleaned from a handful of interviews she'd looked up and read yesterday before she'd come in for the interview.

Taking a chance that the producer was really being on the level, she smiled and said, "Very good," commenting on his "behavior."

"I wasn't trying to lecture you, you know," she told him in case he'd gotten the wrong impression. "I was just putting my opinion out there." And then she shrugged somewhat self-consciously. "My mother says I do that too much."

He instantly endeared himself to her by saying, "Your mother's wrong." She had to really concentrate to hear what he had to say after that. "There's nothing wrong with offering an opinion—unless, of course, you're delivering a scathing review on one of my movies. Then all bets are off."

"Has anyone ever done that?" she asked incredulously. Then, in case he didn't understand what she was asking, she repeated his words. "Given a scathing review about one of your movies?"

He didn't have to think hard. He remembered the movie, the reviewer, what the person had said and when. Why was it that the good reviews all faded into the background, but the one or two reviews that panned his movie felt as if they had been burned right into his heart?

"Once or twice," he answered, keeping his reply deliberately vague. The reviews hadn't exactly been scathing, but they had been far from good.

"Well, they were crazy," she pronounced. "You make wonderful movies."

He laughed at her extraserious expression. "You don't have to say that," he told her. "You already have the job."

"I'm not saying it because I want this job, I'm saying it because I really like your movies," she insisted. "They make me feel good."

"Well, that was their intention," he said, carrying the conversation far further than he had ever intended. He rarely discussed his movies this way. He spent a lot of time on the mechanics of the movie rather than the gut reaction to it. The latter was something he felt would take care of itself. It was just up to him to set the scene.

Chapter Four

"Do you get airsick?"

Lukkas's question came at her without warning.

As she had been doing for more than a week, Yohanna had driven to the producer's Newport Beach house.

She'd turned up bright and early, ready to put in another long day setting the man's professional life in order. He was bringing another project to life, and that involved an incredible amount of details that all needed to be attended to. Every day was a new learning experience for her.

She could hardly wait to get started every morning.

When she'd rung Lukkas's doorbell and he'd opened the door, she had offered up a cheerful, "Good morning."

Rather than return the greeting or say a simple hello, Lukkas had caught her off guard by asking if she'd ever experienced airsickness.

Stunned, Yohanna looked at him for a moment, then replied with a touch of vagueness, "Not that I know of. Why?"

"Good," he pronounced. "Because we're taking a little trip today."

She hung on to the word *little*.

"Anyplace in particular?" she asked when the producer didn't volunteer a destination.

He grinned in a way that made him almost impossibly sexy to her.

"Of course there's someplace in particular." He led the way back to his office. She saw his briefcase on his desk. It was open and he'd obviously been packing it when she'd rung the doorbell. "How many people you know fly around aimlessly?"

"Never conducted a survey on that." She watched him tuck a tablet into the briefcase, putting it between a sea of papers. "Do I get to ask where we're going?"

Lukkas paused, appearing as if he was trying to remember something. "You can always ask," he told her, sounding preoccupied.

"Let me rephrase that," she said out loud. "If I ask you where we're going, will you tell me?"

"I guess I'll have to." He closed his briefcase and flipped the locks into place. "Otherwise, it might be construed as kidnapping."

"As long as I'm on the clock, I don't think it can be called kidnapping." He walked out of his office. She fell into step beside him. "Not unless you tie me up," she put in as an afterthought.

The description made him laugh. Lukkas shook his head. "Did you talk like this at your last job?"

"Oddly enough," she answered, amused, "the topic of kidnapping never came up."

He speared her a long, penetrating look as he armed his security system and closed the door behind them. "So you didn't talk?"

"I didn't say that." She waited as he aimed the remote on his key chain at his car. All four locks flipped open. She got in on her side.

He tossed his briefcase onto the seat behind him, then got in behind the steering wheel. "You ever consider running for elective office? You've got all the evasion maneuvers down pat." Starting up his silver-blue BMW, he commented, "I'll say one thing about you. You've certainly got your wits about you. I like that."

She assumed that the first part of his comment was somehow tied to his query about whether or not she had any political aspirations. She couldn't think of anything she would have rather done *less* than that. Besides, the life she had jumped into, feetfirst, was getting more and more interesting by the minute.

"Then you won't mind telling me where we're flying off to." It wasn't a question but an assumption.

"Don't you like mysteries?" Lukkas asked, playing this out a little longer.

"Just to read, not when I'm in them," she told him honestly. "I like knowing. *Everything*," Yohanna elaborated.

"Does that mean you don't like surprises?" he asked.

Thinking of the way the so-called "layoff" had been sprung on her, there was only one way for her to answer that question. "Only for other people."

"A life without surprises." He rolled the idea over in his head as he squeaked through a yellow light that was already beginning to turn red. "Where's the fun in that?"

Lukkas spared her a quick glance. "You do like to have fun, don't you, Hanna?" he asked.

Finding herself being interviewed for a job by Lukkas Spader had been one giant surprise, but if she said so, he might mistakenly think she was flirting with him. There was no way she was going to allow her attraction to the man get in the way of her working for him.

"Lots of fun to be gotten without resorting to surprises," she pointed out.

On the freeway for all of four minutes, he took the off-ramp that promised to lead him to the airfield he needed.

"If you say so," he replied. "You like Arizona?"

Another question out of the blue. And then she remembered. He'd said something about his new project, a Western, being on location in Arizona. Was that where they were going?

Her stomach began to tighten up.

"I really can't say," she answered truthfully.

"And why is that?"

"I've never been to Arizona," she told him. He probably thought she was some sort of semirecluse. She hadn't been anywhere outside of a rather small area while he, she knew, was an international traveler, going wherever the movie took him.

"Well, Hanna, we are about to remedy that," Lukkas proclaimed.

Her eyes widened just a shade. "We're going to Arizona?" she asked, doing her best to hide her nervousness.

"That would be the natural assumption to make from what I'd just said, yes."

Traffic had gotten a little thicker. He was forced to go just at the speed limit rather than above it.

He hadn't mentioned anything about going on location to her yesterday. When had this happened?

"*Why* are we going to Arizona?"

"Because that's where the movie's going to be shot," he said, referring to his new "baby," a movie he had helped write, one based on his own story idea. "At least most of it. Whatever we can do indoors, we'll take care of at the studio. But there's no way, in this day and age, to be able to fake that kind of background—especially not Monument Valley," he added. He slanted a long look in her direction. "Ever hear of Monument Valley?" he asked.

So far, she seemed like efficiency personified, but that might be because she had him on the rebound from his previous relationship with Janice. He'd leaned on her completely. When she'd told him she was leaving, he'd felt as if his entire foundation was about to crack and dissolve into pieces under his feet.

Hanna had appeared just in time to be his superglue.

"Several of John Wayne's movies were shot there," she told him without pausing to think.

He smiled, impressed she knew that. Impressed with her. Something that was beginning to occur on a daily basis.

"You knew that," he said, somewhat marveled.

"I knew that," she reaffirmed. "So you're going to be shooting this film somewhere around—or in—Monument Valley?"

"No," he answered breezily.

Okay, now she was confused, Yohanna thought. "I don't understand. If you're not shooting there, why did you just ask me if I knew what Monument Valley was?"

"I thought I'd spring a pop quiz on you," he told her.

And then he grinned again. "And maybe Monument Valley will sneak in a time or two when we're shooting background shots for the movie. But right now we're going to be flying to Sugar Springs, Arizona. It's near Tombstone."

On what seemed like a winding road, they were approaching the small private airport that was his immediate destination. It housed approximately half a dozen private single-engine plans. Including his.

The area was a revelation to Yohanna. "I didn't know there was an airport there."

"There isn't," he told her, driving over to the hangar that housed his plane. "It's more like a landing strip than an airport. But the plane isn't very big, either, so it works out."

She looked at him, a queasiness beginning to work its way into the center of her stomach. "You can fly a plane, too?"

"I've got a few hours of piloting under my belt," he told her.

She immediately seized on what she hadn't heard. "But no pilot's license?"

"Not yet." He saw grave concern etching itself into her features. "Don't worry, I'm not the one who's going to be in the cockpit," he assured her. "I've got a pilot on call."

Lukkas was on the private airstrip now. He drove straight toward where his plane was waiting. Arrangements had been made with the pilot the night before. He'd wanted to make sure the plane would be gassed up, inspected and ready to fly by the time he arrived this morning.

"Your color's coming back," he informed her, amusement highlighting his tanned face.

She looked at him, bewildered. "Excuse me?"

"Just now, when you thought I was flying the plane, the color drained completely out of your face. It's back now," he noted.

"Must be the lighting in here," she said, grasping at any excuse. She didn't want him to feel undermined by what had to seem like a lack of faith in him. From what she'd learned, most of the producers had egos the size of Texas and wouldn't stand for any attempts at taking them down a peg or three.

Lukkas didn't appear to have an ego, but it was still too early in the game to tell.

"Maybe," he intoned, appearing to consider her comment about the lighting being responsible for her ghostly pallor a few minutes ago. "Contrary to what you might think, I don't have a death wish, and the only risk I take is when I cast certain performers thought to be washed up in the business by everybody and his brother. What they don't seem to understand," he continued, "is that if you show some faith in that person, they tend to try to live up to that image."

Parked now, he opened his door. "Let's go," he urged, getting out of his car. "Right now we're burning daylight."

He was already walking toward the airplane before she could say a word.

Yohanna wasn't exactly sure why he wanted her to accompany him on this flight. She'd effectively begun to organize his vastly overwhelming schedule so that he could actually have a prayer of staying on top of his agenda. Educating herself as best she could about the man she was taking all this on for, she'd begun to prioritize what absolutely needed to be done and what could wait for another day to come.

She had a feeling the reason Spader was so disorganized was that his mind raced around, taking everything he had to do into consideration, going first down one trail, then another and another. It seemed as though the man's day was filled with a great many starts and no conclusions. Without someone to take charge of the details and put them into a workable order, the producer was headed for a complete meltdown, which would in turn lead to utter chaos in his professional *and* his private life.

And she could do all that right from his office in Bedford. Which was why she didn't quite understand why he was taking her with him to Arizona. Especially when it all seemed rather spur-of-the-moment. At least, he hadn't mentioned anything to her about it yesterday.

"And why are we going there?" she asked.

"Let's call it a final run-through," he told her. "Among other things, I want to look around the town we're renting, make sure nothing modern's lying around to mess up a shot when we're filming. I don't want to be in post-production and suddenly looking at an iPod left on the bar or something equally as jarring."

Well, that part at least made sense. "And what am I going to be doing?" she asked.

"Off the top of my head, I'd say you can be the person taking notes to make sure that I can keep track of everything that occurs to me while I'm doing that run-through." Then he summed it up for her. "You'll do what every organizer does. You'll organize," Lukkas informed her.

Hurrying up the short portable stairs that had been

positioned beside the sleek plane, Lukkas greeted the pilot as he entered the plane.

"Jacob, this is Hanna Something-or-other. She'll be taking Janice's place," he told the pilot. "Hanna, this is Jacob Winter, the very best pilot around."

The pilot flashed a modest smile. "He's just saying that because I didn't crash the plane."

Obviously there was more to the story than just that, Yohanna thought, looking from one man to the other. But if there was, it would be a story for another day, she could tell.

Inclining his head ever so slightly for a moment, the pilot told Lukkas, "We'll be taking off as soon as you strap in."

Lukkas looked at her as if they were equal partners in this, not boss and employee. "Then, let's get strapped in."

A few minutes later Yohanna was gripping the armrests of her seat and holding her startled breath as she felt the single-engine plane begin its takeoff.

This was the easy part, she told herself, but she remained stubbornly unconvinced of this.

"I take it that you don't fly very much, do you?" Lukkas asked, looking at the way her very white knuckles seemed to protrude as Yohanna continued gripping the armrests.

"No," Yohanna answered without looking in his direction.

He thought he heard a slight quiver in her voice. That didn't seem like the young woman he was getting to know. "How often *have* you flown?" he asked.

This time she tried to turn her head to glance in his direction. But something seemed to almost hold her entire body in place. She recognized it as fear and started to mount a defense.

"Counting this time?" she finally responded, answering his question with a question.

"Yes."

She took in a shaky breath. "Once."

That would explain the white knuckles and the death grip she had on the armrests, Lukkas thought. "Then, why didn't you say something to me before we got on the plane?"

She forced herself to breathe normally. It was far from easy.

"Like what? Would you mind driving to this town I've never heard of in Arizona instead of flying? You're the boss," she pointed out. "That means that I'm supposed to accommodate you as best I can, not the other way around."

She kept impressing him when he least expected it. That went a long way in her favor. He'd begun to think that he could no longer be impressed by anything life had to offer. It was nice to know that he was wrong.

"I do like your work ethic, Hanna. This little arrangement just might work out after all." Glancing down at her hands, which were still wrapped around the armrests, gripping them for all she was worth, he told her, "I won't even charge you for having to replace the armrests."

She was acting like a child, not a grown woman, Yohanna upbraided herself. Though it took almost superhuman effort, she forced her hands to let go of the armrests, although it took her a while to get all ten fingers off at the same time.

"Sorry," she murmured.

"Nothing to be sorry about," Lukkas countered. "Lots of people have flying issues."

"You probably think I'm being childish. I mean, I know that the odds against the plane going down are really tremendously low and that, comparably, a lot more people die in car crashes than plane crashes, but what my brain knows and the rest of me knows hasn't become fully reconciled yet."

Yohanna took another long, steadying breath and then let it out slowly, growing just a shade more in control of herself as she did so.

That was when she noticed Lukkas's encouraging, amused smile had completely faded from his lips. It was replaced with a solemnity she hadn't witnessed on the man before.

Obviously something had suddenly changed.

Every single instinct she possessed told her that something was wrong, but as to what, she hadn't a sliver of a clue.

Since she had been the only one talking when this transformation had occurred for Lukkas, it had to be either something she'd said, or a thought that had unexpectedly crossed the man's mind.

If it was the latter, then she was at a total loss how to remedy that. She had no way of discovering what had occurred to him to make him turn one hundred and eighty degrees.

However, if it was something that she had inadvertently said, then the advantage was hers.

But what had she said that could have affected him this way? She'd just cited statistics between plane crashes and car crashes.

Replaying the past few minutes in her head, she decided that it couldn't have been anything to do with plane crashes because Lukkas had still been grinning after she'd mentioned them.

That left car crashes.

Someone he had known must have died in a car crash. The more she went over that abbreviated section of time in her head, the more certain she became that she was right in her estimation.

But there was no way she could just ask Lukkas about that outright. If nothing else, in the long run that would be like pouring salt into a freshly reopened wound just to satisfying her curiosity.

There had to be another way to find out if she was right.

She thought of Cecilia's friend, Mrs. Manetti, who had initially set up her interview with the producer. Mrs. Manetti might know.

And then, she thought as the silence between Lukkas and her continued, there might even be a faster way to find out if she hadn't stuck her fashionably shod high-heeled foot into her unsuspecting mouth.

Her hooded eyes watched Lukkas for any sign that he was about to turn to her or to say something. He seemed very preoccupied with whatever was in the black folder he kept within easy reach, at least from what she'd discerned so far. She quietly turned on her smartphone.

Still watching Lukkas, she pulled up a search engine and typed in the words *car accident* and then his name.

The signal reception was reduced to only two bars, rendering the search engine exceedingly sluggish. She watched the little circle that indicated the site was being loaded go around and around for so long, she felt it was stuck in this mode.

She was about to give up for now and close her phone when she saw the tiny screen in her hand struggle to stabilize both two photographs and the words written directly beneath them.

She'd assumed that the words would become clear first, but it was the photographs—a beautiful young woman in one and a car that looked as if it had been turned into an accordion in the other—that materialized several minutes before the words.

After an eternity the circle stopped swirling and disappeared, leaving in its wake the headline from a newspaper article: Producer's Pregnant Wife Killed in Car Crash.

The article identified the dead woman's husband as Lukkas Spader.

Chapter Five

Stunned and appalled, Yohanna could only numbly stare at the heart-wrenching headline, unaware that her mouth had literally dropped open.

The next moment her brain kicked in and she quickly pressed the home button at the bottom of her smartphone. An array of apps sprang up, very effectively replacing the article as if it had never been there to begin with. Under different circumstances, she would have gone on to read the article, but this was definitely not the time for her to fill in the gaps.

The idea of Lukkas looking over and accidentally seeing what she was reading was just unthinkable to her. It was bad enough that she'd carelessly said what she'd said just now, comparing the crash rate of planes to cars. It didn't matter that she hadn't known Lukkas's wife had lost her life in an event that she had so cavalierly tossed out. Her not knowing hadn't lessened the pain Lukkas undoubtedly felt at the unintentional reminder of his loss.

More than anything, she would have loved to apologize to him, to tell him that she hadn't known he'd lost his wife this way. Until just now, she hadn't thought that he was ever married.

She'd done her homework on him but only partially so. To do her job well, she had been trying to educate herself about Lukkas Spader the producer, not the private man. The one article that had touched on both his professional *and* his private life had referred to him as being one of Hollywood's most eligible bachelors. That, to her, had translated to his not being married.

Had the article been written by a more accurate writer, it would have made some sort of a reference to his being a widower. At least that would have given her some sort of a heads-up.

Yohanna slanted a look in his direction. How did she go about making this right? She didn't have a clue, so for now, all she could do was leave the matter alone.

"We're about to land," Lukkas told her, his deep voice cutting through the fog still swirling around her head. "You might want to secure that." He nodded at the smartphone still in her hand.

"Yes, of course." Feeling like someone who was just now coming to, Yohanna quickly slipped the device back into her pocket.

After a beat, as they began their slow descent, Lukkas quietly said, "They said that she didn't feel any pain."

Yohanna's head jerked up as she looked at him. Had Lukkas glimpsed the article she had pulled up on her phone? She fervently hoped not.

But then, how did she explain the remark he had just made?

"Excuse me?" she said in the most innocent voice she could muster.

"My wife. Her car crash," Lukkas said, filling in the pertinent words. "The first responders on the scene said she died instantly and mercifully hadn't felt any pain. She didn't even have time to react, actually." Then, as if aware that he was speaking in fragments, he told her, "I saw you looking up the article."

There was no point in trying to deny it, Yohanna thought. She wasn't about to insult him like that or by pretending that he could be diverted by some fancy verbal tap dancing. He'd already showed her that he valued honesty.

"I'm so sorry, I didn't know. I wouldn't have made that thoughtless comparison about planes and cars if I had known about your wife."

"I know," Lukkas told her. An extremely bittersweet smile curved just the edges of his mouth. "It's just that, even after almost three years, I'm still not really used to it." His voice took on a wistful tone. "There are times that I still expect to hear her voice, or see her coming out of the kitchen, telling me she's in the mood for pizza when what was really going on was that she'd burned dinner beyond any hope of recognition—again," he added, grinning as he fondly recalled the memory.

"I am so very, very sorry," she told the producer in what amounted to a whisper.

Yohanna felt utterly helpless. She wasn't going to mouth the utterly overused and hopelessly clichéd phrase that she was sorry for his loss because it didn't begin to encompass, in her opinion, the grief the man must have felt and that he still continued to feel.

She remembered when her father had died the summer that she'd turned twelve; for weeks afterward she just couldn't find a place for herself. It was as if every place, both physically and emotionally, felt wrong to her, as if she didn't belong in it. It didn't matter if that place was familiar to her or not, she was still uncomfortable.

It had taken her a long time to make peace with her sense of loss. She couldn't begin to imagine what it must have been like for Lukkas to lose a spouse, not to mention their unborn child, as well.

"Yeah, me, too," Lukkas murmured more to himself than to her.

The next moment she saw the producer unbuckling his seat belt.

"Wait, shouldn't you keep that on?" she asked, afraid her initial careless observation had triggered a reckless reaction from Lukkas.

"Only if I want to try to take this chair with me on location." He pointed to the window next to her. "We've landed."

She blinked and looked out. They were on the ground. How had that happened without her realizing it?

"Oh."

She felt foolish. So far, today wasn't going well *at all*. She'd been so concerned about his feelings of loss as well as how callous he must have thought she'd sounded that she hadn't even paid attention to the fact that the plane had descended and made its landing.

Lukkas pulled down his briefcase from the overhead compartment. "Don't worry, you'll be a seasoned flier in no time," he assured her, verbally moving on and putting a world of distance between himself and the previous topic.

Unbuckling, Yohanna grabbed her things and was on her feet, following him off the plane. As she went, she made a mental note to find the article again when she got home tonight. She wanted to familiarize herself with the details of the story so she wouldn't be guilty of making another thoughtless reference to a very painful period in his life.

The sun, definitely not in hiding when they left Bedford, seemed to have been turned up to High as it greeted her the second she left the shelter of the single-engine Learjet. She shaded her eyes with her free hand, but that still didn't make visibility even an iota more tolerable.

Halfway down the ramp that had been placed beside the plane's open door, Lukkas turned toward her. "Watch your step," he warned. "The sun can be a little blinding out here until you get used to it."

She had a habit of dashing up and down the stairs without bothering to even marginally hold on to any banister or railing. But because Lukkas had specifically cautioned her, she thought it best to slip her hand over the railing and slide her palm down along the bar as she descended. She didn't want him to think that she was ignoring his advice.

Besides, it never hurt anything to be careful—just in case.

There was a silver-green, fully loaded Toyota waiting for them. It was parked well inside the gates. The plane hadn't landed far from it.

"Welcome back, Mr. Spader," the man standing beside the vehicle called out to Lukkas the second they were within hearing range. Of average height and build, looking to be around forty or so, with a thick, black head of hair, the man opened the rear door behind the driver's side, then waited until they reached the vehicle.

"Thanks for coming to pick us up, Juan," Lukkas said to the driver. Then he nodded in her direction. "This is Hanna. She'll be taking Janice's place."

The man he had called Juan nodded at her politely, then flashed an easy smile. "You've got your work cut out for you, Hanna," he told her. "Janice found a way to be everywhere at once."

No pressure here, Yohanna thought. She forced a smile to her lips in response. "I'll give it my best shot."

Lukkas spared her a look before he gestured for her to get into the vehicle first. "You'll have to do better than that to stay on the team," he informed her. "I can't have you just trying, I need you *doing*." He pointedly emphasized the word.

Really no pressure here, Yohanna thought, feeling a little uneasy—but just for a moment. The thing about pressure was that feeling it made her more determined than ever to succeed. She had decided a long time ago to be one of those people who had made up her mind to rise to the occasion rather than to fold under the specter of insurmountable obstacles or to listen to someone when they said something couldn't be done.

She was, at bottom, a doer. It wasn't in her nature not to give something her absolute all.

"Don't worry about me. With all due respect to Janice, I'll do whatever you need done," she replied with quiet determination. "And I'll do it fast."

Listening—even though he looked to be elsewhere—Lukkas inclined his head, as if conducting a conversation with himself.

"We'll see," he said, and then repeated even more softly, "We'll see."

Yohanna squared her shoulders. *We sure will*, she silently promised.

"Did you do this?" she asked Lukkas, wonder clearly shimmering in her voice as, twenty minutes later, she stared at the town coming into view.

At first glance, it was as if all three of them—Lukkas, Juan and she—had crossed some sort of a time-travel portal, one that separated the present from the long-ago past.

Sitting inside a brand-new state-of-the-art vehicle, she found herself looking out at a town that for all the world appeared to have literally been lifted from the late 1800s. Here and there were horses tied to hitching posts outside weathered wooden buildings, the tallest of which was, very obviously, the town saloon. The streets were paved not with asphalt or cement but dirt—hard, sun-baked, parched, cracked dirt.

Rolling down the window on her side, Yohanna leaned out to get a better view. Everything that she would have imagined to have existed in a slightly romanticized version of the Old West seemed to be right here. She began taking inventory.

There was a newspaper office, a barbershop that doubled as a doctor's office, and an emporium that was twice as wide as the other buildings because it contained the only so-called shopping area for the citizens of and beyond the town.

There was another rather dilapidated tiny hole-in-the-wall building, which, she saw as they drew closer, was actually the sheriff's office. One street away, dominating almost that entire block and two stories tall, was the town's one and only saloon. Big and gaudy, the Birdcage Saloon seemed primed for business even at this early an hour in the morning.

"No." Lukkas answered her question. "I found the town like this. It's perfect, isn't it?" She didn't know if he was still talking to her or sharing something with someone in his mind. "Pull over here, Juan," he instructed, pointing.

"Here" was in front of the saloon. Getting out, he waited for her to slide out of the car after him.

When she did, Yohanna looked around in complete wonder, unable to make up her mind whether or not the producer was putting her on. While the town looked weathered, something about it didn't strike her as genuine.

She couldn't put her finger on it, but this old-fashioned Western town didn't appear 100 percent authentic to her, either.

"You didn't help it along to arrive at this Old West town look?" she asked.

She'd initially looked too innocent to be this sharp, he thought. He didn't know whether to be proud that she could be this forthright, or leery of dealing with her on general principle.

In either case, she was still waiting for an answer, he reminded himself.

"I didn't, but Jeff Richards did."

The name meant nothing to her. Yohanna shook her head. "I'm afraid I don't—"

He hadn't expected her to know who he was referring to unless she'd read the article in that popular magazine a few months ago.

"Richards is the one who bought this entire town by paying off its back taxes. It was his idea to turn it into a tourist attraction," he told her. "He was trying to make it into a Tombstone look-alike." He went on to explain. "We're renting it for the duration of filming the exterior shots—and a couple of the interior ones, as well. After that, we fold up our tents—or get into our trailers and drive as it were—and he gets his town back with the added benefit of being able to advertise that *The Sheriff From Nowhere* was filmed here on location."

He smiled to himself about the predictability of the situation. "You'd be surprised what a little publicity like that does to attract people. By the way, while we're renting this town, it'll be your job to make sure Richards gets his checks on a regular basis. You'll also make me aware of any snags, misunderstandings and problems that might crop up due to our arrangement."

"Problems?" she questioned.

"Like fees suddenly being raised or doubled. You'd be surprised what some people try to pull," Lukkas told her.

"Got it," she said, making a notation in her notebook.

That she had written down what he'd said caught his attention. "Why aren't you making an entry on your smartphone calendar?"

"I will," she told him, wondering if he thought she was archaic in her methods. "But I have to admit that I like the feel of putting a pen to paper when I make my notes. This way, I'll wind up with two sets of records about the things I'm supposed to take charge of and keep after."

Yohanna had a feeling this was going to be a lot to contend with, especially since she knew the man's actual handwriting looked to be about preschool level quality. It was difficult to make heads or tails out of some of it.

She would have preferred if he had dictated and recorded his notes into his cell phone. But although it was apparent he felt electronic devices were tremendous work savers, in the long run, he obviously still was very tied to the old-fashioned way of keeping track of the events—large and small—of his life.

"Huh," he murmured in response to her claim of liking the feel of putting pen to paper.

Lukkas couldn't help but wonder if she was being genuine, or if she was merely saying that because she'd learned from someone that he felt the same way about the notes he made to himself.

The veteran producer was the first to admit that he was scattered from here to eternity and the notes he cared about…well, they could still be found somewhere between those two points. He had good intentions, but heaven knew he wasn't organized.

That was where she was supposed to come in.

It was up to her to keep after him as well as to make his hectic world as organized as humanly possible.

"There's Dirk Montelle," Lukkas suddenly announced, giving the man the hello sign when the latter looked in their direction. "He's signed on to direct this little movie," he told her.

The man had a real gift for understatement, she thought. That was a revelation to her.

She would have thought that a man of his capabilities, not to mention the perks he probably had written into his contracts, would have had a giant ego and a way of pounding his own chest and putting everyone else down. She'd known men like that before. Actually *dated* men like that before she'd decided she was better off sitting home alone than being out with one of these egotists, chairing a fan club meeting of one.

But before she could make some sort of a response to his last comment, Lukkas was taking off, striding across the parched and cracked streets to reach the man he had ultimately selected to helm his movie. He'd told her how he'd thought long and hard over making an offer to the director. This was his life's blood up there. That was a hard thing to ignore or even remain neutral about. Finally getting the proposed movie off the storyboards and onto a set with a final script was like having a dream come true. The movie he was now in charge of making had been a secret project of his for the past ten years.

Watching Lukkas pick up his pace, Yohanna shook her head. She picked up her own pace to make up for the head start the man had on her. Yohanna pressed her lips together, looking for strength even though she knew it could have been so much worse.

Even so, she couldn't help wishing that Lukkas would give her some kind of a warning before he took off like that.

She assumed he wanted her to get acquainted with the people working on this film so that when he asked her to do something with one of the cast or crew, she would know who he was talking about.

That meant becoming familiar with the names and jobs of more than two hundred people.

Fast.

Well, she'd wanted something a little more exciting than the work she'd done before, right? Office manager for the law firm had been good, steady work—until it wasn't, of course, and she'd become a casualty of the company merger—but it had also admittedly been dull as dishwater in its day-to-day routine.

This, however, had the makings of some sort of a wild, no-holds-barred adventure in fantasyland. For the moment—and hopefully for some time to come if everything went well—she would be dealing with both the present-day world and the past, and probably the future if what she'd heard about the producer's next project was true.

The words *dull* and *boring* were definitely not words to be applied to this job description, Yohanna thought happily.

"C'mon, catch up, Hanna," Lukkas urged as he turned for a moment in her direction and called out to her. "We don't want this project to start falling behind schedule before it even gets under way."

"No, sir," she responded—only to have Lukkas shoot her a look that stopped her in her tracks.

Instantly she realized her mistake. "No, Lukkas," she corrected herself.

"Hope you learn the routine faster than you learned that," he commented.

"Old habits are hard to unlearn," she told him.

"Didn't ask for an explanation, Hanna," Lukkas pointed out. "Just make it happen, starting now."

She inclined her head rather than open her mouth. Just for now, Yohanna thought that it might be better that way.

Chapter Six

If Dirk Montelle had been cast in a movie, Yohanna thought as she quickly followed Lukkas and drew closer to the director, he would have played a college professor. Montelle looked the type—almost stereotypically so—right down to the pipe that she'd read was never out of arm's reach.

For the most part, the man didn't smoke it as much as he kept it around to chew on its stem. According to an interview he'd given recently, it helped him cope with the countless tensions and crises that went along with being in the business of making fantasies come to life for a brief amount of time.

The longtime veteran director paused for a moment, cutting short his exchange with the person he was talking to, to greet Lukkas. When his steel-gray eyes shifted over to look at her, the affable director grinned broadly and then shook his head, not in a negative way but in apparent admiration.

"So I see you already heard," the director said to Lukkas.

"Heard what?" Lukkas asked as he shook the man's hand.

"About our little crisis. She certainly is pretty enough," the man said appreciatively, taking full measure of Yohanna. "If she can sound believable saying her lines, she's in." Appearing exceedingly satisfied, the director put his hand out to her and introduced himself. "Dirk Montelle. And you are…?"

"Very confused," Yohanna confessed as she glanced from the enthusiastic director to her equally confused-looking boss.

At least it wasn't just her, Yohanna thought with relief.

"Montelle, what the hell are you talking about?" Lukkas asked.

The director's expressive eyebrows rose high on his wide forehead. "You mean you didn't bring her here to replace Monica Elliott?" he asked, referring to the actress playing one of the more prominent supporting roles.

"Why would I want to replace Monica Elliott? The woman's got the mouth of a sailor on shore leave after six months at sea, but the audiences still seem to love her. All her recent films have been hits," Lukkas reminded the director.

Although, in his personal opinion, the egotistical actress was skating on very thin ice and living on borrowed time. Any day now, he expected to see a news bulletin that the twenty-seven-year-old actress had crashed and burned.

"Yeah, well, they're going to have to love someone

else," Dirk told him. "She walked out yesterday, saying that she decided to honor the commitment she'd broken to be in our movie."

Lukkas looked at his director. "Monica had another commitment?" This was the first he was hearing about there being another movie, much less that the high-living actress had broken a contract to film his movie instead.

Dirk nodded. "She said that the first contract predates the one she has with us by fifteen days."

"And what made her suddenly change her mind to switch back?" Lukkas asked.

Dirk raised his wide shoulders in an exaggerated shrug then let them fall almost dramatically. "With her, who knows? Somebody said something about Monica being angry that Angelica Fargo had more lines than she did." The director sighed. "Bottom line is that we're down the second lead." He turned toward Yohanna. "Sure you don't want to give it a whirl?" he asked, sounding almost half serious. "You look about the same size as Monica, so Wardrobe wouldn't be unhappy."

Though flattered, Yohanna's thoughts were focused elsewhere. "Did you see it?" she asked.

Dirk looked at her uncertainly. He hadn't a clue what she was asking. "See what?"

"The other contract," Yohanna stressed. "Did you see the date on it?"

Lukkas realized what his assistant was getting at. "Well, did you?" he asked his director and old friend.

The expression on Dirk's face was that of a man wondering if he had been duped. "Actually, no. I took her word for it. She said something about her lawyer holding on to it. The threat she was silently issuing was that she'd sue and hold up production on the picture if we didn't let her out of this contract."

"What are you thinking?" Lukkas asked Yohanna.

"That she might be bluffing. I could be wrong, but judging by her recent actions—yes, I watch those tabloid programs—that might be something she'd be prone to do, lie to get out of a contract she decided wasn't to her advantage to honor for some reason. It should be an easy thing to check out."

Lukkas turned his attention to his director. "You know anyone on the other set? Someone who might be able to confirm—or dispute—when the contracts for all the major players were signed?"

Montelle suddenly looked very pleased with himself—and impressed with Lukkas's newest addition to his crew. "As a matter of fact, I know a few people."

"Knew there was a reason I hired you," Lukkas quipped. Then he looked at Yohanna. "Nice catch."

"*Possible* catch," she amended.

"Modest, too. Looks as though I got lucky. Remind me to throw some more business Mrs. Manetti's way," he told her. "And while you're at it, give Joanne Campbell's agent a call."

"The actress?" she asked a little uncertainly. Joanne and Monica looked alike enough to be sisters. Why would he need one if he was keeping the other?

"No, the librarian," he deadpanned. "Of course, the actress. The part's a good fit for her."

"But what about Monica?" Yohanna asked him. "Didn't you just say—?"

He held his hand up to keep her from going on. "I want to give her a hard time to show her that it's not good business to create her kind of turmoil on one of my sets. She made Montelle here sweat. Now it's our turn to make *her* sweat. Sound good to you?" he asked the director.

The man's grin said it all, but just in case, he confirmed, "Absolutely. Music to my ears, boss."

His attention back to the director, Lukkas told the man, "If you need me, I'll be in the trailer for a while—" He suddenly paused. "The trailers did arrive, right?"

"Yesterday," Montelle confirmed. "Most of them anyway. The rest are on their way. Should be here by the end of the week. What's a production without glitches?" the director asked.

"A production that doesn't have me eating migraine tablets by the pound," Lukkas responded.

Dirk snapped his fingers as if he'd had a life-altering idea.

"That's how I'll fund my retirement. I'll buy stock in your migraine medication," he said, almost succeeding in keeping a straight face.

"Coming?" Lukkas asked Yohanna after he began walking away.

There he went again. "Would you take offense if I had a bell collar make up for you?" she asked Lukkas, once again quickly striding after him to catch up.

"I don't wear jewelry," he responded, straight-faced.

"Don't think of it as jewelry," she told him. "Think of it as an early warning system. Kind of like with earthquakes."

Lukkas rolled her explanation over in his mind. "I think I like that comparison, but I'm not sure. Get back to me on that," he instructed.

"Right," she mumbled under her breath.

* * *

"This is your trailer?" Yohanna asked, clearly wowed as she walked into it.

He tossed the briefcase he'd brought with him onto the nearest flat surface. "Yes. Why?"

She suppressed a low whistle. "My first apartment was smaller than this. I think my second one was, too."

"Sorry to hear that," he said wryly. "This is my production headquarters when I'm away from the studio. I need the space to think. Small, tight places don't let me think."

"Whatever works," she said agreeably, still taking it all in.

"You can put your things down over there," Lukkas told her, pointing to what looked like a spacious alcove, complete with a compact acrylic desk and a landline.

The latter had her looking at him quizzically. She nodded at it, waiting for him to explain. Why a landline when the logical way to go would have been another cell phone?

"It's my tribute to my past," he told her. "I like blending old and new together. It does nobody any good to let old traditions die unnoticed and forgotten."

"Okaaay," she murmured, drawing out the word.

"And now," he told her, "on that note, I've got several phone calls to make—and if I'm not mistaken, you do, too."

"Right," she agreed, putting down the laptop that she'd packed this morning. Flipping it open, she began initializing her access to the internet.

"Of course I'm right," Lukkas quipped. "That's why they pay me the big bucks." His eyes narrowed just a touch as he looked at her. "That's a joke, Hanna."

Her mouth quirked a touch. "I knew that." Her eyes sparkled with a whimsical glimmer that he found rather compelling.

Perhaps just a little *too* compelling, he silently warned.

Taking a breath to fortify himself, Lukkas said, "Hard to tell at times," and then went off to the section of the custom-built trailer that doubled as a bedroom whenever he remained on a set overnight.

Yohanna found that working for Lukkas Spader on a movie set was a real learning experience. She discovered that while he was the producer on record, there were several positions that bore part of his title and were considered to be under his supervision.

There were assistant producers, coproducers and executive producers to name just a few, and none of them had the sort of responsibility and authority that Lukkas with his simpler title possessed.

She learned very quickly that he took his position quite seriously, relinquishing none of the myriad parts.

He had conceived of the idea for this movie, nurtured it along and then cowrote the script after having written the initial treatment. He'd been involved in the casting of the film, retaining his right of final veto if someone didn't strike him as being right for the part.

According to what she learned from one of the camera crew, Lukkas always took casting approval very seriously, right down to the extras who were to be used in several of the saloon scenes.

He also, the cameraman informed her, tended to use the same crew over and over again, shepherding them from one movie to another. They were, in effect, one large, mostly happy family.

"The man's as loyal as anyone you'll ever be lucky enough to know—pretty rare in this business, let me tell you," the veteran cameraman had rhapsodized.

"How many movies have you made with him?" she asked, curious.

"Five, counting this one," the man, Eddie, had answered as he continued setting up his equipment. "But there're guys here who've been with The Spade from the beginning. He once said that if he liked the quality of someone's work, he didn't see a reason why he shouldn't use that person again."

"Wait, 'The Spade'?" she questioned uncertainly. Were they still talking about Lukkas?

The man nodded. "That's what the crew calls him. Because of his last name," he added.

She had to admit that she wouldn't have thought of that herself. But now that the cameraman had pointed it out to her, she couldn't see how she could have missed that.

"He knows everyone's name. I really don't know how he keeps them all straight. Me, I've got five kids and sometimes I forget some of their names, or get who's who mixed up," he joked. "I never heard The Spade confuse anyone's name with someone else's. The guy's incredible."

There'd be no argument from her on that. But, admiration notwithstanding, she was starting to understand why the producer needed to have someone organizing things for him as he went along. It was apparent that he already had far too much going on in his head to accommodate anything extra.

In all honesty, she was beginning to wonder how the man didn't just implode—or have a meltdown. There was just too much.

* * *

"So how's it going?" Lukkas asked sometime later that day as he came up on her.

"I located Joanne Campbell. Her agent—Jim Myers— said she was in between projects at the moment and would love to have a chance to work with you. Seems you have quite a following," she told him with a smile.

She had to confess that she felt a touch of pride about the matter as well, which she supposed anyone else would have thought somewhat premature. But in all honesty, she was beginning to feel as if she had always had this job. To his credit, Lukkas created that sort of atmosphere on his sets.

Lukkas was quick to wave away the comment she had repeated. "Her agent knows how to sugarcoat his words, that's all. Helps during negotiations."

"Myers wanted to know when you'd like to have Joanne audition for the part."

"No need," Lukkas told her. "She's already got the part." When Yohanna looked at him in surprise, he explained his reasoning. "She has the same build, the same coloring as the Elliott girl and—as a plus—she has a hell of a better attitude than Monica Elliott does." Lukkas had few hard and fast rules on his set, but Monica Elliott had broken one of them. "I don't like turmoil on my sets."

"Turmoil," Yohanna echoed. "I don't see how that's even possible, considering the size of the fan club you've got here." She'd initially decided to keep that to herself, but when something was staring you in the face, there was a tendency to want to at least mention it.

Lukkas clearly looked as if he didn't know what she was talking about. "Come again?"

"I talked to one of the crew members—a cameraman

named Eddie Harrington," she interjected. "From what I gathered, the whole crew thinks that you could walk on water if you really wanted to."

Lukkas frowned at her and shook his head. "Don't exaggerate, Hanna."

"I don't think I am," she told him. "If anything, I'm probably understating it. I don't know if you realize it, but you've got enough goodwill going for you here to mount a campaign for president of the United States if you wanted to."

For a second it looked as if he was just going to laugh in her face, Yohanna thought. And then he just shook his head, dismissing the very notion.

"Being a producer's rough enough, Hanna. Why in God's name would I want to put myself through something like that? And after the hell you go through, you wind up occupying the loneliest seat in the country. No thanks. I'm happy just making movies, giving people a reason to detach from their lives for a couple of hours and just let themselves be entertained."

"That cameraman I talked to also told me that you actually remember everyone's name."

"Is there a question in there somewhere?" he asked.

"Do you? Remember everyone's name," she clarified in case that had gotten lost in the shuffle.

Lukkas shrugged carelessly. "Seems like the right thing to do. Someone works for you, you should have the decency to know their name."

"No argument here," she told him. "But you are aware that that's pretty unique, aren't you?"

He shrugged again. "I really don't have the time to run any self-serving surveys," he told her. "I've got a movie to bring in on time and, if possible, underbudget."

"Well, I'm here to help with that in any way I can," she assured him a tad breathlessly.

Admittedly, she'd gotten a little caught up in the proceedings. Being around Lukkas seemed to do that. Not only that, but she found herself sneaking side glances at the man. Here, on the set, even when he wasn't issuing orders he seemed somehow larger than life.

Great, all you need is to fall for the guy. That'll end your career before it ever gets a chance to start, she chided herself. *Whatever you think you're feeling for this guy, you're not,* she silently emphasized, determined to get a firm grip on her overactive imagination.

"And you're sure about using Joanne Campbell?" Yohanna asked, getting back to the actress they'd discussed.

"Why?" he asked, curious as to why she would question something like this. "You don't think she's right for the part?"

"I have no idea about the part," Yohanna confessed. "I just want to be sure that you're sure."

He relaxed just the slightest touch. "Well, in that case, yes, I am."

"And what would you like to do about Monica Elliott?" She prodded.

That was simple as far as he was concerned. "Let her twist a little in the wind, then send her a text message telling her I've changed my mind and she can go do her other movie. Maybe she'll be nicer to the next director she works with on her next picture."

"You really think she can change her behavior?" Yohanna asked him skeptically.

"Hey, why not?" He was a firm believer in second chances. "I'm in the business of making fantasies, remember?"

"I remember." She brought up another topic that was, in her view, just as important. Possibly more so. "Have you eaten yet?"

Preoccupied, Lukkas was certain he'd heard his all-around assistant incorrectly.

"What?"

"Have you eaten?" she repeated. "I've noticed that you tend to get caught up in whatever you're doing and then you just forget to eat. Not recommended," she told him. "That catches up with you after a while—big-time."

"Auditioning for the part of my mother?"

Yohanna couldn't tell if he was amused or annoyed. She trod lightly.

"No. I just want to keep the job I have," she told him.

"Oh, didn't I tell you?" he asked, looking surprised at his own oversight.

Yohanna narrowed her eyebrows slightly as she looked at the producer, waiting for an explanation.

"Tell me what?" she prompted when he didn't immediately follow up on his previous question.

"That I've decided that you passed the test. You're hired on a permanent basis."

"No three-month probation?" she asked, wanting to be perfectly clear where she stood.

"Consider it month number four," Lukkas answered glibly.

He'd done it again. Left her stunned and falling behind, Yohanna thought. But this time, he also left her smiling to herself.

She figured she was making progress.

Chapter Seven

Hours later she was back on the plane, sitting next to Lukkas and waiting to make the sixty-minute trip to Bedford.

She'd just buckled up when she glanced out the window. The view, or lack thereof, suddenly sank in.

She could never live in a place like this.

"How do they stand it?" she asked Lukkas, staring out into the night.

Making one final notation in his notepad before tucking it back into his pocket, Lukkas slanted a look in her general direction, his attention split. "Stand what?" he asked.

"All that darkness." The fact that there was a new moon didn't help the scenario any. Yohanna suppressed a shiver that traveled along her spine. She'd never cared for the dark. As a child, she'd been afraid of it. "It's like being inside the bottom of midnight."

"Some people actually find the dark soothing," Lukkas told her.

"Not me," she responded with feeling. "The dark can hide things. I like being able to see what's out there at all times."

"At the moment, what's out there is darkness," he said wryly.

For a second she forgot that they were boss and assistant and just responded to him as if they were friends. Friends of long standing because she really was beginning to feel rather comfortable around Lukkas.

Blowing out a breath, she pretended that his teasing ruffled her feathers. "Very funny."

She saw the corners around his eyes crinkling as he made a guess about her childhood. "I bet you were afraid of the dark when you were a kid."

There was a time when she would have protested the observation despite the fact that it was right on the money. But that time was gone. She was more confident now in her own abilities, her own skills. She saw no reason to pretend that he had guessed wrong when he hadn't.

"My night-light was my best friend. It was in the shape of a Saint Bernard." A fond memory entered her mind. Her father had gotten it for her to help her get over her fear of the dark. "If it wasn't on, I couldn't sleep."

"Let me guess. You were a city kid."

She was and she was proud of it. "Born and bred," she affirmed.

Still, even city kids went to the country sometimes, he thought. He remembered his own childhood, squeezed in the backseat between two siblings and what felt like fourteen pointy elbows, desperately trying to look out the window to see where they were—and if they had gotten there yet.

"No long, grueling cross-country trips when your family went on vacation? No camping out or traveling through more desolate areas on your way to somewhere else?" he asked.

She shook her head. There had been no vacations in her childhood. "My father was a workaholic. The word *vacation* wasn't in his vocabulary. But he liked to take me to the local amusement park whenever he could," she told Lukkas in case he thought that she'd been deprived as a child. "We went on long bike rides, played ball in the field behind the high school. I didn't feel as if I was missing anything," she said, anticipating his possible next question. "It was a good childhood as far as it went."

The look on his face said he found that an odd way to put it. "And that was?"

"Until my dad died when I was twelve." An ironic smile slipped over her lips. "After that, my mother went to work and I helped out around the house to try to take up the slack. There was no time for vacations," she assured him.

Hers had been a no-nonsense kind of upbringing from that point on. Her mother had done her best, but there was no way she could have filled the void that her father had left behind.

Something in her voice had Lukkas asking, "You were close to your father?"

"I was," she admitted freely. Her father had understood her, had allowed her to be who she was. If he were still alive today, he wouldn't be trying to set her up with the sons and nephews of some of his friends the way her mother felt she had to. "He told me I could be anything

I wanted to be—as long as I was organized," she added with a laugh.

The sound of her laugh had Lukkas envisioning sunrises over fields of flowers. He smiled. "Is that how it all started? You being so very organized?" He embellished in case she didn't realize what he was referring to.

She nodded. "Yes, that's how it started. What little girl doesn't want to please her father?" Not that it took much. A clean bedroom; her homework done before dinner. These were all things that garnered her father's praise. She missed hearing it. "After he died…for a long time after that I secretly thought if I could just be organized enough, he'd come back." She laughed shortly, shaking her head. Had she *ever* really been that young and naive? "Drove my mother crazy. She'd put something down and before she could blink, I had it back in its place 'where it belonged.'"

She thought back to those days. "I guess to her I was bordering on OCD," she admitted, smiling to herself as she remembered a couple of incidents that had driven her mother particularly crazy. "Before you ask," she continued, "I got over it—partially because I knew what my little organizational campaign was doing to my mother. I knew that she missed my father, too. I didn't want to add to her sadness by making her think there was something wrong with me."

Yohanna understood that she had been monopolizing the conversation. And sharing much too much.

"Sorry," she apologized. "I have a habit of babbling." She felt herself flushing a bit. "You should have stopped me."

The extra color in her cheeks intrigued him. "Why? You gave me some insight into what makes you tick. I thought it was interesting."

And what makes you tick, Lukkas? Yohanna found herself wondering. *What can I ask you without making it look like I'm being overly nosy?*

"Besides," he continued with just a tiny bit of triumph in his voice, "it distracted you."

"Distracted me? From what?"

He gestured toward the window on her left. "We're airborne and you didn't have to squeeze your armrests until they all but fell off."

He was right. They were flying and she hadn't even been aware of the takeoff.

Yohanna looked through her window now. Staring, she could just barely make out dots of lights scattered about in no particular pattern—she assumed they were coming from homes built along the terrain—far below her.

His question about her fears of the dark had taken her back into the past and she'd gotten so wrapped up in revisiting memories of her father, she hadn't even noticed the change in cabin pressure or the powerful surging feeling of ascent.

Still, she felt she had to at least pretend that she had conquered her feeling about takeoffs and didn't need to white-knuckle them anymore.

"Or here's a thought," she suggested. "Maybe I've just conquered my fear of flying."

An amused smile played along his lips. "There is that. Looks as though we'll make a real world traveler out of you yet, Hanna," Lukkas predicted.

They landed in Bedford a little more than an hour later.

Feeling the downward shift, Lukkas opened his eyes.

That was when he realized that he must have fallen asleep sometime in the past fifteen minutes or so.

The long day he and Yohanna had put in had finally caught up to him.

Stifling a yawn, he stretched as best he could in the limited amount of space he had, and then rotated his neck a little. It felt stiff. Served him right for falling asleep sitting up.

Turning his head toward Yohanna, he was surprised to see that she had fallen asleep, as well. Apparently the long day had caught up to her, too.

He was about to gently shake her by the shoulder to wake her when something had him pausing for a second.

Pulling back his hand, he just looked at Hanna for a long moment. She'd been a ball of energy today, never questioning anything he told her to take care of, just finding a way to get it done and quickly.

He knew she'd come to him without any experience in the world where he had made his mark and yet she'd adapted so well and so quickly, it was hard to believe she hadn't been part of the film industry from the very beginning.

And there was something more.

Looking at her like this, her features soft and at rest rather than animated, he could see why his director had thought she was an actress. Aside from being exceptionally attractive, there was something about this young woman…an inherent sweetness that instantly transcended any awkward period that usually existed between strangers as they slowly got to know one another.

Hanna had something, a quality that effortlessly and instantly broke down barriers. That same quality made her someone he instinctively knew he could not only count on but that she could be a confidante, a friend who wouldn't let him down. Someone who would keep his secrets and be there to lend him silent—and not so silent—support when that was what was called for.

Whoa, Lukkas-boy, you're tired and getting carried away here. She's here to take Janice's place, not Natalie's, he reminded himself, afraid of where this was all taking him.

Shutting down any further reaction—*unwanted* reaction, he underscored—buzzing around inside him, he put his hand on Hanna's shoulder and shook it ever so slightly.

When she went on sleeping, he did it a second time, a little more forcefully this time around.

"Time to get up, Hanna—unless you want to spend the night on the plane," he told her.

The sound of Lukkas's voice wove its way into the dream she was having and, along with the jarring motion she felt on her shoulder, abruptly made her come around.

Blinking, Yohanna opened her eyes. She was disoriented for a moment.

"You fell asleep."

It wasn't an accusation but a statement of fact. Nevertheless, it still made her feel like an idiot who had dropped the ball. On the job a little more than two weeks and she was already falling asleep around the boss.

Not exactly a good thing to have happen when it came time to review her job performance.

"I'm sorry. I guess I was more tired than I thought. Are we still in the air?" she asked. Blinking again to clear her vision, she tried to focus as she looked out the window. An array of lights, both near and far, greeted her.

We're home, Toto, she thought with just a touch of whimsy.

"I guess not," she said out loud, answering her own question. And then another thought struck her. "I didn't hold you up, did I?"

"We just landed," he told her. "You slept through that like a baby. See? I told you that you'd get used to it."

She was never one who accepted any form of flattery as if she deserved it. "We'll see how I do when I'm awake," Yohanna replied.

She started to get up and found that she couldn't.

"Um, you might want to unbuckle your seat belt," Lukkas suggested, pointing toward the belt that was still quite buckled in place. "I don't think you're quite strong enough to take the plane with you."

Chagrined, she pressed the release button on the belt—and found that although the buckle made the appropriate noises, it wouldn't separate itself from the metal tongue that had fit so easily into the slot an hour ago.

She tried pressing it again and was on the receiving end of the same result.

Lukkas was already on his feet. When he heard her murmuring in frustration under her breath, he turned around to see what was wrong. He was surprised to find that she was still seated.

"Problem?" he asked.

"I think the seat belt doesn't want me to leave," she quipped drily.

"Let me have a look at it." Sitting next to her again, Lukkas tried to depress the lock and found that it just wouldn't budge. "Let's try this again," he said, seeming to address the words to the inanimate object rather than to her.

His hands on the seat belt, he applied more pressure as he tried to work the ends apart.

That had him accidentally brushing against places that he wouldn't have normally been in contact with—but he had no choice.

Yohanna shifted a little, not because she felt cramped, but because, as Lukkas was trying to free her from the uncooperative seat belt, he seemed to be unaware of the fact that his hands were brushing against her thighs, which in turn caused a heated chain reaction within her.

She was doing her very best not to notice.

She was failing.

Yohanna bit the inside of her cheek, struggling to think of other things.

Struggling to regulate the way she was breathing, as well.

Maybe if she didn't like the man as much as she did, if she actually *dis*liked him, she could easily block the warm shock waves he was unsuspectingly causing to dance all over her body.

But she *did* like him and consequently she *did* feel something spreading through her. Something she knew she shouldn't be feeling—definitely something she *couldn't* react to.

She vehemently didn't want to be one of *those* women; women who slept with their bosses as casually as they changed their clothes.

For his part, Lukkas was trying his very best not to notice that, try as he might not to, he kept brushing his hand against her, fleetingly touching her in places reserved for a lover's caress.

Tendering an apology might be too embarrassing for her, so he pretended not to be aware of it.

But he was.

Exceedingly so.

He could feel the charged electricity crackling between them all the way from the roots of his hair up to the very tips.

This reaction was purely physical and only happening because he hadn't been with a woman since his wife's death. He had never been one of those people who felt some unbridled need to sow wild oats fast and furiously anywhere and anytime he had the opportunity.

To him, relationships were tantamount to the experience, and he hadn't had a relationship since Natalie had died in that senseless crash.

Sitting back, he shook his head. "It's really stuck." He rolled the problem over in his head. "I guess I'm going to have to take drastic measures," he told her.

And just what did he mean by "drastic"?

"You're not leaving me here, are you?" she asked, looking at him uncertainly.

"As a sacrifice to the airplane gods?" he asked with a genuine laugh. "No, what I meant by that is that I'm going to have to cut the belt. Wait here," he told her, getting up again.

"It's not as if I have a choice," she called after him, frustrated and annoyed that she couldn't free herself without all this extra added effort.

She heard Lukkas laugh in response.

He came back ten minutes later, a pair of heavy-duty shears in his hand.

"I was getting worried," she confessed. "You were gone longer than I thought you'd be."

"You'd be surprised how hard it is to find a pair of scissors on a single-engine plane," he told her.

He sat to be closer to her when he made the necessary surgical cut. "Okay, now hold still," he instructed just before he got started.

"The idea of dancing around the cabin has a certain drawback at the moment," she told him, watching as he slipped one of the blades underneath the contrary seat belt.

She held her breath as she saw him grip the scissor handles and very slowly cut through the belt.

The latter was thicker than she had thought and the process was a slow one because, she assumed, he was trying not to cut her, as well.

In what felt like an eternity later, the two sides of the seat belt finally separated, freeing her from her gripping prison.

"You're free," he declared. "This makes you my very first official damsel in distress that I've rescued." He frowned as he looked at the severed belt. "Sorry you had to go through that."

"As long as you got me free, that's all that matters," Yohanna told him, very relieved that it was all over with and that she could finally get off the plane. "Thank you!"

Impulsively, going with the moment, Yohanna stood up on her toes and brushed her lips against his cheek.

Or at least that was her intent when she started.

Chapter Eight

Caught off guard by her closeness and the feel of something whisper soft and silky against his cheek, Lukkas automatically turned his head toward the source of that softness.

And just like that, it wasn't his cheek that her lips were touching. It was his *lips*.

A sense of propriety urged him to pull back. To mumble some sort of an apology even though he hadn't been the one to initiate the action that lay behind this situation.

But needs that far outweighed that sense of right and wrong prohibited him from stepping away from something he'd been missing these past few years. For the first time in all those months, the loneliness that haunted everything he did, that haunted all his waking hours, actually disappeared. The darkness that had hovered over his spirit moved aside and suddenly, just for a second, as he made this intimate contact with another human being, the sun flooded into every aching corner of his soul.

She tasted of strawberry and sweetness.

Most of all, she tasted of hope and, just possibly, salvation.

His salvation.

Horrified at what Lukkas probably thought she was trying to do, Yohanna ordered herself to pull back. All she had wanted to do was to thank him. Granted, this extra step had been an impulsive one on her part, but she hadn't meant for it to turn into anything else, especially not this.

Oh, but it had.

Big-time.

Instead of expressing simple gratitude, she found herself experiencing a wild surge within her veins that she had, until just this very moment, thought was merely the product of overimaginative writers who clearly dabbled in fiction, creating mythical scenarios that could not possibly be achieved in real life.

Except that they could.

Because she was having just such a reaction right now.

She still knew her own name, but as for anything else—where she was, what time it was, things like that— it was all hazy and even now was swiftly dissolving in the heat her body insisted on generating.

Yohanna had no idea how long the kiss continued. One eternity, maybe two. What she did know was that she had never felt this alive before. She felt like someone who could leap over tall buildings, who could do wonderful, wondrous things.

Without being fully aware of what she was actually

doing, she slipped her arms around Lukkas's neck. At that moment she felt his arms tightening around her, felt him bringing her closer so that her body swayed into his. That, in turn, ignited every single inch of her.

She wanted the moment, the kiss, to go on forever. She had never felt this alive before.

And then, as unintentionally as it began, it was over.

One of them had stepped back.

Had it been her?

Or maybe him?

She wasn't sure. One minute, they were all but bound to one another, utterly connected at the lips.

The next, they weren't.

"A simple handshake would have sufficed," Lukkas heard himself saying.

He'd seen the uncertain look in her eyes and knew he had to set the tone if they were ever going to move past this. If he was being honest with himself, all he really wanted to do was to kiss her again, to take her home and get to know every single inch of her.

Slowly.

But that wasn't possible or advisable on so many levels.

"What?"

Stunned, Yohanna looked at him. She replayed his words in her head. "Oh." Belatedly, she realized that he was teasing her and giving her a way to save face at the same time.

She silently blessed him for it.

"Okay, the next time I find myself trapped in my seat and you come to my rescue, I'll remember to shake your hand. How's that?" she asked him, playing along.

Lukkas nodded as he escorted her from the plane and down the metal stairs. Her heels hitting the metal made a rhythmic staccato sound.

"It's been a *long* day. Let's get you home." When he saw her slanting a startled look at him, he clarified, "*Your* home."

"Oh." She was relieved—and yet somehow, just on the fringes of her mind was another feeling lurking.

Disappointment.

Determined not to have Lukkas harbor any sort of doubts about the way she saw her actual job description and the subsequent performance evaluation that would eventually come, Yohanna threw herself into her work, determined to be the ultimate employee. It wasn't hard. She was good at this.

She came in early, stayed late and, bit by bit, brought complete order to what had otherwise threatened to dissolve into an utterly chaotic mess where nothing of any importance could be located—easily or otherwise—when it was needed.

She took to the work waiting to be done around her with amazing precision, organizing Lukkas's schedules, his meetings, all the while making certain that there were no overlaps and that none of the people Lukkas dealt with fell through the cracks.

And as always, she kept lists.

Lists of the people he could count on for financial backing for his project no matter what, and lists of people who needed to be wooed a little.

Or a lot.

In addition, she began to compile files on each of these people, noting their likes, their dislikes, their affiliations as well as the names and ages of their family members. In short, she did whatever it took to round out the mental picture for Lukkas so that he knew exactly who he was dealing with and just how to deal with them. Her research allowed him to always remain two steps ahead of anyone he interacted with.

The first time she showed him what she had worked up—and it was always going to be a work in progress, she assured him, since new people came into his life all the time—Lukkas found himself all but speechless.

The amount of time and effort she had to have put into organizing his life was astonishing.

"You did all this?" he marveled as Yohanna scrolled through the information on one of his new associates, a man who had come on board for the film Lukkas had produced just last spring.

Yohanna curbed the desire to tell him that the tooth fairy was behind all this. She wasn't sure if he could take a joke—or reject it because it wasn't of his own making.

"Yes," she replied instead.

She could see by his expression that he found the work she'd done to be extensive. In her opinion, it had to be. Otherwise, why else bother putting it together in the first place?

"Is Eli the only one you've worked up like this?"

Instead of answering him, Yohanna went back a couple of screens on the laptop, stopping when she pulled up the directory that she had created.

Silently, she scrolled down all the entries.

For the moment it seemed as if there were too many to count.

"When did you have time for all this?" Lukkas asked.

She shrugged. "I found pockets of time here and

there." And then she elaborated a little for him. "I did it when I wasn't inputting your storyboard."

"You did *what* to my storyboard?" he asked uncertainly, glancing at the item under discussion. The storyboard was off to the extreme left-hand side so it would be out of everyone's way until needed.

A film's storyboard was literally a large board on which drawings of the movie were pinned in their proper sequential order. It was the entire movie summed up as succinctly as possible. The director used it to help remind himself of the movie's ultimate focus or message.

Lukkas had asked her just to put up the drawings in their proper sequence.

She was obviously not referring to the corkboard that could be wheeled onto the set if he needed to have it brought there.

"I made up a virtual storyboard and saved it onto a USB drive as well as your smartphone. That way, you can always access it and make changes no matter where you are."

"You sure you never worked in the industry before?" Lukkas asked, scrutinizing her. She had such natural instincts about what was necessary—and what wasn't— he was having a hard time believing that she'd been a complete novice just a few weeks ago.

"I'm sure. I just know how to anticipate a boss," Yohanna replied, flashing her take-no-prisoners smile at him.

"Oh, really?" His tone had her bracing herself, instinctively knowing that he had just decided to throw her a curve. Thinking of it as a challenge, she was ready for anything. "Did your powers of anticipation allow you to anticipate being asked to that premiere and the party afterward that I have to attend?"

Yohanna was well aware of the premiere and subsequent party Lukkas had to attend since he'd had her call each of the major stars in the movie to coax, cajole or plead with them, doing whatever she had to do to get them to promise to appear at the showing.

She had just assumed he'd already had someone to go with. This was a whole new twist she hadn't prepared for and, for a moment, she was at a complete loss as to how to respond.

"You're asking me to attend?" Yohanna asked in disbelief.

He gave her a look that whispered of moderately bridled impatience. "I'm pretty sure I was just speaking English, so yes, I'm asking you to attend the premiere— and the party—with me."

"Why?" The question had slipped out like a stunned whisper.

This man was one of Hollywood's most eligible bachelors. What was the man doing, asking her to attend a premiere with him? *And* the party afterward? He could easily have his pick of any one of a large number of stunning women. She couldn't begin to compete with any of those.

So why was he asking *her* to come with him to this premiere?

"Because if I go alone, aside from speculation about my playing the lonely widower, since I'm the producer and I'm under seventy with all my own teeth, I will be a walking target for any starlet on the rise and willing to go to great lengths to get to the top of the heap. I'll also be easy prey for any backer who has a female relative he'd like to see married or at least involved with someone."

"And you don't want to be that someone," Yohanna ventured.

Lukkas nodded. "Give that young lady a prize," he declared like a carnival barker.

"So you want me to be your beard," she summarized astutely.

The label conjured up the wrong image—at least in his head. "I'd rather think of you as my entanglement repellent."

Yohanna laughed at his choice of words. "That makes me sound like a bug spray."

Lukkas shrugged. He went to his desk to take something out of one of the lower drawers. "Call it any way you see it as long as you're ready to be picked up at five-thirty tomorrow."

She felt her stomach quickening. She wasn't quite as blasé about things as she would have liked to portray. "I know this sounds clichéd, but I don't have a thing to wear for something of this magnitude."

If she thought that would be the end of it, she was sadly mistaken. Lukkas was not a man who gave up easily and he could be just as stubborn as she could.

Possibly more so.

Lukkas reached into his back pocket, took out his wallet and almost without looking selected a credit card, which he then in turn handed to her.

"Here," he told her. "Get something that'll make a good showing at tomorrow's premiere of *Diamonds and Dust*—but not so much that it takes the focus off the movie," he warned.

Yohanna stared at the credit card. Specifically, she

stared at his name embossed on the credit card. She had her own credit cards, but since she had taken over issuing payment checks for his bills, she knew that her cards had a far lower cut-off ceiling than his did.

She looked back up at him incredulously. "You're kidding, right?"

"If I were kidding, laughter would be involved somewhere. Real laughter, not nervous laughter," he attested. "You hear any?"

Yohanna slowly moved her head from side to side. "No."

"Then, I'm not kidding," he concluded. He glanced at the card he had just given her. The same one she was still clutching as if she expected it to either burst into flame or levitate away from her. "You want to take a few hours off to go shopping?"

Her first response was to say yes, but then her stubborn streak kicked in. She was not about to take advantage of either him or the situation—no matter how tempting it might be.

"No, I'll take care of it on my own time," she answered.

Admittedly, Yohanna was still a little shell-shocked over what had just happened, but she instinctively knew what to do to take care of herself—even around dropdead gorgeous men, a club that Lukkas clearly belonged to.

"Have it your way—you do know that there's such a thing as being *too* good to be true, right?" Lukkas asked her.

Lukkas started to leave his office when he stopped to impart one last thought on the subject. "Oh, and by the way, do something with your hair."

Her hand automatically came up to touch the back of her hair. Did he find it lacking? Distracting? Or—what? She needed to know to understand how to remedy the situation.

"My hair?"

"Yes. Wear it up," he answered, waving one hand around in the air as if he were a wand-wielding fairy godmother, able to make things do his bidding with a flick of his wrist. "This is going to be on the formal side."

"Are you *sure* you want me to go with you?" she asked, hoping that he'd change his mind at the final moment.

Lukkas rephrased her question and turned it into an answer. "Am I sure I don't want to be inundated with women who, for one reason or another, see me as a means to an end? Yes, I'm sure. Think of it as part of your job description," he instructed.

"*What* part?" she challenged.

"The part that comes under 'miscellaneous,'" he answered as he left the office.

She stared at his credit card for several moments before she finally put it away into her own wallet. Her fingertips felt almost icy as she handled the card. It represented a great deal of power in its own right, she thought, tucking the wallet with Lukkas's card into the depths of her purse, otherwise known—according to Lukkas—as "no man's land."

A quick but intense review of the contents of her closet that night only told Yohanna what she already knew—she did *not* own a single suitable dress she could wear to a premiere, certainly not something that wouldn't stand out like a sore thumb when she crossed the red carpet beside Lukkas.

She shook her head as she closed her closet. This all still felt so surreal to her. Her, at a premiere. With one of Hollywood's most eligible bachelors. Who would've thunk it?

Whenever she found herself in unfamiliar waters and treading madly, her natural inclination had always been to seek help. But in this case, the only one she could actually turn to would be her mother.

However, she knew if she did, while she would be playing into her mother's fantasy, she would also be opening up such a huge can of worms, she wouldn't have a prayer in hell of ever being able to close it again.

Besides, her mother had already called her several times since she'd started working for Lukkas. The calls all revolved around the same issue. Her mother wanted progress reports and, more specifically, her mother wanted to know exactly how far she had progressed in her relationship with Lukkas.

That there *was* no relationship in progress other than their professional one was not something she seemed to be able to get across to her mother.

It was clear that the woman was absolutely *starving* for romance. Romance in *her* life, not actually in her own, Yohanna thought ruefully. Her mother was one of those women who lived vicariously through their offspring.

Not for the first time, Yohanna wished that she had a sister, or at the very least a cousin she could hide behind or possibly divert her mother's attention to.

But, knowing her mother, she supposed that would blow up in her face, as well.

She could just hear her mother saying, "Why can't you get married and have a husband and kids like your cousin Rachel?"

No, she was better off this way, with no one to be compared to, Yohanna decided.

But she still needed help.

Mentally, she reviewed the women she could call for some sort of advice in a situation like this. And then she realized that there was only one logical candidate.

She fervently hoped that she wouldn't be disturbing the woman, but really, if it hadn't been for her, most likely she would still be sitting in her condo—a condo that would look far less tidy than it did now—out of work and out of hope.

Her present dilemma was both Cecilia's fault and her gift to her, Yohanna thought. In any case, she felt she could attain a sympathetic ear from the woman—as well as a minimum of questions. Cecilia was obviously the kind of lady who cared, but by the same token, she wasn't the kind to pry or to insert herself into someone's life— possibly not even when invited to do so.

Making up her mind, Yohanna picked up the phone and called Cecilia.

Chapter Nine

"Not that I'm not honored as well as touched that you called me to help you pick out something special to wear to the premiere of Mr. Spader's new movie, but why isn't your mother here instead of me, dear?"

After attempting to repress the question during the drive to Rodeo Drive and an exclusive boutique she was familiar with, Cecilia's curiosity had gotten the better of her. She knew that if she found out her daughter had gone to another older woman for advice rather than come to her, she would have been heartbroken.

Cecilia had tried to sound as casual as she could, broaching the question as they walked into the boutique.

Yohanna loved her mother dearly but, in her estimation, that didn't mean she had to put up with her mother's theatrics, and there *would be* theatrics if the woman found out about this.

"Because," Yohanna patiently explained, "if my mother finds out that I'm going to be attending something with my boss that involves walking across a red carpet, I guarantee that five minutes later, she's going to be hiring someone to write the words *Mr. Spader, please marry my daughter, Yohanna* across the sky."

Two sleek, tastefully made up saleswomen started walking in their direction. Cecilia waved them back. To Yohanna's astonishment, the women retreated.

Cecilia obviously had clout here.

"Now, dear," Cecilia was saying, commenting on the scenario Yohanna had just painted for her. "You're exaggerating—"

Yohanna laughed drily as she went to the first display of evening gowns. "No, I'm not. You obviously haven't met my mother."

"No, I have not," Cecilia admitted. "But even if I haven't—"

Yohanna proceeded as if Cecilia hadn't attempted to continue. "She's the one who told me that a real woman cleans her own house and said I was throwing money away on a cleaning service."

Cecilia winced just a tiny bit. "Ah, an old-fashioned woman."

"If the fashions are from the 1900s, then, yes, she is an old-fashioned woman. She is also a very determined woman. Right now, what she's determined about is to marry me off to someone. Anyone short of Attila the Hun is a viable possible candidate. In my mother's eyes I'm in a very precarious place, teetering on the edge of a downhill slope that'll send me sliding right into becoming an old maid."

Cecilia smiled indulgently at her. "Nobody really uses that term anymore, dear."

But Yohanna could only smile, as if her point had been made. "Like I said, you haven't met my mother. What do you think of this one?" she asked, holding one of the gowns up against herself.

"It's not your color," Cecilia pronounced, dismissing the gown with a wave of her hand. Yohanna returned it to its original space as Cecilia began to look through the various gowns. "Have you stopped to think that this event might be covered by one of those cable channels and the camera might pick up your presence there? Since you're attending the premiere with the movie's producer, I can guarantee that cameras will be trained on you.

"This does assume, of course, that your mother watches these kinds of programs. If she doesn't, then you're home free." Cecilia looked at her face and drew her own conclusion. "She watches these shows, doesn't she?"

Yohanna could only nod, feeling a definite pressure from the weight accumulating on her chest. "But every now and then, she does miss one occasionally." There was a breathless, hopeful note in her voice as she mentally crossed her fingers.

"Then, for your sake, I hope she's busy watching something else," Cecilia replied. She debated over a gown, then shrugged and moved it aside. "It's Saturday night. Does she go out with your father, or perhaps some friends?" Cecilia asked hopefully as she went on looking and rejecting gowns one after the other.

Yohanna could only look on, leaving the selection entirely in the older woman's hands because she felt she needed someone steadier than she was to make the final decision.

"My dad died years ago," she said, replying to Cecilia's question. "But Mom does go out with a couple of her girlfriends sometimes. I don't know if it's on Saturday nights or not."

"All you can do is play the odds, dear— That one," Cecilia suddenly exclaimed, gravitating toward a long, light blue gown covered with sequins of a single silver color. The sequins winked and blinked, casting their own beams of light.

Removing it from its hanger, Cecilia offered the gown to Yohanna. "This is perfect for you," she pronounced without any fanfare, cocking her head as if she was studying Yohanna for the first time. "The blue brings out your eyes and it makes you come alive—I mean, more than you already are," Cecilia amended tactfully.

"Understood," Yohanna replied, not wanting the woman to worry about hurting her feelings.

Her mother certainly never had such concerns. There were times that she was convinced her mother went directly for the jugular just to keep her in line.

Too bad it hadn't worked. She was still her own person. She hadn't been brainwashed into believing her mother's ancient mantra. That a woman wasn't complete until she was married.

She was complete, Yohanna thought fiercely. Moreover, she was doing just fine without a male in her life.

And maybe just a little more fine than that, she silently insisted.

"Try it on, dear," Cecilia coaxed, still holding out the gown to her.

Beaming, Yohanna took the gown from Cecilia and headed to the first changing room.

It took her all of three minutes to get out of her own clothes and into the gown Cecilia seemed to have inadvertently stumbled across.

And then it took her an extra two minutes to tear herself away from the reflection in the mirror that she found awe-inspiring and overwhelming.

"Are you all right in there, dear?" Cecilia inquired, raising her voice. Yohanna was taking a long time inside the changing room.

"Just fine," Yohanna called back.

She was still mesmerized by what she saw—a reflection that just couldn't have possibly been her. Instead, the reflection was of a startlingly sexy woman who just happened to be looking back at her.

Yohanna could hardly tear her eyes away, afraid if she did, when she looked back, the reflection would be gone and she'd be left in its stead.

Plain, reliable Yohanna.

She turned slowly to the side, exposing the floor-to-upper-thigh slit in the gown. She absolutely *loved* this gown.

Holding her breath, she ventured out of the change room to present herself to the woman who had brought her here in the first place. She wanted to hear Cecilia's opinion even as she crossed her fingers, hoping that Cecilia would give her stamp of approval on this one. Granted, she could buy it if she had no choice, but in this virgin effort to get just the right gown, she knew she needed backup.

Someone to tell her she was right.

Besides, it would be rather rude not to ask Cecilia

what she thought of the gown. After all, she had been the one who had found the gown.

As for herself, she was half in love with the gown and on her way to proposing to it.

"So?" Yohanna asked hopefully as she very slowly turned in a full circle for the woman's benefit. "What do you think?"

Cecilia's pleased smile said it all. "I think Mr. Spader is going to need a cold shower *before* and *after* the premiere. Also after the party that'll follow."

She'd almost forgotten about that. Maybe Lukkas wouldn't want to attend. "Are you sure there's a party after the premiere?" she asked Cecilia.

"Honey, there is *always* an after-party," Cecilia answered knowingly. "A party before. A party after. The people in the film industry work hard at what they do, so when it's all said and done, they like to party hard, too, sort of to balance everything out," Cecilia explained. "And also because there's always that chance that after the party's over, nothing further comes their way. This is a very, very hard business people have consigned themselves to."

Cecilia paused to take a breath and then smiled warmly again, her eyes crinkling. "I think I forgot to mention the most important part—you look perfect."

Yohanna could feel her cheeks growing warmer. Compliments always embarrassed her. "Thank you— even though that's not possible."

"Why not?" Bemused, Cecilia challenged her opinion, but amicably so.

She'd felt like an ugly duckling most of her life. Her mother had branded her as such, lamenting that it would be difficult to find her a husband because of that. To have

Cecilia compliment her this way was flattering—but it almost didn't feel real.

"Because nothing human is perfect, no matter how hard we might try."

"All right, I'll amend my statement," Cecilia said indulgently. "You're as close to perfect as possible." Cocking her head just a shade, the woman looked at her. "Happy?"

Maybe that reflection in the mirror really *was* her.

"Deliriously," Yohanna responded.

"Wear that," Cecilia instructed, indicating the gown. "And you'll knock 'em all dead," she promised.

Happy that she'd found something and relieved that she didn't have to go on searching for the "right" thing to wear for the better part of the day, Yohanna started to go back to the change room. As she walked, she glanced at the price tag attached to the garment and stopped dead in her tracks.

Surprised, Cecilia came closer to her. "Is something wrong?"

She was still staring at the price tag, all but shell-shocked. "This dress costs around the same amount of money it would take to feed a third world nation for a week."

There was an extremely practical side to Cecilia. "You're not paying for it, are you?" she asked, softness creeping into her voice despite the harsh nature of the question she'd just asked.

"Mr. Spader gave me his credit card," Yohanna confessed.

"Then, charge away," Cecilia urged with a laugh as she nudged her into the change room. "In your producer's pretty green eyes, the money is being put to good use."

As she changed, Yohanna still thought it incredibly wasteful to be using that much money to purchase a simple gown.

"But this money could feed so many kids," she protested, exiting the change area.

"And it will, eventually," Cecilia assured her. "Spader is a very compassionate man. If someone calls him with a hard-luck story, Lukkas Spader is on the phone, calling one or more of his security team to find the caller, and then he delivers the money to them in person."

Cecilia was only repeating what Theresa had already told her about the man. Her friend had been impressed with the size of the producer's heart in an industry that notoriously had no heart.

"Now buy that gown and give that man something beautiful to look at," Cecilia instructed.

Yohanna smiled as she went up to the register.

Directed by Cecilia's keen instincts, Yohanna found herself going to several other stores, notably Neiman Marcus, to buy accessories that she hadn't realized she needed for the night ahead. New shoes. A tiny purse hardly big enough to house a lipstick and a house key. A wrap to throw on her shoulders in case the evening grew chilly. All these things, Cecilia had maintained, were necessary to complete the portrait of a woman who could easily fit into Lukkas's world.

After a while Yohanna had the feeling she was on an endless treadmill and that the shopping would never end.

And then finally, finally—after nearly giving up hope—she was home.

Home with only a few hours to get ready. Her nerves all but went into overdrive. Already worried that she'd somehow wind up putting her worst foot forward, Yohanna tried not to dwell on anything negative.

The butterflies in her stomach were already threatening to hollow out her insides with their ever-increasing wingspan as they perpetually took off and landed.

Being Yohanna, she was ready long before she needed to be. That left her time to pace and to anticipate the worst. The more she did either, the more nervous she became even though she really hadn't thought that was actually possible.

Willing Lukkas to come early, she kept looking at her watch to see how much time had passed.

The hands on her watch were moving so slowly, she felt certain that the minute hand had been dipped in honey.

The inside of her mouth was dry again—something that had been going on all day—actually, ever since he'd asked her to accompany him.

The moment she turned away from the window and began to head to the kitchen, the doorbell rang. She nearly jumped out of her skin, grateful that no one had been there to take in the sight.

Taking a breath, she went to answer the door.

Fully prepared to see Lukkas when she opened the door, she offered him a cheerful "Hi."

"Wow," he heard himself say in response. When the door had opened to admit him, he'd fully expected to see the young woman he'd hired three weeks ago, and instead he was all but bowled over by the absolutely gorgeous woman standing in the doorway.

"Hanna?" Lukkas asked hesitantly.

He couldn't be certain it was her.

The woman standing right in front of him looked like Hanna and yet didn't.

"It's me," she assured him, opening the door wider for him to enter.

Pleasure spiraled through her as she noted the way Lukkas was looking at her.

"I take it by your initial comment that you like the gown."

"Like it?" he echoed. "I think I'm in love with it. You look nothing short of fantastic," he told her with genuine feeling in his voice.

She decided she might as well tell him now rather than later. After all, he was the one putting up money to fund the next project. She couldn't just take more from him because she thought the gown was gorgeous.

"It was awfully expensive," she apologized. "I saved all the tags and, if I'm super careful, I can reattach them and take everything back to the store so that you can get your money refunded."

He caught himself wondering if she was for real and then decided she was. That in turn made her a rarity. And special in his eyes.

"Number one, I don't want my money back," he told her. "If you don't want to keep this gown after the premiere, I guess we can return it. Any money we get will be forwarded to the charity of your choosing. Although, personally, I vote to make it simple and just keep the gown. You never know when you might need to show up somewhere wearing something drop-dead gorgeous to win over the crowd.

"Number two. The sight of you in that dress is well worth any investment into this evening that I've had to make. Now loosen up a little, smile and have fun. You're

walking into a movie theater, not walking your last mile
to get a lethal injection," he reminded her, then prodded
a little further. "Why don't you try smiling? In case you
didn't know—" and he was certain that being Hanna, she
didn't "—you've got a really terrific smile."

Without thinking she raised her hand and brushed her
fingertips along her lips, as if that could somehow allow
her to "see" herself the way he saw her.

"I do?" she asked a little hesitantly. "My mother always
said I put too much teeth into my smile. I guess it made
me a little self-conscious." *Or a lot*, she added silently.

"They're your teeth," he told her kindly, and then reminded her, "You can put them anywhere you want to."

She laughed. "You make it sound as if they were false
teeth I could just take out and leave lying around somewhere."

"I was hoping to coax a smile out of you with that."

"You don't have to coax," she told him warmly. "The
only thing I want from you is to give me your word that
you won't leave me stranded at this premiere."

His eyebrows drew together. "Why would I?" he
asked, perplexed. "The whole purpose of taking you
is so that you can run interference for me, be my shield
against a possible wall of female humanity. If I wanted
to wander off and leave you stranded, I wouldn't have
asked you to come with me to begin with." Lukkas lowered his head a little so that he could gaze directly into
her eyes. "Okay?"

"Okay," she echoed, sounding a little more heartened
than she had a few minutes ago.

"Then, Cinderella, your coach awaits," he told her,
putting out his elbow so that she could hook her arm
through it.

* * *

They arrived at the movie theater—originally *the* Grauman's Chinese Theatre, Yohanna noted with a secret thrill—by stretch limousine. She found the ride exceedingly smooth, but then she was so focused on the evening ahead that she felt she wouldn't have noticed if there'd been a raccoon in the limo with them—unless he'd gotten out of line.

The driver was the first to exit the black, highly polished vehicle. He hurried around to the back and opened the door for her and for Lukkas.

Yohanna got out first.

The cries, calls from fans and photographers vying for their attention, formed almost a deafening wall of noise. She found it almost dizzying in its intensity.

"Don't worry," Lukkas told her, whispering the words into her ear so that she was able to hear them. "You'll get used to it after a while."

She didn't see how.

It was all very different on this side of the TV monitor. Whenever she caught a glimpse of a premiere on TV, it seemed moderately exciting and a tad boring.

This…this was just completely overwhelming. *Boring* was the last adjective she would have applied to the event.

When she suddenly felt Lukkas threading his arm through hers to lead her down the red carpet—*the* red carpet—instant relief flooded through her.

He was still with her.

Just as he'd promised.

Chapter Ten

It was, Yohanna thought the next moment, not unlike being in the center of an all but blinding light show.

Along with the raised voices of reporters who were all vying to snare the majority of Lukkas's attention, she heard the lower somewhat rhythmic sound of cameras going off, automatically snapping photographs while other cameras were videotaping their every move until the next stellar subject came into view.

Her natural inclination was to pick up speed and get away from the noise, the reporters and the flashing lights of their cameras as quickly as possible.

But she wasn't here as herself; she was here in connection with Lukkas. This was his night, not hers, and she was well aware that whatever she did, good or bad, would ultimately reflect on him. That was just the way things were.

So despite the fact that she found being photographed almost nonstop from every single possible angle more than a little unsettling, she reminded herself that this wasn't about her. It was about Lukkas. She wasn't Yohanna Andrzejewski; she was the production assistant who Lukkas Spader had brought with him to this important Hollywood premiere. As such, she had to convey the proper message as well as conduct herself accordingly. In no way was she to act as if she was his "date" beyond the fact that she was attending this premiere with him.

A second later she realized that not only cameras but questions were being directed at her.

"How long have you and Lukkas been dating?" a disembodied voice, a shade louder than the rest, asked.

Here we go, Yohanna thought. She took a breath as inconspicuously as possible, then answered, "We're not." Yohanna flashed a smile in the general direction the question had come from. "I work for Mr. Spader. Bringing me with him to this premiere is just his generous way of thanking me for doing what he considered to be an excellent job." She glanced toward Lukkas as she added, "I'm really excited to be here."

"How about it, Lukkas? Is what she just said true? Or are you really just trying to put one over on the public?" the same loud voice asked.

He had been the subject of endless speculation ever since his wife's funeral. After almost three years he was prepared for these kinds of questions.

"I wouldn't dream of insulting the viewing public that way. The only fantasies I create can be seen right up there on the screen," Lukkas replied genially.

There were more questions, fired at them from any one of a number of people swarming around them. Lukkas politely dealt with several of them, and then, just as politely, begged off.

"That's all for now, guys. The movie's about to start and I make it a point never to be late for my own productions," he explained amicably. His hand on the small of Yohanna's back, Lukkas gently ushered her along with him.

Moving briskly beside him, Yohanna didn't allow herself to breathe a sigh of relief until they were finally inside the theater.

Turning to Lukkas, she confessed, "I had no idea that reporters were this intense." Red carpet or not, going from the limousine to the inside of the theater was almost like being subjected to a baptism by fire.

"Actually, I think they were taking it easier than they normally do," he told her. "The reporters and paparazzi aren't used to me attending premieres with anyone. Not in the past few years anyway," he added, an unmistakable touch of sadness in his voice. He pushed it aside as he smiled at her, approval evident in his eyes. "By the way, you handled yourself very nicely."

He'd made the last sentence sound almost like an afterthought, but the fact that he'd said it at all made her feel as if she was successfully doing her job. She focused on that rather than the fact that his hand was still against the small of her back, ever so lightly guiding her through the lobby.

Warm, delicious pinpricks of heat were darting through her.

"Maybe I can add that to my résumé someday," she responded whimsically. "'Will shill on demand.'"

Laughing, Lukkas promised, "I'll give you a letter of recommendation when it comes time."

When it comes time.

Yohanna rolled the words over in her head, wondering if her actual days of being in the producer's employ were numbered.

The next moment she decided she wasn't going to think about that now. If that did turn out to be the case, it wouldn't be anything she hadn't already been through—and survived. For now, she intended to make herself totally indispensable to the man in every way possible, doing what she was good at.

What she needed to do right this minute was to not react to the feel of his arm around her shoulders as he escorted her inside the actual theater where the huge IMAX screen was located. Shivers were moving up and down her spine, making every inch of her acutely aware of the man beside her.

And she definitely wasn't thinking of him as her employer at the moment.

C'mon, Yohanna, focus. Focus.

The house lights were beginning to dim. She felt Lukkas's arm slip from her shoulders. One contact substituted for another. Before she knew it, he was taking her hand.

Her heartbeat quickened even though she silently insisted that Lukkas was merely trying to make sure she didn't stumble in the darkened theater.

"Our seats are up front," he whispered.

As if on cue, an usher appeared in front of them. He led the way, using a flashlight to illuminate the path down the aisle.

The theater was filled to capacity with not even standing room available, but as far as she was concerned, she and Lukkas were alone in the theater, making their way to the first row.

Progress was achieved in slow motion. The journey down the aisle to the first row felt like an eternity. The only theaters she had ever frequented vied with medium-size living rooms when it came to square footage. This theater was so large it could have swallowed up at least a dozen—if not more—of those theaters. Possibly also a few of the smaller towns.

And then, finally, they came to the row that matched the ticket stubs they'd been given, arriving just as the curtain was being drawn back. A giant dormant screen came into view.

"Just in time," Lukkas whispered, lowering his lips to her ear.

She was acutely aware of his breath as it lightly glided along her cheek and neck.

She struggled hard to keep a shiver from surfacing. She wasn't seventeen anymore, Yohanna silently insisted.

It didn't help.

"Just in time," she echoed, hoping that Lukkas couldn't hear the way her heart had started to pound. Threading her way into the row, Yohanna gratefully sank into her seat as the opening credits appeared on the screen.

Another shaky sigh of relief escaped her lips before she could stifle it. She crossed her fingers, hoping that Lukkas hadn't noticed.

"You never took your eyes off the screen the entire time," Lukkas commented as, nearly two and a half hours later, they made their way up the aisle to leave the theater.

Progress was slow going because it seemed as if every third person they passed wanted to congratulate the producer on the quality of the film he had shepherded into existence.

She told him what everyone else was saying. "It was a good movie."

Rather than gloat, he allowed his natural humility to take over. "You have to say that."

Moving ever closer to the double doors the ushers had opened, she spared him a glance. Didn't he know her at all? She would have thought with the man's keen perception, he would have had a bead on her character—good and bad—by now. Obviously not.

"The only thing I *have* to do is show up on time in the morning and put in a full day's work before I leave for the night," she pointed out. "Empty flattery was not in the job description. And how do you know I never took my eyes off the screen?" she asked. "Weren't *you* watching the movie?"

"I've seen it," he told her drily, then added honestly, "I was looking around to gauge everyone else's reaction to the movie." His voice didn't betray whether the answer to that had pleased him or had caused him concern.

The lights had gone up some, but for the most part, the theater was still rather dimly lit. He couldn't have been able to see far, she thought.

"Kind of dark for that, wasn't it?" she asked.

"Which was why I spent a lot of time looking at you," he told her simply.

That wasn't entirely true. Gauging Hanna's reaction to the movie was only part of the reason his attention had kept being drawn back to her. Something about the young woman kept tugging at him, a connection of sorts that he was both hesitant to explore and yet felt almost compelled to.

He was borrowing trouble, as his grandmother used to say, and his life was already too full. He didn't need any extra complications being wedged into it.

And yet…

And yet nothing, Lukkas reminded himself sternly. People were counting on him for their very livelihood. He had no time to stray off a path he had set down for himself three years ago. A path that was the only thing keeping him sane.

No sooner had he and Hanna finally reached the lobby than they were joined by a tall, blustery man who immediately took his hand and pumped it.

"Judging from the bits and pieces I've been picking up," Darren Thompson, the head of the studio that was set to distribute Lukkas's film throughout the country, told him, "it looks as though you've got yourself another winner on your hands, Spader."

"*We've* got another hopeful winner on our hands," Lukkas corrected. Aware of his abilities as well as the quality of what he produced, Lukkas was always cautiously optimistic in his statements. No one could fault a man for being cautious.

But they could tease him about it.

The studio executive shook his head. "For once in your life, Spader, cut loose, for heaven's sake." The man turned toward Yohanna with no warning. "Help me out here," Thompson requested. "Tell the man how good his movie is."

"I already did," Yohanna told the executive. "But Mr. Spader comes around at his own pace. Nothing anyone can do but wait until he catches up."

"I like her," Thompson said, nodding in Yohanna's direction as he clapped one wide, heavy paw of a hand on Lukkas's back. "Where did you find her and are there more like her?" he asked brightly. "I could use a few level heads working for me at the studio."

Yohanna answered for the producer, sparing him a possible awkward situation. "He found me under a rock labeled Organizer, and I'm one of a kind."

Amused, Thompson laughed heartily. "I believe that, I surely do. Careful, Spader, or I'll steal her away from you." He punctuated the so-called threat with a broad wink.

"Not anytime soon, you won't," Lukkas told him with a good-natured smile on his lips. "I still need her. She's got a lot of organizing left to do before I'm close to being a done deal."

Was he telling the truth or just running interference for her? she wondered. She knew which she hoped it was. But this was work, not pleasure, and she needed to remember that and act accordingly.

"We'll see," Thompson promised, his tone pregnant with self-confidence. "In the meantime, I'd keep her close if I were you."

Lukkas looked at her as they parted company with the studio executive. Close. Heaven knew the directive was appealing. He would have liked nothing better than to keep her close.

Which was exactly why he shouldn't.

This was the first woman he was reacting to since he'd lost Natalie. He had no doubt that this situation consti-tuted his version of a rebound. It would be insulting to his wife's memory and it would definitely be unfair to

Hanna if he allowed himself to begin what would only have an abrupt, unhappy ending in its future.

"Should I be worried?" he asked Yohanna, tongue in cheek.

Not certain if he was being serious or not, she decided her best bet was to act innocent until she could piece his question together.

"I don't know. Worried about what in particular?" she asked.

He put it as succinctly as possible. "That you'll jump ship."

He watched in fascination as the corners of her mouth curved, forming a smile that was all but irresistible in his opinion.

"Not while we're out in the middle of the ocean," she quipped. "Besides," she added on a serious note, "there's still too much to do and I never willingly leave a job half finished. So unless you're planning on letting me go any time soon, just let me do my job and everyone'll be happy."

They were in the theater lobby and discovered that even here the progress to the front doors was incredibly slow moving.

She knew he didn't like being forced to move at this pace. It couldn't even be described as crawling.

"Bet you're glad that this evening's over," she commented. How could so many glittering, beautiful people be crammed into such a small space? she wondered.

"You'd lose that bet on two counts," Lukkas informed her. "I'm not all that glad and the evening's not over."

She wasn't sure if she'd heard him correctly. "It's not?"

"No." He lowered his head to make sure that she heard

him. The noise level had gone up again. "We still have a party to attend, remember?"

She knew that there was an after-party, but she'd just assumed that he'd want to attend it without having her around. "I just thought—"

"Premieres are *always* followed by parties."

His tone of voice didn't leave any room for argument. She took her cue from that. Besides, Cecilia had said as much to her when they had gone shopping for her gown earlier. There was *always* a party.

"Right. What was I thinking?" she quipped, hoping that Lukkas wouldn't feel inclined to make a whimsical guess.

Lukkas allowed himself a short laugh. "The Shadow knows."

Obviously confused, Yohanna paused to look at him quizzically.

Lukkas realized the obscure reference had gone right over her head. "Sorry, that was way before your time— and mine, if you're wondering," he added quickly. "I was raised on old classic programs. *The Shadow* was an old, old radio program. The opening and closing lines were always—"

Yohanna nodded. They were finally outside the theater. After being inside for so long, the cool night air felt almost downright chilly. She pulled her wrap closer around her, silently blessing Cecilia's instincts.

"'Who knows what evil lurks in the hearts of men? The Shadow knows,'" she quoted.

The completely stunned expression on Lukkas's face pleased her.

"You're familiar with that?" Lukkas asked in disbelief.

"Guilty as charged." And then she admitted, "I'm a trivia buff."

Lukkas raised his hand, signaling their position to his limo driver. The same fans who had lined the streets earlier were still there, waiting to catch another glimpse of the film's celebrities.

"You are just full of surprises, Hanna," he told Yohanna with a wide, approving smile.

The limo pulled up, and rather than wait for the driver to hop out and open doors for them, Lukkas opened the rear door, gesturing for Yohanna to get in.

"C'mon, let's get this party over with," he urged. "With a little luck, I'll have you back, safe and sound, in your own bed by midnight, Cinderella."

"You're the boss," she said, sliding carefully into the limousine.

"For now," he agreed.

Yohanna wasn't sure just what he meant by that, but she thought it best to leave it alone. That way, she was able to put her own meaning to things without being disillusioned.

She had to admit she was pleasantly surprised that Lukkas remembered his initial promise to her even at the party. She'd expected him either to wander away or be drawn away by one of the myriad of people—men and most notably women—who were competing for his attention. But each time he did move on to talk to someone, Lukkas ushered her along with him.

And if, by some chance, someone was talking to her at the time, Lukkas waited until she was finished and the verbal exchange was over.

She caught herself thinking that it was almost as if they actually *were* a couple.

Almost.

But she knew there was a fine line between reality and make-believe—especially here, in the very birthplace of make-believe—and she knew the difference.

Still, it was hard not to fall into the very tempting trap of pretending, just for a little while, that things were the way they seemed rather than the way they actually were.

The party continued until after midnight.

Lukkas had checked with her a couple of times to see if she wanted—or was ready—to go home. But each time he asked, she convinced him that she was wide-awake and doing just fine.

Until she was fading and tired.

The next time he asked, she still made the proper protests, but this time he overrode her.

"Save your breath, Cinderella. I'm taking you home," he told her.

She didn't want to be the reason why he had to leave the party. As the producer of what was, by all indications, a blockbuster of a movie, this was his time to shine and she didn't want to spoil that for him. After all, he owed her nothing. He'd already been far more thoughtful than she would have expected him to be.

"No, really," she protested with feeling, "I'm fine. We can stay—or you can stay and I can just get a cab to take me home."

But Lukkas shook his head. "I'm going home with the one I brung," he told her.

His grammar had always been impeccable. Had he had too much to drink? But she'd been with him all night and as far as she knew, he'd only had two flutes of champagne. Maybe *she* was the one out of kilter.

"Excuse me?"

"Never mind," he laughed. "It's just an old saying that used to make the rounds a few generations ago."

"What are you, a time traveler?" she asked, thinking of some of the previous remarks he'd made that sounded as if they had come from another era.

"Sometimes," he conceded. "Did you see *One Foot in the Past*?"

He had just mentioned one of her favorite movies. "Yes, I did. That one really made you think," she told him.

Lukkas grinned with genuine pleasure. "I'm beginning to like you more and more with every passing hour, Hanna." He looked as if he was only half kidding.

Don't get carried away, Yohanna warned herself. He was just going along with the party mood. In any event, she was certain he wouldn't remember any of this on Monday morning.

Still, she thought as he called for his driver, what he'd said to her did have a nice sound to it.

Savoring it for a little while longer wouldn't harm anything.

Chapter Eleven

"Would you like me to come back for you later, Mr. Spader?" the limousine driver asked as Lukkas stepped out of the vehicle and then took Yohanna's hand to help her get out.

Lukkas didn't want to communicate the wrong idea to either his driver or to Yohanna.

"No, Henry. Stay right here. This won't take long," he promised.

Lukkas saw the way his driver eyed him and then slanted a glance toward Yohanna. It was obvious what was going through the man's mind. His driver just assumed that he would be capping off the evening with a dalliance. There was no denying that the woman with him was gorgeous, not to mention approachably tempting.

He knew Henry meant well, but the driver was also wrong. Nothing was about to happen other than his walking Hanna to her door.

Yohanna smiled to herself. "I think your driver expects me to invite you in," she said to Lukkas as he brought her to her door.

He wasn't about to explore that possibility. "I learned a long time ago not to concern myself with what others expect of me. I only need to live up to what *I* expect of me," he told her. They were at her door already. It was time to wrap this up and gracefully take his leave. "Thank you for a very nice evening."

"I should be the one thanking you," Yohanna pointed out. She'd had a really wonderful time.

Yohanna suddenly remembered that she was still in possession of the card he'd given her to buy her outfit. "By the way, here's your credit card back," she said, taking it out of her purse and giving it to him. "I just want you to know that I intend to pay you back for the gown and everything else. Just not all at once," she qualified. The bill had come to a figure that represented six months of regular expenses on her budget.

Lukkas shook his head, dismissing her promise. "You wouldn't have had to buy 'the gown and everything' if I hadn't asked you to accompany me to the premiere, so don't worry about it." He flashed an easy smile at her. "I consider it an investment."

Yohanna caught her lower lip between her teeth, chewing on it as she looked down at her gown. She couldn't have him paying for her clothes. "I don't feel right about this," she told him.

"You might not feel right, but you certainly look right," he heard himself saying, giving voice to the way her appearance was affecting him. "And I appreciate you doing this for me."

He made it sound like a sacrifice on her part when it

was anything but. She couldn't help the smile that rose to her lips. All evening she'd felt like a fairy-tale princess. "All my assignments should be so hard."

Initially, he was just going to bring her to her door and watch her go inside. But he found himself wanting to linger, to stay with her a little longer.

Perhaps even go inside.

But he was afraid of where that might lead, and he wasn't ready to go down that path yet.

And he *definitely* wasn't ready to lose possibly the best assistant he had ever had because of a misstep he felt himself being so tempted to make.

He needed to go.

Now.

"See you Monday," he said, taking a couple of steps back, away from her.

"Monday," Yohanna echoed. Instead of opening her door, she remained exactly where she was, struggling with an urge that had materialized out of nowhere.

She desperately wanted him to kiss her good-night. Just one kiss.

Who are you kidding? You don't want just one kiss, you want more. And "more" is just asking for trouble, you know that.

She had a good thing going here: a job she was quickly growing to love. The worst thing in the world would be to allow a spurt of hormones to ruin that for her.

With effort, she took out her key and unlocked her front door.

A moment later she was closing the door behind her.

She was safe.

Safe from herself.

And never sadder about it than right now.

* * *

Yohanna came to work Monday—as well as all the rest of that week—acting as if there hadn't been a moment there, on her doorstep, when she had ceased to be someone who just worked for Lukkas Spader. She decided to make it a mission in her life to learn as much as she could about the man. There was an underlying sadness that reached out to her. She'd always had an inherent desire to help people heal.

For now, though, she needed to concentrate on getting her job done, which in turn meant helping him get *his* job—the movie—done. And something like that, she was beginning to realize, had a great many moving parts that needed to be attended to.

So for now, she pushed that part of herself, the part that was curious about the man, into the far background and did what she always did whenever she couldn't deal with—or have the time for—her private life: she threw herself into her work.

She organized Lukkas's appointments, revamped his schedule, got in touch with people he had penciled in on his calendar and prioritized his would-be "crises" as they came up.

As a small part of that, she made an effort to learn his favorite foods and took to ordering his lunches and, in some cases, his dinners, as well.

Working diligently, she trained herself to anticipate what Lukkas needed even before he realized he needed it. The upshot of that was that within four short weeks, she had his life running like clockwork. That made her completely indispensable to him.

Unknown to Yohanna, in addition to becoming indispensable to Lukkas, she also became the woman who preoccupied him in unguarded moments.

She also began popping up in his dreams, a fact that both intrigued Lukkas and disturbed him.

The latter reaction was because it made him feel that he was being unfaithful to the wife he'd so adored. When Natalie had died so suddenly, he'd been convinced that his heart would never seek anyone out again. That with the threat of loss moving like a specter in the shadows, he couldn't bear to become involved with another woman since that woman could die and leave him, just as Natalie had.

He could, with some effort, guard his thoughts during his waking hours. But when he was asleep, all bets were off—and all fences were breakable. His thoughts of Hanna would creep in and fanciful scenarios would be constructed that he would never allow when he was awake.

This complicated his life, and Lukkas was trying to cope with that as well as with feelings of guilt while attempting to mount a new production and bring it up to its wobbly feet.

At times it felt as though he was constantly shadow boxing, vanquishing one problem only to have another spring up in its place. On occasion he would consider throwing in the towel—those were the times when Hanna would come through the best.

"Your director's on line one," she told him on a particularly exasperating Tuesday morning, bringing a cordless receiver over to him.

Taking the phone from her, Lukkas frowned slightly. He knew before another word was said that he needed to go back to Arizona to find out what was—and wasn't—going on.

His hand covering the mouthpiece, he said, "Hanna, I'm going to need—"

Nodding, she interjected, "I've already called your pilot. The plane will be gassed up and ready to go within the half hour."

That almost left him speechless. "How long have you been a mind reader?" he finally asked her.

Yohanna didn't let the question go to her head. She didn't read minds; she read body language as well as the particular situation that her subject might be in.

"It comes with the territory," she answered. But she was smiling broadly as she said it.

"Just as long as you do, Hanna, that's all that counts." He made a quick calculation. "I hate to ruin any plans you might have for your evening, but I'm going to need you to—"

She'd anticipated this, as well. "I've got a go bag in the trunk of my car. I just have to get it before we leave for the airstrip."

He could only stare at her. There was no way she could have known that he would be receiving this call from Montelle, his director, nor could she have anticipated what the man would say to him.

"What am I thinking now?" Lukkas challenged, his green eyes narrowing ever so slightly as he looked at her, waiting.

"That's easy." She tried to keep a straight face, but failed within a few moments. Her grin was wide. "You're thinking that you don't know how you got so damn lucky to have found someone like me to anticipate your every need, your every move."

"Not exactly, but close enough," he answered with an amused laugh. "We might have to be there a couple of days. Is that all right with you—or would that be interfering with any plans you have for your evenings?"

"I *have* no plans for my evenings. You have my undivided attention," she assured him. "I signed on for the long haul. This is just all part of that."

He really *had* gotten lucky here, Lukkas thought, looking at her. "Right, but that doesn't mean that you have to be enslaved," he pointed out.

"I'll let you know if I feel as if I've been enslaved. Until then, I believe we have work to do," she reminded him. She pointed to the receiver he was still holding in his hand. "Dirk Montelle is still waiting."

He'd almost forgotten. "Oh, damn."

She went to get her go bag.

It was gratifying to find someone who had as much energy as he had, Lukkas thought a short while later. At the same time, it was also somewhat unsettling. He'd never had anyone match him step for step before. In so many ways, Hanna was the perfect assistant.

He just wished that she wasn't so damn attractive, so *distractingly* attractive, he silently amended, while she was at it. Because once each workday was finally done and they had accomplished—thanks to her—everything he had set out to do, thoughts of Hanna—a civilian Hanna—insisted on creeping into his brain and by her very presence, that caused things to get scrambled in his mind. Things such as priorities—even with Hanna prodding him.

Blocking those kinds of thoughts about her was getting harder to do.

* * *

"How much are you paying to rent this 'town'?" she asked Lukkas as they got out of his rental car. It was more or less a rhetorical question, asked in reaction to the oppressive blast of heat that hit her as she got out of the vehicle.

The dusty, weathered town was standing in for Tombstone for another five weeks. "Tombstone," the town that famously watched history being made and legends being born, did not come cheap.

Lukkas quoted the price he and the company that was behind the tourist attraction had arrived at.

"Enough to keep the locals contented," he added. Anticipating a negative remark from her, he was quick to hedge it. "It might look like a lot on paper, but it's actually a bargain. If we had to have these sets built back on the lot, it would have wound up costing a hell of a lot more than what we are currently paying to rent it," he told her.

That part she was well aware of. Yohanna nodded. "I know. I already ran the figures."

"Of course you did," he quipped. "Do you ever do anything spontaneous?" he asked her.

"Yes." Suppressing a smile, she looked him right in the eye and said, "I applied for this job."

Lukkas inclined his head. "Touché." He turned to the director. "So exactly what's our crisis of the day?"

Dirk Montelle took no pleasure in being the bearer of any sort of negative news. "We're falling behind schedule, and if that keeps up, I'm going to lose our leading lady, who can only give us five more weeks. After that, she's committed to a play they're trying out in LA before taking it out on the road."

Always something, Lukkas thought with an inward sigh. "Any way we can speed things up?"

The director laughed shortly. "I wish. But Maddox fancies himself a method actor. Every scene he's in—and that's practically all of them—he wants to shoot over and over again until *he's* 'satisfied.' See the problem?" Montelle asked, exasperated.

Lukkas dragged a hand through an already unruly mop of hair. His hair insisted on curling in the heat. "I see the problem. What I don't see is a solution without getting someone's feathers ruffled in the process."

Yohanna spoke up suddenly. "Bribery," she volunteered.

Both men turned toward her. "Come again?" Lukkas asked.

"Bribery," she repeated. The idea began to take shape in her mind as she spoke. "Offer Maddox a percentage of the picture if he helps you bring it in on time. Tell him if the movie isn't wrapped by the date that your female lead needs to leave, he doesn't get his piece of the movie. You'd be surprised how many mountains suddenly find they can move when the right amount of money is flashed before them."

Lukkas glanced toward his director.

The latter nodded, pleased with the suggestion. "Might be worth a shot," Montelle agreed.

"Okay, let's do it," Lukkas instructed, then looked at Yohanna. "You want to sit in on this since it's your idea?"

"I think it'll probably go over better with Maddox if he thinks this is something going down just between the guys," she pointed out. "Maddox might be charming on the big screen, but the man is a card-carrying male chauvinist pi—" At the last minute she stopped herself and offered Lukkas a wide smile. "You fill in the blank," she told him.

It was a rather insightful description of the man, Lukkas thought. "Someday, you're going to have to tell me where you picked up all this insight on David Maddox," he said.

The smile on her lips turned enigmatic. "I do a lot of reading," she replied vaguely.

"Yes, but Maddox's true state of mind is kept pretty secret," he told her.

"In order for there to be a secret between two people," she told Lukkas, "one of the two has to be dead. Otherwise, the secret—*any* secret—has a time limit on it. When that runs out, the secret 'mysteriously' becomes public knowledge."

Hanna was right, he thought. For such a young person, there were times when she displayed a very old mind. He caught himself wondering things about her that had nothing to do with the job she did.

"Tell someone to send Maddox to me," Lukkas instructed.

Yohanna fairly beamed at him. "You got it." With that, she took off.

Instead of finding someone to carry out Lukkas's order, she decided to go in search of the actor herself. It took a bit of doing, but she finally found the man sequestered in his spacious trailer.

The actor wasn't alone.

One of the continuity girls was with him. A tray with two full plates sat on the table, but neither party seemed to notice the food. Maddox appeared to be on the verge of seducing a not-so-legal young woman.

That was all the production needed. To be shut down

while charges of seducing a minor were brought up against the actor. It had been known to happen, and that sort of Pandora's box, once opened, couldn't be shut again.

"What are you doing in here?" Maddox demanded angrily when he saw her entering his trailer. He waved his hand at her as if he were brushing aside an annoying insect. "Never mind. I don't care. Just get the hell out."

Yohanna stubbornly ignored the actor. Her attention was completely focused on the young girl instead. "How old are you, Rachel?"

The girl seemed surprised, then immediately became defensive. "How do you know my name?"

"I made it a point to learn everyone's name in the crew," Yohanna replied calmly. "Just like Lukkas Spader does. Now answer the question, please. How old are you?" She already knew the answer to that, but she wanted to see what the girl would say.

"I'm nineteen," Rachel informed her with a toss of her head.

"It seems odd that someone who is in charge of making sure the props are exactly in the same place from one take to the next within a scene can't recall what's written down on her own birth certificate."

Rachel's eyes widened to their maximum capacity. "You've seen my birth certificate?" she asked in confusion.

"Everyone working on this movie set is vetted," Yohanna informed her. "From the guy who delivers the bottled water every other day right on up to the director—as well as the actors and actresses," she concluded, looking pointedly at Maddox.

"I will be eighteen—in another month," Rachel declared nervously, her bravado crumbling.

The next moment, scrambling, she gathered up her shoes and the few items of clothing that had already come off. Clutching them to her, Rachel rushed out of the trailer, leaving the door wide-open because both her hands were wrapped around her clothes.

"I hope you're satisfied," Maddox growled angrily. "You've ruined my morning."

"But I saved hers, so it all balances out in the end," she told the actor glibly.

Getting to his feet, Maddox towered over her by almost a foot. The scowl on his face was practically shooting thunderbolts. "I can have your job," he threatened.

She was not about to be intimidated by a man who tried to take advantage of a naive teenager. "If you can do it any better than I can, you're welcome to it, Mr. Maddox."

His scowl intensified. "You think you have such a smart mouth—"

"No, I don't," she interjected. "What I do have, however, is a smart brain. A brain that tells me if you don't take Mr. Spader up on his offer to generously give you a piece of the film, you are going to be taken to court for a breach of contract—and that's just the beginning.

"People like and respect Mr. Spader. You, however, have a reputation as an impossible actor to work with. If you don't get your act together and start promoting some goodwill, you'll wake up one morning to find that your career is over before you ever hit your prime. And because of your rather lavish lifestyle, which I'm sure you're not prepared to curtail, you'll be in debt before you know it with no way to get back on your feet. This isn't conjecture, this is a sure thing."

She could tell he was having trouble following what she was saying. She didn't know how to spell it out for him any better than she'd already done. Lukkas was a lot better at dealing with narcissistic walking egos than she was.

"Do yourself a favor," she told Maddox. "Learn how to get along with people."

"That's what I was doing with that continuity girl before you scared her away. Getting along," he told her with a leer.

Yohanna didn't trust herself to reply to the actor's ridiculous statement. Instead, she simply urged, "Go talk to Mr. Spader and see if you can't fix things by making 'nice' with the man—"

Muttering contemptuously under his breath, Maddox was out of his trailer before she had a chance to finish her sentence.

Chapter Twelve

With Maddox gone and presumably on his way back to the set, Yohanna was about to walk out of the trailer herself. She stopped just short of the doorway when she thought she heard the actor talking to someone who was right outside the trailer door.

If she came out of the man's trailer just now it might create an awkward scene, so she remained where she was, waiting for Maddox and whoever the actor was talking to, to leave.

Standing there, it was impossible not to listen. After a second she realized that the other voice belonged to Lukkas. Her boss had probably gotten tired of waiting for someone to bring Maddox to him so he had gone to look for the actor himself.

That still didn't change her feeling that coming out of Maddox's trailer at this point would be awkward, so she continued to wait where she was as patiently as she could until the two men stopped talking.

It wasn't long.

Maddox's last remark to Lukkas made her think the actor was heading back to the set and back to work. Score one for Lukkas.

Yohanna decided that the best thing to do was to give herself to the count of five before descending the trailer steps and heading back to the set.

Counting off the numbers in her head, she'd gotten up to four when she heard Lukkas raise his voice and say, "You can come out now. Unless, of course, you want to continue playing hide-and-seek."

Yohanna came out instantly. "How did you know I was here?" she asked as she made her way down the steps. Since he was right there at the bottom step, she was all but toe-to-toe with Lukkas.

"Easy. Maddox looked as if he was a hurricane survivor. The only hurricane I know of in the area is you," Lukkas replied. "And I heard what you said to him in the trailer—the door was left open," he pointed out in case she'd forgotten. "Nice job. You went a little off book," he told her, since she *had* strayed from his initial message. "But in general you've got good instincts."

What had surprised him most of all when he'd listened to her talking to the actor was that she hadn't fawned over the man the way almost everyone else on the set did. "Someone else would have been intimidated by Maddox's fame and personality—"

"I don't like people who abuse their positions—or use it to seduce young, impressionable girls," she added with a frown. She had a feeling that even if Rachel had been underage and the actor had known it, it wouldn't have made any difference to him.

He grinned as he walked back to the center of the set with Hanna. "I kind of got that impression when you read Maddox the riot act."

"No riot act," she denied calmly. "I just gave the man a glimpse of his future if he didn't get his act together and change—like, *immediately*."

Lukkas was having trouble hiding his amusement. The woman was feisty—and he found that to be very attractive. Just like the rest of her.

"So now you're the ghost of things to come in the future?" he asked.

"No, just somebody trying to do her job as best she can."

"Well, I'd say that you've succeeded admirably well," he told her—and then enumerated what she'd accomplished in a relatively short amount of time. "Thanks to you, Rachel's virtue will remain intact—for at least a little while longer—and this film just might get made on time after all." He spared her a rather long, thoughtful look. He couldn't help thinking that he'd gotten lucky all because of an off-chance remark he'd made to Theresa.

"After we wrap up tonight, I'd like to buy you dinner to show you my gratitude." The restaurant in town served good, decent food, but he knew of an excellent restaurant in the next city that served the kind of prime rib that most men only dreamed about.

Yohanna shook her head. "You don't have to do that," she told him.

"You turned Maddox into a human being. Who knows how long that'll last, but I learned in this business to take everything as it comes because things might just fall apart tomorrow. Anyway, after this transformation act with Maddox, it's the least I can do." He stopped short of the perimeter of the town. "I'm not taking no for an answer," he informed her.

"Then I'd better not give it," she replied.

"Smart," he commented. "Now let's get back to work." And with that, he walked into the town with Hanna right beside him.

He was getting very used to that.

It occurred to her as she watched Lukkas in action on the set later that day that the producer was involved in every single facet of the movie. He not only put himself out there to mediate disputes between crew members as well as between the people in the cast when tempers grew short or egos clashed, but Lukkas also made sure he had his finger in every single pie on the set.

Nothing was too large for him to tackle or too small to escape his notice.

Although she considered herself an unharnessed dynamo, just watching Lukkas work made her feel downright exhausted.

But eventually, several would-be crises later, the day finally did come to a close—later than she'd anticipated but still early enough to be within the parameters of the same day.

There were two and a half hours left until midnight as she went to Lukkas's trailer to check for any last-minute instructions he might have for her for the following day.

"There're *always* instructions for the next day," he told her. "But they can wait until morning." He powered down his laptop and closed the cover with finality. "Ready for that dinner I promised you?" Lukkas asked.

She'd thought that he'd forgotten. Stifling a yawn, Yohanna said, "I've been watching you all day. Toward the end, you looked as if you could barely put one foot in front of the other. You need to get some sleep," she advised. "You can buy me dinner some other time."

"Very little placing one foot in front of the other is involved in eating dinner," he quipped. "Another lesson I learned some time ago is do whatever you're planning on doing *now*. There might not be a tomorrow no matter how well you plan for it." There was sadness in his eyes as he added, "So why not celebrate each day as you can before the opportunity is gone?"

He was thinking of his wife, Yohanna thought, wishing there was something she could do to reduce that sadness. But she knew that wasn't possible. Everyone had to work their grief out on their own. The best she could do was to be silently supportive.

Offering him a smile, she said, "I just thought you might be kind of tired after being a superhero all day."

His brow furrowed slightly, the way it did when he was trying to figure something out. "I'm afraid I don't get the reference," Lukkas confessed. "How am I a superhero?"

She enumerated the ways. "Having the patience of Job. Tackling one problem after another. Getting people what they want—"

"When it's possible," he reminded her.

He was the one who decided what could be done and what couldn't. Had they really been in Tombstone, he would have been the marshal of the town, she thought. "You make it possible."

He laughed, shaking his head. "Not that what you're saying isn't really great for my ego, but you're going to have to tone down your image of me just a little. You make it sound as if I have the power of life and death over this little mobile community. You know I don't."

"Figuratively, then," she conceded. The next moment she tried to make him understand just where she was coming from. She figured that she'd observed him long enough to make this kind of judgment call. "Just telling it the way it is. And the way it is, Lukkas, is that you're one of the good guys." She told him in all seriousness, "The world needs more good guys."

He waved off the compliment. "Well, I don't know about the world," he said wryly, "but right now, I need to get something to eat before I start gnawing on the trees around here. So how about it?" he asked, looking at her. "Join me for dinner?"

She didn't like eating alone and she *did* like his company. She had no real reason to beg off. But the thought of driving to the next town—which wasn't all *that* close—was daunting.

"As long as we get something to eat here," she told him. "Because you might be ready to go another round or so, but I'm pretty beat."

"*Here* it is, then," he responded.

As it turned out, the building designated to serve as the local brothel in the movie was actually a restaurant geared to feed the tourists who came through the town seeking local color. It was also where the cast and crew ate their meals.

"Nothing fancy," he told her. "But if you want to stay in town, it's not half-bad."

"Is that your version of a rave review?" she asked, amused at his choice of words.

"No, that's my version of being honest. I'd rather drive

to Scottsdale, but it *is* a bit of a drive, and in the interest of not falling asleep behind the wheel—" he looked at her significantly since he had a feeling that had been her reasoning for remaining in the immediate area "—I thought this was a good alternative."

Yohanna recalled some of the recent reading she'd been doing on life back in Wyatt Earp's time. "Please tell me the restaurant isn't called Big Nose Kate's."

Lukkas laughed. "No, that's the name of the brothel in the movie. I don't know what the restaurant is actually called," he confessed. "Only that so far no one's been rushed to the hospital yet."

"Always a heartening piece of information to know," she conceded.

As it turned out, the restaurant specialized in Mexican cuisine and had several things on the menu that looked appealing to her. She finally decided to get the enchilada ranchero.

"Make that two," Lukkas told the young waitress as he handed her his menu, as well.

The young woman smiled as she looked from him to Yohanna. "Good choice. It's my favorite, too. I'll be right back with your bread," the waitress promised as she withdrew.

Lukkas leaned over in the booth to tell her, "Dirk Montelle wanted me to tell you thanks."

"For?" Yohanna asked.

She couldn't think of a reason why the director would want to thank her for anything. She'd had very few dealings with the director since she and Lukkas had arrived in Arizona this time around.

"Well, Montelle seems to think that you're the reason Maddox is behaving. Maddox is actually satisfied after only a couple of takes of each scene instead of his usual ten or twelve takes. Montelle told me that whatever spell you cast on Maddox, he hopes it's a long-lasting one. According to him, his ulcer has stopped acting up." Lukkas grinned at her. "You might have a career in medicine ahead of you."

She was flattered, but she didn't believe in taking credit when none was due. "You overheard what I said to Maddox. I just played on his insecurities. That wasn't magic. It was just using common sense, that's all."

"I agree," he told her. "But most people…well, they'd rather believe a little hocus pocus was involved. If you took a poll, I think you'd find out that people like believing that something more powerful than them is watching over the world, making things right." He smiled at her. "It makes them feel safer," he told her.

Before Yohanna had a chance to protest again, the waitress returned with the bread and several pats of butter, just as she'd promised. She carried it in on a wooden cutting board and placed it in front of Lukkas.

"I'll be back soon with your orders," she told them before once more retreating into the background.

Lukkas looked at the bread. It was situated in the middle of the cutting board. A sharp knife was next to it. "I guess she wants me to do the honors," he said, picking up the knife.

"I can do that if you like," Yohanna was quick to offer, thinking that perhaps he'd just subtly indicated that he'd rather not do the cutting.

"Not that I don't appreciate the fact that you keep trying to jump in and take care of practically all the details that infiltrate my daily existence, Hanna, but I actually am capable of cutting my own bread," he assured her good-naturedly.

"I never meant for you to think that I thought that you couldn't," she told him.

He surprised her by laughing out loud at her statement.

"Now, *that's* confusing, even without any wine to dull the brain," he joked. "By the way, I'm not offended, I'm amused. I might not have the thickest skin around, but it's definitely thicker than tissue paper," he assured her.

Cutting two thick slices of the warm bread, Lukkas gave her the first piece and took the second one for himself. When she didn't immediately pick up her piece from her bread plate, he nodded at it, saying, "You have to eat it while it's still warm."

"It's bread. How much of a difference can it make?" she asked, dutifully breaking off a piece of her slice and popping it into her mouth.

The instant the bread touched her tongue, she found herself smiling. There was something comforting about consuming the warm slice.

"You're right," she told him.

"It does happen every once in a while," he told her with a conspiratorial wink.

The restaurant was dimly lit. It was also rather noisy and fairly filled with people. Yet when she found herself on the receiving end of Lukkas's wink, she felt as if they were the only two people in the entire place.

With very little effort, her imagination could run away with her.

Don't get carried away. He's just being himself, nothing personal, she silently insisted.

Yohanna struggled to rechannel her thoughts.

"How did you find this place?" she asked him. "This town," she amended. "For the movie, I mean."

Great. You keep talking and you'll really convince him that you're a blithering idiot.

"The usual way," he told her. Then, seeing that she was still at a loss as to what had happened, he elaborated, "I sent out my location scout. Hank usually knows just what I have in mind and he's pretty good about nailing down what I'm looking for.

"We were lucky this place was here," he admitted. "But even if it hadn't been, I would have had sets built on the studio's back lot. With the wonder of CGI available these days, almost anything can be dressed up to look like what you have in mind."

She saw a basic contradiction in that. "If that's what you think, why bother with a location scout?" She would have thought that going with computer-generated imagery first would eliminate the hunt for a perfect location.

Her question brought a smile to his lips. "Because like a lot of people, I like the real thing rather than having to deal with a fake—or worse, dealing with nothing at all, having to pretend that it's there. A lot of actors don't act so much as they 'react.' Having an actual location helps them with that part," he concluded. "Make sense?"

She nodded. "Yes."

He could see right through her. "You'd say that even if it didn't, wouldn't you?"

"I'm not on the clock right now," she reminded him. "I don't have to answer that."

He grinned. Her nonanswer *was* an answer. "You just did," he told her.

Ignoring that, she took a different direction. "Why this story? This picture?"

"Why all these questions?" he asked. "Are you planning on putting out a book about working on this film after we wrap up?"

"You mean like an exposé?" she asked.

"That's exactly what I mean." Had he misjudged her? Was she someone who ultimately gave her allegiance to the man or woman on top, everyone else be damned?

He didn't like entertaining that thought.

"I'm just being curious, that's all," Yohanna admitted. "If you don't want to answer my question, that's okay."

"Who said I didn't want to answer?" he asked. "I was just curious why you wanted to know, that's all. But to answer your question, I've always loved Westerns—what little boy growing up in Texas doesn't?" he challenged, prepared to listen if Yohanna had a contradictory piece of information. But she didn't. If anything, she looked as if she agreed with him. "Anyway, I had so much fun making my first Western a couple of years ago, I decided to do it again."

"Hoping that lightning will strike again?"

It was a referral to the fact that he had won his first film award for the Western he'd just mentioned.

"I'd be lying if I said that it hadn't crossed my mind. But I'm not backing this movie because I'm actively hoping for another award or even another nomination. I'm making this film because I like the story and I believe it'll make a good movie.

"Besides, I really do enjoy the whole process, every step of the way. Especially when I have someone exceedingly competent I can rely on working for me." He could see that her inherent modesty wasn't allowing her to realize he was referring to her.

"In case I'm being too vague about the matter, I'm talking about you, Hanna," he told her, and then got a kick out of the surprised expression on her face. "You're a godsend and I intend to send Theresa Manetti *all* my catering business from here on in."

She'd already made the connection between Cecilia and Theresa. As far as she was concerned, she owed the latter a debt herself. "I'm sure that'll make her very happy."

Seeing that the waitress was heading in their direction with a large tray, Yohanna quickly cleared the table, stacking the small bread plates on the cutting board. The waitress arrived at their table and distributed the two plates. Since their orders were identical, there was no effort necessary to match the customer with the proper order.

The young woman looked from Lukkas to the woman sitting opposite him.

"Please be careful when you're touching the plates. They're very hot. Should you burn your hand anyway, just ask for me. I've always got something with me to take the pain away."

"Prescription drugs?" he asked, not quite able to cast her in the role of someone who distributed drugs, however innocuously.

"Over-the-counter spray," she corrected. "Where would I get prescription drugs?" she asked.

"No clue," he answered, and then confessed, "That was just a wild guess on my part."

Yohanna focused on the conversation. She'd first thought of Lukkas as being exceedingly closemouthed, but she now realized that he only spoke to someone on a regular basis if he considered that person worth the effort.

She promised herself that he would *always* find her worth the effort he put in.

Chapter Thirteen

"I want you to know that I appreciate everything that you've done."

They were halfway through the meal when, out of the blue, Lukkas said that to her.

Yohanna felt her nerves kick up a notch.

This was the way her last boss had begun the last conversation they'd ever had, the one about how her position had been terminated—as had she.

Taking a deep breath, she told herself that this time around she wasn't going to just be a stunned victim who disappeared quietly. This time, if she was being terminated, she would go on her own terms and with dignity.

"But...?" she challenged, waiting for the second shoe—or cowboy boot in this case—to fall.

"But?" Lukkas repeated quizzically, as if he had no idea where the word was coming from.

"Yes, but…" Since he still wasn't saying anything, she filled in the blanks for him. "You've been very happy with my work, but now I have to go."

"You do?" he asked, clearly confused since this was apparently the first time he'd heard this. "Is it something I did?"

Yohanna stared at him. Why was he toying with her? That wasn't like the man she'd come to know.

"Well, yes. You're the one terminating me."

Caught completely off guard, he put down his knife and fork. "Wait—what? I know I made a movie about parallel universes, but I really don't believe in them and I *know* I didn't just terminate you in this life."

Now it was her turn to be confused. "Weren't you just leading up to that? You've been happy with my work up until now, but since I did such a good job organizing things for you, you're all set and no longer need my services."

Lukkas slowly shook his head, as if to clear it of cobwebs. "Unless I'm a victim of some kind of new strain of amnesia, I didn't say any of that."

"Yes, you did," she insisted, and then conceded, "Okay, maybe not in so many words—"

"Not in any words," Lukkas told her, cutting in.

A glimmer of hope began to raise its head. "Then, what *were* you saying?" she asked.

She was partially relieved and yet afraid to go that route in case her premonition turned out to be right. She'd been blindsided once and it had really upset her, but this time around, it would do more than that. It would hurt.

Badly.

"I thought I said it," Lukkas told her. Since there was

a difference of opinion on that, he relented and said, "Well, at least part of it."

"Say it again—" Yohanna urged. "So we're both clear on it."

He paused for a moment, as if recreating the moment for himself. "I said that I just wanted you to know that I appreciate everything that you've done."

She waited. When there was no follow-up, she asked. "And that was it?"

"No," he admitted.

Okay, here it came, she thought. "Okay, go ahead," she urged, resigned to having the next words turn out not to her liking.

"I was going to say that I knew talk, even praise, was cheap and I wanted to show you that I was sincere by offering you a raise."

"A raise?" It took effort to keep her jaw from dropping into her lap. "As in money?" she asked him, rather stunned.

"No, a raise as in my levitating you. Yes, of course, as in money," he told her. "Like it or not, money's the fastest way of communicating approval and pleasure, just like withholding it communicates disapproval. The latter, by the way, has nothing to do with you," he assured her.

With the threat of her just walking out on him over, he resumed eating. "When Janice—your predecessor— left, I was certain I was never going to find anyone to take her place. She was *that* good.

"You, however, not only took her place," he continued, "you have surpassed her, something I never thought would be humanly possible. Janice was on top of *everything*, handling things as they came up. You seem to be able to anticipate what's going to happen, and you do it all effortlessly.

"I just wanted you to know that I might not say anything at the time, but I'm aware of what you're doing and I'm really very impressed with it all. The raise is my way of trying to keep you."

"Keep me?" Did he think she was going to leave? Where had he gotten *that* idea? "I'm not about to go anywhere," she assured him. "I really like this job." When she'd taken it, she hadn't realized just how much she *would* like it.

"Word's going to get out about your efficiency and your effortless juggling act," he told her. It would be just a matter of time before it happened—that much he knew. "There'll be people who will try to steal you away from me by making you lucrative offers and upping the ante. I just want you to promise me that when that happens, not if, but *when*—" he stopped her before she could argue the point "—you'll come to me and give me a chance to match the offer—or top it," he added, thinking that might be more of an incentive to make her remain in his employ.

His eyes pinned hers and he asked, "So do we have a deal?"

She put her hand out to him to seal the bargain. "Absolutely," she promised as Lukkas took her hand and shook it directly over what was left on their plates. "But I think you're talking about something that isn't going to happen."

His opinion differed from hers—and he had experience on his side. "This is a very cutthroat business, Hanna. You'd be surprised what people are capable of just to get slightly ahead of the 'other guy.' Just remember, if there's anything I can do to make things easier for you, all you have to do is tell me."

"Well, there is one thing I can think of right off the bat," she told him, her expression solemn and giving nothing away.

"Name it," he urged.

Her mouth began to show just the slightest hint of a curve. "You could let go of my hand," she told him. "I need it to cut into the second enchilada."

Embarrassed, he flushed. "Oh, sorry."

Her hand had felt so right in his that just for a moment, he'd forgotten he was holding it. The second she said something, he realized he was holding on to her hand like some love-smitten fool and he immediately let it go.

He was reacting to Hanna.

Reacting to her not as an incredibly capable assistant— and quite simply the answer to his prayers—but as a woman.

It had been unconscious on his part.

He had ceased to think of himself as a man, with a man's basic needs, the moment he'd heard of his wife's death. He had been convinced then—and now—that that part of him had shut down, completely and irrevocably, and somewhere along the line, that part of him had just withered away and died.

In his work he was constantly surrounded by countless attractive women of all ages, many of whom thought nothing of using their physical attributes to get ahead.

That sort of thing didn't work with him. He hadn't been tempted, not even one single time. He saw them, noted the "special" assets they brought to the interaction and felt absolutely *nothing*. There hadn't even been any latent stirrings.

For almost three years now he'd viewed situations and women in his capacity as a producer, as someone who knew the benefit of giving the public what they wanted—and the public *always* wanted a young, sexy actress to look at.

But as far as that being something that *he* wanted for himself? That never once even entered into the picture. He felt he was no longer attracted *that* way to women, no matter how sexy or how beautiful.

Until Hanna had come into his life.

Because this live wire of a woman *did* stir things within him that had nothing to do with producing a movie, nothing to do with the hectic agenda he maintained, and everything to do with the inner man he'd just assumed had atrophied from grief.

He was making this pitch to keep her faithful to his company—in effect, to him—because in addition to seeing her as an asset of the highest quality, he simply didn't want to lose *her*. Not just the dynamo of an assistant, not the woman who could keep all those balls successfully in the air, but he didn't want to lose Hanna. Period.

Feeling that way scared the hell out of him for so many reasons. It scared him because he knew what happened when a person became attached to another human being. That sort of a connection left him open to a world of pain if that association should terminate—abruptly or otherwise—for any of a number of reasons.

There was also the problem of guilt.

Guilt because he was going on with his life and Natalie no longer had a life to go on with. Having feelings for someone other than his wife seemed somehow unfaithful, disloyal to her memory.

Natalie deserved better than that.

"Is everything all right?" Yohanna asked him.

Lukkas roused himself and did his best to look as if he hadn't been miles away, lost in thought just now.

"Yes. Why?"

She shrugged, as if she thought perhaps she *had* been overreacting. "You had this very faraway look on your face just now."

"Just thinking about tomorrow's filming," he lied smoothly. Or so he thought.

"Tomorrow's filming," Yohanna repeated, then recited the latest schedule for filming the day after Halloween. "They're doing scene sixteen and scene thirty and the assistant director is doing some secondary background shots of the corral where the gunfight is supposed to take place."

Lukkas could only shake his head in wonder, not to mention in complete admiration. "Like I said, you're absolutely amazing."

She hardly heard the compliment, honing in on the sadness she'd glimpsed in his eyes for an unguarded moment just a minute ago. She was willing to bet that Lukkas hadn't even remotely been thinking about the next day's shooting schedule. Something else was on his mind, something far more personal.

"Listen," she began haltingly, "I might be out of line here…"

"Go on," he told her quietly.

She took another breath, wondering if she shouldn't have said anything, then decided it wasn't in her to turn a blind eye to someone else's pain—especially if that someone else mattered to her as much as Lukkas did.

"But if you ever…you know, need to talk to someone about…anything," she finally said, "I'm a pretty good listener." And then she added with what she hoped was a convincing smile, "Two ears, no waiting."

Not that he planned to tell her anything, but it was nice to know someone cared enough to offer help of a sort.

"I appreciate the offer," he told her. "But the fastest way to lose a friend is to burden them with having to listen to someone go on about things that don't matter to anyone else but them."

"Funny, I was thinking just the opposite," Yohanna told him. "Sharing concerns, things that worry you, that's the ultimate sign of trust, not to mention that something like that promotes bonding."

"Okay, I'll keep that in mind," he told her. Finished with his meal, he set his knife and fork down on his empty plate.

"And in case you forgot this part, it works two ways," he pointed out. "If you ever need to unload, say, about a boyfriend who feels as if you're spending way too much time at work," he elaborated with a smile, "I'm here."

"I wouldn't hold my breath if I were you," she advised.

"You don't believe in complaining?" he asked, curious.

"It's not that," she told him. "I don't have anything to complain about, at least, not in that department."

He took a sip of water to clear his throat. "Let me guess, your boyfriend's perfect?"

"My 'boyfriend' is nonexistent," Yohanna corrected glibly.

Lukkas looked at her, rather surprised. When she'd first come to work for him, she'd said there was no boyfriend in her life. He'd just assumed, as the weeks went by, that that was no longer the case. To find out that he'd assumed incorrectly…well, that pleased him. Pleased him a great deal.

"You don't have a boyfriend?" he asked with an air of disbelief.

Yohanna closed her eyes for a second, desperately trying to ward off a feeling of déjà vu.

"Please don't sound like my mother," she all but begged. "That's her recurring theme. Except that she says that exact same sentence in a much higher voice—almost a screech. That's usually followed by her telling me that her best friend's dermatologist's cousin's son is going to be calling me and I should say yes when he asks me out because, after all, I'm not getting any younger."

Lukkas didn't bother trying to stifle his laugh. "That's very funny."

"Not when you're on the receiving end of the conversation. Trust me on that," she added with more than a little feeling.

Lukkas stopped laughing and looked at her in surprise. "You're serious?"

She nodded. "I only wish I wasn't. I think my mother had posters made up of my high school graduation picture with the caption 'Please date me' written across the bottom. The only saving grace is that the last line has a disclaimer that reads 'Serial killers need not apply.'

"My mother *really* wants grandchildren," Yohanna explained. "All her friends have at least one, if not more. My mother desperately wants to be able to brag about a granddaughter or grandson." There was pity in her voice as she continued, "She feels I've failed her—and she makes sure that I'm aware of that every time she calls me."

As if aware of what she was saying—and to whom—

Yohanna raised her eyes to his. "Wait, how did my offer to be your sounding board turn into my crying on your shoulder?" Embarrassed and aware that she had crossed a line, Yohanna flushed. "I'm sorry. I'm not really sure what just happened here."

He didn't want her to feel embarrassed. If anything, Lukkas felt touched that she'd let him into her world. "Easy. You needed someone to talk to and I just said something to trigger the release. Don't worry about it," he assured her. "As a matter of fact, I kind of like the fact that you felt you could confide in me." When she rolled her eyes in response, he went a step further. "No, really. I think I needed that to remind me just how good I have it."

Glancing down at the table, Lukkas saw that she had finished her meal. That made two of them.

"Would you like any dessert?" he asked and then offered, "I can have the waitress bring back the menu."

"I would *love* dessert," Yohanna responded with feeling, then quickly held up her hand to stop him from waving over their waitress. "But I'd have to wear it. I'm so full, I couldn't fit in another bite—really," she protested.

"Are you sure?" he asked. "We could get it to go." Lukkas saw an impish smile, which totally charmed him. He wondered if she knew that when she smiled like that, she was really hard to resist. "What?"

"I could have it for breakfast." She realized she probably wasn't making any sense to him, so she elaborated, "When I was a kid, I always thought having cake for breakfast was a dream come true. My mother, of course, had other thoughts on the matter. Not to mention that she was very militant about not consuming too much sugar or too many calories. She told me that no man would want to marry me if I looked like the Goodyear Blimp.

"What are you doing?" she asked when he raised his hand to catch the waitress's eye.

"Making a dream come true," he told her simply. "And also asking for the check."

When the waitress came to their table a couple of minutes later he said to her, "We'd like to see the dessert menu, please."

"Right away." The waitress plucked a menu from one of the other waitresses walking by. The other woman was carrying several to the reservation desk.

When she offered the menu to Lukkas, he nodded at Hanna. "It's for her."

"No, really—" Yohanna began to beg off, waving away the menu.

"What kind of cake do you have?" he asked the waitress.

She rattled off four different kinds. When she came to vanilla with pecan sauce, Lukkas noticed a spark in Hanna's eyes. He had his answer.

"She'll take that one," he told the waitress. "Make it to go. Wait, make that two slices to go," Lukkas amended. He saw the quizzical way Hanna looked at him. "Hey, I like cake, too."

"You really didn't have to do that," Yohanna told him after the waitress left to prepare the desserts for transport.

"Sure I did," he argued amicably. "After all, how often does a man get a chance to make a little girl's dream come true?"

She had no answer for that. She could only smile. She was seriously beginning to understand that if there was one thing that Lukkas Spader could do, it was make dreams come true.

For big girls as well as for little ones.

Chapter Fourteen

Lukkas didn't need to look at a calendar.

He knew.

The very date had been burned into his brain, into his heart, since that horrible day three years ago.

Three years.

One thousand ninety-five days ago, his world had ended.

Part of him had desperately hoped that he would find a way to just move on, to block the numbing feelings of loss out of his awareness. For the most part, he'd succeeded.

There were whole chunks of time that he could function without those horrific feelings suddenly ambushing him, destroying everything in its path but the terrible memory of those first few hours, those first few days, where nothing, especially his existence, made any sense.

Those first few days when he couldn't quite understand how he could go on breathing in a world without Natalie in it.

As time went by, the ambushes occurred less frequently. He found a way to function, to be useful. To even continue building his career.

But on the anniversary of his wife's death, it had all come crashing back with a vengeance that first year—and then again the second year.

This year was no exception.

Lukkas could feel himself shutting down even as he struggled not to let it happen.

This year, in an attempt to keep his feelings of loss at bay, Lukkas completely surrounded himself with work—or thought he did.

But because of Yohanna's efficiency, everything was moving so smoothly, he didn't even need to be out on location at this moment. Wasn't really needed anywhere.

Without these artificial roadblocks in place, the grief easily found him.

That morning, Yohanna saw the difference in Lukkas's deportment immediately. There had always been that slight hint of sadness in his eyes. She'd noticed it the very first day when she had interviewed for her job. However, it had been subdued. Today, that aura of sadness seemed to have created some sort of invisible, impenetrable force field around him.

Lukkas was unapproachable and, while not short-tempered, noticeably short with those around him. Including her.

Trying to get to the bottom of the cause, Yohanna waited until she knew he'd be alone in his trailer to broach the subject. Even as she told herself that she should just let things slide, she still found herself going to his trailer and knocking on his door.

She had to knock twice before she heard any response from within. At least, she *thought* she'd heard something, but it could have just been the noise coming from the set.

Taking a deep breath, she tried the door. It wasn't locked.

Because she'd ventured this far, she decided to let herself in.

"Lukkas?"

There was no answer.

Thinking that perhaps he hadn't heard her, she made her way to the rear of the trailer, to the area that had been converted into his bedroom.

That was where she found him.

Lukkas was packing the suitcase he'd brought with him on the plane.

Surprised, Yohanna could only surmise they were flying back to California.

"Are we leaving?" It was the first thing she could think to ask.

Completely involved in his own heartache, Lukkas hadn't heard her come in until she'd spoken. His nerves were very close to the surface and he jumped.

"Don't you knock?" he demanded.

She had never seen him uptight or angry before. The image was unsettling.

"I did. I thought that maybe you hadn't heard me so I tried the door. You didn't lock it."

"And so you thought you'd just waltz right in." It was an accusation more than a statement of fact. An annoyed accusation.

"I think that's self-evident," she responded politely.

Indicating the open suitcase, she asked again, "Are we going back to the studio?"

"I am." His tone made it apparent that he completely excluded her from this.

Yohanna asked, "What about me?"

Lukkas shrugged. "You can do whatever you want to do," he declared, biting the words off.

He wasn't even looking at her, just addressing his words to the contents of his suitcase. But why was he so angry at her? What had she done to bring about such a drastic change?

Yohanna vacillated between just quietly withdrawing and remaining in the trailer for what was shaping up to be some sort of a confrontation.

Tempted, she almost went with the first option. But if she did, she knew that this raw feeling would always be there between them should she somehow still wind up staying in his employ.

For her own peace of mind, she needed to clear this up, whatever "this" was. "Did I do something wrong?" she asked.

He swung around to look at her. "No. You're perfect. Absolutely perfect," he snapped.

"If I'm so perfect, then why are you biting off my head and acting as if you're angry at the whole world— me in particular?"

"Maybe because I am angry at the whole world," he retorted.

Yohanna noticed that he hadn't singled her out the way she had. She became more determined to find out what was going on.

"Because...?"

"Because!" he shouted, slamming down the lid of his

suitcase. He did it so hard, the suitcase fell off the bed. The contents flew out all over the floor.

Yohanna automatically moved to pick up his clothes for him and Lukkas grabbed her by the shoulder, pulling her up.

"Don't!" he ordered gruffly.

At that moment he saw his reflection in the mirror hanging over his bureau, saw the anger that all but distorted his face.

The sight was so startling it abruptly knocked the air out of him.

Dropping his hand to his side, he murmured, "I'm sorry," to her. And then, in a stronger voice, he reinforced his apology. "I'm really sorry. I have no right to take this out on you."

Because he'd apologized, she immediately forgave him. He appeared genuinely sorry and that only made her more determined than ever to find out what was going on. She had spent too much time in Lukkas's company to believe that this was his true nature and the rest had just been a ruse.

Something had gotten to him in a way that she didn't think anything could. Something that seemed to completely shatter him.

And then, suddenly, it hit her. She knew what had caused this transformation.

"Talk to me, Lukkas," she urged him. "Please."

He didn't want to talk, to think, to in any way peel back the layers and make this any worse than it already was.

He tried to make her leave. "Look, I've done enough to you. Please, just go—"

"No," she answered. With that, she planted herself on

the edge of the bed, where she intended to remain until she got him to unload. "I'm not going anywhere. You need to get this out, to talk this through. Lukkas, you really need to get those feelings out before they wind up eating you alive."

Lukkas said nothing as he looked at her, but she could almost feel him struggling with himself.

"I'll start you off," she offered, then quietly continued, "This has to do with your late wife, doesn't it?"

The stricken expression in Lukkas's eyes told her she had guessed correctly.

"What set you off?" she asked. "Did you come across something of hers you'd forgotten was there or—?"

"The accident was today," he said hoarsely, his voice distant, as if he could somehow separate himself from the words he was saying.

Yohanna recalled the article she'd glimpsed on her tablet. He was talking about the car accident that had ended his wife's life.

Her heart went out to him in empathy.

"Each year after my dad died," she said quietly, "on the anniversary of his passing, I wound up reliving how I felt when I watched him slip away— We were at the hospital with him, my mom and I," she interjected.

She saw fresh grief pass over Lukkas's face.

"Well, I wasn't there when Natalie 'slipped away.' I was busy being the big-shot producer on the set," he told her bitterly. "I was supposed to be there with her, supposed to be the one who drove her to the doctor's office for her appointment—but I was too busy and I forgot all about her appointment. We were having our first baby and I *forgot*," he told her, his self-disdain almost palpable. "So, ever the resourceful wife, she drove herself.

The front tire had a blowout. Natalie plowed into a street-light. She must have been so scared—" His voice broke.

"If you had been with her, the front tire would have still had a blowout," she pointed out. "As horrible as it was, her death wasn't your fault," she insisted. "Stop beating yourself up over it."

Yohanna could see that she just wasn't getting through to him. "From what I can piece together, your wife was a wonderful, kind person. She wouldn't have wanted you to do this to yourself. She would have wanted you to honor her memory by being strong and going on with your life," she told him.

He said nothing, but she saw the unshed tears shimmering in his eyes.

Without fully realizing what she was doing, only motivated by the need to offer comfort, Yohanna rose to her feet and put her arms around him. He tried to shrug her off, but she persisted. Slowly, she felt him stop resisting.

"Let it go so you can heal," she urged softly, hugging him harder, doing her best to break through all the layers he'd thrown up around himself, shutting grief in, shutting compassion out.

She wasn't sure just how long she stood there, offering him solace as best she could.

Nor was she really clear as to who made the next move after that.

Whether it was her—or Lukkas.

Whichever did, one minute she was trying valiantly to give him some of her own strength, the strength she'd built up to help her deal with life after losing the father she adored. The very next moment it was as if some sort of spell had been cast, some sort of floodgate had been opened, because that was when her lips were pressed against his.

She could taste his tears—and his pain. Something within her opened up as well, something that not only could offer comfort in the face of grief, but that actually *drew* comfort from the very act of offering it to someone else.

It progressed at almost a breakneck speed immediately after that.

Wanting only to help give voice to his very real pain and, just maybe, to diminish it and its hold on him by that very act, she discovered that there was a solid ache within her, as well. An ache that craved having some sort of real contact, to touch and be touched by another human being in a way that allowed actual souls to touch.

A real sense of urgency all but throbbed in his veins.

Lukkas slanted his mouth over hers over and over again. Each time he did, the stakes were raised. And so was the promise of a reward.

Lukkas had had no idea how much he really needed this sort of contact, a contact he had denied himself because he'd believed that part of him—the part that could be reached by only a woman's touch—had been snuffed out the day his wife had been killed. To find out that it hadn't, that it was, instead, alive and in need of thriving, both dismayed him and thrilled him. To that end he felt utterly confused but alive for perhaps the first time in three years.

Suddenly very much in need to complete this exotic journey he had started, Lukkas undid buttons, coaxed articles of clothing away from the areas that they covered.

The warm flesh he discovered underneath the banished clothing easily started his pulse racing.

And fed a desire for more.

He ran his hands along Hanna's body, his own responding to it the way he hadn't responded to anyone in so long.

It was not unlike coming out of a deep sleep then becoming aware of limbs that had been all but paralyzed such a short while ago. There was no such paralysis, no such numbness, afflicting him now.

Every part of his body was alive and *feeling* every subtle nuance that being here like this with Hanna had created.

In its grip, Lukkas found himself racing to consummate this feeling, to capture it quickly before it was gone and he returned to the isolated, cold, lonely chamber he had existed in until just now.

Yohanna gave him no resistance.

Just the opposite was true.

She enflamed him, fanning the growing fire he had within him until the flames filled out every single corner of his being, leaving no room for grief or regrets of any kind.

Afraid of losing this feeling, of becoming trapped within his self-created prison once again, Lukkas ceased exploring the subtleties of her body and gave in to the overwhelming desire to unite it with his.

One moment his eyes were on hers, their hands delicately interlaced. The next he was driving himself into her and so creating a union where none had been before.

Ever mindful of her, Lukkas watched her face as he began to move. If for any reason at all, she had changed her mind about this, he'd be able to see it and, as hard as it would be for him, he would stop.

There would be deep regret, but he would stop.

But there was no such sign from her.

Instead, Yohanna instantly matched his rhythm. He stepped up the pace.

So did she.

They rose together at breakneck speed, taking the summit together. His arms tightened around her as the internal fireworks came to a head.

For one brief, shining moment, he felt himself both excited and at peace.

Yohanna kissed him, urgently pressing her mouth against his with every fiber of her being. It was as if she wanted Lukkas to know that whatever might come afterward, in this one moment, they belonged to one another and all was perfect in the tiny universe populated only by the two of them.

Yohanna nestled her body against his. She remained there even as the euphoria began to slip away, withdrawing into the same shadows where it had lay hidden, waiting for just that one opportunity to emerge.

Lukkas slowly became aware of everything.

Of the scent of her hair, of the light, sweet taste that her lips had brought to his, of the softness of her skin as her body remained curled into his.

Everything.

No doubt sensing the lull in what they'd just shared, Yohanna raised herself up just enough to lean her arm against his chest and look into Lukkas's eyes.

"So are we still going back to the studio?" she asked, pretending to act as if they hadn't just blown out all the stops and made torrid love together. "Because if the answer's yes, I'm going to need five minutes to pack. Make that ten," she amended, reconsidering, "because I have to put some clothes on first. I don't think your pilot would appreciate my boarding his plane naked."

"I can't see him complaining about that," Lukkas said, playing along. And then he laughed at the absurdity of the conversation. Stroking her hair, which was splayed against his chest, he apologized. "I'm sorry about before."

"Which before?" Yohanna asked cautiously. "Because part of that 'before' was really terrific."

Lukkas was focused on making amends. "I shouldn't have snapped at you like that."

He felt a slight flutter across his skin and realized that she was smiling against his chest. Why that would suddenly make his heart feel full, he had no idea.

"I've endured worse," she told him. "Besides, I'd say that you kind of made up for it." Raising her head again, her eyes met his. Hers twinkled with humor—and maybe a little something more. Whatever it was, it seemed to reel him in.

"I meant what I said the other day, you know," Yohanna told him.

"You said a lot of things on a lot of days," he pointed out, patiently waiting for her to clarify her words.

"You have a point," she conceded. "When I told you that you could talk to me if something were bothering you, I meant it. I really am a good listener and I promise you that whatever you say to me won't go any further than my own ears."

Even though she was trying to have a serious conversation with him, he could feel himself responding to her again. Responding not just to her physically, but to her kindness, her understanding. She was the whole package. Beauty, brains and compassion. And that was rare.

Raising his head a little, he lightly skimmed the tip of his tongue along the outline of her ear. "This ear?" he asked, his warm breath caressing her skin.

She surprised him by maneuvering her body and flipping him onto his back.

"And this ear," she said, turning her head just enough to make her other ear accessible to him.

This time when he mimicked his previous movement, she could feel her whole body responding with a warm shiver that ran the length of it.

She didn't remember all that much immediately after that, except that it was spectacular.

Chapter Fifteen

"So this is the way I find out? When were you going to tell me? Or did you just decide that I didn't need to know?"

Her mother's voice vacillated between sounding indignant and really hurt. Long ago Yohanna had learned that when it came to wielding guilt, her mother was in a class all by herself.

And Elizabeth Andrzejewski had not mellowed with age.

Yohanna frowned. She and Lukkas had returned to Southern California late yesterday. He'd dropped her off at her house while he had gone on to his because he needed to take care of several things.

The blinking light on the answering machine part of her landline had caught her eye the moment she'd entered her house, but for the sake of her own peace of mind, Yohanna had deliberately put off listening to the messages until morning.

Well, now it was morning and here she was listening to her mother lay on the guilt with expert precision. Her mother hadn't been able to reach her while she'd been on location because she'd consciously left her cell phone off. Because unforeseen things had a way of happening, she had left a message on her mother's machine that she was going out of town and couldn't be reached. However, if some kind of *real* emergency came up, her mother could call Lukkas's office at the studio and leave a message. That message would then be forwarded to her as quickly as possible.

Yohanna made sure that her mother would be out having lunch with her friends—something she did every Thursday—before calling. That way she was assured of getting the answering machine. Her reason for this roundabout approach was to avoid fielding the thousand-and-one questions she knew her mother was capable of asking.

The questions that apparently were coming her way now.

"Tell you what, Mom?" Yohanna murmured to her answering machine as it went on playing her mother's far from brief message.

Even though she'd voiced the question out loud, it was purely a rhetorical one. She had a sinking feeling she knew exactly what her mother was referring to and had no doubts that she would be listening to recriminations regarding her "oversight" at length for weeks—possibly months—to come.

The next moment she was proved right. Yohanna took no joy in that.

"You went to a real Hollywood movie premiere with that man, your boss," her mother all but squealed. "Best-looking man you've ever gone out with and did you even *think* to give me a call to let me know? Of course not. I had to find out my daughter was dating a celebrity by watching *Today's Hollywood*," her mother complained bitterly.

"I wasn't 'dating' him, Mother," Yohanna retorted to the answering machine. "I was shielding him."

And now? What are you doing with him now? she asked herself. She honestly didn't have an answer to that, other than the obvious one: that what she was doing with him was having a good time.

"The reporter said that it looked as though Lukkas Spader had finally stopped grieving over his dead wife and was moving on *with his new assistant.* That *is* you, right?" her mother asked with annoyance. "I didn't see anyone else with him in that segment. Just you. My former daughter.

"The woman doing the segment went on to say that you two are an item. An *item.* And you didn't even pick up the phone to tell me, your own *mother.* I raised you better than that. At least I thought I did. Well, let me tell you that is *no way* to treat your long-suffering mother, Yohanna."

Yohanna rolled her eyes. Leaning over the answering machine, she said, "Yes, it is, because I just *knew* you'd be making a big deal out of it. And that's what you're doing," she said, waving a hand at the answering machine. "You're making a big deal out of it."

She sighed, shaking her head. When the time came to actually *talk* to her mother, she knew she wasn't going to say any of what she'd just said, wasn't going to tell her mother to butt out of her affairs—oh, God, her mother would leap on that word, she thought in absolute dismay. No, there would be no indignant comebacks, no angry retorts forthcoming from her.

Instead, she would just sit there, listening to her mother politely, because she would tell herself that, at bottom, her mother meant well and all she *really* wanted for her was just the best.

Meanwhile, her mother thought nothing of making her utterly crazy in the process.

However, her mother and the drama Elizabeth Andrzejewski always created were of secondary importance in the scheme of things. Right now she was far more concerned with what this so-called "breaking news" broadcast her mother had referred to, which she herself as of yet hadn't glimpsed on the air, would do to Lukkas if he happened across it—especially if someone brought it to his attention.

Would the threat of having this labeled a relationship cause him to step back from whatever was building between them? Would he tell her that people would get the wrong idea so to keep things the way they were— professional—he was going to back off?

The very idea of not seeing Lukkas privately anymore felt like a knife to her insides.

But there wasn't anything she could do about that. She was just going to have to be holding her breath until Lukkas found out about the media's current speculation about his life.

Part of her fervently hoped he never would find out because she had a feeling that *that* could very well signal the beginning of the end of their time together. And until just this moment, she hadn't realized that she didn't want it to end. At least not yet.

Not for a while.

A *long* while, she amended.

In all honesty, she had never had a relationship that had actually worked before. There had been a few half-hearted *associations*—for lack of a better word—but they had all simply petered out after a short amount of time.

Maybe it was because, as her mother maintained, she was too picky. But whatever the reason, she had never felt that lighter-than-air feeling she experienced whenever she was with Lukkas. Before she had gone to work for Lukkas, she'd begun to think something was wrong with her. And then she'd met Lukkas and suddenly everything was right with the world.

Her response to Lukkas wasn't just physical—although heaven knew the man, with his well-defined chest, his tight butt and his sleek hips was a feast for the eyes—but he spoke to her on a completely different level.

Spoke to her soul.

Until just recently she had never believed in such things as kindred spirits, never believed in the existence of so-called soul mates. She'd thought it was a term people made up to make themselves feel as if what they had was special and that it would last until the end of time. Usually, it didn't last anywhere nearly as long, and relationship extraction was always rather painful.

But in this case, in *her* case, she felt as if that was exactly what was happening to her. She and Lukkas were quietly building toward something solid. And she wasn't about to have all that work destroyed by some hot-shot reporter or blogger calling unwanted attention to Lukkas and her, to their association.

She wasn't about to allow Lukkas to be driven away from her by a few thoughtless words.

When her doorbell rang, she assumed that her mother had decided to do her "severely wounded mother" act in person rather than leave another message on the phone. Since her car was safely put away in the garage, Yohanna debated pretending she wasn't home.

But her mother was nothing if not persistent. The doorbell rang a second time. And then a third. This could go on indefinitely. She might as well get it over with.

Psyching herself up for a confrontation, Yohanna strode over to the door and yanked it open even as she started talking quickly. "I didn't tell you anything, Mother, because there's nothing to tell! Understand?"

"Sure thing."

Her jaw all but dropped when she saw that Lukkas was standing in her doorway, not her mother.

"Nothing to tell about what, Hanna?" he asked her, coming in.

She waved away both what she'd said and his question regarding it. "Doesn't matter." She knew she had to offer him some sort of an explanation in order not to come off as being too strange. "I came home to half a dozen messages from my mother. The usual thing," she told him, brushing the matter aside and hoping he wasn't going to ask her anything specific about what her mother had said in those messages.

Hope was short-lived.

"And the usual thing is?" Lukkas asked, attempting to coax an answer out of her.

Maybe she did need to begin at the beginning. Sort of.

This definitely felt awkward. "One of those red-carpet reporters took a video of you at the premiere."

"You mean of us," Lukkas corrected. He had been quite aware of the clusters of paparazzi that would have been willing to literally kill one another just to get a clear shot of the two of them.

She nodded. "My mother seems to think that I'm keeping something from her."

Pausing for a moment, he took the wildest guess he could. "You mean like a secret wedding?"

She could only stare at him in complete wonder. "What? No. She knows that no matter how crazy she makes me, I wouldn't exclude her from my wedding. That would be too cruel."

Maybe she had said too much. She had a sinking feeling Lukkas was going to say something about nipping this "romance thing" in the bud and that they were going to have to keep everything aboveboard.

"I'm sorry," she told him.

He furrowed his brow. "Did you do something to apologize for?" he asked her.

"No." Technically, she hadn't, Yohanna thought. There was no way she could have foreseen this sort of a reaction from the voyeuristic press.

To her surprise, Lukkas didn't really need any convincing as to her culpability.

"That's right, you didn't. I knew it was a calculated risk, taking you to the premiere to ward off being 'fixed up' by some of my well-meaning friends and their wives." He moved a little closer to her, his eyes holding hers. "What I didn't calculate into this was my own reaction to you."

For a split second her heart almost stopped beating.

"And that is?" Yohanna asked so softly that had he not been standing so close to her, Lukkas wouldn't have even heard the question.

"That you make me feel again. That very possibly you brought that dead part of me back to life. I'm not going to tell you that I'm ready to do cartwheels and break into song right this minute—I've still got issues to work out," he confided. "But you have made me realize that there just might be a light—albeit a very distant light—at the end of this tunnel I'm traveling through."

Her relief was practically immeasurable. "So you're not going to tell me that my services are no longer needed?"

Where had *that* come from?

"You're kidding, right?" he asked her, surprised she would even think something like that.

"No," she admitted. "I was being very serious."

He laughed. "After you made yourself indispensable to me, got the production running like a well-oiled machine—an *efficient*, well-oiled machine—do you actually think I'd stand dramatically in a doorway and point to the road, saying you needed to hit it and never show your face here again?"

It almost sounded melodramatically ludicrous when he said it that way. Still, she wasn't going to lie about her reaction. Maybe he could even say something to make her feel that she wasn't expendable at this time.

"Something like that," she conceded.

"You're just humoring me. You're way too smart to actually think something like that," he told her with finality.

"So what are you going to do about that story the network's running?" When he raised a brow, she understood that he had no idea which story she was referring to. *Nice going, Hanna.* "The one that has us wildly in love," she clarified.

"What I'm going to do is what I've been doing ever since I first started on this pilgrimage to solidly build up my reputation in this otherwise make-believe world of tinsel, smoke and mirrors. I'm going to ignore the story, ignore the paparazzi—a difficult task, but still doable—and go on doing what I'm good at doing. Producing movies people want to see.

"And in order to do that, I intend to keep amassing a production company comprised of people who are damn good at what they do. And that, in case you have any doubts, most assuredly includes you." And then he paused to look at Hanna. He had left out one important point. "Unless, of course, having those stories and the annoying paparazzi swarming around you like so many blood-sucking mosquitoes with cameras is intolerable to you."

His analogy made her smile. "I think that mosquitoes with cameras are rather intriguing. Far be it from me to run for cover. Actually," Yohanna told him proudly, "I've never run from anything in my life."

"With the possible exception of your mother?" It wasn't a contradiction but an amused question on Lukkas's part.

Yohanna inclined her head, conceding the minor point. "I stand corrected. I have run from my mother. But in my defense, I've only run from her because no matter what I say, my mother only hears what she wants to hear—even if what I say isn't anything remotely close to what she wants to hear."

"Well…" he said, thinking that perhaps he had a very

simple solution to her problem. "Would you like me to talk to your mother in this case, straighten things out for you?"

Yohanna wasn't really clear on just exactly what he was offering to "straighten out." Would he tell her mother that they're just sleeping together, thereby minimizing the importance of what they had? Or was he going to tell her mother that they were just friends?

Not that it really mattered. Because either way, her mother would somehow convert the words into what she wanted to hear.

"I think," she began slowly, examining her words very carefully before she uttered them, "for the sake of my continuing to work for you, you should just abandon the idea of talking to my mother, of even saying a single word to her."

"Come again?"

"Talking to my mother might make you want to permanently terminate our association, if only to make sure that there was no reason for you to ever encounter my mother on a one-to-one basis again," she warned him. For once, she didn't feel as if she was exaggerating.

"Get that notion out of your head," he told her. "That's not about to happen, not from my end. There's nothing your mother could possibly do to make me entertain the idea of sending you away so I wouldn't have to deal with her."

In her heart Yohanna felt she knew better. "My mother would have made Gandhi look around for the nearest gun shop."

He laughed. "She can't be *that* bad."

"Trust me, she can. She's not a bad person," Yohanna quickly interjected so that he wouldn't get the wrong idea. Her mother was a peaceful soul—she was just a harpy. "But she can totally make you crazy inside of five minutes. Sometimes less."

Lukkas began to speak, but she held her hand up to silence him. Cornering his attention, she pressed the play button on her answering machine.

"Listen to a couple of her messages and then tell me that she can't be that bad," she told him.

Lukkas dutifully sat on the sofa and listened to the two messages she had already screened.

When she pressed the stop button, Yohanna looked at him, waiting for Lukkas to react. He remained silent for a very long moment. And then he smiled. "I guess you win this round. Apparently your mother *can* be that bad."

"Told you." It gave her no pleasure to be right this time.

"But she's just motivated by her concern for you," he added.

The addendum to his initial appraisal surprised her.

"I do believe you missed your true calling."

He looked at her, puzzled. "What do you mean?"

"You should have joined the diplomatic corps," she told him. "You obviously know how to twist a phrase to make it sound not just good, but like a compliment." Yohanna took a deep breath. She wasn't finished just yet. This was serious. "I could try to get the story squelched."

"You do that," he told her, "and the media'll really feel as if they're on to something. In my experience, you just hang tight and, eventually, the story blows over and something new becomes the focus of every one of those vultures' attention. Big story or little, the one constant is that they all run their course. I wouldn't worry about squelching the story if I were you. The story will die a natural death," he promised.

Still a bit nervous, she ran the tip of her tongue along her lips, trying to moisten them. "So we're okay?" she asked.

The look in her eyes tugged at something he had been so certain he no longer possessed. His heart.

The smile he gave her said it all.

"We're more than okay," Lukkas assured her. "Unless—"

"Unless?" she asked uncertainly.

Here it came. He was going to tell her that if she thought they had a future, then he'd have to bow out because his heart belonged to the woman he'd been forced to bury.

"Unless this is going to scare you away. Every one of those photographers can be pretty intense and intimidating."

"This *definitely* proves you've never met my mother," she told him with a laugh. "You want to talk about being intense and intimidating, my mother is the national poster child."

"I like her already," he said with a laugh.

Getting into the spirit of the situation, Yohanna grinned. "I will remind you of that statement when the times comes."

"You do that, Hanna. But right now, we've got work to do." He rose from the sofa. "Your chariot awaits, milady."

She got up beside him, as well. The feeling of relief she was experiencing was immeasurable. Smiling into his eyes, she laughed and said, "I could *really* get used to this."

Chapter Sixteen

A few days later Lukkas had to leave town on business for a couple of days. He went alone, asking her to "hold down the fort."

She never thought she could miss someone so much.

It felt as if a piece of her—a vital piece—was missing. The only way she knew how to cope with the stark emptiness she felt was to work. Mercifully, there was still a lot to do so she threw herself into it wholeheartedly.

Anything to blot out the ache.

She was so busy prioritizing Lukkas's schedule for his next movie after the present one wrapped, she didn't notice it at first.

But she sensed it.

Sensed someone watching her.

It was actually more of an edgy feeling than anything else. For the most part she dismissed it, telling herself she was beginning to imagine things, the way anyone running on little sleep and dark coffee might after going at her present pace for more than a day.

But there were sounds she *thought* she kept hearing; sounds suspiciously resembling the clicking noise a camera made when a photograph was snapped. But each time she would look up, her gaze sweeping the general area, she wouldn't actually *see* anything that was amiss.

She considered telling Lukkas when he called to see how things were going, but she didn't want him to think she was paranoid. And she definitely didn't want him to worry, so she went on wrestling with this—at present—unsubstantiated feeling that she was being watched, doing her best to talk herself out of it.

Until she finally caught him.

She was being tailed by a freelance photographer.

"Wait!" she cried as he started to run down her block toward a parked car. "I won't call the police," she promised, heading after him. "I just want to know why you've been taking pictures. You've got me confused with someone else. I'm not anybody," she told the scruffy-looking man with the very expensive camera.

Apparently schooled by experience, despite the fact that, for the moment, he stopped running, the man kept a safe distance between them.

"You are to Lukkas Spader. You're the first woman he's been seen with since his wife died—and he's produced movies with some really hot little babes in them. If he thinks you're special, then the public wants to see you. It's that simple."

Raising his camera, he snapped three more shots in incredibly fast succession—and then he took off again, leaving her to ponder his words.

She tried to see his license number, but the plate was obscured.

Was the paparazzo right? she wondered as she returned to her house. *Was* she special to Lukkas? Or was he just with her to help him transition back to the regular world, the world he'd known before he had lost his wife?

She didn't know.

She only knew that she missed Lukkas something awful. Especially at night. Somehow the dark just made the longing worse. Even her own home felt strange to her.

Without Lukkas to fill the spaces of her evening— which she had gotten extremely used to in a short amount of time—her house felt extra empty, extra lonely.

"I need a dog," she said out loud, her voice echoing back at her as she locked the front door, then walked through the house, turning on lights in each room she came to.

She'd put in another extralong day at the studio today, getting everything prepared for Lukkas so when he got back, he would be ready to roll. She absolutely loved the fact that she had gotten really good at anticipating his needs and requirements when it came to working with him.

The other part of it, anticipating his needs as a man… She was more than happy about keeping her finger on *that* particular pulse, as well.

It was past ten o'clock. She was exhausted but too wired to sleep. A vague hunger nudged at her, reminding her that she hadn't eaten very much.

She went into the kitchen and opened her refrigerator. It all but mocked her as she stared unseeingly into its interior.

Nothing seemed to move her or to tempt her taste

buds. There were several things she could whip up—chicken Parmesan took her less than twenty minutes and she had both the chicken and the extras that went with it. But the idea of cooking for herself held absolutely no appeal for her.

Because she knew she had to eat *something*, Yohanna took out a cherry-flavored yogurt, uncovered the top and then, picking up a spoon, started to eat it as she leaned over the sink.

It took a few moments for the scenario to sink in. And horrify her.

"My God, I've become one of those women who eats out of a container while standing over a sink," she muttered, appalled.

She hadn't been like that before Lukkas had entered her life. She'd been independent and had made her peace with living a solitary life while making the most of it. Now all the freedom in the world couldn't begin to make up for the loneliness that was gnawing away at her.

She missed Lukkas. Missed him so much that it physically hurt.

How had she gotten here? She had absolutely no right to think that Lukkas was going to be a permanent person in her life. She had to live in the moment, not the future. Lukkas was kind, handsome, fun and very approachable. But the man's heart, she sternly reminded herself, still belonged to his late wife, and if she thought there was a way she was going to burrow into that heart and stake a claim to it, then she was going to be horribly disappointed.

She knew that.

Telling herself anything else was just delusional and putting off the inevitable.

Her spoon hit bottom. Somehow she'd managed to consume the yogurt without even realizing it. Or tasting it.

Listlessly, she threw out the container.

Her landline rang just then. She instantly brightened, pushing aside the darkness that threatened to swallow her up.

Yohanna pulled the receiver out of the cradle and put it to her ear. At this point she'd even welcome a call from her mother. Anything to keep her mind from sliding back down into the darkness.

She yanked the receiver up so quickly, she didn't even look at the name on the small screen identifying the caller.

"Hello?"

"How's everything going?"

Her face broke out in a wreath of smiles. Lukkas's voice had a way of reassuring her.

She dutifully gave him a quick summary. "The schedule's coming together. Everything's going to be ready for your review when you get back." Which she hoped was going to be sometime tomorrow—the sooner the better.

"Are you sure about that?"

She thought that was rather an odd statement to make—he didn't usually question what she said—but she gave him the reassurance he was looking for. "I wouldn't tell you if I wasn't," she pointed out.

"What if I get back early?"

Oh, please get back early, she silently prayed. "It's actually ready right now, so you can come back anytime you want," she told him.

"Sounds good," he told her.

The doorbell rang just then.

"What's that noise?" Lukkas asked.

"That's just someone at the door." She was perfectly willing to ignore whoever was there since the most important person in her world was on the phone with her.

"Aren't you going to answer it?" Lukkas asked her.

"I'm busy," she told him, her voice soft and low. "Talking to you." The doorbell rang again, splicing into her sentence.

"Whoever it is sounds as if they're going to be persistent," Lukkas observed, and then advised, "Maybe you should call your security service, just in case there's a problem."

"I don't have a security service," she reminded him.

She closed her eyes as the doorbell rang yet again. There was only one person who didn't give up after a couple of tries.

"It's probably my mother," she said with a sigh. "Hold on."

With that, still holding the receiver in her hand, she went to the front door and opened it.

"I'm not your mother," Lukkas said, closing the cell phone he had in his hand.

She let her portable receiver slip through her fingers. It fell on the floor. She hardly noticed. Overjoyed that he'd come back early, she threw her arms around Lukkas.

"What are you doing here?" she cried.

"Currently?" he asked with a straight face. "Having the air squeezed out of my lungs," he answered with a laugh.

Suddenly realizing that her arms had all but tightened into a viselike grip, she loosened her hold on him.

"Don't take this the wrong way, because I'm thrilled to have you back, but what happened? You weren't supposed to be back for at least one more day, if not more," she told him.

Lukkas shrugged. "I cut myself a little slack. You're so efficient that I figured I could do that once in a while. Besides, I missed you," he told her.

As he began to lower his mouth to hers, he stopped abruptly when he saw them. "Hey, what's this? Tears?" he asked incredulously, lightly touching the damp path the tear had created. "I didn't say that to make you cry."

"Too late," she told him. Up on her toes, she pulled him closer and covered his lips with her own.

Lukkas meant to only kiss her lightly before he told her why he'd *really* cut things short and flown back earlier than planned. But when she kissed him like that, it felt as if everything inside him just began to radiate, to glow.

Accustomed to flying here, there and everywhere at the drop of a hat, fitting in all those different places, belonging nowhere, he hadn't experienced a feeling of homecoming for years now.

"Home" was everywhere and nowhere—until now.

Now *she* was home, he realized. Hanna was his go-to place. His haven.

But all of this hit him afterward. After he had kissed her until his lips were all but numb. After he'd savored every inch of her and made love with her not once, but twice.

Gloriously.

Recklessly.

Lying in her bed, holding her to him, Lukkas searched for the right words to convey all this to her. This and more.

But just when he needed it most, eloquence escaped him.

"I know it's only been a few days, but I've missed

you," he told her, murmuring the words softly into her hair. At first he thought she hadn't heard him, but then he felt her curl farther into him, her arm across his chest tightening.

He felt his whole body quicken in response.

"I missed you, too," she told him, her words floating on her warm breath and skimming across his skin.

He wanted her all over again.

Lukkas struggled to hold himself in check. He needed to get something out in the open first.

"Then, why didn't you call?" he asked. "You didn't even call when you had updates for me."

He'd had to be the one to call, making him feel that he needed her more than she needed him.

"I texted them," she pointed out. "And I didn't want to bother you—or to sound needy," she finally admitted.

"You wouldn't have bothered me," he told her, wondering where she had gotten that impression. "And I really doubt you could sound needy even if you tried."

She was strong and forceful—and soft in all the right places, he couldn't help thinking.

"Oh, you'd be surprised," Yohanna told him.

She'd worried about that more than once—that he would see how much she cared about him, how much she wanted to be part of his life. Because of his past and what the loss of his wife had done to him, she was afraid that he would see her behavior as encroaching on him and he would wind up severing all ties with her.

She didn't know if she could bear that, even if, ultimately, Lukkas had done it for his own good. She wasn't that selfless, even if she wanted to be.

"Does that mean you'd miss me if I were gone?"

Lukkas's question brought her up out of her thoughts with a thud.

It sounded like an innocent question, but she had learned that nothing was really all that innocent.

Feeling as if she was walking on a thin, scarred wooden plank stretched over a bed of quicksand where one misstep would make her disappear, she asked him quietly, "Are you going somewhere?"

Lukkas continued to play devil's advocate. "If I was, how would you feel about it?" he asked. "Would you ask me not to go?"

Her first reaction was that she wouldn't ask him not to go, she'd beg him not to. But she couldn't say that; she didn't have the right.

And, after a moment, that was what she told him, as well.

"If you wanted to go, I wouldn't have the right to ask you not to."

"But if you did have the right?" he asked, continuing to play out the line, waiting for her to tell him what he wanted to hear.

She was doing her best to hold her emotions in check. To be his assistant, not the woman who was in love with him.

"I'd want you to be happy. If going made you happy, then I wouldn't stop you."

Lukkas continued watching her face, searching it for a sign. "So what you're telling me is that you're indifferent," he concluded.

She knew what she was supposed to say, what she *should* say as his assistant, which was the only official position she held. But despite that, something within her just couldn't allow her to continue with the charade she was playing.

"I am *so* not indifferent," she said, contradicting his conclusion.

The look in his eyes seemed to urge her on, so even though she was certain she was probably destroying the tiny piece of paradise she was temporarily claiming as her own, she told Lukkas exactly what was in her heart.

"If I could, I'd ask you—beg you, really—to stay because when you're gone, nothing makes sense to me. I know I've spent the first thirty years of my life without you and I functioned just fine like that. I got through one end of the day to the other, accomplishing whatever it was I was supposed to accomplish. But now everything's changed. All I can think of is how many minutes before I can see you again, before you kiss me again. Before we make the world stand still again.

"I know this isn't what you probably want to hear and I promise I won't try to hold you back when you want to go—but please don't want to go," she pleaded quietly. "Not yet."

He laughed then, and she didn't know if she was on solid ground or if what she'd just said had struck him as ridiculously funny.

All she could do was ask.

"Why are you laughing?" she asked when he continued chuckling to himself.

It took him a second to catch his breath. "Call your mother," he told her.

She stared at him, certain she must have heard wrong. "What?"

"Call your mother," Lukkas repeated, this time far more audibly.

She could see him asking her to do a great many things for him. But never once would she have thought he would tell her to call her mother, especially after what she had told him about her.

"Why?" she asked in hushed disbelief. "Why would you want me to call my mother, of all people?" That, in her book, was akin to having a death wish.

"So you can tell her she can stop trying to set you up with her friends' sons and nephews. Tell her your fiancé doesn't like it."

Her mouth dropped open and she stared at Lukkas in total disbelief. Now she knew she *had* to be dreaming—or at least hallucinating. But she hadn't ingested anything that even remotely had those side effects.

"My what?"

"Fiancé." And then it hit him. He'd left parts out.

"I'm getting ahead of myself, aren't I?" It was a rhetorical question. "I'm assuming you're going to say yes, and I didn't mean to do that. Of course, if you say no, it'll shatter me after I spent all this time looking for— Oh, damn," he muttered as another thought hit him.

"Oh, damn what?"

Instead of answering, Lukkas sat up and looked around the room. Spotting what he was looking for, his jacket, which was on the floor right next to the bed, he leaned over to pluck it up and pull it onto the bed.

Feeling the pocket, he detected the slight bulge and smiled his relief.

"Still here."

Before she could ask Lukkas what he was talking about, he took a small black velvet box out of the pocket, flipped it open with his thumb and held it out to her.

"Hanna, you brought the sunshine back into my life and I don't want to go back to living in the dark."

He took a breath and said the most important words of his life—for a second time. "Will you marry me?"

For the second time, her mouth dropped open. She looked at Lukkas, then at the ring and back again.

"You're serious?"

Lukkas laughed shortly. "I'm naked, holding a ring, with my entire life riding on your answer. This is about as vulnerable as I can get. So yes, I'm serious." He took her free hand into his as he made his case. "I didn't think I could love anyone ever again, or *risk* loving anyone again.

"But you, just by being you, showed me that I could, that my life had meaning again and that it was time to stop sleepwalking through each day. I can't take the ring back, so it's yours no matter what your answer is, but I'm hoping that you'll take me along with it, although—"

Stifling a laugh, Yohanna put her finger against his lips, momentarily silencing him.

"I never thought I would ever hear myself saying this to you, but shut up, Lukkas. You're talking too much and it's not necessary. That's a lot of wasted rhetoric. I've been yours from the very first day."

He still wasn't going to take anything for granted. "Then it's yes? I want to be clear on this," he specified.

"It's *always* been yes," she said.

The phone rang just as he reached for her again. Glancing at the phone's caller ID, she groaned, then picked up the receiver. "Can't talk right now. I'm getting married, Mom. Call you back later." With that, she hung up and looked at her husband-to-be.

"Where were we?"

"Here, I think," he said, pulling her into his arms.

The phone rang again just as he was going to begin kissing her. He intended to create a path that ran the length and breadth of her body.

They ignored the ringing phone.

She would get back to her mother eventually, Yohanna thought. But right at this moment there was something far more important on her mind. She wanted to make love with her fiancé for the very first time.

And she did.

Epilogue

"You really have outdone yourself, you know," Maizie whispered to Theresa as wedding guests filed into the rows of seats that had been set up in the garden behind the hotel.

Theresa was catering yet another affair for Lukkas Spader. This time, though, it was his wedding, and she had pulled out all the stops.

"Using the red carpet to designate the aisle that the bride comes down was truly a stroke of genius," Maizie told her with admiration.

"It just seemed fitting," Theresa replied in the same hushed tone.

Satisfied that everything was running smoothly and that her employees had everything under control, Theresa had allowed herself a small island of time to simply enjoy being a spectator at another one of their success stories.

So far, she, Maizie and Cecilia, in their capacity as Matchmaking Mamas, were batting a thousand.

"From what Cecilia told me, it seems as if Lukkas first fell in love with Yohanna when they attended the premiere of his movie. I saw that photograph one of those awful pushy paparazzi people had taken of the two of them in a weekly magazine. Lukkas had a smitten face if ever I saw one."

Standing beside the two women in the second-to-last row of folding chairs at the outdoor wedding, Cecilia could only agree with her best friends. But she also had a footnote to offer.

"You want to see smitten, take a look at the bride's mother. That woman looks as if she's just died and gone to heaven." Cecilia nodded at a striking woman in blue standing at the rear of the gathering, just in front of the hotel door.

Maizie glanced in Elizabeth Andrzejewski's direction. The woman was positively beaming. "She certainly does look very proud," she agreed.

"Of herself," Cecilia exhorted. "She's telling anyone she can corner that *she* was the one who was responsible for bringing all this around."

"You're kidding," Theresa said, surprised.

"No, I'm not. According to her, she had kept after Yohanna, urging her to go out with her 'handsome boss' until the girl finally did." Cecilia laughed as she shook her head.

"Ladies, be kind," Maizie told her friends, then winked to cast a smidgeon of doubt on her sincerity in this matter. "We all remember what that was like, desperately wanting to see each of our daughters get married to a good man."

"Yes, but we didn't nag them," Cecilia pointed out.

"Actually, we did—if you ask the girls," Theresa reminded her.

Cecilia shrugged off Theresa's words. "Anyway, that's all in the past," she said with a careless wave of her hand.

Maizie looked at the groom, who was standing beside his best man, anxiously glancing toward the rear of the hotel where the bride was getting ready.

"Nice to see another happy couple preparing to spend the rest of their lives together," Maizie commented with an approving smile.

Just then, the orchestra ceased tuning up. Half a second of silence then gave way to the beginning strains of the "Wedding March."

All conversation ceased as the wedding guests turned almost in unison to look to the rear, waiting for Yohanna to emerge from the hotel.

The hush intensified as the guests watched Yohanna walk down the aisle, which was, in this case, the red carpet Theresa had pulled strings to acquire for the occasion.

Initially, Yohanna had been going to walk to the altar alone since her father had died a long time ago and she'd felt the position belonged to him exclusively. But, at the last minute, she changed her mind and asked her rather stunned mother to accompany her on the symbolic walk.

She told her mother it was only right, since the woman had so anxiously wanted to give her away for the past ten years.

"I just wanted you to have someone to love," Elizabeth told her. "Like I had."

"I know, Mom. I know," Yohanna told her, linking her arm with her mother's when the orchestra began to play.

Elizabeth was positively beaming as she walked beside her daughter. She loved to focus on the fact that she was giving her daughter away to Lukkas Spader, a man who was not only good-looking, famous and well-off, but just possibly was the nicest son-in-law on the face of the earth. This was the way she described Lukkas to each one of her friends, all of whom had been invited to the wedding and reception.

Walking down the red carpet, Elizabeth was in her glory. It was an event that she would remember for the rest of her life no matter how long she lived. She said as much, in a hushed whisper, to her daughter. Then followed that up with a question.

"Do you love him, baby?" Elizabeth asked when they were almost at the flower-laden altar that had been built less than a day earlier by some of the scenery crew who had worked on Lukkas's last movie. A fact that Elizabeth would proudly repeat a dozen times over to her friends at the reception, as well.

Yohanna's eyes were on Lukkas, her heart swelling with each step she took that brought her closer to him. "Very, very much," she answered.

"Then, my job here is done," her mother announced, all but bursting with pride.

"Yes, it is, Mom," Yohanna told her with no small relief.

They came to a stop right beside Lukkas. "You're so beautiful it hurts," he whispered to his wife-to-be, a deep smile curving his lips.

Yohanna blushed.

"Who gives this woman away?" the minister asked.

"I do!" Elizabeth cried loudly enough to be heard not

just in the last row but quite possibly inside the hotel lobby, as well.

Lukkas and Yohanna, who only had eyes for one another, were quite possibly the only two people who hadn't heard Elizabeth's loud declaration. The couple was too busy listening intently to the words the minister was saying.

The words that would forever bind them to one another.

It couldn't happen soon enough for either of them.

* * * * *

Don't miss Marie Ferrarella's next romance,
HOW TO SEDUCE A CAVANAUGH,
available July 2015!

In Love with the Boss

From pennies to pearls the Rush sisters are swept off their feet by their handsome bosses!

Sisters Patience and Piper Rush might not have had much growing up but they *always* had each other, through good times and bad. Now, oceans apart, can they find comfort, safety and acceptance in the arms of their drop-dead gorgeous bosses?

In June 2015...
Patience finds herself falling for the man of her dreams in
A Millionaire for Cinderella

And

In September 2015...
Piper's heart is captured by her brooding Parisian boss in **Beauty & Her Billionaire Boss**

Only in Mills & Boon® Cherish™!

A MILLIONAIRE
FOR CINDERELLA

BY
BARBARA WALLACE

Published in Great Britain 2015
by Mills & Boon, an imprint of Harlequin (UK) Limited,
Eton House, 18-24 Paradise Road, Richmond, Surrey, TW9 1SR

© 2015 Barbara Wallace

ISBN: 978-0-263-25142-5

23-0615

Harlequin (UK) Limited's policy is to use papers that are natural, renewable and recyclable products and made from wood grown in sustainable forests. The logging and manufacturing processes conform to the legal environmental regulations of the country of origin.

Printed and bound in Spain
by CPI, Barcelona

Barbara Wallace can't remember when she wasn't dreaming up love stories in her head, so writing romances for Mills & Boon is a dream come true. Happily married to her own Prince Charming, she lives in New England with a house full of empty-nest animals. Occasionally her son comes home as well. To stay up-to-date on Barbara's news and releases, sign up for her newsletter at www.barbarawallace.com.

To Peter, who has the patience of a saint come deadline time, and to the revitalizing powers of coffee and snack-sized candy bars. I never would have written this book if not for you all.

CHAPTER ONE

How LONG DID it take to examine one little old lady? Patience paced the length of the hospital emergency room for what felt like the hundredth time. What was taking so long?

"Excuse me." She knocked on the glass window separating the admissions desk from the rest of the emergency waiting area. "My...grandmother...has been back there for a long time." She figured the lie would get her more sympathy than saying "my employer." Luckily there'd been a shift change; the previous nurse on duty would have called her on it. "Is there any way I can find out what's happening?"

The nurse gave her a sympathetic smile. "I'm sorry, we're really busy today, and things are backed up. I'm sure a doctor will be out to talk with you soon."

Easy for her to say. She hadn't found her employer crumpled at the foot of a stairwell.

Ana's cry replayed in her head. Frail, weak. If only she hadn't been in the other room...if only she hadn't told Nigel he needed to wait for his dinner, then Ana wouldn't be here. She'd be having her tea in the main salon like she did every afternoon.

Patience couldn't help her sad, soft chuckle. A year

ago she didn't know what a salon was. Goes to show how much working for Ana had changed her life. If only Ana knew how she'd rescued Patience, taking her from the dark and dirty and bringing her into a place that was bright and clean.

Of course, Ana couldn't know. As far as Patience was concerned, her life started the day she began cleaning house for Anastasia Duchenko. Everything she did beforehand had been washed away.

The hospital doors opened with a soft whoosh, announcing the arrival of another visitor. Immediately, the atmosphere in the room changed, and not because of the June heat disrupting the air-conditioning. The conversations stilled as all attention went to the new arrival. Even the admissions nurse straightened. For a second, Patience wondered if a local celebrity had walked in. The air had that kind of expectancy.

His tailored shirt and silk tie screamed superiority as did his perfect posture. A crown of brown curls kept his features from being too harsh, but only just. No doubt about it, this was a man who expected to be in charge. Bet he wouldn't be kept waiting an hour.

The man strode straight to the admissions window. Patience was about to resume her pacing when she heard him say the name Duchenko.

Couldn't be a coincidence. This could be the break she needed to find out about Ana. She combed her dark hair away from her face, smoothed the front of her tee shirt and stepped forward. "Excuse me, did I hear you ask about Ana Duchenko?"

He turned in her direction. "Who's asking?"

For a moment, Patience lost the ability to speak. He was looking down at her with eyes the same shade as the blue in a flame, the hue so vivid it couldn't possibly be real. Lit with intensity, they were the kind of eyes that you swore were looking deep inside your soul. "Patience," she replied, recovering. "I'm Patience Rush."

She didn't think it possible for his stare to intensify but it did. "Aunt Anastasia's housekeeper?"

His aunt. Suddenly Patience realized who she was talking to. This was Stuart Duchenko, Ana's great-nephew, the one who called twice a week. Actually, as far as she knew, the only Duchenko relative Ana talked to. Patience didn't know why, other than there'd been some kind of rift and Ana refused to deal with what she called "the rest of the sorry lot." Only Stuart, who managed her financial affairs, remained in her good graces.

"I thought you were in Los Angeles," she said after he introduced himself. Ana said he'd been stuck there for almost a year while some billionaire's family argued over a will.

"My case finished yesterday. What happened?"

"Nigel happened." Nigel being Ana's overly indulged cat.

She could tell from Stuart's expression, he didn't find the answer amusing. Not that she could blame him under the circumstances. She wondered, though, if he would find the story amusing under *any* circumstances. His mouth didn't look like it smiled much.

"He was in the foyer meowing," she continued. "Letting everyone know that his dinner was late. Near as I can guess, when Ana came down the stairs, he started weaving around her ankles, and she lost her balance."

He raised a brow. "Near as you can guess?"

Okay, the man was definitely an attorney; Patience felt she was on trial with all the questions. Of course, that could also be her guilty conscience bothering her. "I was in the dining room polishing the silver. I heard Ana cry out, but by the time I got there, she was already on the floor." She shuddered, remembering. The image of Ana crumpled at the foot of the stairs, moaning, wouldn't leave her soon.

Ana's nephew didn't respond other than to stare long and hard in her direction before turning back to the admissions nurse. "I'd like to see my aunt, please," he said. It might have been said softly, like a request, but there was no mistaking the command in his voice.

The nurse nodded. "I'll see what I can do."

Finally, they were getting somewhere. "I've been trying to get an update on Ana's condition since we arrived, but no one would tell me anything."

"Nor would they," he replied. "Privacy laws. You're not family."

Well, wasn't somebody feeling territorial. Never mind that she was the one who'd brought Ana in and filled out the admissions paperwork. Anyone with two heads could see she cared about the woman. What difference did it make whether she was family or not?

She had to admit, Ana's nephew wasn't at all what she expected. Ana was always talking about how sweet "her Stuart" was. Such a pussycat, she'd coo after hanging up the phone. The man standing next to her wasn't a pussy anything. He was far too predatory. She could practically smell the killer instinct.

Apparently, his singlar request was all they needed, because less than a minute passed before the door to the treatment area opened, and a resident in pale green scrubs stepped out.

"Mr. Duchenko?" He headed toward Stuart, but not,

however, before giving Patience a quick once-over. Patience recognized the look. She folded her arms across her chest and pretended she didn't notice. The trick, of course, was to avoid eye contact. Easy to do when the man wasn't looking at your eyes to begin with.

"I'm sorry to keep you waiting," the doctor continued. "We were waiting for the results of your great-aunt's CAT scan."

"How is she?"

"She's got a bimalleolar fracture of her left ankle."

"Bi what?" Patience asked, her stomach tightening a bit. Hopefully the medical jargon sounded more serious than it actually was.

The doctor smiled. "Bimalleolar. Both the bone and her ligaments were injured."

"Meaning what?" Stuart asked the same question she was thinking.

"Meaning she's going to need surgery to stabilize the ankle."

Surgery? Patience felt horrible. She should have been paying closer attention. "Is it risky?"

"At her age, anything involving anesthesia has a risk."

"She's in terrific health," Patience told him, more to reassure herself than anything. "Most people think she's a decade younger."

"That's good. The more active she is, the easier her recovery will be. You know, overall, she's a lucky woman to have only broken her ankle. Falls at her age are extremely dangerous."

"I know," Stuart replied. For some reason he felt the need to punctuate the answer with a look in her direction. "May we see her?"

"She's in exam room six," the doctor replied. "We'll be taking her upstairs shortly, but you're welcome to sit with her in the meantime."

Exam room six was really a curtained area on the far left-hand side of two rows of curtains. Stuart pulled back the curtain to find Ana tucked under a sheet while a nurse checking the flow of her IV. The soft beep-beep-beep of the machines filled the air. Seeing Ana lying so still with the wires protruding from the sleeve of her gown made Patience sick to her stomach. Normally, the woman was so lively it was easy to forget that she was eighty years old.

"We just administered a painkiller, so she might be a little out of things," the nurse told them. "Don't be alarmed if she sounds confused."

Stuart stepped in first. Patience followed and found him standing by the head of Ana's bed, his long tapered fingers brushing the hair from the elderly woman's face. "Tetya? It's me, Stuart."

The gentle prodding in his voice reminded her of how she would wake her baby sister, Piper, before school. It surprised her. He honestly didn't seem like the gentle type.

Ana's eyelids fluttered open. She blinked, then broke into a drunken smile. "What are you doing here?"

"That fall-alert necklace you refuse to wear notifies me when 911 gets called. I was on my way back from the airport when I got a message."

The smile grew a little wider. "Back? Does that mean you're home for good?"

"It does."

"I missed you, *lapushka*."

"I missed you, too. How are you feeling?"

"Good, now you're here." Her gnarled hand patted his. "Is Nigel okay?"

"Nigel is fine."

"He was a naughty boy. Make sure you tell him I'm disappointed in him."

"I'll let him know." There was indulgence in his voice.

"Don't make him feel too guilty. He didn't mean it." The older woman's eyelids began to droop, sleep taking over once again. "He's stubborn, like you."

"You go ahead and get some sleep, Tetya. I'm back home now. I'll take care of everything."

"Such a good boy. Not at all like your grandfather, thank goodness." She closed her eyes only to open them wide again. "Patience?"

Until then, Patience had lingered at the foot of the bed, not wanting to crowd Ana any more than necessary. Upon hearing her name, she drew closer. "Yes, Ana?"

"There you are," Ana replied. "Thank you."

"You don't have to thank me," she said.

"Yes, I do," the older woman insisted. "You take such good care of me."

Out of the corner of her eyes, she saw Stuart shift his weight and felt the moment his gaze slid in her direction. She kept her attention on Ana and pretended she couldn't see him. "I was only doing what any person would do. Now, why don't you get some rest?"

"Take care of Nigel while I'm here?"

"I will."

"Stuart, too."

She assumed Ana meant for her nephew to help take care of Nigel. Either that or this was the confusion the nurse mentioned, because the man next to her definitely didn't need taking care of. Certainly not from someone like her.

From the tick in his cheek, Stuart thought the same thing.

They stayed until a different nurse came to check Ana's vitals. The small space was barely big enough for two visitors, let alone three, so Patience stepped outside. To her surprise, Stuart followed.

"You know what's crazy?" she remarked. "That foolish cat causes her to break her ankle and he's still going to get gourmet cat food for dinner." A dinner that, she realized as she did the math in her head, was now several hours late. Hopefully he didn't kick cat litter all over the kitchen floor in retaliation. Or worse, break her ankle.

Stuart was watching her again, his face as dour as before. Apparently drawing the exam room curtain closed off more than Ana's bed. "Are you positive Nigel tripped Ana?" he asked.

That was dumb question. "Of course, I'm sure," she replied. "I mean I don't know *for certain*. But, it was dinnertime, and the cat does have this annoying habit of bothering the nearest warm body when he wants to eat. Why are you even asking?" Ana had already told him that the cat had caused the accident.

"Just want to make sure I have all the facts."

Facts? For crying out loud, he sounded as if they were in one of those hour-long detective dramas. "Trust me, you've got all the facts. Nigel is one horrendous pest." Not to mention spoiled rotten. "Besides, who else would trip her? I was the only other person in the house and I…"

He didn't...

She glared up at him through her bangs. "You think I had something to do with Ana's accident?"

"Why would I think that? Ana blames Nigel."

"Because Nigel *tripped* her." His mistrust was serious. Unbelievable.

No, actually, it was very believable. A guy like him, used to the cream of everything. Of course, he'd suspect the help. "Are you suggesting your aunt is lying?"

"Hardly."

"Then why would I be? Lying, that is."

"Did I say you were lying? I told you, I was simply gathering facts. You're the one who read deeper meaning into my questions." Immediately, she opened her mouth to protest, only to have him hold up a finger. "Although," he continued, "you can't blame me if I am suspicious."

Oh, couldn't she? The guy was practically insinuating—not practically, he *was* insinuating that she had pushed a helpless little old lady down a flight of stairs. "And why is that?" She folded her arms across her chest. This she had to hear.

"For starters, Aunt Ana hired you directly while I was in Los Angeles."

So that was it. The man was territorial. "In other words, you're upset because Ana didn't talk to you first."

"Yes, I am." Having been expecting a denial, Patience was surprised to hear him agree. "Normally, I vet my family's employees and you, somehow, managed to bypass the process. As a result, I don't know a damn thing about you. For all I know, you could be hiding some deep, dark secret."

Patience's insides chilled. *If only he knew...*

Still, no matter what questionable decisions she'd made in her life, there were lines she'd never dream of crossing. Hurting a defenseless old lady being on top of the list. "You're right," she told him, "you don't know me."

Yanking back the curtain, she returned to Ana's side.

My, my, quite the bundle of moral outrage aren't we? Stuart ignored the twinge from his conscience as he watched Patience sashay behind the curtain. He refused to feel guilty for taking care of his family. After all, until eight months ago, he'd never heard of Patience Rush. Suddenly, the housekeeper was all his aunt could talk about. Patience this, Patience that. *No need to worry about me, Stuart. Patience will take good care of me. Patience is moving into the brownstone.* And the final straw... *Patience takes care of writing out the checks now.*

With Aunt Ana incapacitated, Patience would have an awful lot of power. Or rather, she would have, if he hadn't come home. He kicked himself for not being around the past eleven months. Now his aunt was attached to a stranger he knew nothing about. Ana might be sharp for her age, but when all was said and done, she was still an old woman living alone who had a soft spot for sob stories. Her big heart made her vulnerable to all sorts of exploitation.

It certainly wouldn't be the first time a pretty young thing had tried to grab a piece of the Duchenko fortune.

Unfortunately for Miss Rush, he was no longer a lonely twenty-year-old looking for affection. Nor was he still naive enough to believe people were as guileless as they appeared. Ana was the only family he had left. He'd be damned if he'd let her be burned the way he had been.

There was the rustle of a curtain, and Ana's gurney appeared on its way toward the elevator. As she passed by, the older woman gave him a sleepy wave. Stuart grabbed her hand and pressed the wizened knuckles to his lips. "See you soon, Tetya," he whispered.

"The surgical waiting area is on the third floor," the nurse told him. "If you want to stay there, we can let you know as soon as they're finished."

"Thank you."

Patience's soft voice answered before he had the chance. Immediately, his mouth drew into a tight line. "You're planning to wait, too?"

"Of course. I'm not going to be able to sleep until I know you're okay," she told Ana.

Ana smiled. "But Nigel…"

"Nigel will be fine," he said. While he wasn't crazy about Miss Rush hanging around, he wasn't about to start an argument over his aunt's hospital gurney. "Don't you worry."

"Besides, it'll do him good to wait," Patience added, "seeing as how this whole accident is his fault." She raised her eyes, daring him to say otherwise. "I promise, I'll go home and feed him as soon as you're out of surgery."

The sedatives were starting to kick in. Ana's smile was weak and sloppy. "Such a good girl," she murmured before closing her eyes.

Oh, yeah, a real sweetheart, he thought to himself. The way she so casually referred to the brownstone as home rankled him to no end. It was like ten years ago all over again, only this time, instead of a beguiling blonde worming her way into their lives, it was a brunette with hooded eyes and curves that wouldn't quit.

Interesting that she chose to downplay her sexuality. A tactical decision, perhaps? If so, it didn't work. A burlap sack couldn't mute those assets. Even he had to admit to a stir of appreciation the first time he saw her.

She was hiding more than her figure, too. Don't think he didn't notice how she looked away when he mentioned having secrets. There was a lot more to Patience Rush than met the eye. And he intended to find out what.

They spent the time Anna was in surgery on opposite sides of the waiting area, Stuart moving chairs together to create a makeshift work area while Patience made do with out-of-date women's magazines. Having read up on last fall's fashions and learned how to spot if her spouse was having an online affair, she was left with nothing to do but lean back in her chair and shoot daggers at Ana's nephew.

Who did he think he was, suggesting she had something to do with Ana's fall? Like she could ever. Anastasia Duchenko saved her life with this job. Every morning, she woke up grateful for the opportunity. To be able to walk down the street with her head held high. To not have to scrub herself raw to feel clean. Finally, she had a job she could be proud of. Be a *person* she could be proud of.

Even if the whole situation was built on a lie, she thought, guilt washing over her the way it always did.

She wasn't proud of her behavior—add it to a long list of regrets—but she made amends every single day by working hard and taking care of Ana. You wouldn't find a better housekeeper and companion on Beacon Hill. She would never—ever—jeopardize the gift Ana had given her.

Tell Stuart Duchenko that, though. If he learned she'd lied her way into the job, he'd kick her to the curb before she could say *but*... And who knows what he'd do if he learned what she used to do for a living before finding Ana? She shuddered to think.

The sound of rustling papers caught her attention. Looking over, she saw Stuart pinching the bridge of his nose. The man looked worn-out. Patience had to admit, for all his jerkiness, he appeared genuinely concerned for his great-aunt. The adoration Ana talked about seemed to run both ways.

"Mr. Duchenko?" A small African-American nurse in a bright pink smock rounded the corner, bringing them both to their feet. "Dr. Richardson just called. He'll be down shortly to talk with you, but he wanted you to know that your aunt came through the surgery without problem and is on her way to recovery."

"Oh, thank goodness." The words rushed from Patience's mouth, drawing Stuart's attention. Their eyes met, and she saw agreement in their blue depths. In this, they were on the same page.

"Can we see her?" he asked.

"She'll be in recovery for several hours, I'm afraid," the nurse replied with a shake of her head. "In fact, considering the hour, they might not move her until morning. You're better off getting some sleep and coming back tomorrow."

Patience watched as a protest worked its way across the man's features. She had a feeling if he insisted, he'd get his way. Better judgment must have stepped in—either that or fatigue—because he nodded. "How long before Dr. Richardson gets here?"

"He said he was on his way down, so I don't think it'll be more than five or ten minutes."

It turned out to be closer to twenty. When he did arrive, Dr. Richardson gave a succinct report, without a whole lot of new information. They'd inserted a plate and some screws to stabilize the break. Ana came through the surgery without issue. They'd monitor her throughout the night for complications. No, he wasn't sure how long she'd need to stay in the hospital.

Still, Patience left the waiting room feeling that Ana was in good hands. Another plus: Stuart was on the phone so she was spared any more accusations. From here on in, she'd do her best to avoid the man.

A pair of angry green eyes greeted her when she unlocked the door to Ana's brownstone. Patience wasn't intimidated. "Don't give me attitude, mister. This whole night is your fault."

With what Patience swore was a huff, Nigel jumped down from the entryway table and ran toward the kitchen. An urgent wail traveled back to her ears a second later. "Puleeze," she called, "like you were ever in danger of starving."

Arms hugging her body, Patience made her way along the corridor, thinking the slap of her sandals against her feet sounded abnormally loud. It felt weird being in the brownstone alone. While Ana went out a lot, the woman was seldom gone past eight o'clock and so her absence hung thick in the emptiness. A gleam caught Patience's eye as she passed the dining room. The silver set she'd been polishing when Ana fell still sat on the table, the cloth on the floor where she'd dropped it upon hearing Ana's cry. The moment replayed as she curled her fingers around the soft material, the image of her savior crumpled at the base of the stairs making her nauseous. Thank goodness, Ana was going to be all right. Tomorrow she would work on making the house perfect for her return. Starting with making sure the tea set gleamed.

Nigel had resumed his meowing. Patience tossed the cloth on the table. "Oh, for goodness' sake, I'm coming. Five minutes will not kill you."

She turned around only to walk into a tall, muscular wall. "What the—" Why hadn't she brought the teapot along with her as a weapon?

Stuart Duchenko arched a dark eyebrow. Even in the partially lit hallway, his eyes shone bright. "Did I startle you?"

He knew perfectly well he had. "How did you get in?"

"Same way you did. With my key." He held up a key ring. "Or did you think you were the only one Ana gave access to?"

"Don't be silly. I didn't hear the doorbell is all." They were way too close. Close enough she could smell the breath mint he'd obviously just finished. She wasn't used to sweet-smelling breath, not from men anyway. It caught her off guard, which had to be the reason she didn't step back at first contact. She stepped back now, and spied a pair of suitcases at the base of the stairs.

Seeing where her gaze had gone, he gave a shrug. "I sold my condominium before leaving for LA. Until I find a new place, this is more convenient than a hotel."

Convenient for what? Keeping an eye on her?

It was as if he read her thoughts. "Ana made the suggestion back when I first left. Of course, I'm sure she wasn't expecting to be in the hospital at the time. My being here won't be a problem for you, will it?" he asked. The gleam in his eye dared her to say that it was.

Patience would be damned if she'd give him the satisfaction. "Of course not. Why would your staying here be a problem for me?"

"Extra work for you. I know you're used to it being only you and Aunt Ana."

Another veiled comment. The man was full of them, wasn't he? "Extra work won't be a problem. Cleaning is cleaning. Besides, like you said, it's temporary, right?"

"We can only hope. I figure I'll stay until Ana gets back on her feet. Make sure there aren't any problems."

What kind of problems? Was he afraid Patience would take off with the silver? Why didn't he just come out and say what was really on his mind?

"You don't trust me, do you?"

"No, I don't."

Finally, the truth was out in the open. She appreciated the bluntness. Beat phony friendliness any day. Didn't mean she wasn't going to set him straight though.

"Your aunt trusts me. Are you saying Ana isn't a good judge of character?"

She stepped back into his personal space, making sure to maintain eye contact and letting him know his answer didn't intimidate her one bit. The posture brought her close enough that she could smell his skin. Like his breath, his body smelled clean and fresh, despite having been traveling all day. An antsy, fluttering sensation started in the pit of her stomach. Butterflies, but with a nervous edge. The notion that she was out of her league passed briefly through her mind.

Stuart's eyes stayed locked with hers. A Mexican standoff, with each of them waiting for the other to blink. "My aunt has a generous heart. I, on the other hand…"

"Let me guess. You don't."

Patience sensed rather than saw his smile. "I prefer to lead with my head. Less chance for mistakes."

"Except, in this case, you're already mistaken."

"We'll find out, won't we?" he said. "Since I'll be living here, we'll have plenty of time to get acquainted. Who knows what secrets we'll learn about each other?"

Patience managed to wait until he disappeared upstairs before hissing. What was it with him and secrets?

You didn't exactly help your cause, did you? Challenging him like that. A smart person would have let his comments pass, refused to give him the satisfaction of a reaction. But, *nooo*, she had to call him out. Might as well hold a sign over her head reading I've Got a Secret!

So much for leaving her past behind. She should have known that a future built on a lie—even an innocent one—wouldn't last. Ana was going to be so disappointed in her.

She bit her knuckle, forcing down her panic. No need to start packing just yet. This bluster was probably nothing more than a scare tactic to put her in her place. To make up for not having a say in hiring her, no doubt. A few days from now, after seeing how well Patience did her job, he'd back off and leave her alone.

It could happen, right?

CHAPTER TWO

THERE WAS A weight vibrating on his chest. He must have left the door open when he came upstairs. "It better be light out, Nigel," he muttered. Freeing a hand from under the covers, he felt around until his fingers found fur. Immediately, the purring increased as Nigel leaned into the touch. A sad voice in his head noted this was the most action he'd had in his bed in way too long. "Hey, be careful with the claws, buddy," he said when the cat began kneading the blanket. "I might need those parts someday." You never knew. A social life might spontaneously develop. Stranger things had happened.

At work, people considered him a workaholic, but the truth was, he'd never been what people would call popular. He discovered early that being a Duchenko heir meant being judged and misunderstood. As a kid, his awkwardness was labeled snobbery. As he got older, his social desirability was measured in terms of his bank account. He had to be constantly on guard, assessing the motives of every person that crossed his path. The one time he hadn't…well, that had taught him two more lessons: Don't let sex cloud your judgment and even family members will screw you over. Except for Ana, that is. Ana was the one family member who loved him for him.

Nigel's head butted his hand, a not so subtle way of saying *more petting, less thinking*. Giving a half sigh, Stuart opened his eyes, then blinked when he saw Nigel in perfect focus. He'd forgotten to take out his contact lenses again. No wonder his eyes felt as if they had sand in them. What time was it anyway? Yesterday had wiped him out so badly he barely remembered falling into bed.

Not too wiped out to go toe-to-toe with the house-keeper, though. It was a bit arrogant of him showing up without warning, but he'd wanted to catch her off guard. To see how she'd react to learning she wouldn't have the run of the brownstone.

Turned out she reacted to the blind side better than most of his legal opponents.

Most of his legal opponents didn't have eyes that lit up like chocolate diamonds, either. Dark and sinfully rich, their spark got his adrenaline going in a way prac-ticing law sure didn't. A guy could make a career out of looking for ways to make those eyes light up.

What was that about not letting sex cloud his judg-ment? Ignoring Nigel's protest, he rolled onto his side and reached for the phone on the nightstand. It was early, he thought, noting the time, but not so early to reach an associate. The ambitious ones practically slept at the firm. A few minutes of scrolling through his con-tacts found him the name he wanted.

Just as he expected, Bob Cunningham answered on the first ring. "Welcome back. I hear congratulations are in order." He was referring to the LA case.

"Too bad the former Mrs. Wentworth didn't come

to her senses last year." Instead, she'd put her late husband's family through hell and sentenced Stuart to months of aggravation, not to mention opening the door for Patience Rush. "There are a couple details to iron out that I'll talk to you about later. In the meantime, I need some background research done. A woman named Patience Rush."

"Is that her real name?"

Good question. Strangely enough, he hoped the quirky moniker was real. "That's for you to tell me." He gave him what details he knew.

"You're not giving the investigator much to work with," Bob replied.

"He's worked with less."

"True. What client number should I bill?"

"SD100." On the other end of the line, there was a soft intake of breath. Stuart seldom used his discretionary fund, but the firm's investigator was the best around. He'd reimburse the firm later.

"Um…"

"What?" Stuart asked.

The associate paused. "This might take a while. We've tapped him for a couple other projects."

And clients always came before personal. Stuart understood. "Just tell him to get to it as soon as he can."

In the meantime, he'd just have to keep a close eye on Patience Rush. Thinking about her eyes, he couldn't help but smile. There were worse jobs in the world.

A short while later, having showered and changed, he headed downstairs only to hear muffled voices coming from the kitchen. One muffled voice actually. He found Patience crouched over Nigel's food dish, brandishing a dustpan and broom. "You'd think a cat who acts like he's starving wouldn't drop pieces of food all over the place," she muttered. "One of these days, I'm going to toss the whole bowl out. Let's see what you do then."

A chuckle rose in his throat. Nigel had a way of making all of them talk as if he understood. He leaned a shoulder against the door frame. "Not a cat person, I take it."

She gasped before looking up at him with a glare. "Do you always sneak up on people?"

There they were again, those chocolate-diamond eyes. He crossed his legs to keep his jeans from growing tight. "I didn't know walking around the house was considered sneaking."

"Then you should walk louder," she replied. "Or wear shoes."

He looked down at his bare feet. "I'll keep that in mind. May I ask what the cat did to earn your wrath?"

"Nigel isn't a cat. He's a four-legged spoiled brat."

As had been all of Ana's cats. His aunt tended to overindulge the strays she adopted. Pushing herself to her feet, Patience swayed her way across the room to the trash can. Stuart found himself wondering if the seductive gait was natural or on purpose. "Sounds like the two of you have a great relationship," he remarked.

"Mine and Nigel's relationship is just fine. Why?" She took her foot off the receptacle latch, causing the lid to close with a loud slap. "Afraid I'll try to push him down the stairs, too?"

"Nah. A woman as smart as you would know hurting Nigel is the quickest way to getting on Ana's bad side."

She gave him a long look. "Was that supposed to be a compliment?"

In a way, yes. He did think she was smart. "If you want to take it as such."

"Gosh, thanks. I'll try not to let it go to my head."

Smart and quick-witted. She was dressed similarly to yesterday in jeans, a T-shirt and a cardigan sweater, her hair pulled back with one of those plastic hair bands. For the first time he looked closely at her features. Yesterday, he'd been too distracted by her eyes, but today he noticed more intricate details like the long slope of her nose and the way her teeth met her lower lip in a slight overbite. A two-inch scar cut across her right cheekbone. Time had caused it to fade. In fact, with makeup, it'd be barely noticeable, but since she was again bare faced, he could see the jagged edges of a cut that should have had stitches. The scar bothered him, like seeing a crack on the surface of a crystal vase. It didn't belong.

Patience cleared her throat. Realizing he'd been staring, he covered his action by adjusting his glasses. This might be one of those rare moments when he was grateful for them. He detested wearing the heavy black frames. The look might be considered stylish now, but it simply reminded him of his younger, awkward days. Then again, maybe a reminder was a good thing, given the awareness swirling around his insides this morning.

He reached for a change of topic. "Do I smell coffee?" There was a distinct aroma of French roast in the air, a unique scent in his tea-drinking aunt's home.

Patience nodded her head toward a stainless steel coffeemaker tucked in the faraway corner. "Cream and sugar are in the dining room. Do you prefer a full breakfast or continental."

"Neither." Was she offering to make him breakfast? Considering the circumstances, he wasn't sure if he should be flattered or suspicious. "Are you waiting on me?" he asked when she took a coffee mug from the cupboard. "Why?"

"Because it's my job," she replied. "I serve breakfast every morning. So long as someone's here, I'll keep on serving it." Filling the cup, she handed it to him.

Stuart stared into the black liquid. What gives? Last night, Patience had made it quite clear that she didn't appreciate his staying at the brownstone, yet here she was pouring him coffee and offering breakfast. Citing her job. Was she truly that dedicated or was this some kind of tactic to throw him off his game? If the latter, it was working.

"Something wrong?" she asked. "Would you feel better if I drank the cup first?"

"All right, you've made your point," he said, setting the coffee cup down. "You didn't appreciate my questioning Ana's accident."

"Not the accident—me. You all but accused me of pushing your aunt down the stairs."

Yes, he had. Now that he thought about it, the accusation wasn't his finest moment. Treating the woman like a hostile witness wouldn't accomplish anything. A situation like this called for a more delicate touch. "I'm sorry," he said. "I tend to be wary when it comes to strangers around my family."

"Well, I tend to have a problem with being accused of crimes I didn't commit," she replied, snapping his olive branch in two. "Now if you'll excuse me, I've got a job to do."

"Can you believe the guy? I think he actually considered that comment an apology."

"Some people aren't very good with apologies." Her sister Piper's face filled the screen of her smartphone. Thank goodness for Wi-Fi and internet chat apps. She so needed a friendly ear right now and Piper was the one person in this world she could trust. Patience called her as soon as she sat down at Ana's desk.

"Maybe he's one of those people," her sister continued.

"Probably because in his mind he's never wrong." She sighed. "I can't believe I'm going to be stuck working for the man while Ana's in the hospital. Talk about a nightmare."

"Oh, come on, it won't be that bad."

"Are you kidding? We're living under the same roof. How am I supposed to avoid him?"

"I doubt he's going to be hanging around the house."

Wanna bet? Patience caught the smirk in his eyes last night. He probably considered the arrangement the perfect opportunity to vet her. Who used words like *vet* anyway? Couldn't he say *check her out* like a normal person.

"I don't like him," she said. "He's…"

"He's what?"

Too imposing. With his unwavering blue eyes and long lean torso. "There's something about the way he looks at me," she said, keeping her thoughts to herself.

"Guys are always looking at you."

"Not like this." Those guys were skeevy. All hands and leers. "It's like he's trying to read my mind." She wasn't used to a man looking at her as anything more than a chick with a nice rack. It was unnerving to have a man look deeper. "Plus, he keeps talking about secrets. I'm worried one of these times I'll slip up and say something incriminating."

"So, don't talk to him. There's no rule that says a housekeeper has to be chatty."

"True." Except she seemed unable to help herself.

"If it helps," Piper added, "I watched a movie the other night where the woman drugged her husband's dinner so he'd leave her alone. You could always try that."

"Oh, sure." It was exactly the laugh she needed. "Because my life isn't enough like a made-for-television movie. Seriously, though, what am I going to do?"

"You could try telling the truth."

Patience shook her head. "I can't."

"Why not? I bet Ana won't care, especially once she hears the whole story. I mean, it's not like you had other choices. Surely, Ana would understand that you did what you had to do."

Maybe, but what about the reason Patience stayed for as long as she did? There were some secrets Piper didn't know and was better off never knowing. That particular shame was Patience's and Patience's alone.

Again, she shook her head. "I'll just have to stay on my toes is all. Hopefully, when Ana starts to feel better, he'll lose interest. A rich, handsome lawyer? I'm sure he's got better things to focus on than the hired help."

"You didn't mention he was handsome," Piper said, giving her a smirk.

"He's…good-looking," Patience replied rolling her eyes. *Handsome* wasn't the right word. "Not that it makes a difference. I'm more concerned about keeping my job."

"You're going to be fine, You're one of the most resilient people I know."

Patience wished she shared her sister's confidence. "Let's talk about something else," she said. She was tired of whining. "How's school?"

"Um…good. French pastries are turning out to be a challenge."

"Bet yours taste fantastic. Any way you can mail me your homework?" She was so proud of Piper. Winning a scholarship to study cooking in Paris. Piper's success made everything worthwhile. "And how's work?" Her sister was earning room and board as a live-in maid. "Your boss must be psyched to have a gourmet cook on staff."

"Frederic doesn't eat home much."

The grainy camera image failed to mask the shadow that crossed Piper's face, immediately sending Patience's maternal instincts into high alert. "What's wrong?" she asked.

"Nothing," Piper replied quickly. "I'm just bummed not to have someone to cook for is all. I miss you."

Homesickness. Of course. Patience should have realized. This was the longest the two of them had ever been apart. Hard as it was on her, it had to be doubly hard on Piper, alone in a foreign country. "I miss you too Pipe. But, hey, we've got Wi-Fi. You can call me anytime you want."

Piper smiled. "Back at you." Offscreen, a noise occurred, causing her sister to look over her shoulder. "Hey, I've got to go," she said. "The boss just walked in. Don't let Ana's nephew intimidate you, okay? You're just as good as he is."

"Thanks. I love you."

"Love you, too."

Patience's smile faded as soon as she clicked off. Piper had such faith in her. It wasn't that she was completely ashamed of everything she'd done in life, she thought, setting the phone aside. Raising Piper, for instance. She couldn't be prouder of the woman her baby sister had become. Giving Piper a chance for a real future had always been what mattered the most. Her baby sister would never have to degrade herself to pay the bills.

A knock sounded behind her, making her start. "You can't accuse me of sneaking up on you this time," Stuart said. "I knocked."

Yes, he had, and he now stood in the doorway with his arms folded like a long, lean statue. It wasn't surprising that he managed to look as regally imposing in jeans and bare feet as he did in a suit. Patience had a feeling he could wear a bunch of rags and still look wealthy. Even the glasses that, on someone else would look geeky, looked more geek-chic on him. Actually, much as she hated to admit it, the frames looked adorable on him.

Some of her bangs had slipped free of her hair band. She brushed them aside to disguise her reaction. "Do you need something?" she asked.

"It dawned on me that I sounded—are you writing out checks?"

His gaze had dropped to the ledger that lay open on the desk. What now?

"I'm reconciling the checkbook. Ana likes a paper record in addition to the online version." She considered adding that his aunt had asked her to take over the task because her math was getting a bit fuzzy, but that would only make her sound more defensive than she did, and she refused to feel guilty for doing her job.

"I never did understand her insistence on two records," He replied. She'd expected a far more snide comment. Walking over to the desk, he studied the laptop screen from over her shoulder. "Seems like way too much opportunity for mistakes."

"I've tried to tell Ana the same thing." As much as she tried not to be, Patience found herself acutely aware of his chest hovering behind her ear. The scent of his body wash lingered in the air. Clean. Crisp. She couldn't help herself; she inhaled deeply.

"You forgot to record check number 3521," he said, pointing at the screen.

Sure enough, there was an unrecorded check. "This is the biggest problem," she said. "Ana always forgets to mark the checks in both places."

"I thought you wrote the checks?"

"I write out the monthly checks for the bills. That doesn't mean your aunt doesn't write out her own occassionally. Especially when she want to give money to the humane society. See?" She pointed to the written ledger. "Check 3521 in her handwriting."

She shifted in her hair, so she could better confront him. "Are you going to question everything I do while you're living here? Because if so, it's going to make for a very long stay."

"I wasn't questioning anything. All I did was point out you missed a check."

Right. And his pointing out had nothing to do with his distrust. "Look," she said, "I know you don't like me—"

"I never said I didn't like you."

Patience blinked. "You didn't?"

"No. I said I didn't trust you. There's a difference."

Not much. "Gee, thanks. I feel so much better."

A hint of color found its way to his cheeks. It, along with his quick, sheepish smile, dulled her annoyance. "I'm not saying this right at all," he said. "I came in because I realized what I said back in the kitchen didn't come out as apologetically as it should have. What I should have said was that I'm sorry for treating you like a trial witness last night. I should have let the matter drop after Ana corroborated your story."

"Actually," Patience replied, "what you should have said was that you're sorry for even suggesting I'd hurt your aunt."

Stuart grabbed the edge of the desk, trapping her between his two arms. Body wash and heat buffeted the space between them, the combination making Patience's pulse quicken. She looked up to meet a gaze that was bright and resolute. "Ana is the only family I have," he said. "I won't apologize for trying to protect her."

This was where Patience should retaliate with angry defiance. Unfortunately, she understood where Stuart was coming from. When it came to keeping your family safe, you did whatever you had to do. No matter what.

Still, she wasn't ready to let him off the hook. "Let's get something straight," she said, straightening her spine. "I like Ana. She's been good to me. Real good. I would never hurt her. I don't care how good your reason is—you are a jerk for thinking otherwise."

They were back to Mexican standoff territory, with their eyes challenging one another. Patience focused on keeping her breath even. She didn't know if it was his scent, his close proximity, or the thrill of having held her ground, but she could feel the adrenaline surging through her. When Stuart broke the moment with a slow, lazy smile, her heart jumped. The thrill of victory, she decided.

"Yes, I was," he said. "A jerk, that is."

"Finally, we agree with something." She sat back, only to realize the new posture placed her in the crook of his arm. Instinct screamed for her to straighten up again, but that would imply she was nervous, and since she wasn't nervous she forced herself to look relaxed. "Apology accepted."

Stuart responded with a low chuckle before—thankfully—shifting positions and releasing her. Patience was surprised how much she missed his scent when it disappeared.

"How about we start over with a clean slate?" he said. "Hi. I'm Stuart Duchenko."

She stared at his extended hand. For some reason, the gesture kicked off warning bells. "Why?" she asked.

"Why what?"

"Why the one-eighty?" A dozen hours ago, he was smirking with suspicion. Now he wanted to be friends?

He'd obviously expected the question, because he chuckled again. "Because you're right, I was being a jerk. And, because Ana would have my head if she saw the way I was acting. Our bickering like a couple of twelve-year-olds won't help her. Therefore, I'm hoping we can be civil for her sake."

He had a point. Ana would expect better of her, as well. "Does this mean you've decided to trust me?"

"Let's not go crazy. I am, however, willing to give you the chance to prove me wrong."

"Well, isn't that mighty big of you." Although, in truth, they had something in common. She didn't trust him, either.

His hand was still extended, waiting for her acceptance. Fine. She could be the bigger person, too. For Ana's sake.

"I'm Patience Rush," she said, wrapping her fingers around his palm.

His grip was firm and confident, more so than she expected. Patience was shocked at the power traveling up her arm.

You're playing with fire, a tiny voice whispered in her ear. Stuart wasn't some sour-smelling creep she could hold off with an expressionless stare. He was a man whose clout and influence could ruin her life. But, like a shining red sign blinking "Do Not Touch," she couldn't resist the challenge.

"Nice to meet you, Patience. I look forward to getting to know you."

"Same here."

She wasn't sure what to say next and, based on the awkward silence, neither did he. The strangest energy had begun humming around them. Wrapping them together, as if the two of them were suddenly on the same page. Weird. Other than Piper, Patience had always made it a rule to keep an invisible wall between herself and the rest of the world. To feel a connection of any kind left her off balance.

Stuart's smile mirrored her insides. Tentative and crooked. "Look at us being all civil."

"Let's not go crazy," she replied, quoting him. "It's only been a minute. Let's see how we do at the end of the day."

"I'm up for the challenge if you are."

Oh, she was more than up for it. If being civil led to him dropping all his talk of "secrets," then she'd civil him to death.

CHAPTER THREE

To HER COMPLETE and utter amazement, he didn't insist on supervising her work. Instead, he left her with a friendly "Don't forget to mark down check 3521." Probably planning to double-check her work later, Patience decided. She took more care than usual to make sure the ledgers were perfect.

After lunch, Stuart went to the hospital to spend time with Ana while she stayed behind to wage war with the brownstone windows. She thought about visiting as well, but decided to wait until evening so Stuart would see how seriously she took her job.

And, okay, maybe part of her wanted to avoid him. Being civil would be a lot easier if they didn't see each other. The energy shift when they shook hands still had her thrown. Ever since, there'd been this inexplicable fluttering in her stomach that no amount of window cleaning could shake. A reminder that she wasn't dealing with an ordinary man, but rather someone a class above the creeps and losers who'd crossed her path over the years. Talk about two different worlds, she thought with an unbidden shiver. All the more reason to avoid him as much as possible.

And so, armed with cleaner and crumpled newspaper, she polished glass until the smell of vinegar clung to her nostrils and there wasn't a streak to be found. As she stretched out the small of her back, she checked the clock on the parlor mantel. Five o'clock. Time to feed the beast. She was surprised Nigel wasn't upstairs with her, meowing up a storm. He wasn't in the hallway, either.

"You better not be hiding somewhere thinking about pouncing on me," she called out as she trotted down the stairs. "I can tell you right now scaring me won't get you on my good side."

"I'll keep that in mind," Stuart replied. He looked impossibly at home, standing at the counter with a cat food can in his hand and Nigel weaving in and around his legs.

"What are you doing here?" she asked, only to realize how abrupt she sounded. They were supposed to be acting civil after all. "I mean, I thought you were visiting Ana." That sounded much nicer.

"I got home a few minutes ago and Nigel met me at the door. Nearly broke my ankle demanding supper."

"No way!" She purposely exaggerated her disbelief. "Good thing you weren't on the stairs." Her smirk couldn't have faded even if she wanted it to. *Go Nigel.* Kitty earned himself extra tuna.

To his credit, Stuart had the decency to look apologetic. "Point made. I was wrong."

"Told you so." Since they were being civil, she kept the rest of her gloating to herself. Instead, she bent down to retrieve Nigel's bowl, making sure she gave the cat an extra scratch under the chin when he ran over to see her. "How is Ana?" she asked.

His expression changed in a flash, growing somber. "They've got her on pain medicine so she mostly sleeps, and the couple times she did wake up, she was confused. The nurses told me that's pretty common, especially at her age." He breathed hard through his nostrils. A nonverbal *but*...

Patience felt herself softening toward the man even more. Seeing Ana so weak had upset her, too, and she had been around to see how active Ana had been. Goodness only knows how shocked Stuart must have felt having missed the last eight months. "I'm sure she'll be back to her feisty self in no time," she said, trying to reassure him. And herself, too, maybe.

"That's what the nurses said."

"But...?" There was a hesitancy in his response that once again left the word hanging in the air.

"Did you know one-fourth of senior citizens who break a hip die within six months?"

"Not Ana." No way was he going down that road. "She'd kill you if she heard you. Besides, she broke an ankle, not a hip, so your statistic doesn't apply."

"You're right. It doesn't." A smile graced his features. Forced maybe, but it erased the sadness from his face. Patience was glad. He looked much better with his dimples showing. Not that he didn't look good when serious, but his appeal definitely increased when his eyes sparkled.

"And Ana would kill me," he added, and they shared another smile before Stuart looked away to finish feeding Nigel. Patience waited until he'd scraped the sides of the cat food can before placing the bowl back in its place. "I was planning to visit Ana tonight," she told him.

"Me too. Right after dinner."

Shoot! She'd completely forgotten about dinner. Normally, by this point in the day, she'd have started cooking, but she'd been so engrossed in cleaning the windows—and trying not to think about Stuart—that everything else slipped her mind. "I…um…" Combing the bangs from her eyes, she caught a whiff of vinegar and winced at the odor. "I hope you don't mind simple. I forgot to get the meat out to thaw."

"Don't worry about it. I'll grab something on the way. I've been dying for an Al's Roast Beef."

"No way."

"What, you don't like Al's?"

"No, I love it." She was surprised he did. Al's was a little hole-in-the-wall near the subway overpass. The kind of place you weren't one-hundred-percent sure passed the health inspection, although it did have the most amazing burgers and roast beef sandwiches. She would have pegged Stuart as preferring something more upscale and elegant, like the wine bar up the street. "Can't beat their barbecue special."

"Would you like to join me?"

Join him? The hair on the back of her neck started to rise, much the way it did when he'd suggested they start over. She didn't trust this warmer, gentler Stuart. Especially since he said he still didn't trust her.

What was he up to?

"We both need to eat," he replied, picking up on her hesitation. "We're both going to the hospital. Why not go together?"

Why not? She could give a bunch of reasons, starting with the fact she should be avoiding him, not giving him an opportunity to dig for information.

"Plus, I owe you an apology for being wrong about Nigel."

"You do owe me that," Patience replied.

"So, is that a yes?" His expectant smile was so charming it caused her stomach to do a tiny somersault. As sure a sign as any that she should say no. Playing with fire, the voice in her head reminded her.

Except that smile was too darn hard to refuse. "Sure," she replied. "Why not?"

She regretted her response as soon as they arrived at Al's. Actually, she regretted it as soon as the words left her mouth and Stuart flashed a knee-buckling smile, but arriving at the restaurant sealed the deal—*restaurant* being a loose description. Beacon Hill types considered the banged-up booths and ketchup stains "atmosphere." Patience considered it dirty. The place reminded her too much of the old days.

"We could do takeout if you'd rather," Stuart said, correctly interpreting her expression. "Go eat by the river."

Patience shook her head. "No. Here will be fine." A picnic by the river sounded too nice, and, frankly, the situation was strange enough without the atmosphere feeling like a date.

This kinder, gentler Stuart made her nervous. They weren't friends—not by a long shot—and she wasn't really sure she bought his apology excuse. So why were they out to dinner together?

After placing their orders, they took seats in a booth toward the rear of the restaurant. One of the cleaner tables, if that was saying anything. Immediately, Patience took out a package of hand wipes and began cleaning the crumbs from the surface, earning a chuckle from Stuart.

"You do realize you're off the clock, right?" he asked.

"You want to eat on a dirty table?" she shot back. She was beginning to dislike his laugh. Rich and thick, the sound slipped down her spine like warm chocolate syrup, making her insides quiver every time she heard it. Doubling down on her cleaning efforts, she did her best to wash both the crumbs and the sensation away. "I don't even want to think about what the kitchen looks like," she continued.

There was a splash of dried cola near the napkin dispenser. She went at it with vigor. "Piper would have a nutty if she saw this place."

"Who's Piper?"

Drat. She didn't realize she'd spoken aloud. This really was a mistake. Not five minutes in and she'd opened the door to personal questions. Fortunately, Piper was the one personal subject she could talk about forever. "She's my sister."

"Let me guess, she's into cleaning, too?"

"No, cooking." Her chest grew full. "She's studying to be a chef. In Paris." She made a point of emphasizing the location.

"Is that so?"

Based on the spark in Stuart's eye, Patience decided it was admiration and not disbelief coloring his voice, and her pride expanded some more. "She was accepted last fall. It's always been her dream to become a famous chef."

"You must be proud."

"Proud doesn't begin to cover it. I think she's going to be the next Top Chef, she's that talented. Ever since she was a kid, she had a knack for taking ingredients you'd never thought would go together and turning them into something delicious. Once, I came home and found her making jalapeño pancakes."

"Were they any good?"

"Believe it or not, they were. Although she got flour everywhere. Took me all night to clean the film from the countertop." A waste of time since the roaches came scrounging anyway. The thought only made her smile fade a little. As always, her pride in Piper's talent over-ruled the bad.

Their conversation was interrupted by a group of col-lege students settling into the booth behind them. Their laughter barely disguised the popping of beer cans.

"I forgot this place was BYOB," Stuart remarked. "We could have brought a bottle of Merlot to go with our meal."

"I'm not sure this is a Merlot kind of place," Pa-tience replied.

"Good point. Beer then."

She tried and failed to stop her grimace.

"You don't like beer?"

"I don't like the smell." He wouldn't either if he'd spent years breathing sour, stale air.

Stuart was clearly curious, but thankfully he didn't push. At least not right then. Instead, he stretched his arms along the back of the booth, the position pull-ing his shirt taut across his torso and emphasizing the contours beneath the cotton. Patience wondered if he realized he was the most superior-looking man in the place.

"So, your sister's dream is to become a famous chef," he said. "What's yours?"

To make sure Piper's dream came true. Patience busied herself with pulling napkins from the dispenser. "I don't know what you mean."

"Oh, come on. Surely you didn't always want to be a housekeeper?"

He was fishing. Looking for clues about this so-called agenda he thought she had regarding his aunt. What would he think if she told him her childhood hadn't allowed for dreams or aspirations? Or that there was a time when even being a housekeeper seemed out of her reach? Would he trust her more or less? Patience could guess the answer.

"I thought we called a truce," she said, dodging the question.

"Hey, I was just making conversation. I didn't realize I'd asked you to reveal a state secret."

He had a point. Maybe she was overreacting just a little. It certainly wasn't his fault he'd stumbled too close to a bad topic. "Teacher," she said softly. "When I was little, I wanted to be a teacher."

"There now, that wasn't so hard, was it?" Damn him for having a charming smile as he spoke. "What changed your mind?"

"I grew up," she replied. The words came out sharper than she intended, causing a stunned expression. "And my mother died, leaving me to raise Piper." She was probably telling him way too much, but she figured revealing some facts was smarter than acting prickly. "Hard to go to school and raise your kid sister." Not that there was money for school to begin with, but he didn't need to know that.

"I'm sorry. How old were you?"

"Eighteen."

"That must have been tough."

"We managed. How about you?" She rushed to change the subject before he could ask anything further. "Did you always want to be a lawyer?"

He laughed again. "Of course not. No little boy wants to be lawyer. I wanted to be a professional baseball player."

"What happened?"

"I grew up," he said, repeating her answer. In his case, instead of sounding prickly, the words came out sad, despite his clearly trying to sound otherwise. "Turns out you have to have athletic ability to be a professional athlete—or a child athlete, for that matter."

Looking at him, she found his protest a bit hard to believe. "You look pretty athletic to me," she said. His arched brow made her blush. "I mean, I'm sure you weren't as bad as you make it sound."

"I had bad eyes, allergies and childhood asthma. Trust me, no one was ever going to confuse me with Babe Ruth. Or John Ruth for that matter."

"Who's John Ruth?"

"Exactly." He grinned, and she got the joke. He was worse than a guy who didn't exist.

"So," he continued, "with the Hall of Fame out of the picture, I found myself steered toward the family business."

"I thought your family business was mining?" Ana was always talking about Duchenko silver.

"Not since the turn of the century. Grandpa Theodore turned it into law. Thankfully. Can you see me coughing and squinting my way through a silver mine?"

No, she thought with a laugh. He definitely belonged to suits and luxury surroundings. His choice of words did make her curious, however. "You said steered. You didn't choose?"

"Sometimes you find yourself on a path without realizing it," he replied with a shrug.

Patience could sure relate to that, although at its worst, his path couldn't hold a candle to the one she'd landed on. "Do you at least like it?"

"For the most part. There are days when I'd rather be in the mine."

"No offense," she told him, "but I'll take the bad day of a rich lawyer over the bad day of a poor maid anytime."

"Don't be so sure," he said. "You've never had to draft a prenuptial agreement for your step-grandmother."

At that moment, the girl at the counter called out their order, and he slid from the booth, leaving Patience to wonder about his answer. Writing some document hardly seemed a big ordeal.

Stuart returned a few minutes later with a tray laden with food. The smell of fresh beef made her stomach rumble. Grimy location or not, Al's did have good burgers.

She waited until they'd divided the burgers and French fries before picking up the conversation. "How is writing a prenuptial so awful?" she asked him. "It's not like unclogging a toilet or something."

"You wouldn't say that if you met Grandma Gloria."

"Harsh."

"Not harsh enough," he said, biting into his burger.

So Patience wasn't the only person Stuart had issues with. Maybe he didn't like outsiders in general. Or was it only women? "She had to have some redeeming quality. I mean if your grandfather loved her…"

"Grandpa Theodore *wanted* her. Big difference."

"She must have wanted him too," Patience replied. She wasn't sure why she felt the need to defend this Gloria person, unless it was because exonerating Gloria might improve her own standing in his mind.

"She wanted Duchenko money." There was no mistaking the venom in his voice. "And she went after it like a heat-seeking missile. Didn't matter who she got the money from, or who she had to hurt in the process."

Like who? The way his face twisted with bitterness made her think he was leaving something out of the story. It certainly explained why he had issues with her befriending Ana.

"This Gloria woman sounds lovely."

"Oh, she was a real peach. Did I mention she turned thirty-four on her last birthday?" he added abruptly.

"Thirty-four?"

"Uh-huh."

"Hasn't your grandfather been dead for…"

"Ten years," he supplied. My grandfather died ten years ago."

Making Gloria…ew. Patience wrinkled her nose at the image.

"Exactly. And now I'm stuck dealing with her for the rest of eternity."

Patience took a long sip of her cola. His comments had opened the door to a lot of questions, about many of which she had no business being curious, and yet seeing his frown, she couldn't help herself. "Ana doesn't talk much about her family," she said. "Other than you, that is.

"Unfortunately, there wasn't much love lost between Ana and Grandpa Theodore. From what I understand, they stopped speaking to each other around forty or fifty years ago. People were shocked when she traveled to his funeral. She told them it was only out of respect for me."

"Wow." To not speak to your sibling for decades? She couldn't imagine going more than two or three days without talking to Piper. "That must have been some fight."

"True. I asked Ana once, but all she said was Grandpa Theodore stole her happiness."

"How?" Ana seemed like one of the happiest people she knew.

"Beats me. I remember my father grumbling once that he wished my grandfather would make things right this one time, so whatever happened was his fault. Unfortunately, unless Ana decides to open up, we might never know."

"Your poor dad. Sounds like he was stuck in the middle."

"For a little while anyway. He uh…" His eyes dropped to his half-eaten meal. "He and my mom died in a car accident when I was fourteen."

"Oh." Patience kicked herself for bringing up the subject. "I'm sorry."

"It was a long time ago."

Time didn't mean anything. There was nothing worse than having the ground yanked out from under you, leaving you with no idea where you belonged, what would happen next, or who would catch you if you fell. The teenage Stuart would have held in the pain, put on a strong face. She could tell by the way he held himself now, closed and protected.

Just like her. *No one should be forced to grow up before they're ready.*

Again, it was as if she'd spoken her thoughts out loud, because Stuart looked up, his blue eyes filled with a mixture of curiosity and gratitude. "I'm going to go out on a limb and say you grew up earlier than I did."

His words twisted around her heart. If only he knew... For a crazy second, she longed to tell him everything, thinking that he, having been in her shoes, might understand. Reality quickly squashed her fantasy. He'd never understand. The two of them came from two different worlds. Rich versus poor. Clean versus dirty. Sitting here, sharing childhood losses, it was easy for that fact to slip her mind.

"It's not really a contest I wanted to win," she heard herself answer.

"I don't suppose anyone ever does." Picking up his soda, he saluted her with the paper cup. "To happier subjects."

That was it? No questions? No probing? Patience studied his face, looking for evidence that the other shoe was about to drop. She saw nothing but sincerity in his smoky eyes.

"To happier subjects," she repeated. She'd gotten off easy this time.

Or had she? Stuart smiled over the rim of his glass, causing her insides to flip end over end. All of a sudden, Patience didn't feel she'd gotten off at all. More like she was falling into something very dangerous.

"Ana seemed a little more with it tonight," Patience remarked a few hours later. They were walking along Charles Street on their way home from the hospital.

"Yes, she did," Stuart replied. The change from this afternoon made him hopeful. Interesting, how his aunt's improvement seemed tied to Patience's arrival. Much as he hated to admit it, the housekeeper and his aunt had a real rapport. Patience was so, well, patient, with the older woman. Gentle, too. Getting Ana water. Making her comfortable. Everything about Patience's behavior tonight screamed authenticity. If her kindness was an act, Patience deserved an award.

Then again, he'd seen award-worthy performances before, hadn't he? He'd purposely brought up Gloria over dinner to gauge Patience's reaction, thinking the topic of fortune hunters might at least cause her to reveal some kind of body language. Instead, he got sympathy, felt a connection…

"You're frowning." Patience remarked.

"Sorry, I was thinking how little Ana ate this evening."

"She never eats much. You know that."

Yes, thought Stuart, but he needed something to dodge her question.

They walked a few feet in silence. The night was balmy and clear. Combined with the warm breeze, it created an almost romantic feel to the air around them. Stuart stole a glance in Patience's direction. She had her arms folded across her chest, and her eyes were focused on the pavement. Even so, he could still sense the undulating of her hips. It was, he realized, unconscious and natural. Otherwise, he suspected she'd attempt to downplay the sensuality the way she did her figure and her looks. Hell, maybe she was trying and failing. She certainly wasn't having much luck minimizing the other two.

That plastic hair band was failing, too. Strands of hair had broken free, and covered her eyes. One of them needed to brush the bangs away so he could see their sparkle again.

He rubbed the back of his neck instead.

Patience must have mistaken the action for him being warm. "You can definitely tell it's going to be the first day of summer," she remarked.

"Longest day of the year. Did you know that after tomorrow, every day gets a few seconds shorter? Before you know it, we'll be losing two and a half minutes a day. Sorry," he quickly added. "I did a graph for a high school science fair. The fact kind of stuck with me."

"In other words, you were blind, asthmatic, unathletic and a science nerd. No wonder you gave up on baseball."

He felt his cheeks grow warm. "For the record, I'd outgrown the asthma by then."

"Glad to hear it."

"Hey, we can't all be homecoming queens."

If he didn't know better, he'd swear she hugged her body a little tighter. "I didn't go to many school dances," she said.

Another piece to what was becoming a very confusing puzzle. One moment she was sexy and sharp-witted; the next, her eyes reminded him of a kitten—soft and innocent. What the heck was her story? He was no closer to knowing if Patience had an agenda than he was this morning. They might say you get more flies with honey, but all he got was more questions.

Along with a dangerously mounting attraction.

Cool air greeted them upon entering the brownstone. Stuart shut the front door and turned on the hallway light. Nigel, who had been sitting on a table by the front window greeted them with a loud meow before running toward the kitchen.

"For crying out loud," Patience called after him. "It's only been a few hours."

At the other end of the hall, the meows grew louder and more indignant—if such a thing was possible. She rolled her eyes, earning a chuckle from Stuart. He said, "You think he's bad, you should have met the other Nigels."

There were more? "You mean he's not the first."

"Actually, he's the third. Nigel the Second lived here while I was in law school."

"Wow, Ana must really like the name Nigel." Either that or the woman wasn't very good at pet names.

"I asked her once why she gave them all the same name,' Stuart added. "She told me it was because they all have Nigel personalities."

"If that's true, remind me to avoid guys named Nigel."

Their chuckles faded to silence. Patience toed the pattern on the entryway carpet. What now? There was an awkward expectancy in the air, as if both of them knew they should do or say something. The problem was, neither knew what.

At least Nigel had stopped his meowing.

"Thank you for dinner,' she said finally.

"You're welcome." He smiled. "Maybe we've got this being civil thing down."

"Maybe. I have to admit, you're not bad company when you aren't accusing me of things."

"Never fear, tomorrow's another day," he replied. Patience would have laughed, but there was too much truth to his comment. This temporary truce of theirs could break at any time.

"By the way," he added, you're not such bad company yourself. When you aren't dodging questions."

"Like you said, tomorrow's another day." She turned to leave only to have her left foot tangle with something warm and furry. Nigel. She maneuvered herself awkwardly, trying to avoid stepping on the darn cat. Her ankle twisted, and she pitched sideways, toward the stairway. That caused her right knee to buckle, and before she knew it, she was falling in a heap.

Stuart caught her before her bottom touched the floor. "Stupid cat," she muttered.

"Are you okay?"

"I'm fine. Nigel on the other hand might have used up another one of his nine lives." She looked around, but the creature was nowhere to be found.

"He ran upstairs," Stuart replied, helping her to her feet.

"With his tail between his legs, I hope. If you didn't believe me before about Nigel causing Ana's fall, you have to believe me now."

"The evidence is definitely in your favor. Are you sure you're okay?"

"Positive. My butt didn't even hit the ground."

"Good. Hate to see you bruise something you might need," he said with a smile.

That's when she realized he still held her. His arm remained wrapped around her waist, pulling her close, so that their hips were flush. The odd angle gave Patience little choice but to rest her hand on his upper arm,

They might as well have been embracing.

He smelled of soap and laundry detergent. No aftershave—a testimony to his innate maleness that he didn't need anything more. Awareness—no, something stronger than awareness—washed over her, settling deep in the pit of her stomach.

Fingers brushed her bangs away from her temple. Barely a whisper of a touch, it shot straight to her toes. Slowly, she lifted her gaze. "I've been wanting to do that all night," he said in a voice softer than his touch.

"I—I'm growing out my bangs. That's why they keep falling in my face." Why did she think he wasn't talking about her bangs?

Maybe because his attention had shifted to her mouth. Staring, studying. Patience caught her lip between her teeth to stop it from trembling. All either of them needed to do was to move their head the tiniest bit and they would be close enough to kiss.

"I should check on Nigel…" She twisted from his grasp, combing her fingers through her hair in a lousy attempt to mask her abruptness. She needed to…she didn't know what she needed to do. The blood pounding in her ears made it hard to think.

She needed space. That's what. Turning on her heel, she headed upstairs, forcing herself to take one step at a time. She lasted until the second flight, when Stuart was out of sight, before doubling the pace.

Smooth going, Patience, she thought when she finally closed her bedroom door. Why don't you break out in a cold sweat while you're at it?

What on earth was wrong with her anyway? She'd dealt with literally dozens of unwanted advances over the years. Losers, pushy drunks, punks who couldn't keep their hands to themselves And she freaks out because Stuart touched her hair? The guy didn't even try anything.

Oh, but you wanted him to, didn't you? That's why

she'd bolted. In spite of everything that had gone on between them in the past twenty-four hours, she actually wanted Stuart Duchenko to kiss her.

Heaven help her, but she still did.

CHAPTER FOUR

THE NEXT MORNING, Patience woke up with a far clearer head. Tossing and turning for half the night did that for a person.

When she thought things through, Patience wasn't really surprised that she was attracted to Stuart. Along with being handsome, he was the polar opposite of every man who had ever crossed her path. Sadly, that difference was exactly why she had no business kissing or doing anything else with him.

Throwing back the covers, she stretched and headed for the shower. Back in her and Piper's old apartment, a long hot shower was her way of scrubbing away life's dirt. The close, fiberglass stall had been her oasis. This morning, she was using Ana's Italian marble shower to rinse away last night's fantastical thoughts. There was probably some kind of irony in that. All she knew was she had to go back to keeping her distance before she made a fool of herself or, worse, said something she shouldn't.

The brownstone was empty when she finally came downstairs. A quick look toward his bedroom door—because she needed to prepare breakfast, not because she was thinking about him—showed Stuart was already awake. Up and out, apparently. A good thing, Patience told herself. She still wasn't sure how to explain her behavior last night, and Stuart's absence gave her the space she needed to come up with one.

Nigel was sitting by the kitchen door. The food littering his mat said he'd already had breakfast. There was coffee in the coffeepot, too.

"He sure is making it hard to stay unaffected, isn't he, Nigel?" She gave the cat a scratch behind the ear. "But we're going to do our best."

Just then the front door opened, signaling the end of her solitude. With a soft meow, Nigel trotted toward the entryway. "Hey, Nigel," she heard him greet. "Told you I'd be back."

Patience rubbed her arms, which had suddenly developed goose bumps. Amazing the way the air seemed to shift every time he entered a building. Like the atmosphere needed to announce his arrival.

And thank goodness, too. She turned to the door at the same time he entered, and if she hadn't been forewarned, her knees would have buckled underneath her completely.

He'd lied last night. No way the man walking into the kitchen was an unathletic nerd. His thin cotton tank might as well be nonexistent, the way it clung to his sweaty body. She could see every muscle, every inch of nonexistent fat. His arms alone…were lawyers allowed to have biceps that illegal? All those thoughts she had about his being commanding and superior? They doubled. And she'd thought he might kiss her last night? Talk about being a fool.

"Good morning." He barely looked in her direction as he made his way to the refrigerator. "Going to be a scorcher. You can feel the heat in the air already." Grabbing a bottle of water, he downed the contents in one long drink. "Did you sleep all right?"

Clearly last night's encounter hadn't affected him. "Fine," she lied, ignoring the hollow feeling threatening to take hold of her insides. "You?"

"As well as anyone with a furry bed warmer can sleep. Nigel has apparently appointed me the substitute Duchenko."

"I noticed you fed him. And made coffee. Thank you."

"Since I was awake first, it seemed only logical. Plus, Nigel would never have let me leave the house, and I wanted to get a run in before it got too humid."

"I didn't know you were a runner."

"Grandpa Theodore's idea. He thought it would help keep my lungs strong. The habit just sort of stuck." As he talked, he crossed the kitchen to the side where she stood. Patience gripped the counter a little tighter. Even sweaty, his skin smelled appealing. Instead of stale and dirty, it was the fresh, clean scent of exertion.

"I called the hospital before I left. Ana had a good night," he said, reaching into the cupboard for a mug.

He offered her a mug, as well, but Patience shook her head. Sharing coffee together felt too domestic and familiar.

"Oh, good. I was thinking of taking her some of her favorite tea and cookies when I visited her today. Since you were concerned about her eating and all… what?"

He was giving her one of those looks, where he seemed to be trying to read her mind. "That's very thoughtful of you."

"You sound surprised."

"Actually…" His expression turned inward. "I'm beginning not to be."

"Thank you. I guess." Maybe he was finally realizing she wasn't some kind of criminal mastermind out to take his aunt's money or whatever it was he suspected her of being. Maybe this meant he would back off and her insides could unwind.

Or maybe not, she corrected, taking in his muscular arms.

"Don't get too comfortable. I'm still keeping an eye on you." Damn, if the smile accompanying the remark didn't make her insides grow squirrelly. He finished pouring his coffee and headed toward the door. "I'm planning to stop by the hospital before work this morning. If you'd like, I can give you a ride."

"Thanks," she replied as Stuart left to get a shower. Sitting in close quarters with him while they wove through traffic was not her idea of fun. She'd bet he had a tiny Italian sports car so their knees could bump on every turn, too.

"Like I said," she remarked to Nigel, who had returned and was weaving in and out of her legs, "he's making it awfully difficult."

Stuart took the stairs two at a time. So much for the restorative powers of a good run. Five miles and his thoughts were still racing.

Not just his thoughts. All he could say was thank goodness Patience wasn't trying to look sexy or he'd have a heart attack.

It was time he accepted the fact that he'd gone from finding the woman attractive to being attracted to her. His fate was sealed the second his arm slipped around her waist. She fit so perfectly, her hips aligning with his as though they were meant to be connected…

Giving a groan, he kicked his bedroom door shut. It was all that damn tendril's fault. If the strand had stayed tucked in her band where it belonged, he wouldn't have been compelled to brush the hair from her face, and if he hadn't brushed her hair, he never would have considered kissing her.

And oh, did he consider. He owed her a thank-you for bolting upstairs. Kept him from crossing an improper line with his aunt's employee.

Raised a few more questions, too. Mainly, what made her flee in the first place? Stuart swore that for a few seconds before Patience took flight, he saw real desire in her eyes. Did she back off because she realized the mistake they were about to make or because of something more? The lady sure had her secrets.

Maybe he could find out what they were. That is, if he could keep his attraction—and his hands—to himself.

Surprisingly—or perhaps not so surprisingly—Patience left for the hospital without him. The hastily scrawled note pinned to the coffeemaker said she needed to stop at the tea shop to buy Ana her Russian caravan tea. "A reasonable excuse," he said to Nigel. But the tea shop was only a block away, and in the direction of the hospital. He would have gladly waited while she ran her errand.

No, more likely, she wanted to avoid being in the car with him. For him to care about her decision was silly, but care he did. Why didn't she want to ride with him?

Unfortunately, any answer had to wait because when

he arrived at the hospital, his aunt was awake. Someone had raised her bed so she was sitting upright. Patience stood by her head, brushing out her hair. Stuart watched as her arm moved with long, slow strokes, each pass banishing the tangles of hospitalization. "Do you want to leave the braid down or wear it coiled?" he heard her ask.

"Coiled," Ana replied. "Of course."

He smiled. His aunt always insisted on looking as regal as possible. She was wearing the serenest of expressions. Her eyes were closed and the hint of a smile played across her lips. For the first time since he'd come home, she resembled the Ana he remembered.

His chest squeezed tight, his heart and lungs suddenly too big for his body. He was afraid to cough lest he spoil his aunt's moment.

"Good morning." The moment ended anyway, as Dr. Tischel, Ana's primary care physician boomed his greeting from behind his shoulder. *"Lapushka!"* Ana greeted with a smile. "How long have you been standing there?"

"Not long. I didn't want to disturb your beauty session." He locked eyes with Patience only to have her break the gaze and resume brushing. "How are you this morning, Tetya?" He kissed Ana's cheek.

"I don't know," she replied. "How am I, Karl?"

"Remarkably lucky, for one thing. You're too old to be rolling down staircases. We all are."

All the more reason not to stare at women two-thirds your age, thought Stuart. The good doctor's gaze had locked itself to a spot below Patience's neck. The housekeeper had angled her body toward the wall, but that didn't stop the man's blatant assessment.

"Will she be able to go home soon?" Stuart asked in a loud voice, drawing the man's attention. A question to which he already knew the answer, but then he wasn't asking because he wanted information.

"I'm afraid not," the doctor replied. The man didn't even have the decency to look embarrassed. "You took a nasty fall, Ana."

He lifted the sheet from where it covered the upper part of her legs. On the leg without a cast, a large bruise turned Ana's kneecap purple. Dr. Tischel touched around it, causing Ana to wince.

"Knee's pretty tender," he said, stating the obvious. "You're definitely going to have to stay off your feet for a little while."

"Are we talking about a wheelchair?" Stuart asked. He was having trouble imaging his great-aunt managing crutches as the moment.

"At the very least," the doctor replied. "For a little while anyway."

"Don't worry," Patience said. "I'll push you around the house."

"Oh no, the brownstone has way too many stairs," Dr. Tishcel said. "That's what got you in trouble in the first place. The rehab hospital has a terrific orthopedics wing. They'll take good care of you."

"What?" In spite of her pain, Ana stiffened. "You're sending me to another hospital? For how long?"

"Depends," Dr. Tischel replied. "At least a couple of weeks."

"A couple weeks!" Patience and Ana spoke at the same time, although he was pretty sure their furor was for two different reasons. Stuart tensed at the announcement himself, and he'd been expecting the news since the day Ana fell. Two weeks sharing a house with Patience. Alone.

"I'm afraid so," Dr. Tischel replied. "We want to make sure that ankle heals properly. I'll give them a call this afternoon and check on availability. With luck there's a bed open and we can transfer you tomorrow.

"In the meantime," he said, pulling the sheet back over her legs, "I want you to try and sit up in a chair for a few hours."

Ana gave an indignant cough. "Don't know why if I'm just going to be laid up in another hospital bed."

"Because the movement will do you good. You don't want to develop blood clots, do you?"

"No, she does not," Stuart answered. Seeing the doctor was getting ready to leave, he rose from his chair, hoping to keep the man from giving Patience another once-over. Granted, he shared Dr. Tischel's appreciation of her beauty, but the woman wasn't standing there for his viewing pleasure. He held out a hand. "Thank you for your help."

The gambit failed as the older man shook his hand only briefly before reaching across Ana to grasp Patience's. "It's my pleasure. Ana has always been one of my favorite patients."

Ana coughed again. "Favorite, my foot," she grumbled once the doctor left. "Stupid old fool wants to stick me in a nursing home."

"Rehab facility, Tetya." Stuart replied. Out of the corner of his eye, he caught Patience wiping her hand on her jeans. Apparently, she wasn't impressed with Dr. Tischel's behavior this morning, either. "It's only for a little while. You'll be back at the brownstone before you know it."

Ana shrugged. She looked so sad it made Stuart almost want to tell her Dr. Tischel had made a mistake. In a way, he understood. The news probably did sound like a sentence. She was losing her freedom.

He grabbed her fingers. "I'll visit every day, I promise."

"And me," Patience said. "I'll even find out if I can bring Nigel so you can see him, too."

"Will you?" Ana's face brightened. "I've been so worried about him. He acts tough, but on the inside, he's really very sensitive."

"I'll do everything I can. I promise."

Stuart watched while the two women talked about the cat, his chest squeezing tight again. The soft, caring tone in Patience's voice mesmerized him. She sounded so genuine; it made him want so badly to trust her intentions.

Could he?

Just then, Patience reached over to brush a strand of hair from Ana's face, sending his mind hurtling to the night before. Parts of his body stirred remembering how soft Patience's hair had felt sliding through his fingers. How on earth was he going to spend two weeks with Patience, get to know her and keep his attraction under control?

"Oh, no!"

Ana's cry shook him from his reverie. She sat straight, her face crumpled in distress. "What's wrong, Tetya?" he asked.

"The humane society dinner dance. I totally forgot, but it's tonight."

Was that all? Stuart let out his breath. "Looks like you'll have to miss this year's festivities."

"But I can't," Ana said. "I'm being honored as the volunteer of the year. I'm supposed to be there to accept my award."

"I'm sure people will understand why you're not there, Tetya. You can have your friend, Mrs. Calloway, accept on your behalf."

"Ethyl Calloway is not my friend," his aunt snapped.

Stuart should have remembered. Ana and Ethyl weren't friends so much as friendly society rivals. The two of them had worked side by side at the Beacon Hill Humane Society for years, competing to see who could do more to further the organization's good work. As a result, hundreds of homeless cats and dogs had found new homes. Personally, he thought it incredibly fitting that Ethyl accept the award on his aunt's behalf, but what did he know?

"Missing the ceremony isn't going to diminish what you've done for the shelter," Patience said. "People will still know about your hard work."

To Patience's credit, her comment worked. Ana settled back against her pillow, her agitation fading. "Will you accept the award for me?" she asked.

Stuart cringed. The humane society dinner dance was a nightmare of society women and their spouses who made it their mission to offer up single granddaughters to every eligible bachelor who had the misfortune of attending. Those without granddaughters used their time to strong-arm donations. The last time Ana had convinced him to attend, he'd left four figures poorer and with a pocket full of unwanted phone numbers. But the organization was Ana's pride and joy. Accepting her award was the least he could do.

"Of course I will," he told her.

His aunt and Patience exchanged an odd look. "What?" he asked.

"I think she meant me," Patience said.

The blush coloring her cheeks couldn't be as dark as the one heating his. "Oh. I didn't…"

"I had no idea you'd be home this week," his aunt said, her eyes looking deeply apologetic, "and you know how I hate to attend alone."

"You're more than welcome to go in my place," Patience added. "I don't mind."

No kidding. Her eyes were practically begging him to say yes, they were so hopeful-looking.

Unable to see the silent exchange, Ana waved the offer away. "Nonsense. You never go out. This is your chance to dress up and have a good time. Stuart will go with you."

"I will?" The painkillers had to be making Ana loopy again. Take Patience to an event where holding her in his arms would be encouraged? Bad idea.

"Someone has to keep the men from pestering her," Ana said. "You know how persistent some of those people can be."

Yes he did. In that sea of gray hair and pearls, Patience was going to stand out like a star. A welcome distraction for every senior man there.

Stuart wasn't sure if what he felt was jealousy or wariness on their behalf. "Ana's got a point," he said. "There is no reason why we shouldn't go together."

"See, dear? Stuart's on board.

He could see the moment Patience accepted her fate. Her shoulders slumped ever so slightly and she nodded. "All right."

"Good, it's settled. Stuart will go with you to the

dance, then tomorrow you can both fill me in on all the gossip." Ana relaxed a little more, the smile from earlier returning to her face.

"If you don't want to attend together, I'll understand," Stuart said when they stepped into the corridor a short while later. "I know Ana backed you into a corner. I'll be glad to deal with these people on my own."

Why? Was he trying to do her a favor or did he think she wouldn't fit in at the society function? Patience had to admit the second question had crossed her mind more than once.

She also had to admit that Ana hadn't backed her into anything. As soon as she suggested Stuart go along, her entire body broke out in excited tingles. Which, now that she thought about it, was a far bigger problem than not fitting in. Unfortunately...

"It's too late to back out now. Ana's expecting a report from both of us."

Patience wished she could read what was behind Stuart's long sigh. He ran a hand over his features, and when he finished, the face he revealed was an expressionless mask. "Very well," he said. "We'll go, collect her award, and make it an early night. That way, neither of us has to spend more time at this party than necessary."

Good idea, thought Patience. Less time for her to get into trouble.

So why did she feel disappointed?

CHAPTER FIVE

PATIENCE SMOOTHED THE front of her dress, then smoothed it again. Why hadn't she gone shopping this afternoon when she had the chance? The little black dress she pulled out of the closet was too short, too tight and too tacky. Everything about her screamed *cheap*.

It hadn't mattered when she'd thought she was attending with Ana. Or maybe it hadn't mattered *as much*. While naturally she wanted to please Ana, the older woman didn't make her stomach tumble.

Stuart shouldn't either, remember?

A knock sounded on her door. "Patience?" So much for not affecting her stomach. The sound of his voice made the butterflies' wings beat faster.

She draped a scarf around her shoulders, hoping that the draped material might camouflage her cleavage, smoothed her dress one more time and slipped into her pumps.

The heels were way too high. Would anyone notice how banged up her black flats were?

"Patience?"

Face it, she'd look out of place no matter what she wore. Best she could do was wear a smile and hope Stuart wasn't too horrified by her appearance.

Taking a deep breath, she opened the door.

Afraid of what she might see in Stuart's face, she avoided raising her eyes past his torso. That view was intimidating enough as it was. He was in full lawyer mode in a black suit similar to the one she remembered from the emergency room. This time, he finished off the outfit with a blue tie, the color of his eyes. To her embarrassment, Patience noticed her scarf matched. Made them look coordinated. *Like a couple.*

Maybe he wouldn't notice.

"Sorry to keep you waiting," she said.

"No worries. It was…worth the wait." There was an odd hitch to his voice. Mortification, maybe? Still afraid to look up and see, she pretended to pay attention to the steps as they headed downstairs.

"The Landmark isn't too far from here," he said. "Would you like to walk or drive?"

Once again, she faced the specter of being in a dark closed space with him. "Would you mind walking? I could use the fresh air." Anything to get the butterflies to settle down.

"Are you sure?" She didn't need to ask to know he was referring to her high heels. If only he knew how many hours she'd logged in shoes like these. A few blocks' walk would be a piece of cake.

The night air was surprisingly comfortable. A gentle breeze greeted them as they stepped onto the stoop. While Stuart locked the door behind them, Patience looked up at the darkening sky. A handful of early stars twinkled hello, and she made a quick wish that the night would turn out all right. Remembering their conversation from the night before, she asked, "How much daylight did we lose today?"

Stuart chuckled. "None, actually. The drop in daylight doesn't start for a few more days."

"So yesterday's explanation was wrong?"

"Generalized. I didn't realize I was going to be quizzed."

His hand hovered by the small of her back, guiding her down the steps. Patience made sure to walk quickly so as to avoid contact. "I'm sorry Ana strong-armed you into coming with me."

"I thought we covered this at the hospital. She strong-armed both of us."

"Yeah, but still I thought I should apologize. To be honest, I'm surprised you haven't said anything about the fact she and I were going together. I thought for sure you'd comment on it being part of my agenda."

"I thought about it, but since I know how badly Ana likes to have someone attend these things with her, 'll give you a pass." He flashed a smile. "Don't get used to it, though."

Patience added it to her list. Right after "going to parties with Stuart."

They stopped to wait for the traffic light. "I've never been to one of these kinds of events before," she said, while they waited for the light to change. "Any chance they'll present Ana's award early?"

"Nope. They need incentive for people to stick around. How else would they get them liquored up enough to bid on the silent auction items?"

"You ever bid?"

"Are you kidding? Those society women are worse than mob enforcers. You'd be amazed at the stuff they've convinced me to bid on. And for how much."

Patience fought a smile picturing Stuart fending off a parcel of senior citizens. "Did you win?"

"Twice. Once I won a gym membership. That was useful. The other time it was a romantic getaway to Newport, Rhode Island."

"Romantic weekend, huh?" She fought back the intense curiosity that rose up with his answer. Who was the lucky woman? In her mind, she pictured someone smart and sophisticated and who always wore the perfect outfit. Since his dating life wasn't her business, she settled for the blandest response she could think of. "At least you won something fun."

"So my secretary said."

"You took her on the trip?"

"No, I gave it to her as a bonus. She took her husband."

There was no need to feel relieved, but she was anyway.

They reached the Landmark just as a limousine pulled to the front door and a couple stepped on to the curb. Seeing the way the woman's diamond cocktail ring sparkled from a block away, Patience's palms began to sweat. She was supposed to mingle with these people? What was she going to talk about with them? By the way, what furniture polish does your cleaning lady use?

"Hey, you okay?"

She nodded, and adjusted her scarf. "I'm glad you're here is all. I'm a little..." Why not admit the truth? "I'm a little out of my league."

"Why?" he said. "It's just a lot of people dressed up and showing off."

A lot of people who hired people like her. No, correction. Who hired cleaning ladies. They wouldn't let her in the door, let alone hire her, if they knew her story.

"What you should really worry about is whether the chicken will be any good." His hand molded to the small of her back. The warmth of his touch spread up her spine, giving her courage. It was only for a few hours. She could do this.

The couple they saw were waiting for the elevator when they entered the lobby. It took less than ten seconds for Patience's confidence to flag. The same amount of time it took for the husband to smile and check out her legs. She wished Stuart's hand was still on her back. Then she could pretend he was with her by choice, and, by extension, the entire room would think so too. Instead, his fingers barely brushed her as they boarded the elevator.

Ethyl Calloway greeted them at the ballroom door. She was a tall, handsome woman who, like their companion on the elevator, was decorated with expensive jewelry. "Stuart! It's so good to see you." She kissed the air by his cheek. "How is Anastasia doing?"

"Much better," Stuart replied. "Already chomping at the bit to get back to her volunteer schedule. We had to practically tie her to the bed to keep her in the hospital."

"Well, at her age, it's best she not push herself too soon."

Her age? Ethyl wasn't much younger. The way the corner of Stuart's mouth was fighting not to smile, he was thinking the same thing. "Knowing Ana, she'll recover so fast she'll make the rest of us look lazy," Patience said.

Ethyl looked over as though she was noticing her for the first time. "Hello—Patty, isn't it?"

"Patience."

"Right. Ana mentioned she gave you a ticket. I'm glad you could make it. You'll be accepting Ana's award for her, right?" The older woman turned her attention back to Stuart. Actually, she physically turned toward Stuart and, in doing so, turned her back to Patience. Not on purpose, she told herself. Even so, she found herself blocked from the conversation. While Stuart nodded and went over details, she stood awkwardly to the side, smiling at the people who glanced in her direction.

"Lucky us," Stuart said, once Ethyl freed him from her attentions. "We're sitting at the front table."

"What does that mean?" From his sarcasm, she guessed not anything good.

"We get our rubber chicken first."

"Oh."

"And we get to sit with Ethyl. Take good notes. Ana's going to want a blow-by-blow recap." He pointed across the crowd to a congregation in the corner. "Looks like the bar is over there. I'll buy you drink."

They wound their way through the crowd, a difficult task as every ten feet some acquaintance of Ana's stopped them to ask for a medical update. After one very familiar-looking man inquired, she touched Stuart's arm. "Was that…?"

"The mayor?" He nodded.

Yep, she was out of her league. Please don't let me do something stupid

"Wine?" Stuart asked when they finally reached the front of the bar line.

Patience shook her head. "Sparkling water, please." Alcohol would go straight to her head, and she needed to keep her senses as sharp as possible. Another man walked by and checked out her legs. She gave the hemline a tug, on the off chance she could cover another quarter inch or so.

"You look fine." Stuart's breath was gentler than the breeze as he bent close and whispered in her ear. "Just a bunch of people…"

"Dressed up and showing off." She repeated his lesson for his benefit. Certainly her insides weren't listening. Her skin crawled, positive she was being evaluated by every person in the room and coming up short. What was that phrase about putting lipstick on a pig?

How she envied Stuart and the effortlessness with which he fit into his world. "I bet you go to a lot of these kinds of parties," she said to him.

"Only when I absolutely have to. Crowds and parties aren't really my thing."

"Really? But you look so at home." Everyone did, except for her.

"I'll tell you a secret." He leaned in close again. Damn, if he didn't smell better than the flower arrangements. "It helps if you think of all this as one big game," he said.

Distracted by the way his lips moved when he whispered, Patience nearly missed what Stuart said. "A game?"

"One big contest. Society's version of who's the biggest. Everyone's trying to prove they're better than the other."

"You make it sound like the whole room is a big pile of insecurity."

"Isn't it?"

"Including you?" she asked, although she couldn't imagine Stuart ever having a reason to be insecure.

"I've had my moments. Hard not to when you're raised by Theodore Duchenko." His eyes looked down at the glass in his hand, studying the contents. "My grandfather would make anyone feel insecure. He was what you'd call 'larger than life.'"

She was beginning to think life under Theodore Duchenko wasn't much of a picnic. "And stepgrandma?"

A shadow crossed his features. It might have been a shadow from one of the people in the crowd, but Patience couldn't be sure. Whatever it was, the passing left his expression darker than before. "Gloria is a case unto herself."

What did that mean? Before she could ask, he was steering her toward a group of tables lining the side wall on which were displayed a collection of wrapped baskets, photographs and other items. "The infamous silent auction," Stuart announced. "Everything a person couldn't want, dutifully accompanied by a heaping serving of guilt." He pointed to an easel next to the table where a large poster sat. Above the photograph of a big black Labrador, a caption read, "He's got so much love to give; if only someone would love him back." The dog's big brown eyes grabbed Patience's heart and squeezed.

"Admit it," Stuart said. "You want to adopt a puppy now, don't you. Or at least bid on a membership to the wine-of-the-month club." Patience took a long drink from her glass. The puppy and the wine weren't the only things she wanted and couldn't have.

The two of them spent time reviewing the various items up for auction, with Stuart predicting how much he thought the final bid would be for each one. Despite his sarcastic commentary, he too bid on a few items, including a customized kitty tree for Nigel and, to Patience's surprise, a braided gold bracelet. "This is for Ana right?" she teased. "Because I'm not sure your assistant's husband would like you giving his wife jewelry."

"Who says I wasn't planning to give the bracelet to you?"

She laughed. Wistful quivers aside, that was hardly likely. "Exactly what you give the girl you don't trust."

"You don't think I would?"

"I think…" His eyes dared her to believe his offer. "I hope you're joking," she said.

"You're not into expensive jewelry?"

Not if it came with strings attached, and that was the only kind of expensive jewelry she knew of. "I think Ana would enjoy the gift more."

There was something very off-putting about the way he reacted to her response. Rather than laugh or look disappointed, he gave her one of those soul-searching stares.

She was about to ask him if she'd said something wrong when Ethyl Calloway reappeared with a silver-haired gentleman behind her. "This is Bernard Jenkins from WZYV," she said, stepping in front of Patience— again. "He's emceeing tonight's award presentation. Since you're accepting Anastasia's award, I thought you two should meet."

On the emcee's arm was the most statuesque blonde Patience had ever seen without a stripper pole.

The woman introduced herself as a Natalie Something. "We met last year at the bar's program on the revised probate laws," she said, pumping Stuart's hand with enthusiasm.

"That's right," Stuart replied. "You're with Ropes Prescott. Good to see you again."

The conversation moved into a mishmash of names and companies Patience didn't know. She could see why Bernard became a deejay. The man knew how to talk. And talk. Patience put on a pretend smile and used the time to examine the lovely Natalie. Her little black dress was current. In fact, Patience was pretty sure she'd seen a picture of the dress in a fashion magazine last month. The woman knew all the "in" jokes too. Every time she laughed, she would toss her mane of blond curls and let her fingers linger on Stuart's jacket sleeve. Patience squeezed her glass. She'd wanted to know what kind of woman Stuart would date. She had a pretty good idea now. Her stomach soured.

Meanwhile, Bernard Jenkins gave her a wink.

"Excuse me," she murmured. Without bothering to see if anyone heard her, she slipped away in search of a few quiet moments in the ladies' room. The draped tables used for guest check-in were empty save for a solo volunteer who was packing unused papers into a box. She smiled as Patience walked by, the first smile she'd received outside of Stuart's all night.

"People dressed up and showing off," she repeated to herself. Was it really all a game, like Stuart said? If so, he had to be one of the winners. It was so obvious when you compared him to everyone else in the room.

"Isn't this a pleasant surprise."

Dr. Tischel came strolling out of the ballroom, with a smile as broad as the rest of him. "Twice in one day. Fortune must be smiling on me."

"Hello, Dr. Tischel."

"Karl, please." Spreading his arms, he drew her into

an unexpected hug. Pulling her close, he held on so tightly Patience had to angle her spine to prevent his hips from pressing against hers. Antiseptic and cologne assaulted her nostrils, making her grimace.

After a beat longer than necessary, she managed to extricate herself. "Is Mrs. Tischel here, too?"

"Last I heard she was in Salem with all the other witches." He laughed at his joke.

Patience took a step backward. His eyes had that glassy sheen she knew too well. She looked to the check-in table, hoping the volunteer might help, but the woman had conveniently disappeared. And she could forget Stuart. He was probably so busy talking to the lovely Natalie he didn't realize she was missing. Looked like she would have to deal with the situation the same way she'd solved problems her whole life. On her own.

She took another step backward. Distance was always the first solution. "Ana was looking better when I left her this afternoon." A safe topic always helped, too.

"Ana? Oh, Ana." He waved a sloppy hand through the air. "She's a tough old bird. Are you here alone?"

Thank goodness, a way out of this conversation without causing a scene. "No, I'm here with Ana's nephew, Stuart. In fact, he's probably——"

"The one whose girlfriend dumped him?"

"I wouldn't know anything about that," she replied. Other than thinking that if true, the woman was a fool. "I should be getting back——"

The doctor grabbed her upper arm, preventing her from passing. "Let me buy you a drink."

His hot, stale breath made her want to gag. "No."

Shoving the man with enough force that he tottered sideways, she broke free and hurried back into the ballroom.

A half dozen pairs of eyes turned in her direction. Of course. Pay attention now, after she no longer needed anyone's assistance. Wasn't that always the way? For crying out loud, but she was tired of being stared at. She looked down at her dress. Her scarf had been pushed aside during her scuffle with Dr. Tischel, revealing her ample cleavage for all the world to see. No wonder the good doctor had hit on her. She looked like a two-bit hooker.

"There you are."

The crowd parted and there was Stuart threading his way through the guests, his eyes glittering with a different kind of brightness. One that suggested he was actually glad to see her. "I was wondering where you went. Is everything all right?"

He was looking her up and down, taking in the disheveled scarf and goodness knows what else. "What happened?"

"Nothing." Patience didn't want to talk about it. Her arm hurt from where Dr. Tischel had grabbed her, and she was starting to get a headache. "I'm not feeling well is all."

He arched a brow. Why, she didn't know. She was telling the truth. She didn't feel well. "I'm—"

As if on cue, Dr. Tischel lurched by them, his shoulder striking her shoulder blade and pitching her forward. Stuart caught her by the arms before she crashed into him.

"We meet again," the doctor said. A lewd smile unfurled across his face as his eyes locked onto her exposed neckline.

In a flash, Stuart was between them, blocking the doctor's line of sight. "Maybe you should get some coffee," he said, his tone making it clear he didn't expect an argument. When the doctor had left, Stuart turned back to face Patience. "Are you all right?"

Everyone was looking at them. Patience could feel the stares on her skin, worse than before. A tiny sob escaped before she could stop it. "No," she said.

"Come on." A warm arm wrapped itself around her shoulder and guided her toward the door. "Let's get some air."

Stuart led her to an unused conference room down the hall. There weren't any chairs, but it was private. "Was he the reason you wanted to leave?"

"I ran into him outside and he got a little grabby."

"Jeez. What is it with old guys and young girls? Did he hurt you?"

"No. I'm fine." Wrapping her arms around her body, she stared out the window at the traffic on Newbury Street. She hated that she let Dr. Tischel's leering get to her. The old guy was no worse than any of the others. "I thought these people would be different."

"Different how?"

"Better, I suppose. Stupid, I know." She should have known better.

Stuart joined her at the window. His nearness made her feel warm and safe, and, while she knew she shouldn't, Patience let the sensation surround her. "Sometimes I wonder if I'll ever be more than a hot body to people."

"Hey—you are more." Gripping her shoulders, he forced her to turn around and look at him. "Way more."

If he knew how dangerously good his words made

her feel… "Not to guys like Dr. Tischel," she said. As far as she knew, there were way more of his kind than anyone else.

"Dr. Tischel is a drunken moron," Stuart replied "In fact, first thing tomorrow, I'm going to talk to Ana about switching physicians. A guy who drinks like that? I don't want him anywhere near her."

"Can we not tell her about the grabbing part? I don't want to upset her."

"I suppose that means punching him out on the dance floor is out of the question too?"

He was being purposely outrageous, and it worked. Patience smiled. "Yes, it is."

"Too bad. It'd be fun to watch the old guy fall. Nice to see you smiling again though. There's nothing worse than seeing a pretty woman looking sad. I can say you're pretty, right?"

Color flooded her cheeks. He could say anything he wanted. The man had her completely under his spell at the moment. "Thank you," she said.

"For what?"

"Being so nice. You didn't have to be." It was true. He could have let her go home in a taxi cab and wiped his hands of her. Instead, here he was making her feel… special.

"What can I say? Didn't you watch me at the silent auction table? I'm a sucker for sad brown eyes."

Patience tried to blush again, but fingers caught her chin, forcing her to hold his gaze. "I can't help myself."

"Sorry." She couldn't think of another response, her brain having short-circuited as soon as he touched her. The connection reached far deeper than her skin. Stuart didn't know it, but he was the first person besides

Piper to ever talk to her this way, as if she was a person, whole and worthwhile. Cracks formed in the wall she'd so carefully built to keep the world from closing in.

"Don't be." His touch shifted, fingers tracing their way along her jaw and across her cheek. Patience knew exactly what he was tracing. Like so much about her, the jagged line could be covered but never completely erased. She'd cut herself falling off a table. A painful reminder of what happened when a person got too close.

Stuart was breaking that rule right now. Scary as the thought was, she longed to sink into his touch.

"You still want to go back to the brownstone?" he asked.

"No,"

"Good." One word, but it—and the smile that came along—made her feel more wanted than all the words in the dictionary could.

The cracks grew wider.

He held out his hand. "Let's go get Ana her award."

Stuart still wanted to punch Karl Tischel in the nose. What was it with rich old men and young women—did they think that every woman belonged to them?

Or just the women Stuart was with?

Thinking of how many times he'd caught Tischel leering at Patience, his fingers curled into a fist. Three strikes and you're out, Doc.

When had the fight become so personal? Was it when she'd answered her bedroom door looking like an eleven-point-five on a ten-point scale? Or when he saw her walk into the ballroom pale and shaken? When had he gone from being attracted to the woman to caring about her feelings? Damn if her likability wasn't getting to him, too.

They managed to get through dinner and the awards presentation without incident. Unless you counted Bernard Jenkins's pompous droning. Honestly, did the man ever come up for air? The guy spent the entire meal giving Patience and Ethyl a grape-by-grape account of his recent trip to the Tuscan vineyards.

Bernard's date, Natalie, wasn't much better. When she wasn't agreeing with Bernard, she was laughing and tossing her hair as though every word Stuart said was the most fascinating thing she'd ever heard. The woman reminded him of Gloria. Continually on the lookout for a brighter horizon. Aging local celebrity or rich lawyer. Nerdy law student or elderly silver magnate. They made their decisions based on whatever put them on top.

Ethyl was at the podium announcing the winners of the silent auction when a flash of movement caught his eye. Turning, he saw Patience texting away on her cell phone. Suspicion tried to take hold but failed. Tonight, he was suspicioned out.

"I'm sending Ana a picture of you accepting her award," she said when she noticed he was watching.

"I don't think she's awake at this hour."

"No, but this way she'll see it first thing in the morning, and I get extra brownie points." Her smile knocked the wind from his lungs.

"And finally, the gold bracelet donated by Basmati Jewelers was won by Paul Veritek." A smattering of applause floated across the room.

"You didn't win," Patience said. "Sorry."

"I'll live." He wasn't sure what had possessed him to bid on the bracelet in the first place. Seeing Patience's bare wrists had him offering up a bid without thinking. In a room filled with expensive jewelry, the simplicity stood out. But then, she didn't need jewelry, or makeup for that matter, to stand out, did she?

"And that concludes our program," Ethyl announced. "We look forward to seeing you next year."

"Guess that means the evening is over," Patience said.

"All but the dancing." Right on schedule, a Big Band standard began to play. As he watched couples making their way to the dance floor, Stuart was suddenly gripped with the desire to join them.

"Feel like dancing?"

"I thought you said you wanted to leave right after the ceremony."

He did. He also told himself putting his arms around Patience again was the worst idea ever, but now he couldn't think of anything he'd rather do. "I changed my mind. A few dances might be fun."

"I—" He'd caught her off guard, and she was struggling with what to say. The hesitancy made his palm actually start to sweat like a high schooler.

"Okay," she said finally. "Why not?"

His thrill over her acceptance was like a high schooler's, too.

He led her to the far edge of the dance floor, where the crowd wouldn't swallow them up, and pulled her close. Last night's embrace had been tentative and accidental, but here on the dance floor, he was free to hold her as close and for as long as he liked.

They moved in sync, their bodies slipping together in a perfect fit. Not surprisingly, Patience moved with a natural rhythm, her lower half moving back and forth like the waves in an ocean. Or like a lover meeting his thrusts. Stuart rested his hand on her hip and savored every shift beneath his fingers.

The song ended, and another ballad began. And another. They danced and swayed until the deejay announced it was time to say good-night.

Patience lifted her head from his shoulder. Her eyes were as bright as he'd ever seen then, with a sheen that looked suspiciously like moisture. "Thank you for chasing Dr. Tischel out of my head," she whispered.

That was all it took. Something inside him started to fall.

They walked up Beacon Street in silence, both of them pretending to act matter-of-fact even though they both knew their relationship had changed. How and why could wait until later. Right now, Stuart was content listening to the click-clack of Patience's heels on the sidewalk and reliving the feel of her curves beneath his hands. As for Patience, she was letting her fingers glide along the fence lining Boston Public Garden. "A fancy cake for Mrs. F," she said in singsongy tone under her breath.

"Whose Mrs. F?" he asked.

She flashed him a nostalgic-looking smile. "It's from a bedtime story I used to read to Piper about a man delivering cakes around Boston. A fancy cake for Mrs. F who lived on Beacon Hill. I think of the line whenever I see this row of houses."

Another memory involving raising her sister. Interesting how easily she shared those memories yet said so little about her own childhood. Beyond what he'd pulled out of her over dinner, that is. It was as if she didn't have a childhood of her own, Considering the shadows he'd seen in her eyes last night, maybe she hadn't.

So many pieces of her he didn't understand, so many parts unrevealed.

The story she described was one you read to a young child. "How old is your sister anyway?"

"Piper? Twenty-two."

Eight years younger. "So you read your sister a bed-time story when you were a kid?"

There was a stutter in her step. "Yeah, I did."

"I'm guessing your mom worked nights."

"Um…not really. She was just…busy." The evasive-ness had returned, only this time what she didn't say came through loud and clear. If he had to guess, he'd say she'd started raising Piper long before their mother passed away. A child raising a child. He'd been right; she hadn't had a childhood of her own. She *was* like those damn dogs on the humane society poster, only in-stead of sympathy or guilt twisting in his gut, he wanted to wrap Patience in his arms and hold her tight and tell her she never had to be on her own again.

"I'm—"

"Don't." Stepping in front of him, she cut him off. "You're about to say you're sorry, and I don't want the sympathy."

"Okay, no sympathy." He understood. Sympathy was too much like pity. "How about admiration?"

"How about nothing? I did what I had to do. Trust me, I didn't do anything special," she said, turning away.

Except that Stuart didn't trust her, or had she forgot-ten? Had he forgotten for that matter?

They kept walking until they reached the State

House, the moon reflecting off its golden dome. Around the corner, Stuart spotted a trio of staggering silhouettes making their way from Park Street station. Patience was walking a few feet ahead. Her curves made her the perfect target for drunken comments. Stepping up his pace, he positioned himself on her right, creating a buffer. The group came closer, and he saw that two of the three were women teetering on high heels. The pair clung to the shoulders of the man in the middle, a pasty-looking blond who looked like he spent most of his time in dimly lit places. Their raucous laughter could be heard from ten feet away.

Stuart stole a look in Patience's direction before slipping his arm around her waist. She looked back, but didn't say anything.

As luck would have it, the trio reached the signal light the same time as they did. The man made no attempt to hide his ogling. "Come join the pah-ty, baby," he slurred, alcohol making his Boston accent thicker. "We're gonna go all night."

Patience's body turned rigid. He tightened his grip on her waist, letting her know he'd keep her safe.

The drunk slurred on, oblivious. "This dude knows what I'm talking about, doncha? Life's too short. Gotta grab the fun while you can. I did." He slapped one of the women on the rear, and she let out a giggly yelp. "Me and these ladies are just getting started."

Just then, a public works truck drove up, its bright headlights lighting their slice of the street.

"Oh, my God," one of the women cried out. "I know you!" Pushing herself free, she stumbled closer, her oversize breasts threatening to burst free from her tiny camisole top. "You work at Feathers. I danced right after you. Chablis, remember?"

Patience didn't reply. She stared straight ahead. When the light changed, she stepped off the curb and started walking. Stuart had to step quickly to keep up.

"What's the matter, you too good to talk to me now? That it?" Chablis asked as she followed. "Hey, I'm talkin' to you."

A crimson-nailed hand reached out to grab Patience's shoulder, but she quickly turned and dodged the woman's touch. "You have the wrong person," she hissed.

When they reached the opposite side of the street, Chablis looked to make one more attempt at conversation only to have her friend tug her in the opposite direction. "Come on, baby," he slurred. "We don't need them. We got better things to do."

"Yeah, Chablis," the other woman whined. "Give it up. That witch ain't owning up to nuthin'."

"But I know her," Chablis insisted, as if her knowledge was the most important discovery in the world. As she let her friends drag her away, she continued to swear and complain about being ignored. "She always did think she was better than us," Stuart heard her mutter.

"Sorry about that," he said to Patience.

"It's no big deal. They're just a bunch of drunks."

Perhaps, but the pallor of her skin said they'd upset her more than she let on. Poor thing had probably had her fill of drunks by this point.

A beer can came hurtling in their direction, rattling the sidewalk a few feet shy of where they stood. "Hey!" Chablis yelled, her voice sharp in the night. "Does your boyfriend know he's dating a stripper?"

Stuart might have laughed if Patience hadn't stopped

in her tracks. When he looked, he saw the color had drained from her face.

A sick feeling hit him in his stomach. "She's got you confused with someone else, right?" he asked.

Even in the dark of night, Patience's eyes told him everything he needed to know. There was no mistake.

Chablis was telling the truth.

CHAPTER SIX

"IT'S TRUE, ISN'T IT?" he asked. "You were a—a..."

Stripper? He couldn't even say the word, could he?

Stupid Chablis. Patience never did like the woman. For a second, she considered blaming everything on the rambling of a drunken trio, but one look at Stuart's face snuffed that idea. The thought had been planted in his head, and no amount of denial would chase it away. Eventually, he would dig up the truth. No reason to drag the ordeal out longer than necessary.

How stupid for her to think the night would end on a good note. Like she would ever earn a fairy-tale ending.

Folding her arms across her chest, Patience held on to what little dignity she could. "We prefer the term 'exotic dancer,'" she said, pushing her way past him.

"Where do you think you're going?"

"Where do you think? To the brownstone to pack my things." With luck she would get there before the tears pressing the back of her eyes broke free. Now that Stuart knew about her background, he was bound to ask her to leave her job with Ana. Hadn't he said that he didn't want Dr. Tischel anywhere near his aunt. Surely he would feel the same about Patience.

Well, she might have just lost her job, and her home,

but she would not lose her composure—not on the streets of Boston and not in front of him.

There were footsteps, and Stuart was at her shoulder, grabbing her arm much like Dr. Tischel had. With a hiss, she pulled away. The look of regret passing over his features was small compensation.

"You're not even going to try and explain yourself?"

Patience had never felt more dirty and exposed as she did under his stare, but she managed to hold herself together. "Why should I? You don't want to listen." No, he would judge her like everyone else had. The same way she judged herself. Why stick around to listen to condemnations she'd said to herself?

Stuart blocked her path. "Try me." Between the shadows and his stony expression, it was impossible to read his thoughts

They weren't the words she had expected to hear, and Patience hated how they made her heart speed up with hope. "You're really willing to listen?"

"I said I would. Don't you think you owe us an explanation?"

Us, as in him and Ana. With the shock of discovery wearing off, guilt began to take hold. She owed Ana way more than an explanation, but the truth was a good place to start. "Fine, but not here. Please." Out of the corner of her eye, she caught the silhouette of a person standing in a window. "I'll tell you everything when we're at the brownstone." Then she'd move out and never bother him or Ana again.

Neither said a word the final few blocks. Such a different silence compared to when they had left the hotel.

Then, the air had hummed with romantic possibility. This long walk was nothing but cold.

Naturally Nigel was waiting for their return, meowing and running back and forth for attention. Without a word, they walked into the kitchen so she could give Nigel his midnight snack. Attending to a cat's needs had never taken so long.

"You ready to talk?" he asked when she'd finished rinsing the can.

"Not much to say." She'd already decided to give him the shortest version possible. Less misery that way. "I needed money and dancing was the only job I could find that would pay me enough."

Minus the part where she turned down the offer twice before finally giving in, and only then because her creepy boss at the burger place wouldn't give her more hours unless she slept with him.

"Interesting." He pulled out a chair and motioned for her to take a seat. "Now how about you give me the full version?"

The full version? Her heart hitched. She'd never told anyone the *whole* story. "Why do you care about the details? It is what it is."

"Because I care." The words warmed her insides, until she reminded herself he meant "about the details." He was, after all, a lawyer. Naturally, he'd want to collect all the facts.

Question was—how many facts did he need? She'd buried so much of her story that even she wasn't sure of everything anymore.

Taking a seat, she wiped the dampness from her palms on her dress. "Where do you want me to start?"

"Try the beginning."

"I was born."

"I'm serious."

"So am I." Where *did* she begin? "I suppose every-thing really started when Piper was born. My mom—don't get me wrong, she wasn't a horrible mother. I mean, she didn't beat us or let us starve or anything like that. She just wasn't into being a mom, you know?"

A quick look across the table said he didn't, but she plowed ahead. "I think she thought a baby would keep Piper's dad around, but..."

She shrugged. That was her mother's pipe dream, not hers. "Anyway, as soon as I got old enough, she left taking care of Piper to me. But I told you that already."

"'A fancy cake for Mrs. F,'" he recited. "How old were you?"

"Twelve or thirteen? Thirteen, I think. It wasn't that hard," she added quickly. As was the case whenever a person looked askance at the arrangement, her de-fensiveness rose up. "Piper was a good kid. She never caused trouble, always did her homework. Plus, she could cook."

"A thirteen-year-old taking care of a five-year-old. You didn't resent it?"

Her automatic answer was always no. For some reason—the way Stuart looked to be reading her mind maybe—the answer died in favor of the truth. "Some-times, but I didn't have a choice. She was family. I had a responsibility."

From behind his coffee cup, she saw Stuart give a small nod and realized if anyone understood the im-portance of family responsibility, he would. After all, wasn't his devotion to Ana the spark that had led to this conversation?

She continued. "When my mom died, Piper and I were left alone. I promised her we would stay together no matter what."

"And that's why you needed the money? For Piper?"

"Yeah." She stared into her cup, unsure how to continue. Talking about Piper was the easy part. It wasn't until after their mom died that the story turned bad. "My mom left us broke. Worse than broke. Actually. I didn't know what else to do."

"What about assistance? There are programs…"

"You don't understand. It wasn't that easy." How could he? Man like him, who never wanted for anything.

"But surely—"

"We were living in our car!" She hurled the answer across the table, the first time she'd ever acknowledged what happened aloud. "We were afraid if we told anyone, Piper would end up in child services, and I swore that wouldn't happen." In her mind, she saw her sister's frightened face, heard the desperation in her voice. She squeezed her eyes shut, but the memories stayed all the same. "I couldn't break my promise to her. We were all each other had. Losing her would have been like…like…"

"Losing your own child."

"Yes." His answer gave her hope that he understood. Opening her eyes, she stared across the table, silently pleading her case. "I would have done anything to keep her safe. Anything."

This was the place in the story where she should stop. Having justified her actions, there was no reason to share any more. The problem was that talking about the past was like cracking a glass. Once begun, the crack didn't stop spreading until it reached its nat-

ural end. And so the words continue to flow. "There
was this guy who lived near us. Named Ben. He was
always hitting on me, telling me how hot I was. Used
to tell me a girl built like me could rake it in at the club
where he worked. I always ignored him. Until I didn't
have a choice anymore."

Unable to sit still any longer, Patience pushed herself
away from the table and crossed to the back window.
Her distorted reflection stared back at her in the glass.
"It was January. We hadn't eaten all day. I'd lost my
job—we didn't have money. Piper had a cold. Sounds
like one of those over-the-top TV movies, doesn't it?"
she said with a hollow laugh.

"Go on."

"I didn't know what else to do," she whispered. The
desperation and shame she'd felt that fateful day returned as fresh as ever, rising up to choke the air from
her lungs. "I told myself it was only for a little while.
Until Piper and I were on our feet." The delusion of
youth and hopelessness.

"How long did that take?"

Why was he asking? He could guess the answer.
Until she went to work for Ana.

"That's the trick life plays on you," she said, resting her head against the glass. "You tell yourself it's
only for a few weeks, a few months tops. Next thing
you know, a few months turns into a year. Two. After
a while, you start to think maybe you can't do any better. I mean, you've got no experience, so any job you
can get doesn't pay nearly as much and that's assuming you could even get another job. Who's going to hire
someone who danced on a table?"

"Table? Is that—?"

"Yeah. A drunk grabbed my ankle." Her breath left a smudge on the pane. Using her scarf, she wiped the mark away. If only life could clean up so easily. "Sometimes I think, if only I'd held out one more day…

"I can still feel their eyes on me," she whispered. "At night. Watching me with their dull, glassy eyes. Fantasizing about what they want to do with me." She slapped a hand against her mouth to keep from gagging as the memories began to choke her. A sob broke through anyway. "They made me feel so dirty."

"Shh." Once again Stuart was there, his face joining hers in the glass. Didn't matter that he wasn't touching her, his proximity was good enough.

"But I kept my promise," she said. "I kept us off the streets and I gave Piper a normal life." Of all the regrets she had in her life, keeping Piper safe wasn't one. "Whenever things got really bad, that's what I would tell myself. *I kept my promise.*"

Behind her, Stuart let out a long, loud breath. An echo of her own exhaustion. She hadn't expected to share so much. Telling Stuart details she'd never told anyone…the ordeal left her raw and exposed. "You said you wanted the long version."

"Yes, I did."

There was another sigh. Patience imagined him washing a hand over his features as he tried to digest everything. What would he think if he knew the one detail she'd kept back? But how could she tell him when she could barely admit the secret to herself?

"I know you think I had some big agenda, but I didn't. I ran into Ana and she confused me with a job applicant. I let her believe that's who I was and interviewed for the job." She turned so he could see she was being as honest as possible. "Ana was the first person besides Piper who ever treated me like I mattered. I swear I would never hurt her. I just needed to get out."

"You do matter," Stuart whispered.

She hated the way his words warmed her from the inside out. More so, how she couldn't help following them up with a pitiful "I do?"

"Yeah, you do." His thumb brushed her cheek, chasing away tears she didn't know had fallen. "And you deserved better."

She was too tired to argue otherwise. He'd asked for her story and she'd told him. "If you want me to leave, I will," she told him. She'd lied, and deception came with a price. Thankfully she'd squirreled away enough money so she wouldn't have to worry about living on the streets this time around. If she kept her expenses low, she'd be all right. She was a survivor.

"You don't have to leave," Stuart told her. "We all have things in our past we regret."

Tears turned her vision watery, but they were happy tears this time. "Thank you...I know I should have told the truth from the start, but I was afraid if Ana knew what I was, she would want nothing to do with me. And then, of course, you arrived, talking about how you didn't trust me and..."

"I was pretty inexorable, wasn't I?"

"If that's your way of saying you were acting like a jerk?" She was finally beginning to relax. "Then yeah."

"I'm sorry about that. You can blame Gloria."

Right. The step-grandmother. "I think I'm beginning to dislike her as much as you do."

"Trust me, that's not possible."

It was, once again, a comfortable silence wrapping around them. Patience felt lighter than she had in months—since the day she accepted the job, really. It was as if a thousand pounds had been lifted from her shoulders. Maybe, if she was lucky, the rest of her story would die a silent death, and she could enjoy that relief, as well.

"It's late," Stuart said. "You look exhausted."

She was drained. And sad, in spite of her relief. This wasn't how she'd expected the night to end. There had been magic in the air on that dance floor. For a little while she'd felt like Cinderella at the ball. But it was time to come back to reality. Having told her story, there was no way Stuart would ever look at her the same way again.

How could he? She was no longer a housekeeper; she was a housekeeper who used to take her clothes off for money.

"If it's all right with you, I think I'm going to go to bed."

"Yes, of course. I'll see you tomorrow. Good night."

"Good night." She had moved to leave when the need to say one last thing stopped her. "Thank you again for understanding." He'd probably never know how much it meant to her. On so many levels.

She expected a simple *you're welcome* in return, mainly because there didn't seem to be anything more to say. But Stuart didn't utter a word. Instead, his hand reached out to cradle her cheek. Patience's breath caught. How could a man's touch be so gentle and yet so strong? Her body yearned to lean into his hand. To close her eyes and let his strength hold her up. He swept his thumb across her cheekbone, stopping at the top of her scar. After what felt like forever, his hand dropped away. "Good night."

Patience's heart was racing so fast she was convinced it would reach her bedroom first. Twice in two nights, she'd come dangerously close to breaking the rules when it came to keeping her distance. The third time, she might not be able to walk away.

He'd wanted to know her secret. He finally did and, man, was it a doozy. Never in a million years would he have imagined Patience was…had been…he couldn't even think the word. That she'd been forced to make those kinds of choices… It made him sick to his stomach to think that in this day and age she'd felt there was no other way.

Took guts, what she'd done. And strength. Real strength. She was barely an adult and yet she'd kept her family together.

If her story was true, that is, and not some ploy for sympathy.

Immediately, he shook the distrust from his head. Damn, but he'd become such a skeptical jerk. Patience was telling the truth. He saw it in her eyes. At least he wanted to believe that's what he was seeing. He wanted to believe her as badly as he wanted to hold her. Which, he thought, washing a hand over his face, was pretty damn bad.

They were two very scary realizations.

"Nigel, why do you insist on being in the one place that makes doing my job difficult?" Patience narrowed her eyes at the cat, who, as usual, was ignoring her question. He was too busy poking at imaginary enemies in Ana's dresser drawer.

It'd been twelve long days since the dinner dance,

and she was finally starting to believe that she was keeping her job. Stuart hadn't brought up the confession again. Of course, he also made himself as scarce as possible. He was on his way out the door when she woke up, and away until she went to bed. Except for that first morning when they'd recapped the dance for Ana, he'd even taken to keeping a different visiting schedule. None of his avoidance surprised her. Understanding was one thing, wanting to associate with her was another.

Back at the club, they had a saying: Prince Charming ain't walking through that door. No matter how good-looking or how amazing some guy might seem, the two of you weren't going to ride off into the sunset on his white horse. She was smart enough to know the same rule applied to housekeepers and their bosses. Say she and Stuart had slept together that night. It wouldn't have been anything more than a short-term fling, right? Being help with benefits wasn't her style. What self-respect she had, she'd like to keep, thank you very much.

So Stuart avoiding her was a good thing. Honestly.

"Will you quit it?" She found a way out of her thoughts in time to catch Nigel snagging the lace on a pair of Ana's undergarments. "I'm pretty sure Ana wants her clothes unmolested," she said. The cat pawed at the air as she took the panties away and refolded them. Feeling bad that she'd disturbed his fun, Patience scratched behind his ear. She had a feeling part of Nigel's more-than-usual peskiness was because he missed Ana. Their promise to bring him for visits, it turned out, had been a bad idea. Nigel treated the rehab facility as he did the brownstone and wandered at will. It had taken her almost an hour to find out what room he had moved into for naptime.

"Ana will be home in another few days. In the meantime, how about you give me ten more minutes, and then we'll have a good long petting session."

As usual, Nigel wasn't interested in bargaining. He wanted his attention and he wanted it now. Somehow he managed to wedge his head and paws into the drawer opening, and began chewing on something.

Patience rolled her eyes. "What are you doing now? Please tell me you're not trying to eat Ana's underwear." She opened the drawer and saw that the cat had found a box and was attempting to bite the corner of the cover. Her sorting and taking things the past few days must have unearthed it from the bottom of the drawer.

"You really do want to eat everything in sight, don't you?" Lifting them both free, she plopped Nigel on the bed before placing the box on the bureau. As soon as she was finished, she'd put the box back safely at the bottom of the drawer.

A knock sounded behind her. "Somehow I didn't picture you as a granny panties kind of girl," Stuart said. The sound of his voice made her stomach tumble. Swallowing back the reaction, she glanced over her shoulder. "I'm putting away Ana's laundry and packing some new items. You know, for a woman with expensive tastes, she has the most disorganized drawers I've ever seen."

It didn't skip Patience's notice that only a week before, he would have questioned what she was doing rather than make a joke. While she was touched by the show of trust, she sort of missed the protection her defensiveness gave her. When he was nice, it made keeping her distance that much harder.

"Surprised to see you here so early," she said. Here at all, really.

"We closed shop early for the holiday, and since Ana takes her post Physical Therapy nap around this time, I figured I'd work at home."

"That's right, tomorrow's Fourth of July." With all the coming and going, she'd forgotten the date. "Ana told me once how she usually has a barbecue on the roof deck."

"Barbecue in the sense that she has a caterer bring in barbecued chicken," Stuart replied. "She and her humane society buddies have been doing it for years."

"She must be devastated to have to cancel."

"Not as much as you'd think. Last I heard, Ethyl was moving the event to the rehab hospital."

Patience envisioned Ana, Ethyl and the others invading the rehab terrace with their catered dinner and cocktails. "Maybe I should be devastated on behalf of the hospital."

"Don't be. I'm sure there's a donation involved." He sat down on the edge of the bed. It was the longest and closest they'd been together since the dance. Patience studied the hands clasped between his legs. All too clear was the memory of those hands holding her close. Fingers burning a hole in the fabric of her dress. She turned back to the underwear drawer.

"Sorry I haven't been around much lately. Work has been slamming," he said.

Even the weekends? "You don't have to explain your schedule to me." Or make excuses, for that matter.

"I know, but..." The mattress made a settling noise, and she imagined him shrugging. "But I didn't want you to think that after the other night, I was...well, you know."

"Yeah." She knew. She wasn't sure she believed him, but she knew.

"Anyway, I was wondering what you were doing tomorrow."

Patience's stomach dropped. He was going to tell her he was hosting some kind of event himself, wasn't he? If she wanted a distance reminder, being asked to wait on his friends would certainly fit the bill. "It's a normal paid day off," she told him, "but if you are planning something…"

"Actually, I was wondering if you would mind checking out a condominium with me."

"What?"

"You know the new luxury tower they built near the Leather District? One of our clients is the developer. Sounds like a pretty awesome property."

"I'm sure it is." Weren't most million-dollar properties? Patience tried to ignore the pang in her chest. From the very start, Stuart had said this living arrangement was temporary. Now that Ana was close to being discharged, there was no reason for him not to look for a place of his own. What did the decision have to do with her, though?

"I was hoping you'd check out the property with me. Give me your opinion."

"The housekeeper's point of view?"

He grinned. "I was thinking more of a female point of view, but if you want to weigh in on how difficult the place will be to keep clean, feel free. Don't feel like you have to though. I know it's your day off, but if you do say yes, I'd make it worth your while."

"Worth my while, eh?" Talk about loaded language. She shivered at the potential prospects. "How?"

"I will personally show you the best seat in all of Boston for watching the fireworks."

Patience chewed the inside of her mouth. Goodness, but it was impossible to say no. Especially when the idea of sitting with him beneath the stars was so seductive.

"Sure." There'd be plenty of time to kick herself for the decision later. "What time?"

"After lunch. I figured we'd go see Ana, then meet up with Nikko. He's the developer."

"It's a—plan." She almost slipped and called it a date. Luckily she caught herself at the last moment.

What she should have been trying to catch was Nigel. Tired of being ignored, he leaped from the bed to the bureau. Problem was, he miscalculated the distance. His front paws connected with the box she'd set on the bureau, flipping it end over end. Off flew the cover, sending the contents flying.

"Bad kitty," she said. The admonishment was useless since Nigel had already bolted from the room in embarrassment.

"Here, let me help you." Stuart crouched by her on the floor, his unique Stuart scent filling the space between them. Patience had to struggle not to close her eyes and inhale. "The box was in Ana's drawer," she explained. "Nigel started chewing the cover so I moved it to the bureau." To keep it out of his reach. So much for that idea.

"Looks like a bunch of photographs."

Mementos was more like it. Patience spied newspaper clippings, tickets, playbills, what looked like drawings scribbled on napkins. Piper had kept a similar box when she was a kid.

She picked up one of the newspaper clippings. The article was written in a foreign language.

"French," Stuart said when she showed him.

"Don't suppose you can read it?"

"Sorry. Russian."

And she'd barely made it through Spanish. "This is where we need Piper."

The date said it was from the early fifties. Ana would have been just out of high school. Patience couldn't help wondering what had made her hold on to the article. The photo accompanying the article featured a trio of men standing together in front of a painting. Nothing very exciting. She was about to put the clipping in the box when one of the names jumped from the page.

"Stuart, look." She pointed to the caption. "One of the men is named Nigel Rougeau. Think it's a coincidence?"

"I don't know. The name Nigel had to come from somewhere." He slipped the clipping from her fingers and studied it closer. Like a lawyer examining evidence, Patience thought. "Looks like this was taken at some kind of art show. The wall is lined with paintings."

"But which one is Nigel?"

"Well, I can't say for sure, but based on the names listed in the caption, I'd say the one in the middle." He pointed to the bearded man with intense, dark eyes. "In fact…" He picked up one of the scattered photographs. "Here he is."

Sure enough, it was the same bearded man, only this time he was leaning against a motorbike. There were other photos, too. Nigel on the beach. In a café. One showed him standing in what looked to be an artist's studio, looking very serious and artistic as he dabbed paint on a canvas. Whoever he was, he'd obviously played a very important role in Ana's life. Important and personal.

"We should put these away," she said. It didn't feel right, poking through Ana's past. "This is obviously something very private or she wouldn't have stashed the box in her underwear drawer."

"You're right. This is none of our business." One of the pictures had fluttered a few feet away. Leaning forward, Stuart picked it up and was about to add it to the box when he froze. "Well, I'll be," he muttered.

"What?" Patience looked over his shoulder. It was another studio photo, not very different from the other one, except for maybe a few additional paintings on the wall.

"Check out the painting to the left of the easel."

It was nude portrait. A large one featuring a woman sprawled on a sofa. She was smiling at the artist, as if they shared a secret. Even in the background of a snapshot she could feel the intimacy. But why did Stuart want her to look?

"Don't you recognize the face. The smile?"

Patience studied it closer. "No way…" The smile was the same one that had greeted her the day she took the job. "Ana modeled for him?"

"More than modeled, I'd say. Which," he said, dropping the photograph into the box, "has me feeling extra slimy for poking around."

"Yeah, definitely." Looked like Ana had her own secrets. Patience could respect that.

With the items collected, she reached for the box cover only to have Stuart reach at the same time. Their hands collided, his fingers skimming the tops of hers. Patience stilled. It was but a whisper of a touch, but it brought her skin to life with a tingling sensation that enveloped her entire body.

For most of her adult life, Patience had avoided physical contact. Look, don't touch. That was the rule. But with Stuart, even the lightest of touches had her craving more. She longed for him to take her hand. Pull her into his arms and hold her like he had the night of the dance.

She needed to back away before she lost her head. One look at Stuart's eyes said he was fighting the same battle.

"I'd better put this away before the contents spill again," she said, her voice a whisper.

"Good idea."

They stayed put, each waiting for the other to move.

"I—"

"Yeah," Stuart completed for her. He pushed himself to his feet, then offered a hand to help her up. Patience declined. Better she stand on her own two feet.

"I'll let you know what time we're going to meet Nikko tomorrow."

Who? The condominium. How could she forget. "I'll be here," she told him.

Stuart looked about to say something, only to think better of it. With one last look, he turned and left the room.

She didn't realize how badly she wanted him to stay until his footsteps had faded away.

CHAPTER SEVEN

"WE APPRECIATE YOU opening the office for us on a holiday, Nikko. I hope we didn't screw up your plans."

"Are you kidding? My wife's got her sisters at the beach house for the weekend. I'd rather do this than deal with holiday traffic any day."

Stuart and Patience shared a smile as the realtor herded them onto the elevator. While Nikko chose the floor, Stuart made a point of positioning himself in the middle. It was no secret that his client had a roving eye. The man had already stolen a glance at Patience's behind. Stuart wasn't going to let him steal another.

From the start, it had bothered him to see men checking her out. Knowing her secret, however, added a layer of protectiveness. He felt compelled to keep her from being objectified. Especially by men like Nikko Popolous.

Okay, perhaps he was doubly compelled to protect her from Nikko, whose silver hair and good looks had half the women at the firm sighing with longing.

For her part, Patience dressed in her usual nondescript style. Flowing sleeveless top and cropped jeans. He wished he knew a way to tell her that disguising her figure wasn't working. It wasn't her figure that turned men's heads—it was the whole package.

He ran his thumb across his fingertips remembering how close he'd come to kissing her yesterday. Clearly a dozen days of keeping his distance had done nothing to kill his attraction. Like that was a surprise.

But wouldn't acting on his desire make him no better than Karl Tischel and the other creeps? Worse actually, since a week ago he'd been telling her he didn't trust her. She deserved more respect than that.

"This is one of our prime corner units," Nikko was saying as he unlocked the door. "The natural lighting is out of this world."

Patience let out a small gasp as they stepped inside. "This place is amazing!" A poker-faced negotiator, she was not.

She was right, though. The condo was nice. Hard-wood floors, tons of windows.

"The open floor plan makes this a great place for entertaining," Nikko told them.

Stuart was more entertained by the sparkle in Patience's eyes as she ran a hand across the top of the kitchen island. "Everything is so clean and new."

"Top-of-the-line, too," Nikko told her. "The cabinets are solid cherry."

"There's a double oven! And a wine cooler." She smiled at Stuart. "Piper would go crazy if she saw this place."

"You need to check out the terrace. Wraps around the whole unit. Gives you another two hundred square feet. And the best part is, you don't have to share with the other tenants." The realtor slid open one of the window panels and stepped outside. "Check out this view," he said to Patience.

Stuart guided Patience out into the hot, humid air, resisting the urge to place his hand against the small of her back. The way her shirt fluttered when she walked suggested the material was light and thin. If he touched her back, he'd feel straight through to her skin and that would open up far too many problems.

"Great view, huh?"

It was nice; you could see Boston Common in the distance.

"Bet it's great at night," Patience remarked.

"Oh, at night it's spectacular," Nikko said. "There's another door that leads out here from the master bedroom. You think the kitchen was a nice setup, wait till you see the bathroom. My own bathroom isn't this fancy."

The sales patter continued while Nikko led him back into the condo and down the hall. Stuart didn't listen. A sales pitch was a sales pitch. All he wanted was a place to sleep that accrued a good return on investment.

Damn, but he'd grown jaded.

Once upon a time, he might have hunted for a home instead of an investment. When he was younger. Someplace like what he remembered sharing with his parents.

Of course, maybe things would be different if he were condo shopping with someone. Someone whose eyes sparkled with excitement.

The bathroom was impressive. Designer vanities, giant sunken tub in thecorner. "Beat's Ana's claw-foot tub, doesn't it?" he said to Patience.

There was no answer.

"I think she stayed on the terrace," Nikko remarked.

Indeed, when Stuart stepped through the bedroom slider, he found her in the same place as before, her attention fixed on some faraway point.

He had to stop and grab the railing as desire rolled through him. Why was keeping his distance a bad idea again?

It wasn't until he walked closer that he saw the sadness behind the faraway gaze. "Everything all right?"

"Great," she replied. "Why wouldn't it be?"

He settled in next to her. "You tell me. You looked a million miles away."

"I was thinking how you could fit my old apartment into this place's living room."

"It's the lack of furniture. Makes the space seem bigger."

"No, our apartment was that small."

There was regret in her voice that didn't belong. "Bet it was easy to clean," he teased.

He got the smile he was hoping for. "Didn't take long, for sure."

Nor, Stuart bet, did the apartment ever feel empty and cold. "And, you had your sister."

"True. I'd pick small over losing her in a second, even if she did take over the bathroom when she hit high school. There was only one electrical plug that could handle a blow-dryer," she said when he chuckled. "For four years, I was lucky to get my hair dried in time for work."

Patience would never believe him, but he envied her. Her closeness with her sister, that is. Despite everything the two of them had endured, they'd always had each other to cling to. He wished he had that kind of support. Sure, he had Ana, but their closeness hadn't really de-

veloped until he came east for law school. Before that…
well, no wonder Gloria was able to charm him blind.

Looking to the ground, he concentrated on plowing
little piles of grit and dirt with his shoe. "My grandfather's house was big," after a moment. "It actually
had wings."

"You mean like in west wing, east wing—that sort
of thing?"

"Uh-huh." Though his attention remained on the
ground, he imagined her eyes widening. "There were
literally days when I wouldn't see Grandpa Theodore
even though we were in the same house."

"Not at all?"

"Not unless I went looking for him." Attempts that
were met with varying degrees of success.

"I'm sorry."

No, he didn't want her sympathy any more than she
did. "He was…busy," he said too, to steal her word.

Patience slid her hand to the left until their fingers
aligned, her little finger flush with his. "I understand."

Yeah, she did, thought Stuart, but then he'd known
as much for a while. Same way he knew that as lonely
as his teenage years had been, they were a cakewalk
compared to hers.

He itched to cover her hand with his and entwine
their fingers. Would she pull away if he did?

"The view is irresistible, isn't it?" Nikko stepped
onto the terrace, making the decision for him. The realtor waved his phone. "Sorry. My wife couldn't find
the air pump. Don't know why—the thing's right in the
center of the garage."

"Are you telling this guy he needs to buy?" Nikko
asked Patience.

She laughed. "I think that's up to him."

"Maybe, but I did bring you here for input. What do you think?"

"I think this is the most amazing apartment I've ever seen outside of Ana's brownstone."

"Those brownstones are great, but they come with their headaches. Like parking. Brownstones don't come with parking," Nikko said. "And did you see the cedar closet in the laundry area? Solid cedar, not veneer. A moth would need a drill to get at your winter wardrobe. To put something like that in custom would cost you a fortune."

As opposed to spending a fortune on a condominium that already had one. Stuart was about to reply when he realized Nikko had been directing his remarks to Patience. He was assuming it would be her wardrobe hanging in the cedar closet.

Patience, staying here. The idea didn't strike him nearly as improbable as it should. On the contrary, the longing from earlier reared again, tendrils spreading up and across his chest. He hadn't realized until just now that when he left Ana's brownstone, he would be leaving Patience behind. Strange as it seemed, he'd grown used to sharing a space with her. He would miss her presence. That's what the ache in his chest was all about. He was going to miss having company.

"All I'm saying is that most people would have at least slept on the decision," Patience said when they got back to the brownstone.

"I don't know why you're so surprised. You said yourself the place was amazing."

"It is. But I didn't mean for you to whip out your

checkbook and write a down payment." Last thing she wanted was the responsibility of having influenced his decision. Picking up Nigel's dish, she headed to the cupboard. "How do you know there isn't someplace better out there?" she asked, pulling out a can of Salmon Delight.

"There might be, and if I were looking for the perfect apartment, that would be important, but I'm not. This place is close to my office, and a good investment. I had pretty much made up my mind to buy if the space was halfway decent."

If that was so, why invite her?

"I really did want a second opinion," he replied when she asked. "If both of us liked the space, then I knew the condo was a winner."

"Oh, sure, because I've so much experience buying luxury property. You do realize when I said it was the most amazing place outside of the brownstone that it was also the only other high-end place I've ever looked at."

"You sell yourself short. You zoned right in on the areas I wanted an opinion on. The laundry room, the kitchen, the living space."

All the cleaning woman areas of expertise. She winced and tried to take the compliment the way he meant. "The kitchen was nice."

"So I could tell by the way your eyes lit up." Okay, now she was blushing. He was studying her eyes?

"Here I thought I was being so calm and sophisticated."

"You were being yourself, which—before you make a comment—is exactly what I wanted. You'll argue otherwise, but you're not very good when it comes to hiding your thoughts."

"I'm not?" Impossible. She'd spent years cultivating her stone face. She knew how to block out the audience with the best of them.

However, she had been off her game since Stuart moved in. Did that mean he knew how badly she'd been struggling to keep her attraction at arm's length?

Luckily, Stuart couldn't see her face or he'd really be able to read her feelings. The overheated cheeks were a dead giveaway.

"How else do you think I figured out you were keeping secrets? Your eyes gave you away. They always do," he said. "I see it all the time in depositions. Body language is a killer. Although in this case…you weren't exactly hiding your enthusiasm."

"I did gush a little, didn't I?"

"A little?" Patience didn't have to be a body language expert to read the amusement on his face.

"Okay, a lot," she conceded. "That didn't mean you had to buy the place. I don't think I could be that impulsive." She had trouble buying anything on a whim. What if you needed the cash later on?

"I told you, I had already decided—"

"Before we got there. I know what you said, but this afternoon was still the first time you saw the place. That, to me, is impulsive. How do you know you got the best place?"

He shrugged. "It's just a condominum."

"Just?" His comment made it sound as if he was settling, and while Patience wasn't expecting him to gush about the place like her, she had expected him to at least care about where he lived.

"I work seventy to eighty hours a week," he explained. "I'm hardly ever home. As long as the place is close to my office and can fit a bed, that's all I care about."

So he was settling. Patience wasn't sure what saddened her more: that or how little he had in his life. Something Karl Tischel said at the dinner dance popped into her head. *The one whose girlfriend dumped him.* Was work the reason? Or did he work because he'd been dumped? Either way, his life sounded lonely. Correction. He sounded lonely, Patience realized.

Apparently, she wasn't the only one who couldn't hide her emotions.

Even so, she shouldn't want to reach out and comfort him the way she did. Certainly not after watching him spend a million dollars without blinking an eye. What more proof did she need that they were from different worlds?

And yet his loneliness spoke to a place deep inside her, making her feel closer to him than ever.

"What's with the take-out bag?" In Stuart's hand was a large white paper bag with handles. On the way home, he'd insisted they stop at the local market. He made her wait outside while he went in, only to return a few minutes later with a bag of food. Patience had been curious then, and she was doubly curious now. She leaped on the topic as the perfect change of conversation.

"Dinner," he replied. "I seem to recall promising you a picnic and fireworks."

"Yes, you did. The best seats in Boston, you said."

"Trust me, they are."

Nigel sauntered into the kitchen and crouched by his empty food dish, waiting for Patience to fill it. The minute Patience crossed his path, he began weaving around and between her legs. "You're lucky we aren't on the stairs," she told him.

"Don't you mean *you're* lucky?" Stuart replied. "As far as I can tell, Nigel isn't the one who gets hurt."

"True." Patience thought of the photographs they'd found yesterday. Ana had once said Nigel had a "Nigel personality." If the original was as pesky as his namesake, that might explain why he wasn't around anymore.

Behind her, Stuart was unpacking the tote bag. She saw containers loaded with potato salad, fried chicken, fruit and chocolate cake—enough to feed a full army. "So where is this awesome picnic spot?" she asked. "Near the Boston Esplanade?"

"Nope. The roof."

"Ana's roof?"

"Sure. That's why the humane society insists she throw the summer barbeques here. You won't find a better view, not even on the Esplanade."

He pointed to the utility closet in the corner of the kitchen. "Is the portable radio still on the shelf?"

"I think so."

"Great. Grab it and a couple of glasses, will you? I'll go set up the table."

The rooftop deck had been something of a marvel to Patience. Before her accident, Ana had ocassionally taken afternoon tea up there. In Patience's old neighborhood, a deck meant a place to keep a couple plastic chairs or small table for eating outside, but Ana's deck was an outside living room. No plastic chairs or cheap furniture here. Instead, there was a love seat and matching chairs. Floor lamps, too. Four of them, one in each corner so as to light the entire space once the sun went down. Potted evergreens and other plants brought nature into the arrangement while a pair of heaters added warmth in the colder weather.

One of her first major housekeeping projects had been to bring the cushions indoors and cover the furniture. Then, as she did now, she found herself in awe that such a beautiful room could exist outdoors.

It was a perfect summer night, made for sitting under the stars. A three-quarter moon hung high and yellow in the cloudless sky. Before them a mosaic of rooftops and lights spread as far as the eye could see. The beacon atop old John Hancock Tower glowed blue, telegraphing the beautiful weather to anyone who needed reminding.

Stuart was opening a bottle of wine when she arrived. "You don't mind, do you?" he asked her. "If you'd rather, there's water…"

"No, wine would be great." Even if it did make the atmosphere feel more date-like. "After all, it's a holiday right?"

"Right. What's Independence Day without a toast to freedom?"

Walking over to the edge of the deck, Patience looked out across the city. "I can see your apartment building from here, I think. Over there." She pointed to a tower in the distance. "I can't remember if I could see Ana's roof from the terrace or not."

"We'll have to stand outside and wave to each other someday to find out." He appeared at her elbow, carrying a glass of wine in each hand. Handing her one, he raised the other. "To freedom."

Patience gave a slight smile as she raised hers in return. "One of us achieved freedom today. How long before you move?"

"The end of the month, I think. I want to make sure Ana's mobile enough before I go, so as to not put all the burden on you."

"That's sweet of you."

"I want to." Perhaps, but Patience didn't harbor any illusions. He was looking out for Ana because he loved his aunt, not her.

Not that love had anything to do with anything.

"Did I say something wrong?"

And here she thought staring at her glass would keep her eyes from giving her away. "Just thinking a month wasn't that far away. Ana will be sorry to see you go."

"Ana?" He moved in tighter, giving her little choice but to turn and meet his gaze. Questions hung in the back of their blue depths. He knew she meant both her and Ana, but she couldn't bring herself to admit it.

"Don't be silly. You know she adores you. It has to be killing her to be in the hospital while you're here in the brownstone."

"It's killing me," he replied. "Seeing her laid up reminds me of how old she's getting. And how frail."

"Part of me wants to think she'll be here forever," he added, contemplating the contents of his glass.

Patience could feel the regret pressing down on his shoulders and rushed to reassure him. "We always want to think that the people we love will stay forever. I'm as guilty as you are. I want to believe Piper will be part of my world forever, but someday she's going to have a life of her own. It's already started."

"You make it sound like she'll forget you exist."

"Forget no, but she'll have other priorities beyond her

big sister." The way it was supposed to be. She hadn't sacrificed in order for Piper to stay by her side.

"Maybe you'll be too busy having a life of your own to notice."

Doing what? Cleaning? "Oh, I'll have a life, but I want more for Piper. I want her to have everything. Love, family, a home."

"Who says you won't have those things, too?"

She'd love to have them, but they seemed too far out of reach. Easier to wish happiness for Piper. "Maybe someday," she said, speaking into her wine. "At the moment, I'm happy where I am. Working for Ana."

"You know you deserve more, right?" His fingers caught her chin and turned her face toward him. "Right?" he repeated.

Patience wanted to tell him to stop being so kind. Things were easier when he'd been suspicious. At least then she knew the dividing line. Attraction bad, distance good. When he was sweet and tender like this, the line blurred. She could feel the cracks in her invisible wall growing bigger. Pretty soon there would be no wall at all to protect her.

But she couldn't tell him any of that—not without admitting his growing hold over her. "Maybe someday," she repeated with a smile. Stepping away from his touch, she looked to the Esplanade, the long expanse of green lining the Charles River. "You're right, this is the best picnic spot. You can see the Hatch Shell," she said, jumping once again to a safe topic. The area around the open-air stage glowed white from all the spotlights and television trucks. "I swear I can hear the music."

"I'm not surprised. We're close enough." Behind her, Patience heard shuffling, and suddenly the music grew louder. He'd turned on the radio simulcast. "There," she heard him say, "that's better than straining to catch a stray chord. Sounds like the concert just started. Plenty of time before the fireworks."

"Do you know," Patience said, stepping away from the view, "that I've never seen the July Fourth fireworks live?"

"Really?"

"Nope. Just on TV. Piper was afraid of loud noises so I never took her. We stayed home and watched them on TV instead."

"How about when you were a kid? Sorry." He seemed to realize his mistake as soon as he spoke.

"That's all right. There are worse things to miss out on." She took a plate and started helping herself to the food. "How about you? What did your family do on Fourth of July?"

"Nothing. I was at camp, learning important wilderness survival techniques, like how not to lose your inhaler while hiking."

She laughed.

"I'm not kidding," he said. "I lost that sucker twice one summer. Kept falling out of my pocket."

"I'm sorry," Patience said, "but I'm having a hard time picturing you as this awkward asthmatic."

"Remind me to show you my high school graduation photo someday. You'll believe me then."

"Well, you're definitely not awkward now."

"Thank you." Stuart's smile had an odd cast to it, almost as if he didn't quite believe her. Which was ridiculous, because surely he knew what kind of man he was, didn't he?

They ate in silence, letting the music fill in for conversation. It never failed to surprise Patience how comfortable just being with Stuart could be. Simmering attraction aside, that is. Maybe it was more that she never felt uncomfortable with him. Never felt like he was trying to mentally undress her. Even those moments of intense scrutiny, when his eyes bore down on her, weren't about her figure, but rather what was inside. With him, Patience never felt like less than a person.

It was a gift she'd never forget.

Feeling a lump begin to rise in her throat, she reached for her wine. This wasn't the time for tears.

"How do you think Ana's party is going? She seemed pretty excited when we saw her this morning."

"Going great, I'm sure." Stuart smiled while wiping the grease from his fingers. "No doubt she and her cronies have commandeered the entire hospital sunroom and put the staff to work. Those ladies can be a force to be reckoned with. Don't be surprised if we show up tomorrow and hear they had the whole hospital involved."

Patience could picture the scene. "They'll miss her when she's discharged." She sipped her wine thoughtfully. "I'm surprised you're not at a party yourself."

"I promised you a picnic for viewing the condo with me."

"We could have done it a different night." He must have had better options than spending the night with her.

"No, I said I'd show you the best place to see the fireworks. Besides, I wanted to."

Patience tried not to get too excited by the remark. Unfortunately, she failed. The idea that Stuart had chosen her warmed her to the core. "I hope your friends aren't too disappointed."

"They'll survive, I'm sure." He stared at his drink, looking as if he was debating saying more. "I don't— I don't have a lot of friends. At least not close ones."

"I'm surprised."

He looked up. "Are you? In case you haven't noticed, I tend to be rather suspicious of people."

Because of Gloria? Wow, his step-grandmother had really done a number on him. Or was there someone else who'd hurt him, too? The woman who "dumped him" maybe?

"Dr. Tischel told me about your ex-girlfriend," she told him.

"What did he say?"

She was right—the way his spine straightened told her that his step-grandmother hadn't been the only woman to burn his trust. "Not much. Only that she broke up with you."

"He didn't say anything else?"

Like what? Seeing Stuart on alert had her curious. "No. He didn't even mention her name." The fact he'd brought up the subject at all had made Patience think she wasn't just any girlfriend but rather someone who had broken his heart.

Stuart's reaction all but confirmed her theory. Waving away the comment with exaggerated indifference, he sat back in his seat. "Dr. Tischel was drunk and looking to spread gossip is all."

Patience wasn't so sure. Dr. Tischel had spoken pretty offhandedly for a guy trying to gossip. In fact, he sounded more as if he was repeating news everyone already knew.

She was about to ask for Stuart's version when he held up his hand. "Listen," he said. The orchestra was playing a medley of Big Band songs. Memories of swaying in each other's arms came rushing back, the onslaught overwhelming all other thoughts. One look at Stuart's darkening eyes told her he remembered, too.

"Let's dance," he said, setting down his glass. It wasn't a request but a command. The assertiveness sent a thrill running down her spine. Her hand was in his before she could think twice.

"What are the odds?" she heard him murmur as he pulled her close.

"I don't know." And she didn't care. She would dance to anything if it meant being able to spend time in his arms. You are such a goner, she thought as she rested her temple against his shoulder.

"This is the first time I've ever danced without mile-high heels," she said. "I feel short."

His chest rumbled beneath her ear. "You could always stand on tiptoes."

"That's okay, this is perfect." More than perfect. Closing her eyes, she let the moment wash over her. Who knew when they'd share another one? "Much better than the dinner dance."

Stuart pulled back and his eyes searched hers. "You mean that, don't you?"

There was something about his voice. In a way he sounded surprised, but a bigger part of him sounded pleased, as if he'd made a great discovery.

"You still don't trust me to tell you the truth, do you?" After everything she'd shared about her past...

"That's just it, I do," he said, pulling her close again. "For the first time in a long time, I do."

They swayed in silence. Patience lost herself in the music and the sound of Stuart's breathing as they turned around and around, their feet and their bodies in perfect sync. The roof, the streets below, the entire city—all fell away except for the two of them.

The song ended, replaced by the slow mournful strands of the "1812 Overture," Boston's signal the fireworks were on their way. Patience clung tighter, wishing the moment would never end.

"Gloria," Stuart whispered suddenly. The name made Patience's insides chill.

"The girlfriend who broke up with me. It was Gloria."

CHAPTER EIGHT

Dear God. Was he saying…? "You had an affair with your step-grandmother?" It was a lousy question, but she had to ask. Gloria was, after all, married to a man sixty years her senior. It would be only natural that she might turn to someone young and virile.

Besides, the alternative would be that Gloria chose Theodore over…

"No affair."

Her stomach sank. Exactly what she'd feared. "She left you for your grandfather." The *ew* factor increased. What kind of woman would prefer an old man to…to Stuart?

She already knew the answer. "She was after the money."

"Yeah." He broke away. Patience tried to grab his hand to pull him back only to miss the mark. "I should have realized. I mean, she pursued me—that alone should have been my first clue."

"Why?" Patience didn't understand. She pictured women coming on to Stuart all the time.

He laughed at her question. A soft, sad laugh. "Asthmatic and awkward, remember? Well, awkward anyway. This was almost fifteen years ago," he rushed to add. He must have guessed she was about to argue the point. "I hadn't grown into myself yet. When it came to things like dating, I was pretty clueless. Gloria on the other hand…let's say she'd grown into herself years earlier. When she started showing interest in me, I thought I was the luckiest guy in the world. Couldn't wait to introduce her to Grandpa Theodore. Talk about a stupid mistake."

"She started chasing after him."

"Hey, why settle for the nerdy grandson when you can snag the mother lode, right?" The bitterness in his voice told the rest of the story. Along with his eyes. He could try to make a joke out of the betrayal, but she could still feel his hurt. As he'd said before, the eyes gave away everything.

Having told his story, or as much as he intended, he made his way back to the coffee table. "Although to be fair, Grandpa Theodore did his part, too." Snagging his wineglass, he drained the contents. "In a way I'm grateful to them," he said, reaching for the bottle. He started to pour, only to change his mind, and set it back down. "They taught me a valuable lesson."

"Be careful who you trust."

"Exactly. I promised myself I would never—ever—get taken in again. Wasn't long after that I came out here and connected with Ana."

Who became the one relative he could trust. Patience understood now why he'd been so suspicious of her when they'd met. Like her, Stuart had built himself an invisible wall. Granted, he'd built his for different reasons, but the purpose was the same: self-defense. So long as he kept the world at a distance, he would be safe.

He'd shared his history with her, though. To think he'd allowed her to see a part of him few people ever saw. Tears sprang to her eyes, she was so honored. What little there was left of the walls protecting Patience's heart crumbled to dust.

It was a mistake. Every bit of her common sense knew better. A woman like her, a man like him. Temporary, at best. But she couldn't help herself. The need for distance forgotten, she brushed her fingers along his jaw.

"Gloria was a fool," she whispered, hoping he could read in her eyes the words she wasn't saying.

"Are you sure?" Stuart whispered back. He wasn't asking about Gloria, but about her. Was she sure she wanted to cross the line they were toeing.

The answer was no, but surety had long since fallen by the wayside in favor of emotion. Patience melted into his arms as his lips found hers.

In the distance, fireworks exploded over the Charles River. Neither noticed.

The first thing Patience noticed in the morning was the pressure bearing down on her chest. She opened her eyes to discover Stuart lying next to her, his arm flung possessively across her body. Remembering the night before, she smiled. Funny, but she expected the morning after to be uncomfortable, with regrets darkening the light of day, but no. She was so happy she felt as if her chest might explode.

Her smile widened as Stuart gave a soft moan and moved in closer. "Morning," he murmured. With his voice laced with sleep, he sounded young and unjaded.

Blue eyes blinked at her. "I see you."

"I see you, too."

"No, I mean I can see you. I fell asleep wearing my contacts again."

"Again, huh? Happens often?"

"More than I want to admit." He rolled to his side. "In this case, though, I blame you."

"Me?" she asked, rolling to face him.

"Uh-huh. You distracted me."

"Oh." She was going to strain her cheek muscles if she kept smiling this way. "I didn't hear any complaints last night."

"Oh, trust me, there are no complaints this morning, either."

They lay side by side, his arm draped around her waist. The intimate position felt so natural it was scary. "But I better not hear any jokes about my glasses."

"I like your glasses. They give you a sexy hipster look."

Stuart laughed. It was a sound everyone should hear in the morning. "Maybe we should get you some glasses." His smile shifted, turning almost reverent. "You really mean what you're saying, though, don't you?"

"Doesn't make a different to me whether you wear glasses or not. You could wear a sack over your head for all I care. Well, maybe not a sack. I kind of like your face."

"I like yours," he said, brushing her cheek. Her face. Not her body. Patience loved the way he looked at her. He didn't see her as an object or even as an ex-stripper. As far as Stuart was concerned, she was a person. Someone worthy of respect.

But do you deserve it? The question came crashing

into her brain, reminding her that, in spite of all her confessions, there was still one secret she'd kept to herself. Stuart trusted her enough to tell his story. Maybe she should trust him with the rest of hers?

His fingers were moving south, tracing a path over her shoulder, tugging the sheet away from her skin.

"Stuart…?"

"Mmm?"

"I—" She arched into the sheets as he nuzzled the crook of her neck. "Nothing." He made it way too easy to give in.

Ana was talking a blue streak. "…need more events like last evening's. I asked Dr. O'Hara to get me the CEO's phone number. When I'm settled back home, I want to make a donation and tell him to earmark the money for entertainment. As I told Dr. O'Hara, patients need distractions, and he agreed. I have to say, I wasn't sure I was going to like him but he's much less condescending than Karl. Plus, he has a lovely wife, so he won't be bothering Patience. Are you listening to me?"

"Of course, I am. Dr. O'Hara's condescending."

He wasn't even close, was he? Stuart could tell from Ana's arched brow. "Sorry, I was thinking about… something else." This morning, to be exact. And last night.

"Obviously." His aunt settled back against her pillow. Time in the rehab facility had improved the sharpness of her stare, which she used to full advantage. "So what is it that has you smiling like the cat who ate the canary? It's unlike you."

"I'm in a good mood is all. I found a condo yesterday. On the other side of the Common."

"Does that mean you'll be moving out?"

"Not for a while yet."

The disappointment left Ana's face. "Good. I'm not ready for you to leave yet."

Neither was he. It had dawned on him this morning that leaving would mean leaving Patience behind. Unless they continued whatever it was they were doing at his place. Was that what he wanted?

Pictures of her standing on his terrace flashed through his head.

"You're smiling again. Must be a very nice apartment."

"It's not bad. Patience came with me to check the place out. She liked it."

"Really? I didn't realize you valued her opinion? I got the impression there was tension between the two of you."

"We…" Damn, if his cheeks weren't getting warm. "We worked that out."

"Did you, now?"

"We talked."

"I'm glad. She's a lovely girl, isn't she?"

"Um…" He pictured her face when she woke up this morning. Hair mussed. Sleep in her eyes. She was far more than lovely. She was genuine and honest. He could trust her.

The realization hit him while they were dancing. Scared the hell out of him. At the same time, he'd never felt freer.

"Stuart?"

"You were right, Tetya. She's terrific."

He could tell the second his aunt put two and two together. Her pale blue eyes pinned him to the chair. "Are you having an affair with my housekeeper?"

Stuart ran a hand across the back of his neck. His cheeks were definitely crimson now. Thankfully, his aunt took pity on him and waved her question off. "You don't have to say anything. I know a besotted look when I see one."

"I'm not sure I'd say besotted." A word from this century, perhaps.

"Use whatever word you want. I'm glad."

"You are?"

"Of course. You let what happened with Gloria keep you from falling in love for way too long. Killed me to think Theodore crushed *your* heart, too."

Who said anything about love? He was about to tell Ana she was reading too much into the affair when something his aunt said caught his attention.

"Too?" This was the first time his aunt had ever referred to the bad blood between her and his grandfather. He thought of the memory box buried at the bottom of her drawer, of cats all bearing the same man's name, and his heart ached for the woman he'd grown to love as a grandmother. What had his grandfather done? He had to ask. "Are you talking about Nigel?"

"Don't be silly? What would your grandfather have to do with my cat?"

She was a worse liar than he was. The way she suddenly became interested in smoothing her sheets gave her away. "I meant Nigel Rougeau," he said.

Her hand stilled. "Who?"

"I saw the photographs, Tetya. The ones in your drawer."

"Oh."

"I know it's none of my business...I've just always

wondered why. What could my grandfather have possibly done to make you cut us off?"

"Oh, *lapushka*, I was never trying to cut you off. What happened was a long time ago, before you were ever born."

"You mean what happened with Nigel?"

She nodded.

She didn't get to say anything further. Footsteps sounded outside the hospital door and, a second later, Patience appeared. Stuart couldn't believe the way his pulse picked up when he saw her.

"Hey," she greeted in a shy voice that screamed all the things they'd done overnight. "I was bringing Ana something to eat. I didn't realize you'd be here."

"I decided to visit during lunch so I could get home at a decent hour," he replied. His answer made her blush, probably because they both knew why he wanted to get home early. The pink ran across her cheeks and down her neck, disappearing into the collar of her T-shirt. She looked so incredibly delectable Stuart had to grip the sides of his chair to keep from kissing her senseless.

"I brought you a chicken salad sandwich," she said, setting a bag on Ana's bedside table. Then, noticing his aunt's distraction, she frowned. "Am I interrupting something?"

"Ana was about to tell me about Nigel Rougeau." That made Ana look up.

"She was the one who found the box," he explained.

"We weren't trying to pry, I swear," Patience said. "I put the box on the bureau while I was organizing your drawer and Nigel—the cat—knocked it on the floor. We saw the name when we were picking up the mess. I'm sorry."

"Don't be, dear. It was probably Nigel's way of demanding attention." Ana gave a long, sad sigh. "He never did like being kept a secret."

She meant Nigel Rougeau. Realizing this, Stuart and Patience exchanged a look. Apparently cats and their namesake shared personality traits after all.

"Maybe it's time I told our story," Ana said, smoothing the sheets again.

"Should I leave?" Patience asked. "Let you talk about family business…"

"No, dear. You can stay," Ana told her. "You're like family."

Stuart could tell Patience was still wavering, so he grabbed her hand and pulled her into the chair next to his. "Please stay."

She looked down at their joined fingers. "This is okay, too," he said. "She knows."

"Oh." The blush returned.

"Nigel loved when women blushed. He used to say every woman's cheek has its own special shade. He was a painter I knew in Paris."

"You were his model. The painting on the wall."

"He and I preferred the term *muse*. Our relationship was far deeper than artist and model." She sighed. "He had such talent."

The reverence in her voice took Stuart aback. "Why didn't you mention him before?" he asked. Why keep a man she so clearly worshipped a secret?

"Some things are too painful to mention." Next to him, Patience stiffened. They both understood all too well what Ana meant. "You don't have to tell us now, either," Patience said.

"Yes," he agreed. "We'll understand."

"No, I want to. I'm sure he's furious that I've stayed quiet this long." Ana spoke in the present tense, as if he were in the room with them.

"We met the summer I graduated high school. I was on a grand tour, being bored to tears with tours of cathedrals and palaces and had sneaked away to see some of the more forbidden parts of Paris. Instead, I met Nigel. It was love at first sight. When the tour moved on, I stayed behind."

Her voice grew gravelly. Stuart reached over and poured her a glass of water. As he handed the drink to her, he saw her eyes had grown wet. "We were going to do great things in the art world. He would paint, I would be the inspiration. The Diakonova to his Salvador Dali."

"What happened?" Patience asked. The two of them leaned forward, curious.

"Your grandfather happened, of course. You know our parents passed away when I was a child." Stuart nodded. Losing your parents young seemed to be Duchenko tradition.

"Because he was the eldest, Theodore became my legal guardian. When he found out Nigel and I were living together—Nigel considered marriage a bourgeois institution—he went crazy. He flew to Paris to 'bring me home.' Said he would not allow his seventeen-year-old sister to ruin the Duchenko name by living in sin with some two-bit, fortune-hunting painter. I always wondered whether if Nigel had been more successful, if Theodore might have had a different view."

She paused to take another drink before continuing. "And then, he saw Nigel's work."

"The painting hanging in the studio."

His aunt gave a wistful smile. "That was one of so

many studies. Nigel was a student of the human form and being his muse…"

"He studied your form the most." Patience's comment earned a blush. It was the first time Stuart ever saw his aunt color in embarrassment.

"Your grandfather was doubly furious. He told me in no uncertain terms that if I didn't come home and live like a proper lady, he would destroy Nigel's career before it had ever started."

Patience gave a soft gasp. "Surely, he didn't mean…"

"I'm sure he did," Stuart replied. "Grandpa Theodore could be ruthless when he wanted to be." Didn't matter who was involved. His sister, his grandson.

Reading his mind, Patience squeezed his hand, the gesture replacing the emptiness inside him with warmth. Grateful, he pressed her fingers to his lips.

"What did you do?" he asked Ana, knowing the answer.

"What could I do? I was only seventeen. If I refused, it would be the end of Nigel's career, and I couldn't do that to him. He was born for greatness."

So, instead, she sacrificed her happiness for his sake. Stuart wanted to strangle his grandfather.

"You must have loved him very much," Patience whispered.

"He was my soul mate." Ana smiled a watery smile, only to have it melt away seconds later. "I told Nigel, I'd come back. That as soon as I was eighteen I would find him. We could use my money to protect ourselves from Theodore's influence."

"But you didn't go back." She'd moved to Boston and never returned to Paris.

A tear slipped down Ana's face. "There was nothing

to go back to. A few weeks after I left, Nigel was killed in a motorcycle accident. He always rode too fast…"

Her voice grew wobbly, and the tears fell more frequently. "Later I heard Theodore had hired someone to purchase all his paintings of me and have them destroyed. All his work gone forever."

"Oh, Tetya." There were no words. Stuart jumped to his feet and wrapped his arms around her, anger toward his grandfather building as Ana shook silently against him. Here he'd thought marrying Gloria was the old man's low point. He couldn't be more wrong.

A comforting warmth buffeted him. Patience stood by his side, her hand gently rubbing circles on Ana's back. "I'm so sorry," she whispered.

Giving a sniff, his aunt lifted her head. While her eyes were red and puffy, Stuart saw the familiar backbone finding its way back. "My sweet child," she said, swiping at her cheeks, "why are you apologizing? You didn't do anything. Either of you."

Her absolution did little to alleviate the hurt he felt on her behalf. "But if I'd known…"

"What? You'd have called him on his behavior? Theodore knew what he was doing. He was a selfish man who didn't care who he hurt."

No, thought Stuart, he didn't.

She touched his cheek, tenderly, like the surrogate grandmother she'd become. "I'm just glad he didn't destroy your heart the way he did mine."

"Me, too." Although he'd come damn close.

Emotionally and physically worn-out, Ana dozed off a short while later. Patience waited by the doorway while Stuart tucked the older woman in and gave her a goodbye kiss.

* * *

"This explains why she named all the cats Nigel," Patience said, once they stepped into the corridor. "She was keeping her lover's memory alive." It broke her heart to think of Ana—sweet, gentle Ana—spending a lifetime mourning her only love. How could Theodore ruin his sister's happiness like that? All because she'd dared to fall in love with the wrong kind of man?

Life really did stink sometimes.

Out of the corner of her eye, she saw Stuart looking back over his shoulder. "I knew my grandfather could be cold, but I always thought what happened with Gloria was a case of him being seduced. Now I wonder..." Rather than finish the sentence, he looked down at the linoleum. Didn't matter. Patience could guess what he was thinking. In spite of what he said regarding his grandfather's involvement, he still placed the bulk of the betrayal on Gloria's shoulders. Ana's story shifted the blame more evenly. "Ironic, isn't it?" he said. "My grandfather being so intent on protecting the Duchenko name and fortune, only to make a spectacle of himself decades later by marrying a fortune hunter himself?"

"You heard Ana. He was selfish. Selfish people only care about what benefits them."

"True." He left out a deep breath. "Goes to show, you really can't trust anyone."

"That's not true." Patience rushed to keep the walls from reforming. "You can trust Ana. And you can trust me." Staring directly at him, she dared him to look into her soul and see her sincerity. "I swear."

"I know." He went back to studying the floor.

This morning, Patience had joked about his glasses looking sexy and hip. At the moment, however, he just looked lost. It felt like the most natural thing in the world to wrap her arms around her waist and hold him close. He started at first, but it wasn't long before he hugged her back, his chin resting on her shoulder. "I'm as bad as he was, you know that?"

"What are you talking about?" Pulling back, she frowned at him. "If you're talking about your grandfather, you couldn't be more wrong." The two men were day and night. "I've seen how much you care about Ana. For crying out loud, you've been in here visiting every day since the accident. You make sure she has the best doctors, the best therapy. Hell, you went to the humane society dinner dance for her."

She pressed herself tight in his arms. "You could never do what your grandfather did to Ana," she whispered in his ear. Or what his grandfather had done to him. "Not in a million years."

"You sound pretty confident."

"I am," she replied with a smile. "There's a reason Ana sings your praises so much. You're a good man, Stuart Duchenko." Her heart echoed every word.

Stuart squeezed her tight, and for a second Patience thought she felt his body shake. The moment didn't last. Slipping out of her embrace, he crossed the hall and moved to a new doorway. There he stood, staring into an unoccupied room. "My pity party must sound pretty pathetic to you."

Because, he was saying, she'd had it so much worse. Maybe so, but as she'd told him before, it wasn't a contest. "Everyone needs reassurance once in a while."

"That so?" A smile made its way to his face as he leaned against the door frame. "Well, in that case, I hope you know how awesome you are, Patience Rush. I'm damn lucky our paths crossed."

On the contrary, she was the lucky one. She was falling deeper and deeper by the second.

"Thank you for being here." Leaning forward, he kissed her. A long, lingering kiss, the tenderness of which left Patience's head spinning. "See you back home?"

Not trusting herself to speak, she nodded. If there was any chance that she could keep her heart from getting involved, that kiss chased it away for good.

CHAPTER NINE

THAT NIGHT, THE two of them lay on the deck's top sofa, legs and bodies entwined like spaghetti, making out like a pair of teenagers. Patience swore Stuart had turned kissing into an art form. One moment his kisses were possessive and demanding, the next they turned so reverent they brought tears to her eyes.

All the while Patience fought the voice in her head warning her that he'd eventually realize she wasn't good enough.

She was saved from her dark thoughts by Stuart tugging on her lower lip with his teeth. "I think I'm love with your mouth," he murmured.

Words muttered in the throes of passion, but Patience's heart jumped all the same. She forced herself to treat the remark as lightly as he intended it to be. Running her bare foot up Stuart's leg, she thrilled at the way her touch caused a soft groan. "What does *lapushka* mean?" she asked.

Stuart raised himself up on his elbows. "Seriously?"

"I'm curious." And she needed the distraction. He might have been only talking about her mouth, but the word *love* required her to take a step back. "I know *tetya* means aunt..."

"*Lapushka* means little paw. And before you ask, I have no idea why she calls me that."

"I like it. *Lapushka*." She drew out the second syllable. "It's sweet."

"Better than *mon petit chou*. French for my little cabbage," he added when she frowned.

"I thought you didn't know French."

"That was the extent of my knowledge."

"At least now I have something to call Piper next time she calls."

Stuart didn't answer. A faraway look found its way to his face. Patience touched his cheek to call him back to the present. "You're thinking about what Ana told us this afternoon, aren't you?"

"Grandpa Theodore took so much from her. She could have had a completely different life." He cast his eyes to the cushion, but not before she caught a flash of regret. "I keep wondering if there isn't some way I could fix the damage he caused."

"How? Unless you can turn back time, I don't think you can."

"Actually…" With a moan that could best be described as reluctant, Stuart rolled onto his side. The separation wasn't more than a few inches, but Patience felt the distance immediately and shivered. "I was thinking about that this afternoon."

"About turning back time?"

"Sort of."

Now he had her interest. She shifted onto her side as well, propping herself on one elbow so as to give him her full attention. "What do you mean?"

"I was thinking about the painting we saw in the photograph. Ana said Nigel painted all sorts of studies of her."

"Yes, but she also said your grandfather paid some-one to buy all of them."

"But what if he didn't? I mean, what if he wasn't able to buy them all. Ana made it sound like there were a lot of paintings and sketches. It's possible one or two of them survived. Grandpa Theodore was powerful, but he wasn't omnipotent. In spite of what he thought."

"Do you really think a painting exists?"

"It's possible, and if one does, then Ana could have back a piece of what she lost. Might not be much, but…"

It was a wonderful, beautiful gesture that deepened the feelings that were rapidly taking control of Patience's heart. "But Nigel died years ago,' she reminded him. "How would we ever find out about his paintings?"

"We can at least try. I did a little searching on the internet this afternoon. Apparently Nigel had a sister."

"Really? Is she still alive?"

"Alive and living in Paris. If anyone knows what hap-pened to his artwork, it would be her. All we need is for someone to go talk to her. You wouldn't happen to have any ideas who we could call, do you?" he asked, brushing the bangs from her face.

"Funny you should ask—I do." She matched his grin. "I'm sure Piper would be glad to help. She knows how important Ana is to me. I'll call her tomorrow. With luck, she can arrange to talk to Nigel's sister this week."

"That would be great. Thank you."

He didn't have to thank her. "After everything Ana has done for me, this is nothing. I'd love to find this painting as much as you." And give back to the woman who saved her a piece of her soul mate that was big-ger than a box of memories and a string of cats bear-ing his name.

Thinking of the cats made her giggle. "What's so funny?" Stuart asked.

"Nothing. I was thinking, if the cats all had Nigel's personality, does that mean he never stopped eating?"

"Interesting question. We'll have to ask Ana someday.

"In the meantime," he said, rising above her. "It's still the middle of the night in Paris. We've got a few hours to kill before we can think about calling your sister."

"Is that so?"

"Uh-huh." He gripped her waist and quickly flipped her beneath him, causing Patience to let out a high-pitched squeal. "Looks like we'll have to find something to pass the time," he said, dipping his head.

Patience met him halfway.

Despite claiming her older sister "owed her," Piper was more than happy to visit Nigel's sister, just as Patience knew she would be. "Stuart and I really appreciate this," she said to the younger woman.

"Stuart, huh?" Piper's face loomed large as she leaned toward the screen. "How are things going with the two of you? Is he still cool with, you know, the club?"

Patience's mind flashed to a few hours before, in Stuart's bed. "Seems to be," she replied.

"See? I told you he'd understand. It's not like you went to work in that place because you liked dancing naked on tables."

"Of course, I didn't," Patience replied with a wince. She wondered if the memory would ever stop making her stomach churn. "And you're right. Stuart says he understands."

"Wait—what do you mean 'says he understands'? Don't you believe him?"

"No, I believe him. Stuart's been great."

"Then what's wrong?"

"Nothing." Patience shook her head. How could she explain that Stuart being great was the problem. He was too great while she was…well, she sure as heck didn't feel worthy. Sooner or later, this dream had to end. A soft sigh escaped her lips. Too late, she remembered Piper was on the other end of the line.

"Patience?"

Blinking, she came face-to-face with Piper's scowl.

"What aren't you telling me?" her sister asked.

"Um…" She bit her lip and prayed her sister's old cell phone camera wouldn't pick up her blush.

It was a fruitless wish. "Oh, my God! Is something going on between you and your boss?"

"He's not my boss," Patience said quickly. "He's my boss's great-nephew."

They were splitting hairs and they both knew it, which was why Piper asked, "What exactly is the difference?"

"The difference…" There was no difference, but she didn't want to admit it. Calling Stuart her boss only reminded her they weren't from the same world, a reality she was trying to ignore for as long as possible. Acknowledging that reality would only lead to others, like Patience not being good enough for him. "The difference would be the same as you dating either your boss or his next-door neighbor." she finally said.

Just as she knew she would, Piper rolled her eyes at the lame example. "Please. The only neighbor I've met is an eleven-year-old boy, and my boss doesn't even…"

"Doesn't even what?" For some reason, her sister had stopped midsentence, and her gaze was focused on a point off camera. "Piper?"

"Sorry, I lost track of what I was about to say. And you still haven't answered my question. Are you dating Stuart Duchenko?"

"For now, yes."

"No way! That's great!" Piper beamed from ear to ear. "I'm so happy for you."

"Don't go making a big deal. We're having fun together, that's all. It's nothing serious."

Of course she still hadn't mentioned the other thing. After Stuart distracted her yesterday—not that she'd fought too hard—there hadn't been another good moment. Then again, when was there a good time to share something so humiliating? It wasn't exactly something you could blurt out. *Hey, Stuart, by the way, dancing naked wasn't the only thing in my past I didn't tell you about. There's also this little police matter...*

She switched the subject back to Nigel Rougeau's sister and hoped Piper believed her.

At least one of them should.

"And this," Stuart said, "is the firm library. Home away from home for any decent first-year associate."

He snuck a kiss to Patience's temple while pointing out the shelves, causing her knees to wobble slightly. Not because of the kiss but from the intimacy it implied.

"Was it yours?" She pictured his dark head bent over the books late at night.

"Are you kidding? See that desk by the window? If you sit in the chair, you can still feel the imprint from my butt cheeks."

Patience choked back a snort, causing a pair of heads to look in their direction, only to return to their work as soon as they spied Stuart. "Don't look now, but I think they're afraid of you."

"Well, I can be pretty scary, you know."

"I know I was terrified when I first met you."

"I could tell by the way you sauced off."

"That's not even a real word." Giggling, she slapped his sleeve. One of the heads looked up again, and she couldn't help indulging in a moment of smug pride. *That's right*, she wanted to say, *your boss is entertaining me.*

It was an illusion, of course, this image of being a couple, but she was willing to let herself enjoy the fantasy for as long as it lasted. Later today, Ana would be coming home, and soon after Stuart would be moving out, bringing an end to their affair. When that happened, she would confront the emotions she was fighting to keep buried.

Until then, she'd let the illusion have control.

"The partner's dining room is next door," Stuart said. "Would you rather eat in there or in my office?"

That's why she was here. With Ana returning home, Stuart had invited her to lunch to discuss what she needed to do to get the brownstone ready. "You're the host. I'll let you decide."

"My office it is. That way I can ravish you after we eat," he whispered in her ear.

Patience's knees wobbled again. The way his voice grew husky, she could listen to his whisper all day long. "Sounds good to me."

"What part? The eating or the ravishing?" Either. Both. She welcomed the privacy, too. Previous moment aside, she felt uncomfortable walking around Stuart's law firm. Although she'd exchanged her jeans for an ankle-length skirt and tank top, she still felt out of place amid the power suits. "What are you talking about?" Stuart had remarked when she'd mentioned her fears. "No one expects my date to look like she's heading to court."

"They would if she was a lawyer," she countered.

"But she's not. She's you."

He had no idea how his response made her heart soar.

"Bob was looking for you," a woman called to them when they reached his office.

"I know," Stuart replied. "I got his emails. If it's about the Peavey case, tell him to send the brief directly to John Greenwood."

"He said this was about another project. A report you asked him to assemble."

There was a sudden stutter in his step. While they weren't touching, Patience could still feel Stuart's body tense. "Oh," he replied. "Tell him I'll talk with him later." Even his voice sounded tight.

"I'm keeping you from something important, aren't I?" she asked.

"Nothing that can't wait."

But she was. His whole demeanor had changed on a dime. Lighthearted Stuart had disappeared behind a shadow. All of a sudden, he was frowning, the playful gleam gone from his eyes.

"Seriously, if you have work to do, I can—"

"No." He practically shouted the word. For some reason, it made the hair on her neck stand on end. "Whatever Bob has to say can wait."

"But if he's trying so hard to talk with you…" Multiple emails and personal visits—it had to be important.

Stuart shook his head. "I already know what he wants to tell me, and it's not important at all."

"Okay. If you say so." No need pressing the issue, even though she wasn't sure she believed him. "Bob can wait."

"Exactly."

Stuart's office was a mirror image of him. Attractive and elegant. If this was the reward, no wonder those associates worked so hard.

She stood in the center of the room while he closed his office door and then turned to her with a mischievous grin.

"Are we planning to eat?" she asked him.

"Eventually." Taking her hand, he led her to the luxurious leather chair that dominated the back of his desk. "First things first. I believe I said something about ravishing."

"I distinctly remember you saying after we eat."

"Sue me. I lied."

She would have made a joke about being in the perfect place to do so had he not completely derailed her thoughts by slipping his arms around her waist. She tumbled onto his lap without argument.

His eagerness never ceased to amaze her. Every time he kissed her felt like the first time, passionate and needy.

She let out a whimper when he broke away. "Sadly, not being able to lock my door prevents a proper ravishing. That will have to wait until later."

"Your aunt will be home."

"She has to sleep eventually. And, if I recall, they're

installing her bed on the first floor, which means we can be as loud as we want." He slipped off the strap of her tank top and nipped at the exposed skin.

Goodness, but she would going to miss this when he left. Putting her hands on his shoulders, Patience pushed gently away. One of them had to add some space; otherwise, it wouldn't matter whether his door locked or not.

"I thought we needed to talk about Ana's new living arrangements," she said. Stuart groaned, but he didn't argue.

"The medical supply company delivered the bed this morning," she continued. "Is Ana okay with the arrangement?" After discussing it, she and Stuart had decided to move his aunt to the first floor for the next few weeks. Dr. O'Hara had been concerned about her going up and down stairs. Stuart and Patience were concerned she might trip over Nigel again.

"She's not crazy about the idea, but I think Dr. O'Hara convinced her she was doing the smart thing. I told her you'd bring down a lot of her personal items and set up the front sitting room as much like her bedroom as possible."

"Linens and nightstand are already down. And when I left, Nigel had taken up residence on the bed." She'd passed the cat curled up in the center of the mattress, the same location he claimed on Ana's regular bed.

"So long as she has Nigel, she'll be more than comfortable," Stuart replied. "Speaking of...have you spoken to your sister yet?"

"No. I got a message from her this morning saying she wanted to video chat, but we were unable to connect. I don't know if she's managed to look into Ana's painting, though."

"She has. I got an email from her just before you arrived."

"You did? Why didn't you tell me?"

The index finger trailing down her arm gave her the answer. He'd been distracted.

"Did she say if she learned anything?" she asked, ignoring the goose bumps ghosting across her skin.

A slow smile broke across Stuart's face. "Looks like we were right. A dealer did buy the contents of Nigel's studio right after his death—I'm guessing that's the man Grandpa Theodore hired—but it turns out that Nigel sold at least a couple pieces before his death. She gave Piper the name of the gallery owner who brokered the transaction. Piper and her boss were going to talk to him tomorrow."

"That's great! Wait." Patience paused. "Did you say her boss was helping her?" To hear Piper talk, the two of them barely had contact.

"Maybe he's helping her translate."

That would make sense. Piper's French was shaky. "Let's keep our fingers crossed the gallery owner kept decent records."

"Fingers, toes, and anything else you can think of," Stuart replied. "I really want to make this happen for Ana."

"Same here." Especially if success meant Stuart would have a smile, as well. Patience was pretty sure she'd do anything to see that.

Stuart didn't take two-hour lunches. Not unless there was a business meeting involved. But, with Patience, the time simply got away from him. Moreover, he didn't care. If he didn't have work to finish before Ana's discharge, he would have been perfectly happy to let the lunch go on for three or four hours. The woman was so damn easy to talk to.

Easy to do a lot of things with, he thought with a smile.

You, pal, are in deep, aren't you? For once, he let his subconscious speak freely. He *was* in deep, and, to his amazement, the thought didn't set off alarm bells. Why should it? Patience wasn't Gloria. Patience didn't pretend to be something she wasn't or tell him what she thought he wanted to hear. Instead, she was content to be with him—the real him. The one who wore thick glasses and talked about sunset differentials. Even at his most besotted, to steal his aunt's word, Gloria didn't make his insides feel light and joyful, the way Patience did. So, Stuart didn't freak out at the notion he might be falling. In fact, he could see himself falling a lot deeper.

Someone cleared his throat. Stuart looked to the door, saw who it was and cringed. "Hey, Bob. Come on in."

The overly tall, overly eager looking attorney stepped inside and closed the door behind him. No doubt meant as a gesture of confidentiality, it made Stuart wince nonetheless. "The investigator tracked down the information you needed," he said, brandishing a thin manila envelope. "I know it took a little longer than expected, but we had a couple big cases come through, and since this was personal and you hadn't followed up…"

"I thought I sent you an email telling you to cancel the investigation."

"You—you did?" The color drained from Bob's face. Associates hoping to be on the fast track hated to make mistakes, Bob more than most. "I didn't see one."

"A few weeks ago." The Saturday following the dinner dance. Stuart distinctly remembered typing out the message before going to bed. Right before Nigel jumped up and demanded attention.

Damn. Was it possible he hadn't hit Send? Now two people who didn't need to know were aware of Patience's secret.

Bob mistook his wiping his hand across his face for displeasure. "I am so sorry. The note must have gotten buried somehow...I..." He thrust the envelope at Stuart. "Are you sure you don't need this information? I mean, it's pretty interesting reading, I'll say that."

"You read it?"

Again Bob paled. "Um, only to make sure the report was complete. I wasn't trying to pry..."

Like hell he wasn't. The investigator's notes were probably too salacious to pass up. He gave Bob a dismissive look, letting the associate know he was unhappy with his performance. "Doesn't matter," he made a point of saying. "I already know everything the investigator might have found."

"You do?" Bob said. "Even the criminal record?"

Criminal record? Please no. Stuart squeezed the arms of his chair tight enough to snap them. It took every ounce of his control and then some to keep his face free of reaction. "Yes, even that."

"Oh. Okay. I'll go finish the brief for Greenwood then."

"You do that," Stuart replied. "And Bob?" Man, but it was hard to talk with nausea rising in his throat. "If you ever get a personal project from a partner again? Mind your own business."

The associate nodded before exiting as quickly as possible. Leaving Stuart alone.

With the manila envelope.

It had to be a mistake. Patience had told him every-thing, right? And he trusted her.

But what if…the possibility made him gag.

Only one way to be certain. He tore open the en-velope.

"Dammit!" He slammed his fist on the desk, ignor-ing the pain shooting to his elbow. It was nothing com-pared to the hurt tearing through his insides. There, fastened to the top of the report, was everything he didn't want to know.

"All right, Nigel, let's get this straight. This is Ana's new bed, not yours. Meaning you will give her space to lie down when she and Stuart get home from the hospital, okay?"

Which, Patience checked the clock on the mantel, should be in an hour or so. She smoothed the wrinkles from Ana's comforter. The setup might not be ideal, but it would work for a month. Who knows? Ana might de-cide she liked living on the first floor.

We can be as loud as we want. A delicious shiver ran down her spine as she remembered Stuart's com-ment after Dr. O'Hara suggested the new arrangement. "Might as well make the most of what we have while we have it, right, Nigel?" she said, combing her fingers through Nigel's fur.

Suddenly, the front door slammed with a force so hard it made the frame rattle against the wall. Stuart appeared in the doorway, wild-eyed and out of breath.

"Stuart, what's wrong?" Instinctively, she took a step backward. He looked like a madman. The pupils in his eyes were blown wide, and while she'd seen them black with desire, she'd never seen them like this. "Did something happen to Ana?"

"Ana's fine."

"Then what?" This was not the man she had spent lunch sharing kisses with. This man looked like he wanted to…

Oh, no. She spied the crumpled papers in his fist. Pain began spreading across her chest, sharp like a heart attack. Why couldn't the past have stayed buried for a little while longer?

"I can explain," she said.

"Oh, I bet you can." His voice had gone dead. "I bet you have a whole slew of explanations at the ready."

"Stuart—"

"I trusted you," he spit. "When you said you told me everything, I believed you, but you were lying."

"No," she said, shaking her head. "I was telling the truth."

"Oh, yeah?" He stalked closer, waving the papers in his fist like they were a club. "Then tell me. Why do I have a police record telling me you were a prostitute?"

CHAPTER TEN

THE ACCUSATION HUNG between them, a fat, ugly cloud. Patience wished she could turn herself into Nigel. He'd run under the bed when Stuart slammed the door.

"This is what you were really hiding, wasn't it? You didn't want Ana to know who she'd hired. What she'd hired."

What she'd hired? How dared he? "I am not a prostitute."

"Your police record says otherwise."

"Police records don't tell the whole story." A few sentences typed on a form. How could it possibly cover all the details?

Tell that to Stuart, though. His outburst seemed to let out some of his steam, making the anger more of a slow boil. Patience preferred the outrage. Folding his arms, he settled in a nearby chair, his eyes burning holes in her skin.

"Then by all means, enlighten me," he said. "I can't wait to hear the long version."

"Why should I bother? You've obviously made up your mind." Worse, she wasn't entirely sure she could blame him after hiding the truth the way she had.

"Try me."

Patience almost laughed, the comment was so close to his words the night of the dance. The night she should have come clean. He'd been willing to listen then. Now she wasn't so sure.

In his chair, Stuart sat waiting. Her own personal judge and jury.

She took a deep breath. "You ever been to a place like Feathers? It's not some upscale bachelors' club. It's a dive, with divey people. Some of the girls—a lot of the girls—did stuff on the side to make extra cash."

"But not you."

"No!" she snarled. She got it. He was angry and hurt, but to even suggest… How many nights had she spent in his arms offering herself to him, body and soul? She didn't share herself like that with just anyone, and he should know that.

Stuart must have realized he'd crossed the line, as his voice lost its sharp edge. "How did you get lumped in with the others then?"

"One night, the cops raided the club, and hauled us all downtown. My lawyer said it would be too hard to fight the charge and I'd be better off pleading out to avoid jail time."

"Too hard for whom? You or him?"

It was the first civil thing he'd said since walking in, and it was a question she'd asked herself dozens of time. "I just wanted the whole thing to go away so I did what he said. I didn't want to risk breaking my promise to Piper.

"And that," she said, sinking onto the edge of the bed, "is the long version."

Neither of them said anything for several minutes. Patience stared at the floral duvet, counting the various blossoms. A tail brushed her ankle. Nigel making his escape to the kitchen. The lucky guy

Finally, Stuart broke the silence. "If all this is true, why did you lie? I might have understood if you'd told me first."

"Because I wanted to forget the night ever happened. I felt dirty enough. To admit I not only danced like a cheap whore, but I was arrested like one, too?" No matter how tightly she wrapped her arms around her midsection, her stomach still ached every time she thought about it. "Do you have any idea how it felt the other night, having to tell you about my pathetic past? I wanted to salvage a little bit of dignity." And also cling to him a little bit longer.

None of that mattered now. Patience had seen the loathing on Stuart's face when he walked in.

"All I ever wanted from this job was respect."

"You had my respect."

Had. Past tense. Her insides ripped in two. Hadn't she known from the beginning getting involved with Stuart was a bad idea. *Don't drop your defenses*, she'd told herself. *The crash would be worse if you let yourself care.*

Well, she hadn't listened, and the crash was killing her.

Stuart stood and crossed to the window. "I trusted you." The same words he'd said when he first came in. Violating his trust had been her biggest crime of all.

Except…

"Did you?" she asked suddenly. "Did you really trust me?"

"You know I did. I told you about Gloria, for crying out loud."

"Then how did you find out about my record?" Last time she looked, there wasn't a criminal record fairy handing out information. A person had to go searching for it. "I don't believe it. You had me investigated didn't you?"

"I—" He couldn't even look her in the eye.

"You did. Unbelievable." Sitting here, making her feel bad about her violating *his* trust, when all the time… "Face it, *lapushka*." She drew the word out as sourly as she could. "You never trusted me all, did you?"

"That's not true." Stuart shook his head.

Right. And she was the Queen of England. Suddenly, the brownstone was much too small for the two of them. She needed to leave right now.

"Where are you going?" Stuart asked when she stalked toward the foyer.

"Out." Unless she was fired, she still had the right to come and go as she pleased. "I need some air."

She noticed Stuart didn't try to stop her. Looked like the fantasy truly was over.

Well, like she always said, Prince Charming ain't walking through that door. Instead, *she* was walking out.

"Patience?" Soft though it was, Ana's voice still managed to echo through the brownstone. "Where is she? I thought you said she was waiting for us at home?"

"I thought she was," Stuart told her. A lie. He'd been *hoping* Patience was waiting for them. He had no idea if she'd ever come back after walking out.

This was his fault. If he hadn't been such a jerk when he'd found out about her arrest. But he'd been hurt, and he'd lashed out.

A soft meow sounded behind them. "Nigel, my sweetie pie. Did you miss Mommy?" His aunt hobbled over to the stairway. "He looks like he's lost weight. Don't you think?"

"Maybe. I don't know." At the moment, he was more concerned with Patience's whereabouts. "Maybe she went to the store."

Ana was trying to scratch an excited Nigel's head without falling over. "But she knew we were on our way. Why wouldn't she wait until we got here?"

"Perhaps she went to get something for your return. Tea, maybe." But he'd already discounted his theory soon as the words left his mouth. "Or maybe she's upstairs and can't hear us in her room." An equally lame suggestion, but he clung to the possibility.

"Tell you what," he said, scooping up Nigel. "Why don't I show you what we've set up in the front parlor? Then, while you and Nigel are having a good reunion, I'll go see if I can track down Patience."

But he was pretty sure he knew the answer. The air in the brownstone was different; the silence thicker than usual. By the time he went upstairs and spied Patience's open bedroom door, he was certain.

He stood in the doorway while his heart shattered. The bed where they'd made love this morning had been stripped to the mattress, the bedding folded in neat piles waiting to be washed. She'd left the closet door open. One lone hanger, the only sign the space had ever held clothes, lay on the floor.

A blue scarf hung on the doorknob. He recognized it as the one Patience wore to the dinner dance. Balling the cloth in his fist, he pressed it to his cheek, and inhaled deep. He remembered the way her scent had teased him while they'd danced. The memory mocked him now. The pain in his chest threatened to cut him at the knees.

Dear God, but the house already felt emptier. *And it was all his fault.*

On the bureau lay an envelope with Ana's name scrawled across the front. No goodbye for him, he thought sadly. He didn't deserve one.

"Is she upstairs?" Ana asked when he returned.

"No. She's gone."

"What do you mean gone? I don't understand." Her eyes narrowed when he handed her the envelope. He was doing a lousy job of hiding his feelings, and she knew it. "What's going on Stuart?"

"It's complicated," he replied. "You should read the letter."

"Do you know what's in it?"

"No." But he could guess.

"What does she mean she couldn't bear to face me after I found out?" Ana looked up with a frown. "Found out about what?"

It was the question he'd been dreading. "Patience…" Staring at his hands, he searched for the right words. "Turns out she was keeping secrets." Briefly, he told her about Patience's arrest and her job at Feathers, doing the best he could to leave out the gory details. When he finished, Ana looked back to the letter that was on her lap. "I'm sorry, Tetya."

"I figured her story had to be something pretty awful for her to lie about it."

"She was afraid—" He whipped his head around. "You knew she was lying?"

"Of course, I did. Surely you don't think I'm that

naive." Her glare chased off any possible response. "I could tell she was hiding something during her interview. It was obvious she didn't know a thing about being a proper housekeeper. And the way she stuttered on about forgetting her agency paperwork…the girl is not a very good liar, you know. After she left, I spoke to the agency, and they told me the real candidate had gotten stuck on the subway."

Stuart owed his aunt an apology. She was far sharper than he gave her credit.

"Wait," he said, backing off that thought. "If you knew she was lying, why did you hire her? Why didn't you call her out on the story?"

"Because the poor dear was clearly desperate. Leaping at the chance to clean house?"

"Still, for all you knew, she could have been trying to rob you." The questions were moot at this point. He was simply looking for grounds to justify his mistrust. Hoping for some sliver of a reason to prove he wasn't an arrogant, jaded fool.

"Nonsense," Ana replied. "Patience couldn't hurt a fly. Anyone who spends five minutes with her can tell that."

Yes, they could. Even he, with all his suspicion, had recognized her gentle sweetness. It's why he'd fallen so hard in spite of himself.

"Besides, Nigel liked her and he doesn't like just anyone. That alone told me I could trust her. As for not asking her story…I figured when the time came, she would tell me what I needed to know."

In other words, his aunt had decided based on the opinion of a cat who, sadly enough, was a better judge of character than he was.

"In a lot of ways, Patience reminds me of the animals at the shelter," she told him. "Lost and looking for a place to call home. I know it was a rash decision—a dangerous one, even—but I couldn't turn her away."

"When you put it that way…" It didn't sound so rash at all. Simply confident in the goodness of human nature. Something he'd always had trouble with. He thought he'd conquered his mistrust, but apparently not.

"She has a way of getting under your skin, doesn't she?" Now the guilt arrived, strong and harsh. He'd managed to do what his aunt couldn't: chase Patience away. He'd let her sweetness frighten him and turn him into a bully.

"I've really screwed things up, haven't I?" he said.

"Yes, you have."

Ana never did believe in mincing words. "What do I do?" He looked to her face, hoping in her wisdom she'd have a solution.

"For starters, you can get me my housekeeper back. I care too much for her to lose her."

"Me, too," Stuart whispered. He should never have overreacted the way he did when he'd read Bob's report. If he'd acted calmly, Patience might be here with him right now. Instead, he'd let his heart give in to suspicion. And she was gone.

"She's never going to forgive me."

"You'll never know until you try."

When he shook his head, she reached over and took his hands, her gnarled grip stronger than he expected. "Listen to me. I had the chance to fight for my Nigel. I didn't and I lost him forever. I don't want to see the same thing happen to you. You have already missed out on so many years of happiness because of Theodore and that gold digger he married. Patience is your second chance. Don't be like me, lapushka—fight for her."

His aunt was right. He couldn't give up on Patience. He had to find her if only to apologize for being an ass. "How did he track her down, though? He doubted she'd left a forwarding address at the bottom of her goodbye note. But....

There was one person Patience would contact no matter where she ran off to. One person she would never desert. And he had that person's email address. A kernel of hope took root inside him.

Rising, he kissed Ana on the cheek. "I'll be right back."

"Where are you going?"

"I've got to send an important note to someone in France."

"You look lousy."

"Back at you." Patience knew exactly how she looked. Tired and depressed. Same way she felt. "The beds at this place are like boards on stilts. I was tossing and turning half the night." She missed the big comfy bed she had at Ana's.

She missed a lot of things she had back at Ana's.

But that was in the past. With a swipe of her hand, she brushed away her bangs and the painful thoughts. "I've got possible good news, though. The front desk clerk told me they're hiring at the new Super Shopper's Mart. I'm going to go apply today."

"Good luck."

"Thanks." She'd need it. She couldn't afford to hide away in a hotel room forever. Eventually, she was going to have to find a new job and a new place to live. Preferably soon, before she drained her savings and found herself living in her car. Again.

Funny how things came full circle.

"I just hope they don't ask for a lot of references. Or ask too much about my previous position."

"Maybe if you called Ana…"

"No." Patience cut that suggestion right off. That possibility died when she'd walked out.

She hadn't meant to leave so abruptly. Not at first, anyway. When she'd stormed out of the brownstone, she'd truly intended to just clear her head. Problem was, the more she walked around Beacon Hill, the more upset she got. At Stuart for being so damn suspicious of everybody. At the world for being so unfair in the first place.

But mostly at herself for being stupid enough to think she could bury the past. And for letting her guard down. She'd let herself care—more than care—and now her insides were being shredded for her foolishness. In the end, she'd decided she couldn't face seeing Stuart or Ana again, and so when Stuart had left for the hospital, she'd packed her things.

"Don't you think you're being drastic?" Piper asked.

"Trust me, I'm not. You should have seen Stuart's face," she added in a soft voice. For as long as she lived, she wouldn't forget how the betrayal and anger darkened his features.

"Probably because he was mad you didn't tell him. Stinks when people keep information from you."

Patience winced. "I know. I'm sorry." The other night she'd broken down and told Piper about the arrest. Her sister had been ticked off over being kept in the dark, too, although she'd softened when Patience had explained how it wasn't news you shared with your preteen sister.

The thing was, Piper was right. If she'd told Ana everything from the beginning, she wouldn't be in this position. Granted, she probably wouldn't have gotten the job, but she also wouldn't have had to deal with Ana's disappointment. Or with Stuart's. Which, when she thought about the past couple weeks, would have been the best thing of all.

Sure would hurt less, that's for sure.

"I'm not really upset anymore," Piper told her. "Stuart might not be, either. Maybe he decided that the past doesn't matter."

"Right, that's why he had me investigated. Because my past doesn't matter." She still couldn't believe he'd crossed that line. Well, actually, she could believe it. Stuart had said from the beginning he had trust issues. Still… "Who does he think he is, judging me? I may not have made fantastic decisions, but I always had the best intentions. I got you an education, and I kept us off the streets."

"Hey, no arguments from me," her sister replied. "I think you're awesome."

And to think she had been feeling guilty about not telling him. Turns out her subconscious knew best. The only thing telling him about the arrest would have accomplished would be to put the regret in his eyes that much faster. At least this way, she'd eked out a few more days with him.

"I never should have let myself…"

"Let yourself what?" Naturally Piper heard her. When would she learn to keep her thoughts quiet?

She considered brushing the comment off, but Piper wouldn't let her. When she was a kid, she'd made Patience repeat every under-the-breath phrase ever muttered. Maybe talking would lessen the ache in the chest. "Let myself start to care," she said.

"You really like him, don't you?"

Way more than liked. She missed him the way she would miss breathing. "Not that it matters. I told you before, we were having a fling, nothing more, I mean, face it—even if I'd told him everything from the start, he could never seriously love someone like me. We come from completely different places."

"So? Why can't people from different worlds fall in love?"

"Do they? When's the last time someone from our neighborhood got swept off their feet by a millionaire?" *Prince Charming ain't walking through that door.*

"That's not what you used to tell me."

"You're different," Patience immediately replied. "I raised you to be better than the neighborhood."

"I know. You always said I was just as good as the next person."

"You are."

"Then, aren't you?"

Closing her eyes, Patience let out a long, slow breath. "This is different."

"How?"

Because, she wanted to say, the world wasn't black-and-white. Equality in a human sense didn't mean equal in the eyes of society. And while Stuart had no right to judge her as a person, there was a huge difference between not judging someone and falling in love with them.

"Trust me, it just is. A guy like Stuart doesn't want to spend the rest of his life with an ex-stripper."

Before either sister could keep the argument going, a knock sounded on her hotel door. "Who on earth would be banging on my door this time of morning?" Patience asked, frowning. Housekeeping didn't start for another hour.

"Patience, are you in there?"

The sound of Stuart's voice came through the wood, causing her heart to panic. "It's Stuart," she whispered. "He's here." How had he managed to track her down? The only person who knew her location was…

"You didn't," she said with a glare.

"He asked me to contact him as soon as I knew where you were staying. He wants to talk with you."

"Patience, I know you're in there. Please open the door."

She looked over her shoulder before glaring at her laptop where her sister's face was the picture of apology. "What makes you think I want to talk with him?"

"How about the fact that you look like hell? Give him five minutes. What if he's sorry?"

"Sorry, not sorry—I told you, it doesn't make a difference."

"And I think you should hear him out."

"I'm going to keep knocking until you answer," Stuart called from outside.

He would, too. A knot lodged itself at the base of her skull. A ball of tension just waiting to become a headache. Patience squeezed the back of her neck, trying to push the tension away, but the feeling was as stubborn as the man banging on her hotel door.

"Patience?"

"Fine. One minute! I am so going to kill you when you get back to Boston," she hissed at her sister.

"I love you, too," Piper replied.

Whatever. Patience slapped the laptop closed. Might as well get this over with. A quick glance at the mirror told her she really did look terrible. She started to comb her fingers through her hair, thought better of it and went to the door.

"What?" she asked, through the chained opening.

Stuart's blue eyes peered down at her. "May I come in?"

"Anything you need to say, I'm sure you can say from out there." Where she was safer. The mere sound of his voice had her insides quaking. Goodness knows what standing close to him would do.

"You sure you want me airing our dirty laundry so everyone else in the place can hear us?" he asked.

Damn. He had a point. "Fine. Five minutes." Sighing, she unlatched the door and let him in. Immediately, she knew it was a mistake. He had on his weekend clothes. Faded jeans and a T-shirt. The look made him appear far more approachable than his suit. She didn't want him approachable. She wanted to keep her distance.

He jammed his hands into his back pockets. "How are you?" he asked.

"I was doing fine until you got my sister involved," she replied.

"You don't look like you're doing fine."

"How I look isn't your business anymore." Nevertheless, she pulled her sweater tightly around her, feeling exposed in her T-shirt and sleep shorts. "What's so important that you needed to track me down?"

"You left without saying goodbye."

"I left a note."

"For Ana."

"Maybe Ana's the only person I wanted to say good-bye to."

"Ouch."

If he expected an apology, he was mistaken. "Is that all you came about? To critique how I said goodbye?"

"No. I came to find out why you left."

He was kidding, right? "Isn't it obvious?" She started to make the bed, fussing with the sheets the alternative to losing her temper. Did you really think I would stick around so Ana could fire me for lying to her?"

"No one was going to fire you."

Patience stopped her fussing. "Okay, pity me then."

Stepping away from the door, Stuart walked to the opposite side of the bed. The queen-size space suddenly felt too small a buffer zone. The rumpled sheets did nothing but remind her what it felt like to be under the covers with his arms wrapped around her.

"No one was going to pity you, either," he said. "Ana knew from the very beginning. Well, not the specifics, but she knew you lied your way into the job."

"How?" She wasn't sure she should believe him.

"Apparently you're not that good an actress."

What did he say the other day? Body language always gives people away. Here she thought she was fooling everyone, when in reality the only fool was her.

She sank to the bed, her back to him. "If Ana knew… why did she hire me?"

"You know Ana and her thing for strays."

Yeah, she did. Ana believed all creatures deserved a good home. Obviously, she'd believed Patience did, too. A lump rose in her throat, bringing tears. Ana was a greater gift in her life than Patience ever realized.

Suddenly, she felt like the world's biggest jerk. "You're right. I owed her a better goodbye. I'll call her."

"Better yet, why not come back?"

"You know I can't do that."

"Why not? I told you, she doesn't care. *I* don't care."

Behind her, she heard his soft cough. "Look, Ana's not the reason I came. I came to apologize for the way I overreacted the other day. I was a jerk. I should have trusted that you had a good reason for not telling me about the arrest."

"You hired an investigator."

"Yes, I did," he said. "When I first got to town and was worried about Ana. But that was before I got to know you."

"Stop." Next, he'd start saying how much he'd come to like and admire her or some other meaningless sweet talk. Her heart was hurting enough as it was. "I get it. Really, I do. Shame on me for not expecting it."

"Excuse me?"

He came around the foot of the bed until he stood by her knees. Patience immediately fought the urge to scoot backward, to where their personal spaces couldn't merge.

With a swipe of her hair, she gave her best imitation of disinterest. "In a way, the timing couldn't have been better. I mean, we both know we were ending things soon. This way we got the messy part over with."

"What are you talking about?"

"Do you really need me to spell it out for you?" She had to give him credit—he actually sounded incredulous. "A millionaire and an ex-stripper who cleans toilets? Hardly a fairy tale. I knew from the beginning it was temporary."

He met her attitude with one of his own. Arms folded, he scowled down at her with eyes that pinned her to the spot. "Wow, you've got everything all worked out, don't you?"

"I'm a realist. I know how the world works."

"And how would you know what I was thinking? You didn't stick around long enough to find out. Hell, you would have walked out the night of the dinner dance if I hadn't pressed you for an explanation."

He leaned into her face, bringing his eyes and lips dangerously close. "You know," he said, his voice low, "you keep talking about me not trusting you, but I'm not the only one with trust issues. You were so certain you knew what I was thinking, you didn't give me the chance to give you the benefit of the doubt. Maybe, if you'd told me about your arrest. Let me in…"

"I let you in as much as I dared," she told him. "If I told you every lousy thing that's happened in my life, you'd…"

"What? Be disgusted. Throw you out?"

"Yes."

"Bull. You only let me in when circumstances pressured you. If Chablis hadn't crossed our paths, I'd never have found out about Feathers. Trust works both ways, babe." Taking a deep breath, he stepped away.

Patience hugged her midsection. Without Stuart's presence to warm it, the air became cold and empty feeling. "Big words coming from a guy who was still investigating me after we started sleeping together," she murmured.

Her words hit their mark, and he winced. A small

consolation. "That was a mistake," he said. "I meant to call Bob off."

"Of course, you did." He simply forgot, right? "Let me guess, the voice in your head telling you I wasn't good enough wouldn't let you. A woman with her background—no way she could be any good," she whispered, mimicking.

"That's bull."

"Is it?" She wondered. "Why else would a person 'forget' to stop an investigation?"

"Because I was distracted."

"By what? What could possibly be that distracting?" Why she was even bothering to push the issue she didn't know, other than that she needed to hear him admit the truth.

But his answer wasn't what she expected. "You," he said. "You distracted me."

"With what? My banging body."

"No, by being yourself. I forgot to call Bob because I was too busy falling in love with you."

Love? This had to be his idea of a cruel joke. He couldn't really be in love with her. Could he?

Slowly, she raised her eyes and looked into his. There was so much honesty in their blueness it hurt. "How can you love me? I'm—

"Sweet, wonderful, smart…"

"But the things I did. The life I led."

"Sweetheart, those are things you did. They aren't you, not the way you think," he told her. Suddenly, he was in her space again, his hands cradling her cheeks. "I'm in love with Patience Rush. The woman who was willing to do anything, including sacrifice herself, to keep her sister safe. Who survived despite all the hell life threw at her. The woman who was strong enough to pull her and her sister up from that world. That's the Patience I'm in love with."

A tear slipped down Patience's cheek. "When I think about all those years in the club…"

"Shh. Don't think about them. They're in the past." He kissed her. As gentle and sweet a kiss as she ever experienced. She wished she could hold on to the moment forever.

"Come home, Patience," he whispered.

Fighting not to cry, she broke away. "I can't…"

Stuart looked like she'd slapped him. Disappointed and hurt. His expression made the ache in her heart worse. "Can't or won't?" he challenged.

"Can't." Might as well be honest. The past was too much a part of her to let it go. What if a week from now he changed his mind when he'd had time to think? The rejection would be too much to bear.

"I think you should go," she told him.

"Patience…"

She shook him off before her resolve could crumble. "Please. If you respect me at all…"

They were the magic words. Stuart took back his touch. "Fine."

He stopped when he got to the door. Patience didn't turn around, but she heard the pause in his step. "Just remember, all my anger and mistrust was because you were keeping secrets. I never once judged you for your past. If anything, I have nothing but respect for how you survived. Too bad you can't cut yourself the same deal."

CHAPTER ELEVEN

THE TUBE IN the neon *e* was burned out, turning the sign into "Fathers." Patience grimaced at the unintentional creepiness.

She wasn't sure what she was doing here. After Stuart left, she'd tried to call Piper back, but her sister didn't pick up, so she'd spent the day sitting on the edge of the bed, replaying Stuart's accusations in her head. She'd spent the night lying in bed doing the same. At first she was angry. How dare he accuse her of having trust issues? Talk about the pot calling the kettle black. Eventually, however, her emotions turned to the important statements. *I love you*. His declaration scared her to death. How could he love her? *Her*. What did the two of them see in her that she didn't see?

When she finally got out of bed, her thoughts led her here. She stared at the broken neon sign wondering if inside held the answers she was looking for.

The front door of Feathers hadn't changed in her absence. The faded black door was still covered with stains, the source of which she never wanted to know, and the beer stench, so strong it seeped through the bricks to reach outside, still made her gag. Familiar as it was, however, she felt as if she was standing in someone else's memory, as if she'd stumbled across an old photograph in a thrift store. Could it be that she'd changed that much in less than a year?

Back when she started at Feathers, she'd had one dream and one dream only: to give Piper a better life. She'd succeeded, too. In fact, she'd go so far as to say she'd done a damn good job. Not only had she given Piper access to a better life, but all of her sister's dreams were coming true.

Did she dare dream a dream for herself now?

Don't let anyone tell you you're not as good as anyone else. How often had she drilled those words into her sister's head? Maybe she'd have done better to drill them into her own.

Stuart loved her. She loved him. She'd probably loved him from the moment he walked through the emergency room doors. Could she trust their love would last?

Then again, two months ago, she hadn't thought love was possible. Not for her, at any rate. She'd started the relationship with Stuart adamant she wouldn't risk her heart and look what happened: she'd fallen in love, anyway. Being with him had made her feel special. And if she could feel that good while believing their relationship to be a fantasy, how good might she feel if she opened her heart to it completely?

"Well, will you look who's come back." Like a miniskirt-wearing gift that kept on giving, Chablis ambled around the corner. She had a cigarette in her hand. Smoke break. Patience always did find it laughable that taking their clothes off was okay but smoking inside was against the law.

The dancer tapped ash onto the sidewalk. "What's the matter? Boyfriend dump your stuck-up behind?"

she asked, before taking a long drag. Smoke filtered through her magenta-lined lips. Guess you ain't better than us, after all?"

"You know what, Chablis…?" Patience paused. A week ago—even a day ago—Patience might have thrown Chablis's smack talk back in her face. She no longer felt the need. Chablis was stuck in a world Patience no longer belonged in.

"You're right. I'm not better than you. I'm not better than anybody." She smiled. "But I'm no worse, either."

Since Patience didn't expect the dancer to understand what she was saying, it wasn't a surprise when Chablis's face wrinkled in confusion. "Whatever." She reached for the door handle.

Through the gap, Patience saw the dimly lit scenery from a lifetime ago. Once again, it was like looking at someone else's photograph. Stuart was right—Feathers was in her past. The future was what she dared to make of it. That was something else she used to tell Piper. *Don't be afraid to go for your dreams.* High time she took her own advice.

And this time, she was going to do without lying or hiding from who she was. Stuart said he loved the real her? Well, the real her was who he was going to get.

"Excuse me, miss?"

The male voice startled her. Stiffening, she turned, expecting to find a customer. Instead, she came face-to-face with a young police officer.

He gave her an apologetic smile. "Is everything all right? You look lost."

If he only knew. "I was," she told him, "but I think I know where I'm going now."

"Do you need directions? Trust me, you don't want to go in there. It's no place for a lady."

Patience looked at the closed door of her past. "You're right," she agreed. "I think I'd much rather go home."

"You can't manage without a housekeeper," Stuart told Ana. They were having a lousy excuse for breakfast—his version of scrambled eggs and coffee—in the kitchen. Or rather he was. Pieces of Ana's eggs somehow kept landing on the floor for Nigel to eat. She'd been protesting his cooking the past three days. "What will you do when I move out?"

"You could stay."

"Sure." They'd had this argument before, too. "How about I adopt a cat and name her Patience, too. People won't talk."

He knew why his aunt was dragging her feet. She was hoping Patience would change her mind and come back. Stuart hoped she'd come home, too, but he was a realist. It'd been three days since he poured his heart out in Patience's motel room. Three days since he said he loved her. And they hadn't heard a word. Whether he wanted it to or not, life had to go on.

The doorbell rang. "That's the candidate from the employment agency. I'll go get her. Try to keep an open mind," he said.

"If an open mind means telling her no, then fine, I'll keep an open mind."

Rolling his eyes, Stuart left the kitchen, Nigel chasing after him. "I hope you're planning on being cooperative," he told the cat. Otherwise, this was going to be a long morning. He opened the front door...

And froze in place.

On the threshold stood Patience, dressed for work in her blue work shirt and capris. In her hands, she held a feather duster. "Rumor has it you need a housekeeper."

She was back. The hopefulness behind her smile made him want to pull her into his arms then and there, but he resisted. This was her decision; he needed to let her play it out her way.

He settled then for smiling. "Did the employment agency send you over."

"No. I'm just a woman who's made a lot of mistakes looking to start over. I don't suppose there's a place for someone like me here?"

"Oh, there is." He pushed the front door wide. "Come on in. There's a little old lady in the kitchen who's going to be thrilled to meet you."

"Just her?"

"Me, too."

"Good." She smiled. "Although I should warn you in advance. I'm very much in love with this lawyer I know."

Stuart's heart gave a tiny victory cheer. "Sounds like a lucky guy."

"I'm the lucky one. Like I said, I made a lot of mistakes, and am hoping he—you—will give me a second chance."

Now he gave in and pulled her close, kissing her with everything in his heart. "You don't have to ask twice," he told her.

Patience wrapped her arms around his waist. To Stuart it felt that she was afraid he'd disappear. "I'm sorry I didn't trust you," she said into his chest.

"Same here. This time we'll trust each other."

"That's a new thing for me—to trust someone. I

might stumble a little bit." She looked up, her eyes as bright as the brightest chocolate diamond in the world. "Will you be patient with me?"

"Patient with Patience?" Grinning at his lame joke, he kissed the top of her head. "I don't think that's going to be a problem. Both of us are going to screw up, sweetheart. But as far as I'm concerned we've got all the time in the world to teach each other. Forever even."

Her arms squeezed tighter. The word *forever* was scaring her, he knew. Someday it wouldn't, though. Someday she'd realize she was so loved that forever was the only possible time frame.

"Forever sounds like a good goal," she said finally, her bravery increasing the admiration he held for her. "I love you, Stuart Duchenko."

He'd never believed three words more. They'd get to forever. He knew they would. "I love you too. Now…" Giving her a reluctant last kiss, he shut the door. "How about we go make an old lady's day?"

A meow sounded at his feet. "You, too, Nigel."

Together, the three walked toward the future.

Two weeks later

"Why is the phone ringing in the middle of the night?" Stuart groaned. "Don't they realize we're tired?"

"Poor baby. They probably don't realize how hard furniture shopping was for you." Patience grinned at the pout she spied before he covered his head with his pillow. The two of them and Ana had spent the day shopping for Stuart's new condominium. He was scheduled to move out at the end of the week. Ana was disappointed, until she learned Patience would be staying put. For now. As madly as they loved each other, both she and Stuart decided they should take their relationship one step at a time. Eventually, Patience would move in, but for now, there was no need to rush. Like Stuart said. They had forever.

Forever was such a nice-sounding word. Patience believed in it a little more every day. Turned out Prince Charming not only walked through the door, but he stuck around, as well.

"Whoever it is, tell them they're insane," Stuart muttered from beneath his pillow. "Then get under these covers so I can do unspeakable things to you."

"I thought you were sleepy?" she whispered, snatching the phone off the end table.

A hand snaked around to splay against her bare abdomen. "I'm awake now."

She answered without bothering to suppress her giggle. There was only one person who'd call at this hour and she wouldn't care. "Piper?"

"Greetings from England." There was a pause. "I'm not interrupting something, am I?"

"Not yet." She slapped Stuart's roaming hand. "What are you doing in England?"

"Helping your boyfriend, of course. And I have good news, and more good news. Which one do you want first?"

"Start with the good news."

"We found Ana's painting."

"You did!" She sat up. "That's wonderful."

"That's why we're in England. The gallery in Paris gave us a lead on a collector here who purchased one of Nigel's paintings. Turns out, the painting is of Ana.

Almost identical to the one in the background of the picture Stuart emailed."

Seemed silly to be moved to tears over a nude painting, but Patience's eyes started to water. After all these years, Ana was finally getting a piece of her Nigel back. "Ana is going to be so thrilled when she hears the news."

Hearing his aunt's name, Stuart immediately sat up, too, and mouthed the word *painting*? Patience nodded. He pressed a kiss to her cheek.

"Even better, the owner is willing to sell. Tell Stuart I'll email him the name and contact information."

"Thank you so much for doing this, Piper." Ana meant so much to her and Stuart. That they could finally reclaim this piece of her past was but small repayment. "Thank Frederic, as well."

"I will. Now, do you want the other good news?"

Patience looked at the man sitting next to her, feeling overwhelmed with good fortune. She didn't think it was possible for life to get better. However, Piper certainly sounded happy, so she was definitely curious. "Yes. What's the other good news?"

"Well…" There was a long dramatic pause before her sister finally replied.

"I got married."

She nearly dropped the phone. "Did you say married?" How? When? *Who?*

"It's a long story," Piper said. "Do you have time?"

Was she kidding? For news like this, Patience had all the time in the world. "I couldn't hang up now if I tried." She settled back to hear what her baby sister had to say.

By the end of Piper's story, Patience had tears in her eyes. Stuart was right there, his strong arms ready to provide solace. "You going to be okay?" he asked, when she hung up the phone.

"She did it," Patience whispered. "Everything I ever dreamed for her. She did it." Her heart felt so full she thought it might burst.

One of her tears escaped. Stuart brushed the moisture from her cheek and she smiled, thinking about their first night on the roof. "I was so certain Piper would be the only one of us to find love and have a happy ending."

"And now?"

She shifted in his arms, so she could look into the eyes of the man who'd captured her heart the moment he walked through the hospital door. "Now, it looks like I was wrong. Because I can't imagine a happier ending than being with you."

* * * * *

If you loved this book and want to
enjoy Piper's story too, watch out
for BEAUTY & HER BILLIONAIRE BOSS
by Barbara Wallace, available in
September 2015!

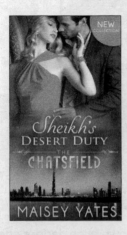

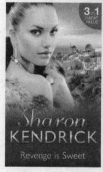

MILLS & BOON®

Cherish™

EXPERIENCE THE ULTIMATE RUSH OF FALLING IN LOVE

A sneak peek at next month's titles...

In stores from 19th June 2015:

- **The Millionaire's True Worth** – Rebecca Winters *and*
  His Proposal, Their Forever – Melissa McClone

- **A Bride for the Italian Boss** – Susan Meier *and*
  The Maverick's Accidental Bride – Christine Rimmer

In stores from 3rd July 2015:

- **The Earl's Convenient Wife** – Marion Lennox *and*
  How to Marry a Doctor – Nancy Robards Thompson

- **Vettori's Damsel in Distress** – Liz Fielding *and*
  Daddy Wore Spurs – Stella Bagwell